THE GAME CHOSE ME

A Novel by
Ebony Stroman

PUBLISHED BY

EBANDTE INC. PUBLISHING

"A BOOK BY EBANDTE GOTTA BE GOOD!"

GW00646419

Published by:
Ebandte Inc. Publishing
P.O. Box 341147
Jamaica, NY 11434
WWW.EBANDTE.COM

Library of Congress Control Number: 2004117457
ISBN – 10: 0-9749298-1-6
ISBN – 13: 978-0-9749298-1-1
© Copyright 2004 by Ebony Stroman-Clarke

THE GAME CHOSE ME CREDITS
Written by Ebony Stroman-Clarke
Edited by Danté Clarke
Cover model Latierra Kittrell
Cover graphics & design by www.apollopixel.com
Text formation by Jonathan Gullery & Ebony Stroman-Clarke

Printed in USA.

IN LOVING MEMORY OF:

LEON ANTONIO CLARKE
FEBRUARY 11, 1971 – MAY 5, 2001

&

SCOTT RAGLAND
AUGUST 10, 1969 – NOVEMBER 28, 2004

We lost both of these brothers to acts of violence.
Both of them were somebody's son, brother, father &
uncle. When will we learn to stop killing each other?
Scottie & Tone, both of y'all are truly missed. You will
always be alive in our hearts!

Acknowledgements

God, I thank you so much for the good and the bad. Mom, I know you're smiling! I miss you and love you dearly, you my girl!

Dante, only joy comes to mind when I'm thinking of you. You are truly heaven-sent just for me. Eve couldn't have said it better; I'm riding with you whether I'm in "The passenger side of your Bentley or the number two bus." (smile) I love you! Even though I met you when I was sixteen, I wish I would've met you sooner so I could've loved you longer. You are truly what love and happiness is all about. I see your dreams baby and I understand your nightmares. You're stuck with me for life (smile)! To you I dedicate my life!

Melodia, you are truly a work of art. You are more than just my sister; you're my friend, my little helper, my biggest critic and biggest fan! Let's not forget the **HUSTLER** in you! I knew you had it in you girl! I love you! To you I dedicate my undying love!

Latierra, you're so precious and so mature. Who would've thought my baby sister would grow up to be a big girl like you are. You're lovely, precious, pretty, smart and breaking me and Dante's pockets with all these Jordans you want (just playing, smile). Thanks for being the cover model for this book. I really love you and I hope you know you're special! To you I dedicate my undying love!

Emily, my sister from another mother, you are my special star and I'm glad you're a part of my life!

Of course I have to thank all of my supporters from my hood in Baisley to the massive support from Harlem world, all up and down 125th street to 145. Thanks to everyone in the Bronx up on Fordham Road, Parkchester and all over. Thank you to my brothers locked in the belly of the beast for making me and Dante's first novel **THE HOOD** a great success! I am in love with all of y'all. Keep reading and I'll keep writing!

Thanks to everyone who carries the titles **EBANDTE INC. PUBLISHING** puts out. All the street vendors, distributors, book stores, etcetera, THANK YOU!

Suga, you know you're always my number one! I love you! To my mother-in-law, Ms. Clarke thanks for all the things you do. One day God will answer all of your prayers.

Kamal! You are the hustlers' hustler!!! The way you're devoted to making sure **EBANDTE** becomes a great success is crazy! The cold days, the long rides – whatever it is you're always there. Thank you!! You are truly what your name means; perfection!

To Al (the bus driver) didn't I say I was gon' give you a shout out!? THIS IS YOUR BIG SHOUT OUT! (LOL). Thanks for bringing me back and forth upstate to visit my husband. You always get me there safe and on time!

Thanks to any and everyone who helped **EBANDTE INC. PUBLISHING** in small ways as well as in big ways! From Steph Lova and DJ Red Alert at Power105.1, to Glen at **CAPITAL ONE RECORDS,** Whip and Rock at **ROCK HOUSE ENTERTAINMENT** & Peewee Kirkland.

MANIFEST ENTERTAINMENT GROUP, I see you! Keep doing what y'all do! Mark Anthony author of **"PAPER CHASERS"** & **"DOGISM"** thank you so much for everything!! You are a blessing Mark! Treasure E. Blue author of **"HARLEM GIRL LOST"** I see you on ya grind; I'm so proud of you! You are one gifted brother. You'll always be my big bro. I'm waiting for that next book to drop. Tenille & Chyna...I bet y'all thought I forgot y'all – please! Y'all heads are too big for me to forget y'all (Smile)! Chyna, I don't know why they gave you a gun...I'm staying far away from you! Tenille, you better run too (LOL).

If I forgot you; you probably forgot me a time or two before but it's okay. I'm not mad at anyone, I love everyone. I hope everyone loves me too! Good luck & may God bless you all!

Dedication

This book is dedicated to my readers near and far. Y'all have supported me and welcomed me with open arms. Your hard earned dollars that you've spend on my books did not go in vain, I see y'all, I love y'all, I appreciate y'all and I'm happy you're on my side! This book is dedicated to you!

A Message to the Reader

Too often we substitute age for experience. The value of experience is overrated, usually by people who nod wisely and speak stupidly. Embarking upon my journey of writing and publishing it was often thought and said that I was too young to know about **THE HOOD**, I was too young to write about **THE HOOD**. Nevertheless with the help of my husband; Dante, I wrote, produced, marketed and sold **THE HOOD** to thousands of loyal supporters just like you. Then there are those people who do not read "these types of books." To those people I ask one simple question: why? God made all of us different, special and unique. Therefore all our stories are not the same. I to read different types of books; 48 Laws of Power; Unlimited Power; Rich Dad, Poor Dad; The Greatest Salesman in the World, Who Moved My Cheese, Assata and the list goes on. However I know and understand there's a lesson to be learned from **ALL** things; therefore I do not limit my resources. I'm wise enough to know that I know nothing at all. Only he or she who lives forever learns **ALL** things. Since I've not been granted the luxury of eternity I try and absorb all the knowledge I can throughout the duration of my lifetime. This is why I can read the above named books and absorb and apply the jewels these books bring; then turn around and read books like Coldest Winter Ever, Let That Be the Reason, Unfallen Roses, etcetera and learn lessons from these books as well. So remember, it's not the book…it's what **YOU** take from the book. Am I getting through to you or do I sound crazy? On that note I'll leave you with this; only the strong goes crazy, the weak just goes along. Which one are you? God Bless.

THE GAME CHOSE ME

Fuck the world and don't ask me for shit is my attitude nowadays! I remember when there was a time I wore my heart on my sleeve, but shit, not anymore! Those days are long gone. Today a motherfucker couldn't get me to piss on them if they were on fire, especially those trifling ass three "aunts" of mine, *if that's what you wanna call 'em*, and a nigga...Please! Need I say more? But I also remember when there was a time I would let you piss on me and I didn't have to be on fire for you to do it - as long as that paper was right, but I'll get to all that in a minute. Right now let me bring you into my world to as far back as I can remember, and, I'll tell you all about the life and times of 'Mahogany Princess Woods.' After you've entered into my world you'll see that this ain't me. This is what the fuck they made me!

Chapter 1

The Beginning & End

"Happy-birthday-to you! Happy-birthday-to-you! Happy-birthday-to-Mahogany! Happy-birthday- to-you!"

"Yeaaa, Princess you're fifteen now! Blow out your candles so you can open your gifts."

That was my mother. She always called me by my middle name 'Princess.' She always called me Princess because she said that's exactly what I am and I should always be treated as such. She figured if she called me Princess it would remind me of who and what I am.

I remember that fifteenth birthday of mine like it was yesterday even though it was ten long years ago. It was at my home in Forty Projects located in Queens, New York. Forty PJ's was like its own little community within a community. There were about ten brick buildings; some of them stood eight stories high and others stood only four stories high. All ten buildings took up the space of three blocks. Parallel to the PJ's were houses, a store, a supermarket, a Chinese restaurant and liquor store. Whenever the summer time came you best believe everybody was outside and forty was having some big event keeping Queens on the map. My birthday wasn't in the summer time; it was at the end of September so I never had the pleasure of throwing my party outside – it was always in my apartment. I still remember my fifteenth birthday party. There was lots of people present; aunts, cousins, friends etc. Everyone was eating and dancing having a good time at my mother's expense. I was having such a good time I didn't know whether to laugh or to cry because everything was so sweet. My birthday cake had a beautiful picture of myself on it. All my favorite songs were being played. If I didn't know any better I would've thought DJ Red Alert knew it was my birthday the way he kept playing my favorite songs over the airwaves.

My mother was a very generous person. She always believed in feeding everyone. So it was no surprise that my parties always had lots of food, goodies, drinks, etcetera. The whole neighborhood knew it to. Therefore my parties always had a lot of uninvited guest year after year. My mother always let the kids who were less fortunate into my parties to get a bite to eat and just have a good time. In my early years I didn't understand and I would protest against her letting the "bummy kids" into my parties. Year after year my protest fell upon deaf ears. My whining was to no avail so I finally gave up. I learned to party with the "bummy kids," I also learned to like it, but most of all I was learning to understand why my mom did what she did.

A guaranteed guest at my party was sure to be this one "bummy kid" named Dey-Dey. Each year Dey-Dey would show up fatter and funnier than the year before, but nothing was funnier than the year of my fifteenth birthday. I remember Dey-Dey wearing his tight superman shirt *looking like he was nine months pregnant* with ashy black high-water jeans, while stuffing his face with cheese doodle after cheese doodle. Just the sight of him would make anyone laugh. On top of that Dey-Dey always wanted to be the center of attention. The only thing he loved more than the cheese doodles and fried chicken he stuffed his face with was the dance contest. He couldn't dance one bit, but that didn't stop him from trying. What really motivated him was the twenty dollars my mother gave to the winner of the contest. Dey-Dey would get on the floor and bust a sweat tryna win that twenty dollars. He looked so funny not only were the other kids laughing at him, but so were some of the adults. Every year he won the twenty dollars, not because he could dance, but because "he earned it" my mother would say.

On my fifteenth birthday he won fifty dollars because he danced so hard his foot busted out the sole of his sneaker! He was dancing so hard to the point where he didn't even realize his foot was out of his sneaker until the kids standing in a circle around him stopped chanting "go Dey-Dey, go Dey-Dey" and started pointing and laughing. My mother handed him fifty dollars right there on the spot! My parties were always fun and everyone always had a good time!

I always stayed dressed to kill, each year I would rock a outfit better than the one I rocked the year before. On my fifteenth birthday I was laced in the baddest chocolate-brown leather skirt suit. To compliment my suit I wore my brand new light brown Gucci boots with the G's all over them. You couldn't tell me I wasn't the shit! I truly was the shinning star of the party. My mom never danced or anything, she was basically making sure everyone one else was having a good time. I remember her prancing around our home looking fabulous as usual. My mother was a very light skinned woman with shoulder length light brown hair. Time was no enemy to her body, she didn't have saggy breast or a loose booty, she was still in shape her body was tight!

I still remember everything I got. I remember my mother turning the music completely off minutes before the party was s'pose to end, which bought the entire room to a complete stand still. She made an announcement for everyone to gather around. Once everyone complied she kissed me on the cheek and fixed my collar. Just as I was about to ask my mom what was so important that my favorite LL Cool J song had to be stopped, she handed me a small black box while saying,

"Princess in this box is something very special. Once you've opened it I'll explain exactly what it is."

I opened the box, inside laid a thin platinum necklace with a platinum and diamond key on the necklace. I gave my mother the look that says, "What's so special about this?" Since every mother knows their child my mother looked at me and said, "Princess that key on the necklace is not just any key, that key is the key to my heart."

While saying those words my mother grabbed the heart on her necklace which she wore around her neck. With the deepest sincerity she spoke.

"That key is the only key that can open my heart. Princess I would like you to use that key to open my heart right now."

As my mother said those words tears formed in my eyes. I used my key to open the heart around her neck. Once the heart was opened, my mother removed the necklace from around her neck. She pointed to the picture inside of the heart as she held it in her hand and said, "This is a picture of you at your first birthday party."

I looked at the picture and began crying. I was wearing a pretty pink dress with white trimmings. My socks were ruffled like my dress, on my feet were white patent leather shoes. And a tiara sat on my head full of curls. My mother wiped the tears from my eyes and continued speaking.

"Darling I want you to know and understand that no matter what you do or no matter where life may take you, you are always in my heart. So if there's ever a day that you're feeling down just use your key to open my heart so you can see that you are always my number one and you'll always be my Princess."

After that speech I was so emotional I almost forgot where I was, but my younger cousin Shiane opened her big mouth to remind me.

"Oh Mahogany you are so phony! You know those ain't no real tears, and if they are I don't see any reason that you have to cry! I should be the one crying! Every time my birthday comes I just get a home made cake and one outfit or a pair of sneakers, but not little Miss Mahogany! Aunt Cynthia always gotta OD! Look at all ya stuff. You got money, jewelry, clothes, a bike and a leather jacket so you need to take those tears and shove them up your…"

"Shiane you better cut it out! That is your cousin and my niece so be nice to her before I have to pop you right in your mouth! I told you about that, now apologize!"

That was my aunt Charlene. Aunt Charlene always had to put her only child Shiane in her place about her big mouth. Even though Shiane was only fourteen sometimes she would act as if she was forty-one. Shiane was big for her age she could pass for eighteen years old easily. She had buckteeth, tight eyes, short hair that stopped just below her chin and bad skin. To make matters worse her skin was high yellow so it was easily noticed. From the way her body was shaped it wasn't hard to tell she had her share of steak and potatoes. She looked just like her mother, the only difference was, my aunt Charlene was a little thicker and she always wore her hair in a curly weave. Her skin was bad too, but not as bad as her daughter's skin. They were both high yellow with tight eyes and buckteeth though. This explains why they stayed mad at the world even though my aunt Charlene would always try to front like she loved me so much.

Aunt Charlene always made Shiane apologize whenever her mouth was out of order, but Shiane's apologies really didn't mean shit to me because Shiane would apologize then go right back to saying some slick shit. Usually Shiane's words didn't bother me. I would just shatter her world with one phrase. That phrase was usually, "Don't hate me 'cause you ain't me." Whenever I said that Shaine would get pissed! She knew I was speaking the truth, the only thing she would usually say to me was, "Mahogany you think you're all that but you're not. If you didn't have clear light skin with long hair and green eyes you would look a mess."

After Shiane would say things to let me see clearly just how jealous of me she was, I'd laugh in her face while combing my pretty, light-brown, long hair and blink my eyes so she could see just how pretty and green they were with a pair of long eyelashes to compliment them. Once I did that Shiane would really get pissed and we would end up fighting. Depending on whose house we were fighting at we would both get a beaten, not by each other but by my mother. My mother would lecture us and beat our asses to the point that we wished we would've never fought. But when we fought at Aunt Charlene's house she would usually take her daughter's side then put on a front when my moms came to get me. Aunt Charlene would say things to my mother like, "Cynthia, those two girls was at it again and I had to put both of them in their place. I didn't hit them because I figured that's just kids being kids, you know how they do, fight one minute and love each other the next."

Aunt Charlene would tell my mother lie after lie. She talked about how she did this and how she did that, but the reality of the situation was she ain't do shit! She didn't even stop us from fighting, if anything she was the instigator. I would hear her telling her daughter things like, "If you don't whip her ass then I'ma whip your ass" or "don't let nobody hit you first. Always be the one to throw the first punch." I never told my mother what was going on because my mother was a firm believer that a child should stay in a child's place. So whatever my aunt told her is what my mother believed. After a while my mom got hip to the game and she didn't allow me to go over Aunt Charlene's house as much. Whenever Shiane came to visit us my mother would let her know from the beginning that she wasn't having it. My mother would always say, "With a family like ours, who needs enemies?" I didn't quite understand what my mother meant each time she said that phrase when I was younger but boy-o-boy did I learn in time.

My other two aunts Charmaine and Brenda weren't

any different. Aunt Charmaine was cute, short and chubby, with caramel skin. She always wore her hair in braids. Aunt Brenda was a slim brown skin woman who always wore her hair in a ponytail. She had stains on her teeth from all the cigarettes she smoked. Aunt Charmaine would always tell me how I was her favorite niece and how she loved me so much, but that was only when my mom was looking. As soon as my mom turned her back aunt Charmaine would turn into a completely different person. Aunt Charmaine had three kids, all of whom my mother looked out for whenever it came to holidays, birthdays, back to school shopping or just because. I was my mother's only child and when it came time to buy something for my birthday, graduation or something like that; my aunts would always say, "We didn't get Mahogany anything because we don't know what to get for the girl that has everything." That was their lame ass excuse. Aunt Charmaine would always say "Mahogany I saw something that I wanted to get for you but you'll have to wait 'til the fifteenth." I guessed the fifteenth never came on her calendar because every year she would say that famous line, and every year I never received anything from her, not even a card but I ain't sweat it. My mom always made sure I had everything I wanted and needed. I knew the real reason my aunts didn't buy me anything was because they didn't want to. I knew if a person really wanted to do something for you and it was from the heart they were gonna do it regardless. So I didn't really care much for them or their excuses, in fact, excuses are what I expected from them. My attitude towards them was plain and simple, "Fuck 'em!"

Aunt Brenda didn't have any kids. Yet she was always

EBANDTE INC. PRESENTS . . . *THE GAME CHOSE ME*

broke, don't ask me why and don't ask me how because your guess is good as mine.

My father couldn't stand any of them and all three of them knew it. He would usually tell my mother, it was a shame how her own sisters could be so jealous of her. My pops was a street dude. He was killed when I was twelve years old. Even though him and my moms weren't together, he always made sure he took care of me. He made sure my moms was alright too.

Many people would say I looked just like my pops. They said the only thing my moms gave me was her light skin and her long brown hair. The rest of my features came from my dad like my green eyes and my pretty smile. My dad was a fine chocolate brother, he wasn't Jamaican but he wore his hair in short dreadlocks that always stayed neat. I could tell my parents still loved each other and I still believe if my pops wasn't murdered; him and my moms would've gotten back together. If you let my moms tell it, she says they would've never gotten back together. She always admits she loved my dad and always will love him, but she said the two of them could've never gotten back together because, "He wanted to live for the streets" and she wanted "To live for Jesus."

The one thing I appreciate about my parents break up was it was civilized. Most of the people in our neighborhood thought my parents were still together because of the respect they had for one another. My dad stopped by our house so often it was hard for anyone to tell they were broken up. He even brought gifts for me and my mom. My dad had plenty of money and he didn't mind spending it, my mom was a nurse. It was part of those two reason why my aunts always barrowed money, clothes and jewelry from my moms. They always felt like my moms had it like that therefore they didn't have to buy me anything or return any of the money they barrowed from her. Some people would call us "hood rich" because we lived in the projects, but we had almost everything that money could buy. The reality of the situation was, most of the material things we had came from my dad, he always made sure we wanted for nothing. Sometimes my mom would get stubborn and not accept his gifts. Like the time when my dad offered to move me and her out of the projects and into a house. My mom refused to use his "blood money" to move into a house. She said she'd rather save her money like she's been doing and move herself into a house "legally." I loved my dad and I know he loved me. When he was killed I was devastated. Of course I didn't get all the extravagant things I used to get when he was alive. My moms was taking care of me and taking care of herself all alone. Plus she made sure all the bills were paid while still saving money to buy a house. But my mom wasn't a slouch, even though I wasn't getting extravagant things I was still fly, all my gear was always up to date. My moms wouldn't deprive me of anything she just did what she could and I understood that. I understood my father made easy money in the streets while my mom had to work long, hard eight-hour shifts to take care of us. That's why it was easy for me to understand if I told my dad I liked a leather jacket, sneakers, or a piece of jewelry, he would get the jacket or sneakers in every color. Plus buy the whole set to the piece of jewelry I liked. While my mom would only be able to buy one or two of the jackets or sneakers I liked, and one piece of jewelry instead of the whole set. But no matter what my mom brought for me I was grateful! I know everything she did for me was from her heart, and I was still a fly little bitch.

Through all the ups and downs I could tell that my mom was hurt about my father's death. It's almost like she felt guilty about something, or she knew something that the rest of the world didn't. After my father's death I noticed my mom started attending counseling. She made it her business to keep me active as possible. My mom put me in dancing school. She also started paying for me to take singing lessons.

I loved singing with a passion. I always wanted to become a famous singer. Sometimes I would daydream about becoming a famous singer and going on the popular radio stations to promote my CD. I'd picture myself saying things like, "I would like to thank my mother and father and everybody else who held me down, and for those of y'all who didn't; eat a dick. And to everybody who doesn't have my CD already; go cop three of them 'cause you gon' need one for the house, one for the car, and one for the plastic 'cause it's a classic." After my daydreams I would always laugh to myself just thinking about how things would really be if I became a famous singer.

When my birthday party came to an end I was so happy to get everyone out of my house so I could relax and get ready to floss my new fly shit in school the next day. To me school wasn't just a place to floss. I had dreams and goals so school was important. On top of that, my mother wouldn't buy me shit if I didn't maintain at least a B average. And I was far from a fool so even though I had dreams of becoming a singer, I had a back up plan just in case I didn't make it. My back up plan was to become a psychiatrist so I could help all the nuts in this fucked up ass world or at least try too. Yup, I had big dreams and big goals, and I was going to big places 'cause I was destined to succeed. I was a sure winner and when I got up that next morning I was going to school.

The next day I was up and ready for school bright and early. This wasn't just a regular school day, this day was special! It was the day after my birthday, a half of day in school and my mother didn't know anything about it. What really made this day so special was; it was the day that I promised to give up my virginity to Jamel!

Me and Jamel was dating for six months, we didn't have sex yet. He was nineteen, out of school and fine!! Jamel was six-one, brown skin with a low cut Cesar. His hairline always seemed to be cut perfectly straight. His teeth were beautiful! On top of that, the way he always licked his wet juicy lips was enough to make any bitch's pussy wanna jump out of their panties and onto his face. Even though me and Jamel was creeping because I didn't want my mother to know I was dating an older guy, we got to see each other often. We lived in the same neighborhood. Whenever I was coming from the store or on my way home from school, I'd see Jamel standing on the corner. He would nod his head which was the signal for me to go into the building. Once I entered into the building Jamel would enter shortly after me. We would go into the back staircase and kiss and feel up on each other. Jamel did most of the feeling and I just let him. When I would wear skirts Jamel didn't waste anytime fingerpoping me. One time he even rubbed his dick on my pussy, that day we came so close to fucking, the only thing that stopped us was a crackhead creeping through the back door. The crackhead scared us so bad we stopped everything we was doing. Once Jamel noticed it was a crackhead and not a nosey neighbor or something, he yelled at the crackhead and told him to get the fuck out of the staircase! He went on yelling at the crackhead saying, "Yo if you tell anybody you saw us back here I'll fuck you up myself! Don't make me do it man 'cause I'm telling you I will! Now hurry the fuck up and leave!"

I never saw a crackhead run so fast I couldn't help but to laugh. Once the crackhead was out of our sight Jamel tried to pick up were we left off, but I said "Hell no!" I was too nervous. That's when Jamel got upset and started licking on my ear while whispering, "Mahogany, why you actin' like that? You know I care for you and you know I wouldn't do nothing to hurt you. You my little wife. You the only girl who made me even wait this long before I hit it. If you was anybody else I would've been left you, but I can't leave you 'cause I care for you. I'm tired of playing games with you Mahogany, I thought you was a big girl, when you gon' show me?"

As I tried to respond he put his finger over my lip and said, "Ssshhh, we don't have to do it now, but think about what I said." Then he kissed me on my forehead as he put his finger inside of my pussy. He took his finger out, licked it and said, "Uhm...vanilla, I really care for you Mahogany, do you care for me?"

My response was, "Yes!"

Jamel replied, "Let me hear it then, tell me you care..."

That was the day I decided I would let Jamel break my virginity. I knew all that shit he was kicking in my ear was game, but I didn't give a fuck! On top of that I had my hot ass friend, Jackie whose been fucking since elementary school in my ear telling me how good sex felt.

Jackie told me I had to suck my man's dick if I don't want him to leave me. Whenever Jackie spoke, I listened 'cause if anybody knew about sex, it was Jackie.

Me and Jackie was the same age, we was cool as ice. We lived in the same projects. Both of us were pretty and fly and we knew it, especially Jackie. Jackie just knew that the sun didn't shine 'til she got up. Jackie had pretty brown skin, a banging body and long black curly hair. She would let anybody know in a minute, man or woman that she was the shit!

Jackie lived with her mother, her mother's boyfriend, and her two older brothers. Jackie's brothers were hustlers. They spoiled her and they kept her fly. Their mother was a recovering drug addict, she didn't really have time to watch Jackie, she was too busy tryna keep herself clean and sober. That's why Jackie's brothers made it their business to make sure Jackie was always taken care of. They were so use to taking care of Jackie that when their mother recovered they just continued taking care of Jackie like they always did. Another thing I loved about Jackie was, she spoke her mind. After I told her what happened in the staircase with me and Jamel she said, "Girl even though I can't stand Jamel's ass, he is fine, fly, older, and he has a hot car! Not only that, he has so many girls sweating him, but he's with you, a young girl, instead of those older girls who will do any and everything to and for him at the drop of a dime. You better realize what you got while you still got it 'cause you know what they say, 'What one girl wont do the next one will' and I know you don't wanna lose ya man just 'cause you ain't giving up the ass."

After that conversation with Jackie I knew what I had to do. I called Jamel later that day and I told him I would allow him to break my virginity the day after my fifteenth birthday, which at the time was two weeks away. Jamel looked too good for me to let him get away, especially over something as simple as giving up some pussy. I figured how bad could it be? I had to get fucked one day anyway, so it might as well be with him and it might as well be now. I had my mind made up that the day after my fifteenth birthday was the day I was gonna fuck Jamel, suck his dick and let him make me a woman. Plus Jackie said it felt good! So I made up my mind to fuck my man. Jackie even made up a poem for me to say in my head before I went to sleep for my last two weeks of being a virgin. I practiced it faithfully every night.

Dick is not the enemy, dick is your friend,
after you ride dick, dick will make you grin,
but you gotta suck some dick and lick some balls
if you want that nigga with the good dick
to be all yours,
and if you do it right dick will spend the night
and he'll wake up in the morning
looking for you in the day time with a flashlight,
but you gotta do it right and deep throat that shit,
'cause if you don't then dick will move
on to the next bitch.

I laughed myself to sleep thinking about Jackie's poem. I knew in two weeks I was no longer gonna be Jamel's "little wife" instead I was gonna be his "Freak bitch!" Everything was planned perfect. Since I had a half of day at school, Jamel was supposed to pick me up from school in his fly ass Lexus. We didn't want everyone in our business so we were going straight to a hotel in Long Island without making any stops. Later Jamel would drop me off around four o'clock at the bus stop located a block away from my building. This way if anyone saw me, I'd be alone and look like I was on my way home from a full day at school. It was the perfect plan.

When two weeks finally arrived I was so excited, but nervous at the same time. So far everything was going according to my plans. The only bad thing was my mother was home from work. It was her day off, but even that wasn't so bad 'cause me and Jamel was going to a hotel. Plus since my mom didn't know about my half of day in school, when I got home at four-thirty she couldn't or wouldn't be suspicious because four-thirty was the usual time I arrived home from a regular school day.

When me and Jamel arrived in the hotel room he didn't waste anytime throwing me on the bed and undressing me. He knew we only had three hours to do the damn thing! I was excited for two reasons, one; because I was getting my virginity broken and it was with Jamel, and two; because I was in a hotel room with a guy! Besides going on trips with my parents, I've never been inside a hotel room.

Once Jamel stripped me down to my panties and bra he took a moment to tell me how sexy and beautiful I was. My body was petite, but it was shapely, and after all the cocoa butter I used on it daily; it was super soft. When Jamel finished praising my beauty he laid me on my back, opened my legs real wide and told me to relax. He moved my panties to the side then began sucking my clit. Jamel was using his tongue to eat my pussy and blowing on it using his soft sexy lips. After a while of doing that Jamel laid me on my stomach as he began massaging my back all the way down to my butt. Suddenly I felt a warm hard object in between my legs. It was Jamel's dick. His dick was so big and my pussy was so tight, he couldn't slide his dick in the first time he tried so he began eating my pussy some more. This time my pussy got real wet and I was jumping and moaning. My legs were shaking uncontrollably. All the wetness from Jamel's tongue plus the juices from my wet pussy was on my inner thighs. At that moment I knew Jamel would be able to stick his big, fat, hard dick inside of my wet pussy with no problem, but I didn't want Jamel to stick it in just then. I kept thinking about what Jackie said about keeping your man. So as Jamel finished eating my pussy, he was positioning himself to climb on top of me, but before he was able to, I grabbed his dick and started jerking it. I could tell by the look in his eyes not only was he surprised with my bold actions, but he was loving every minute of it. Then I shocked him even more when I got on my knees while both of us was still in the bed, I put my ass in the air and my face in between his legs as I began sucking his dick and licking his balls just like Jackie said I should! I didn't know what the fuck I was doing, but I sure wasn't gon' let him know that. I tried to suck his dick like I was a pro! I kept Jackie's poem in the back of my head so I deep throated his dick every chance I got. However I sucked his dick that day it must have felt good to him too because he didn't waste anytime cuming inside of my mouth before I spit that warm, salty, nasty shit out.

As I ran to the bathroom butt ass naked to wash the nasty taste out of my mouth, Jamel bent me over the sink and slid his dick in between my legs. When it finally went inside of my pussy I was screaming like hell and asking myself, how the fuck could this feel good to Jackie? But after a few more strokes, I understood what sister girl was saying! Jamel's dick was feeling good to me. After Jamel came all over my ass cheeks both of us got in the shower, he washed my body and I washed his, he even washed away my bust cherry. As Jamel washed in between my legs he couldn't help himself, he just had to stick his dick inside of my slippery, wet pussy one more time. Once me and him was out of the shower; we couldn't help ourselves and we continued to fuck about two or three more times until we fell asleep in each others arms.

I was awoken by the sound of the hotel phone ringing. When I answered, it was a male's voice saying, "Time is up." I just said, "Okay." as I placed the phone back on the receiver. I rolled over to wake Jamel up. I told him what the guy called and said. Looking at my watch I realized it was seven-thirty in the evening! Immediately I jumped out of bed while tryna find my panties screaming, "Oh shit! Jamel look at the time! My mother's gonna kill me, it's already seven-thirty and it's gonna take us at least a half-an-hour to get home from here! And how am I gonna explain why my hair is wet!?"

Jamel was moving in slow motion like I just drained the life out of him while yawning and saying, "Just tell her you went to the pool."

After I looked at him like he was crazy I said, "Jamel, its September not July, if you think my mom will believe that lame ass excuse then you must be smoking that shit you selling."

The whole ride back I was so nervous. All I could do was think about which lie could I tell my mother? I called

Jackie from Jamel's cell phone to see if she called my house. If she didn't, I was gonna lie and say I was with her. But it didn't look like that plan would be working, no one was answering Jackie's phone, which was strange. Then I was thinking about saying I was at the library, but I was pretty sure my mother being the nervous person that she is, checked the library already so that wouldn't work.

By the time I arrived in my projects it was eight-seventeen. I had a thousand lies to tell my mother, but I wasn't sure about which one I should use. I knew it definitely had to be a lie involving me and no one else, I was pretty sure she called all my friends she could think of. So I decided I would go in the house and see what kind of mood she was in. That would help me determine which lie I would tell. Before I exited Jamel's car we kissed as he said to me, "You know you really mine now, right?"

Showing my pearly whites and licking my lips I shot back, "I know. I just hope you know!"

Winking his eye he came back with the magical words I've been waiting to hear all night, "I love you Mahogany."

That wasn't Jamel's first time telling me he loved me, but it was special because he rarely said it, and the times that he did say it was because I asked him to say it. So after he said that, I wasn't even thinking about the trouble I was gonna be in. To me it was worth it just to hear Jamel say those magic words. When I was standing outside of Jamel's car, I stuck my head inside his window to give him one last kiss then I grabbed his dick while saying, "I'll call you tomorrow when I get home from school, but if I don't call you then that means I can't call you." Jamel grabbed my arm and told me, "Nah, I got a better idea, I'm picking you up from school tomorrow 'cause I know I'll wanna see ya pretty little face even if it is just for ten minutes."

Blushing I replied, "Okay I love you, I'll see you tomorrow."

Now I definitely knew any trouble I was in was worth it 'cause like Jackie said, I sucked his dick real good, now he didn't wanna leave me alone. I was loving every minute of it! I loved the way Jamel took control of me. I knew I would love fucking and sucking his dick for the rest of our lives.

When I arrived in front of my building I saw police vehicles, some marked and some unmarked, but I could tell they were all police vehicles. Seeing police vehicles in my neighborhood was not unusual. A lot of times police were raiding drug houses in that area or harassing local drug dealers. But on this night I was nervous because I thought my mother might've gotten so paranoid that she called the police to report me missing. In my mind I was hoping that really wasn't the case. When I exited the elevator on the fourth floor I saw nothing but police, some uniformed and some in plain clothes. I knew right then and there it was nothing I would be able to say or do to get myself out of this trouble I was in. As I walked closer and closer towards my apartment I noticed yellow tape, I saw my Aunt Charlene and my Aunt Brenda hugging and crying. As I tried to run and find out what was going on I was stopped by an officer holding his hand up.

"May I help you?"

Giving him much attitude I replied, "Yes I would like to know what's going on in my apartment."

"Ma'am who are you?"

"I'm the person who lives in 4B with my mom, now if

you'll excuse me I would like to find out what is going on."

"Ma'am I'm afraid we can't let you enter the premises, this is a homicide scene."

After the officer made that statement I screamed, "A WHAT!!!"

My scream was loud enough for everyone near my apartment to turn around including Aunt Charlene and Aunt Brenda. Immediately the two of them raced towards me with open arms saying, "Mahogany baby, calm down everything's gonna be alright, we're gonna find the bastard or bastards who did this."

With tears in my eyes I backed away from them biting my bottom lip as I replied, "Aunt Charlene, Aunt Brenda I know y'all ain't saying what I think you're saying."

Aunt Brenda took a step towards me, "Calm down baby, she's in a better place, heaven last always."

With my faced drowned in tears I screamed, "I know somebody better tell me I'm dreaming, somebody better wake me up, I know that my mother is not dead, not my one and only, not her!"

Grabbing my hand Aunt Charlene came closer towards me, "Mahogany baby, come on let's go outside with Aunt Brenda so we can all get some fresh air. You don't need to be right here, not right now."

Spazzing I said what I felt in my heart, "No I think y'all got it twisted because I definitely need to be right here, right now 'til somebody tells me what the fuck is going on!"

Chapter 2

New Life...

I stood all alone in a giant warehouse. Nothing but snakes surrounded me. The faster I tried to get away, the closer they came.

"Don't let them get me! Please don't let them get me!" I screamed.

"Run Mahogany! You have to run! Don't let them get you!" a woman's voice yelled.

I ran towards the door. The knob was broken, I couldn't get out. I turned to look back. The snakes were getting closer. I rushed toward a huge window inside the warehouse. I looked up. I knew there was no way I could reach the window, it was too high.

"Don't let them get you!" it was the same woman's voice. I kept hearing the same voice but I didn't see anyone.

"Where are you? Help me! Please help me! Why do you keep telling me to run and you're not doing nothing! Help me!" I cried.

"Watch out its right behind you!" the woman screamed.

I turned around; the snake had its mouth wide open.

"Noooooooooo!" I screamed.

"Mahogany wake up! Wake up! Why the hell are you screaming?" When I opened my eyes, Aunt Charlene was standing over me.

"Oh my God!" Shiane screamed. She threw a pillow then continued, "Ma she probably having another one of those stupid dreams! I can't take another night of hearing her screaming. Can you let her sleep in your room!?"

"Shiane be quiet!" Aunt Charlene shot back. Shiane sucked her teeth.

"Mahogany, sit up," said Aunt Charlene. I sat up. My heart was beating fast. My pillow was wet from sweat and tears.

"Were you having another dream?" Charlene asked.

"I think so," I replied.

"Were you having these dreams before your mother died?"

"No, I started having them three months after she died."

Aunt Charlene shook her head, "Well pretty soon it'll be one year since she's been dead. I'm trying to be patient with you, but I don't know how much longer I can take this. You're gonna have to learn to control these dreams. You can't keep waking me and Shiane up every night."

"You could say that again," shouted Shiane.

I ignored Shiane and continued speaking to Aunt Charlene, "I don't know why I keep having these dreams. I just can't control them. Maybe if I knew the stupid cops finally arrested my mother's killer I'd feel better."

"If you're waiting for the cops to do something, you're wasting your time. The only piece of evidence they have is the baseball bat your mother was beaten to death with.

They ain't even got a witness. Even if somebody in that projects did know what happened, you know just like I do. Once the police ask them something, they ain't see shit!"

Shiane hopped off the top bunk, "Ma, I'm going in your room. I do not feel like being bothered."

I shot Shiane a look that could kill. She sucked her teeth then wobbled her fat ass into her mother's room.

"I'm sorry I keep waking y'all up Aunt Charlene."

"Don't be sorry, it's done. Next time just control them, that's all."

"It's not that easy."

"Well, you better do something because this is getting ridiculous."

"I'll try."

"Don't try, just do it sweetheart."

Shiane came wobbling back into the room wrapped in a sheet.

"What's wrong with you?" her mother asked her.

Shiane sucked her teeth, "I can't go back to sleep now. Why couldn't Mahogany move in with Aunt Brenda or Aunt Charmaine?"

"Why can't you go on a diet!?" I shot back.

"Mahogany, relax okay?" replied Aunt Charlene.

"Don't tell her nothing ma. Next time I'ma just punch her in the face!"

"You ain't punching nobody!"

"Mahogany!" screamed Aunt Charlene. Then she continued, "Do you wanna get your hair done today?"

"Yes," I replied.

"Alright then shut up. I'm sick of repeating myself."

"Uh-uh, that's not fair ma. I know you ain't just taking Mahogany to get her hair done today. You promised next time her check came, we was all going to get our hair done!"

Aunt Charlene looked at her only daughter, "Did I say you wasn't getting your hair done?"

"So I'm going to Tammy's shop too?" Shiane asked.

"Yes, we all are," Aunt Charlene replied.

Shiane started jumping up and down. Aunt Charlene started laughing.

"Sit down child. Stop acting like you ain't use to nothing."

I looked at Aunt Charlene, "If all three of us are going to Tammy's we better get there early. Today is Saturday so I know it's gonna be packed."

Shiane stopped jumping around then looked at me, "She swear she know everything! I cannot stand her sometimes!"

Aunt Charlene ignored her daughter, "I'm trying to leave no later than ten o'clock." Charlene looked at the clock on the wall then continued, "It's a quarter to eight now so we could start getting ready."

"Aunt Charlene, by the time we get to Harlem Tammy's shop will be packed! If we leave around that time we'll definitely be in there all day."

"It shouldn't take that long, we taking a cab out there," Aunt Charlene replied.

"I told you she thinks she knows everything," Shiane added.

I sucked my teeth then headed for the bathroom. Aunt Charlene started laughing.

"Shiane you crazy," I heard her say.

• • •

Upon arriving in Tammy's shop I could've died! The place was filled to its capacity. Ladies were everywhere sitting down, standing up, under the dryer, at the sink. I knew this would be a long day. Through all the people, rollers, magazines and blow dryers Tammy still managed to spot me.

"Is that my girl?" Tammy smiled making her way over to me.

"Hey Tammy," I greeted her with a kiss on the cheek.

Looking at her watch she let me have it, "Now you know ya butt should've been here as soon as I got here. You would've been in and out by now. Since when have you been coming here at a-quarter-to-twelve? It's Saturday too! Did you fall and bump ya head miss-missy?"

Tammy always treated me as if she was my big sister. I didn't mind at all, in fact I was happy with the treatment she gave me. Tammy was my idol, she had it going on! From the hottest designer clothes to the colorful minks and butter leathers, Tammy was fly! About fifteen years my senior Tammy was everything I wanted to be. She was tall, pretty, fly, owned her own shop. She even drove a BMW. Sister didn't look a day over twenty-five.

Tammy's been my hairdresser since I could remember. My mother brought me to Tammy's shop every week to get my hair done since I was ten. I think that's around the time Tammy opened her own shop. Since then a lot has changed. Tammy no longer did other people's hair. Of course I was an exception to that rule.

I admired Tammy so much that I even wanted to marry a man just like her husband Randy. Uncle Randy was a straight up gangsta! He took on the role as my uncle after seeing me with his wife so much. I guess he just got tired of me calling him Mr. Randy all the time. He said 'Mr.' made him feel old. Ever since then I've granted his wish of calling him Uncle Randy. He granted me the nickname of 'Lil Mama.' Uncle Randy was a big time player in the game. He had the streets of Harlem on lock! Everybody knew it.

The way Tammy and Uncle Randy treated me, the average person would've thought there was really some type of blood bond between us. Him and Tammy was real hurt by the sudden death of my mom too. They sent a car full of roses to my mom's funeral. They always showed much love.

Demanding an answer to the question Tammy just asked me she stood firm in one spot with her hands placed on her hips and one eyebrow raised, "Hello miss-missy. Since when did you start coming at a-quarter-to-twelve? Am I going to have to call Uncle Randy and tell him his Lil' Mama don't love us anymore?"

"You wouldn't go there."

Now folding her arms and tapping her foot she replied, "Yes I will go there I'm waiting."

I stood there speechless as Tammy began counting, "Ten-nine-eight-seven-six…"

One of Tammy's workers's yelled from the back of her huge shop, "Tammy, you have a phone call."

Tammy shook her head and said, "Saved by the bell." I giggled then blurted, "But I live in Brooklyn now, remember?"

Tammy gave me that 'Oh yeah' look then held one finger up signaling she'd be back in a minute. Just as I grabbed a magazine off the receptionist table Tammy reappeared faster than she left.

Surprised I turned to her, "That was fast."

Rolling her eyes and shaking her head, "That was a pain in my ass. Now back to you miss-missy, you know I'm gon' hurt you right?"

"But you love me, Tammy."

Grabbing me by my wrist and placing the magazine back on the receptionist desk Tammy whispered, "Play along." I knew what she was up to. So I just smiled as she ran her game for everyone within close range of us to see what was going on, "Well what took you so long? I thought you were never coming back! Did you have to build the store you said you were going to when you came earlier today?" She winked at me, I just followed her lead. I could hear the clutching of girls teeth plus feel the burning stares piercing through my back. It was clear that no one was really buying Tammy's lie. However, Tammy didn't really care and neither did I. Only one person was bold enough to say something.

"Uhm, Tammy I think you should do my hair first, Mahogany can wait." Tammy turned to look at the person who dared to challenge her authority as she replied, "And you are...?"

"I'm Charlene, Cynthia's sister, Mahogany's aunt."

"Okay, you're the one Mahogany's staying with now right?"

"Yeah, you know I had to look out for my niece. I told her ya shop would be crowded 'cause I remember how crowded it was the last time I came. Anyway like I was saying she can wait because my do needs to be done first. I like the way you did my hair before, can you do it the same way?"

Frowning Tammy replies, "Refresh my recollection

when did I do your hair?"

Charlene carried on like her and Tammy was the best of friends. Even though she'd only been to her shop once before today, "Girl stop playing! You know we go way back. I was with Cynthia a while back when you did both of our hair. You don't remember? Cynthia got spiral curls and you hooked my curly weave up."

Tammy looked confused, "Actually that's highly unlikely because I don't do weaves. Are you sure it was me?"

Charlene had the look of frustration written all over her face as she looks Tammy up and down, "I could've sworn it was you. I know it was close to a year ago but I really think it was you. If it wasn't you then you must have a twin because homegirl looked just like you." Charlene completes her statement by rolling her eyes. Tammy snapped her finger and replied, "Okay, okay I remember now."

"Um-hm," Charlene mumbled while Tammy continued,

"It was my sister Dasia who did your hair that day. We're not twins but we damn sure look alike. She's not here anymore. Dasia opened her own shop out in Queens. If you'd like I can give you the address."

Charlene looked insulted, "I'm already here now. I'm not going all the way to Queens when I came all this way, who else here does curly weaves?"

"I wasn't implying that you go all the way to Queens. I was just giving you her address in case you wanted to visit her in the future. If you'd like the same style you had before then that shouldn't be a problem. Most of the girls here can do that style. Someone should be with you in about forty-five minutes."

"Why do I have to wait that long when Mahogany gets her do done now? We came together."

With much attitude Tammy spits, "Mahogany has an appointment. She's been coming every week since I could remember."

"Oh, I guess that makes it okay. Although I can't recall making an appointment for just Princess Mahogany," replied a sarcastic Charlene.

Tammy takes a deep breath, "Like I said - someone will be with you shortly." Looking in Shiane's direction Tammy spoke again, "This must be your other sister, are you getting a curly weave today too?"

Shiane answered Tammy, "Do I look like I can be her sister? For your information I'm her daughter." Charlene co-signed her daughter's disrespect with her laugh. Tammy looked like she was ready to kill them both as she cracked a devilish grin, "Someone will be with you too."

Me and Tammy disappeared to the back of the salon so I could get my usual wash-and-set. Shiane and Aunt Charlene sat and waited to be rescued by the next available weave needle and thread.

Aunt Charlene had a bad attitude the entire ride back home. She was pissed off for two reasons; one because she didn't like her hair and two because she didn't like how Tammy catered to me but not to her and her daughter.

My hair was looking banging as usual. I couldn't wait to floss my style. Upon arriving in the house I ran to the ringing phone.

Ring...Ring...Ring.

Out of breath I answered, "Hello."

"Where you was at?"

I had to look at the phone and repeat myself, "Hello?"

"You heard what I said so get to talking."

Sassy as I wanted to be I replied, "Daddy? I could've sworn my daddy was dead."

"Well I'm ya new daddy, now gimme kiss."

"Oh really? Jamel, you need to cut it out."

"Oh, first I can't know where daddy's girl was all day. Now I can't even get a kiss."

"It's Saturday, you know where I was today and m-wha. Are you satisfied now, you got a kiss and you know my whereabouts."

"Nope, gimme another kiss."

"M-wha, m-wha, m-wha!"

"Now that's better. What was you doing?"

"I just walked in the door and I was about to..."

"Got-damn! Can we be in the house for more than five minutes before you get on the damn phone!" screams Charlene as she walks in the kitchen and sees me on the phone.

"The phone was ringing soon as we walked in the door, I just answered it. I didn't call anyone if that's what you're thinking."

Jamel speaks through his end of the phone, "Tell that fat bitch to shut the fuck up."

"No, you shut up," I replied to Jamel. However, Aunt Charlene thought I was talking to her.

"What did you just tell me to do Mahogany?"

"I wasn't talking to you Aunt Charlene."

Jamel enjoys a laugh at Charlene's expense, "Ha, ha, ha. That's who you need to be telling to shut up."

"Let me call you back."

"You won't be calling anybody on my phone. Shit, I

have people to call too."

"Call me back later please."

Jamel breaks, "Fuck that! I'm coming to get you right now! You don't have to deal with that bullshit. We could go to the movies or something." Click, Jamel hung up the phone.

"Who were you on my phone with?" asked Charlene.

Shiane puts her two cents in, "From what I heard, somebody called 'daddy,'" Shiane laughs at her own joke. I give her an evil look while putting her in her place, "Get some business of your own and stay out of mine please."

Aunt Charlene snapped, "I asked you a question Mahogany."

I mumble, "What is this tag team?"

"WHAT!?" says Charlene.

"Nothing, I was on the phone with Jamel."

Charlene's attitude changes and a smile appears on her face, "Well why didn't you say that?"

I frown, "Would it have mattered you need to use your phone right?" I walked out the kitchen with an attitude. As I went to me and Shiane's bedroom I sat on the bottom bunk staring at the cream colored walls. Charlene decided to come question me as she takes a seat next to me, "So how is Jamel doing? I haven't seen him in a minute."

"Jamel is fine, I guess."

"Oh, now you guess?"

"Guessing is all I could do. I haven't spoke to him for a few days. Then when I did you had to use the phone right?"

"You real funny Mahogany you know that?"

Shiane screams from the kitchen, "Ma, come mere!"

"Hold on a second Shiane," Charlene rises to her feet

as she heads toward my bedroom door. Standing in the frame of the door she speaks, "Is Jamel coming over here today?"

"He's on his way now."

"Good because I need to hold a few dollars from him until later on in the month."

"Hold up, didn't you just get some money today and don't you already owe him money from before?"

"In the famous words of Mahogany, 'get your own business and stay out of mine please.'" Charlene walks out the room laughing. I feel like hitting her with a brick! Instead of hitting her with a brick, I fall back on the bed as I watch an episode of *It's a Different World*. Inside I really am wishing I was living in a different world.

Jamel couldn't have come at a better time. I'm finished watching television and my nap is over when he knocks on my apartment door. I already know it's him before Shiane rushes pass me to open the door.

"Hey Mel, Mahogany is sleeping. Do you wanna chill in the living room with me until she wakes up?"

I creep up behind Shiane and immediately interrupt, "Mahogany is right here." Shiane sucked her teeth, rolled her eyes and brushed pass me as Jamel entered. We headed to the plant filled living room to sit on the burgundy colored couch. Kissing me on my cheek Jamel speaks, "What's up sexy?"

"What was she saying to you before I came?" I asked with my arms folded.

"Who, ya fat ass cousin? Don't even sweat that. I'm with who I came to see. Do you miss me?"

"You know it. But this little act Shiane puts on every time you come to see me is getting ridiculous. I'm getting real sick and tired of her games."

"Yo, what did I say? Fuck her, all I want is you.

"I know baby but it ain't even about who you want. A blind man can see any man choosing me over her any day. My point is that chick is real disrespectful. I'm really getting fed up."

"Cute, conceited and can't take it no more should be your slogan."

I hit Jamel with a pillow, "Shut up silly."

Tickling me Jamel replies, "Now I'm silly, huh, huh, huh?"

I'm laughing uncontrollably while trying to stop his tickle attack. "Okay, okay, you got it! You're not silly you're the best, the best from the east to the west, now stop!" Jamel stopped tickling me but we both continued laughing. Interrupting our moment Shiane came into the living room wearing short shorts and a t-shirt begging to be noticed. "What's so funny, Jamel, Mahogany?"

Jamel looked at Shiane with disgust, "What do you want?"

"Oh it's like that?" Shiane replied.

I stood to my feet and answered her, "Yes it's like that!"

Jamel grabbed my shirt to pull me back down next to him. "Yo, fuck her, let's bounce." Shiane stood with her mouth wide open, "What did you just say Jamel?"

"I wasn't talking to you so it really doesn't matter."

"But you were talking about me so it really does matter."

"Shiane go back in the bedroom please," is what I suggested.

"Why don't you make me, Mahogany?"

I laughed at her while saying, "You really don't want

that sweetheart."

"Oh, I really do, please make my day!"

Aunt Charlene came racing into the living room, "What is all the fuss about?"

"Mahogany is showing off in front of Jamel."

Charlene looked at Shiane, and then she looked at me, her eyes landed on Jamel to whom she spoke to completely forgetting what she raced into the living room for, "Hey Jamel, when did you get here?"

"What's up? I been here for a minute. Me and Mahogany was just about to leave though."

"Oh really, can I come to." Charlene laughs, "Let me stop. Where are you two going?"

"We gon' catch a flick."

"Y'all sure go out a-lot. You must have a-lot of money Jamel."

"Not even I just like to show Mahogany a good time."

"Well that's too bad because I am broke as hell. Mahogany was just about to ride with me to pick up some money." I cut in, "I was?"

Charlene replies, "Yes you were, but if I could somehow get my hands on a few dollars right now, it wouldn't be necessary for you to take that ride with me."

Jamel laughs, "What's a few dollars?"

A smile appears on Charlene's face, "Nothing big one or two hundred dollars will do. It'll just hold me over until I pick up the money I'm s'pose to pick up."

Jamel goes in his pockets and peels off some twenty dollar bills, "I got eighty dollars for you."

Charlene snatches the money out of Jamel's hand, "That'll do!" I am so embarrassed but that doesn't stop Charlene from carrying on. "So, Jamel, you know if my sister was still here, she would never even allow you two to go out like y'all do or even visit one another."

Jamel raises his eyebrow, "Oh yeah?"

"Hell yeah, lucky for you I'm cool as they come. Long as you and Mahogany ain't killing each other or making a whole bunch of babies I could careless about what y'all do. Shit, we all human and we all got needs. I say if you can't be good be careful; if you can't be careful, please don't name it after me."

Jamel looks at me as I put my head down. Charlene carries on, "I'm a old hoe. These young girls today will do a little bit of everything for a whole lot of nothing. Back in my day if a nigga came at me he knew he had to come correct or he didn't come at all. Try telling that to these young hoes today and they think you 'hating' on them. This is why I keep my mouth closed, my legs crossed and just count my ones."

Jamel's outburst of laughter stopped Charlene from proceeding with her story, "Ha, ha, haaa, haaaa! You more funny than a little bit!" replied Jamel still tryna catch his breath.

Shiane couldn't help but to put her two cents in, "I don't see what's so funny." Shiane looked at her mother, "Ma, what you just said made a lot of sense. Hoes like Mahogany…," was all Shiane was able to get out of her mouth before I lunged off the couch to pop that bitch!

As Jamel tried to restrain me Charlene grabbed her daughter while laughing at the whole ordeal. Shiane's laugh told me she thought everything was funny as well.

Vexed I spit, "I'm happy this is all game to you! We'll see whose laughing when I'm through stomping a mud hole in you Shiane!"

Charlene's laughing face turned real serious as she replied, "Mahogany, you better relax and learn to watch your mouth..."

Cutting her off I spoke, "Shiane is the one calling people 'hoes' but I'm the one who needs to relax!?"

"That's what the fuck I said! And if anyone is gon' be stomping a mud hole in anybody up in this bitch its' gon' be me! So you better remember who you're talking to before you get your life smacked away..."

I tried to cut in, "But..."

"But my ass," Charlene cut me off then continued, "You lucky I didn't hit you, jumping off the damn couch like you a fucking superhero!"

I sat there crying as Charlene continued insulting and embarrassing me, "Yeah I said it, WHAT! Now hit me like I'm a fucking little girl and that'll be suicide for sure!"

I didn't understand where any of this was coming from. I didn't understand how the whole 'hoe' topic started, nor did I understand why Shiane and Charlene wanted to be all up under Jamel. I was the only one he cared to see. I was hurt, lost and confused. What I did understand was I'd never ever allow Jamel to visit me there again under any circumstances.

As Jamel hugged me, we made our way to the door. Charlene still felt the need to show off. She ran her mouth, "Jamel when you get sick of dealing with immature, sensitive little girls Shiane will be right here. She may be young but..." was the last thing Charlene said before Jamel cut her off.

"Yo, check this out, you should feel real low right now. Here you are a grown ass woman playing little fucking kid games! You and your daughter on your best day couldn't touch Mahogany on her worst. Even a blind man can see that. So please stop tryna impress me because I'm not impressed. I don't want ya daughter, straight like that! So what I suggest you do is go take that eighty dollars buy you and your daughter some hamburgers and be happy. I'm already with the lady I plan on being with." With that said me and Jamel stepped as Charlene and Shiane stood there in the state of shock looking stupid.

Chapter 3

Time Will Tell...

Fresh out of the shower on a Saturday morning, I'm feeling good. The season is Fall but that didn't stop the sun from shining. Even the birds were chirping, who said nature didn't show love to the PJ's? Life is good...

Wrapped in nothing but a towel I'm dancing around me and Shiane's room, happy I'm home alone. I listened to the smooth sound of Sade coming through the speakers.

On this day I'm s'pose to be with Shiane and Charlene getting our hair done. However, for some strange reason they 'forgot' to wake me up for the third time in a row. I'm not sweating it. I finally figured out Charlene doesn't want pay for my hair to get done anymore.

In the meantime I look for my pretty pink Gucci shirt with the matching sweater as I prepare to visit Jamel at his home in Forty PJ's. After minutes reveal my search to be unsuccessful, I decide to wear my purple shirt with a pair of blue jeans that fit me like a glove. Since my hair is desperately in need of Tammy's touch I decide against wearing it out, instead I put it in a bun leaving a few loose strings out. I look simple but sexy.

Arriving at Jamel's house I'm greeted with a wet, juicy kiss. Completely shocked I ask Jamel, "What was that for?"

Jamel replies, "That's for you being you. I just wanted to show you how much I miss you."

Smiling, I cross my arms and look at him, "Oh really?"

Jamel laughs, "Yes really."

"What are you up to?"

"Why do I have to be up to something?"

"Because I know you, Jamel."

"Nowadays a brother can't love his lady without being up to something huh?"

"Not you, brother."

Jamel touched my bun then asked, "Why are you wearing your hair like that?"

Feeling uneasy about my hair I replied, "You don't like it?"

"No, I like it. I like it a lot. I was just wondering why all of a sudden you wanna wear it like that. I'm use to seeing you with it out."

"Well, Charlene stopped bringing me to Tammy's shop. So until I get a boyfriend who's gonna get my hair done the bun stays. Besides, isn't change good?" I knew Jamel would do anything for me. This is why I wasn't surprised with his response, "You gon' let that fat funky bitch decide how you gon' do ya do, nah, un-uh! From now on you getting ya hair done every week. I'm paying for it!"

I smiled then put my arms around Jamel's neck as I gave him a kiss on his cheek, "You're the boss."

"That means you can't get mad at the boss, right?"

I took a seat on Jamels' king-size bed that took up most of the space in the bedroom of his tiny project apartment, "Uh-o."

"What you 'uh-oing' about?"

"Let me hear it."

"Let you hear what?"

"What do you have to tell me?"

Jamel paused then looked at me with the puppy face that always gets my panties wet, "I just wanted to make a little change in our plans."

I shook my head, "Here we go. I didn't come all this way for you to change the plans. I came over here because I was your only plan."

"Weren't you the one just preaching about how good change is?"

"You can't use what I say against me."

"I just did."

I looked at Jamel who was still looking like a sad puppy before replying, "I'm listening."

"You remember my man, Sha, right?"

"The one that's' locked up?"

"Yeah, he was locked up but he just came home today. They had my nigga for five years!"

"So you wanna party and bullshit with him."

Jamel hugs me until both of us are laying flat on the bed then he gives me another wet kiss as he speaks, "That's why I love you baby! You're so young but yet so mature and so smart."

Breaking loose from his grip I reply, "Yeah, Yeah, Yeah. Where y'all going?"

"They having a party for my man in the city tonight."

"So what time you plan on coming back?"

"Ain't you spending the night?"

"Yeah."

"Well aight then, you gon' see me and we gon' chill. Plus I'ma give you some. I know that's what you want, nasty!"

I giggle, "Shut up!"

"It's true, I think I created a nympho."

"You ain't create nothing!"

Jamel licks his lips, "You want some right now?"

I tilt my head towards the head of the bed then reply, "Come on."

Jamel laughs, "Look at you!"

The moment is interrupted by a knock on Jamel's apartment door. Jamel leaves the room to answer the door. I kick off my shoes to relax my feet as I get cozy on his bed. When I'm comfortable I pick up the remote control then turn the television to a music video station.

After five minutes pass Jamel makes his way back into the bedroom only to tell me he's leaving. This is when I sat up. I looked at the time on the FM/AM radio that rested on his night stand. Before I could say a word Jamel spoke, "That's Sha at the door right now, we about to be out. Gimme a kiss."

"Why are you leaving right now, I thought the party isn't until tonight? It's not even noon yet."

"Come on mommy, can you just let a nigga live?"

"Well what am I s'pose to do until you come back?"

"Lay down, relax, read a book, watch a movie or keep watching that," says Jamel as he points to the music videos.

"What if your mother comes back?"

"Oh, now you a stranger, as long as you been fucking with me why you acting brand new now? You know just like I know my mother ain't coming from Tony house no time soon. You might as well say she live wit the nigga. She spends more time at his house way in west bubble fuck than she do here anyway."

I laugh as Jamel keeps talking about his mother and her boyfriend, "And if she did come home so what, you acting like she don't know who you are, like y'all ain't ever met. This is my house plus you my girl. You better recognize. Let me find out you scared of your own shadow, is that it, you don't wanna stay alone baby?"

I hopped up off the bed as I walked toward Jamel.

"Alright shot-caller, since you the boss go get me something to eat before you leave, then you can be on your merry way." I kiss him on the cheek.

Jamel digs in his pockets. He pulls out a crisp one-hundred dollar bill then hands it to me.

"I don't have time right now, order something or walk ya ass to a store to get something to eat."

"Well you must think I'm eating for ten, huh?" I said as I looked at the hundred dollar bill.

"Nope, not even. You know I ain't Rockefeller, that's for your food today plus the money to get your hair done tomorrow."

"Well mister know-it-all please tell me how am I s'pose to order some food, you know ain't no delivery man coming to the projects. Second of all how am I s'pose to get my food, whose gonna lock the door?"

Jamel snaps his fingers and digs in his pockets again. He separates his house keys from his car keys then places the house keys in the palm of my hand.

"Here, take my keys. That means don't disappear 'cause a nigga will be locked out. I ain't tryna hear you was up the block or around the corner or wit Billy-Joe." I cut

Jamel off, "Shut up silly!"

"Don't play wit me girl."

I blow him a kiss, "Besides getting something to eat the only other place I'll go is probably upstairs to Jackie's house."

"Ya hoe ass friend? Do not let that bitch step one foot inside my house!"

"You and Jackie need to cut it out!"

"Fuck Jackie!"

"Stop being so mean!"

"Tell her to stop being such a hoe. I gotta go, Sha is waiting. Gimme kiss." I kiss Jamel then he leaves the room.

• • •

Stepping off the elevator all I hear is loud music blasting. The music is so loud that it's making the walls vibrate. As I approached Jackie's apartment door I see it's cracked open. Entering into Jackie's apartment I see her dancing and singing in her living room using a brush as her microphone. I creep up directly behind her then yell in her ear, "BOO!"

Jackie jumped, screamed and grabbed her heart all at the same time. When she noticed it was me she grabbed the remote off of her black leather couch, she pressed a button. The music came to a complete stop as she pushed me, "BITCH!"

I replied while laughing, "I know."

Jackie was still shocked when she spoke, "You scared the shit out of me!"

I took a seat on the leather recliner which faced the big screen television. I sat giggling. Jackie was still popping shit, "You almost gave me a fucking heart attack!"

"Maybe next time you won't leave your door open, with your back turned and music blasting."

"Maybe next time I might just cut the hoe that creep up on me like that."

"Maybe you'll learn to stop popping shit, how 'bout that?"

"Shit, a bitch is weak too! You lucky it was you. If you was anybody else I would've cursed you the fuck out, straight up! Then I would've kicked ya ass out!"

"Save ya bullshit, aight. You sure didn't look weak getting ya freak on over there on the dance floor," I pointed.

Taking a seat Jackie calms down, "Don't let a bitch fool you, that wasn't energy. That was the I-just-got-some-new-good-dick dance!"

My mouth dropped open, "Who!" was what I demanded to know.

Jackie looked at me like I was crazy as she rubbed her coochie real nasty like then replied, "Me! I just got some new dick!" like she was trying to relive the moment.

I rolled my eyes, "I know that part. I wanna know what dick made you happy like this. Who is he?"

Jackie smiled, "Well, he's twenty-three years old, tall, dark and handsome. He just came home and..."

I cut her off, "Sha!?"

Jackie laughed, "Well damn bitch! Who the fuck told you?"

"It doesn't take a rocket-scientist to figure that out. You don't waste any time, do you?"

"Time is money and money is time."

"Well the nigga just came home, so I know he ain't got much of either."

"But what you don't know is that nigga is fucking thorough!"

I raise one eyebrow, "And?"

"And niggaz is gon' bow down to him."

"So what's you point?"

Jackie looked at me like I was crazy. "My point is when niggaz start paying him homage and throwing that paper at him left and right, who is the bitch he gon' remember? The bitch who put it on him soon as that ass got home!"

"Girl, you are a trip!"

Jackie pulled out a cigarette. She lit it then replied, "A trip I ain't, a smart investor I am."

"You got your brothers to take care of you. As long as you got them you know you don't need anybody else."

"Oh please, Antoine is too busy chasing this new bitch. Jason is on some other shit right now. Shit, I learned to be a hoe from them. Mother made 'em mother fuck'em."

"No you didn't."

"Yes the fuck I did."

"What's up with Jason anyway? I haven't seen him in a month of Sundays."

Blowing smoke through her nostrils she replies, "He aight, why?"

Waving my hand back and forth in front of my face in an effort to keep the smoke away I speak, "Just asking, when you started smoking?"

"I only smoke when I'm stressed."

"That's a lame excuse. How much stress could we have at sixteen anyway?"

Jackie sucked her teeth, "It's hard for me to believe I'm only sixteen. Sometimes I feel more like sixty-one. Can you believe you've been staying in Brooklyn for a whole year now?"

"That year seems more like an eternity. Shiane and Charlene give me more headaches than a little bit. Why you think I'm always over here?"

"We already know the answer to that. You just come to see that bitch-ass Jamel."

"Well right now I'm seeing you, what you gotta say about that?"

"That's only because Sha and Mel went shopping and shit before they go to Sha's party tonight."

I shake my head, "Well dayum bitch! How you know?"

"When I give up the pussy I get privileges, I know everything! Gimme a week I'll have Sha's social security number."

"You ain't no good."

"No sweetheart, I'm all good. I call it the power of the p-u-s-s-y."

• • •

"Baby, first I was a little upset, now I'm getting really worried. This is the fourth time I've paged you. You still haven't called me back yet. I don't wanna beef with you, I don't wanna argue with you. I just wanna make sure you're okay. Please give me a call as soon as you get this message. I love you." That was the message I left Jamel at 4:48 in the morning. I hadn't seen or spoke to Jamel since he left the house a little before noon. Worried was an understatement at this point. I was sick just thinking about shoulda, coulda, woulda tales. The only thing I could think of was to call Jackie hoping she knew more information than I did at this point. I picked the phone up and dialed Jackie's number, 522-1943. I listened to the phone ring waiting to hear Jackie's voice. My prayers were answered when Jackie answered her phone with sleep in her voice, "This better be the prince of Egypt calling to give me a whole lot of his royal dollars."

I whispered, "No this ain't the prince of Egypt it's Mahogany."

"You ain't the prince and you ain't got a dick calling this time of morning!? I'm hanging up…"

"Wait!" I replied in the same whispered tone then continued, "You seen or heard from Jamel or Sha?"

"Why the fuck are you whispering?"

"I don't know," is what I replied as I wondered *why am I whispering,* then I started speaking at a regular tone, "Just answer my question," I demanded.

Jackie replied, "Damn! Give a nigga some pussy so now you think I'm his keeper. Hell no I ain't hear from him or that thing he's with. And quite frankly…,"

I cut Jackie off, "Jackie, I'm serious. I haven't seen or heard from Jamel since he left here earlier. I know he went to a party and he's just tryna have a little fun with his boy but he didn't even call. This is why I'm concerned, this is way out of his character, Jamel isn't like that. He would've at least called. Do you think something happened?"

"I think this is a case of a nigga just being a nigga. Trust me I got two brothers. I know how their trifling asses get down so to me ain't nothing new under the su…," was all Jackie got out as the sound of gun shots interrupted our conversation, POW…POW…POW…POW…POW! I spoke first, "Was that gunshots!?"

A sarcastic Jackie replied, "We'll it ain't the motherfucking Fourth of July so I guess it was gun shots."

"Oh my God, please let Jamel be okay! Mel where are you call me back baby!" I wined.

Jackie tried to comfort me, "Mahogany don't worry about it I'm pretty sure Mel is okay. That's probably just them stupid ass niggaz outside ain't got shit else to do. They probably got one gun. They happy about it, so they tryna hit a bird. What they should be tryna do is hit them niggaz that robbed their punk asses," Jackie joked trying to lighten up the moment so that I could be more at ease.

"Jackie, I'm scared what if…"

Jackie cut me off, "What if you overreacting, matter fact, let me call my brother so I could see what the fuck is going on. If anybody knows he'll know. I'll call you right back."

We hung up the phone.

I knew Jackie didn't like Jamel but she was just being a friend to me. This is why she tried to relax me, plus find out exactly what was going on. I appreciated that.

Just as a tear rolled down my cheek fearing the worse, I heard a loud knock at the door then the knob twisted.

"Who is it?" I replied trying to make my voice sound deep and intimidating. I heard the loud knock again then the sound of Jamel's voice, "Come on man, open up the fucking door!"

I was so happy to hear the sound of his voice that I ran to open the door. Jamel brushed passed me making his way to the bedroom without saying two words to me. I was shocked! I stood there still holding the door wide open wearing nothing but a t-shirt and panties as if I was waiting for someone else to enter. Coming back to reality I closed and locked the apartment door as I headed to the bedroom. Jamel was fully clothed, stretched out all over the bed barely leaving enough room for me to get comfortable. I turned on the light inside the dark room and spoke, "Is something wrong with your fingers?"

Jamel sat up, "What?"

I folded my arms and rolled my eyes, "You heard what I said! Is something wrong with your fingers?"

"Yo, be easy aight."

I moved closer toward Jamel as I repeated what he said making more of a question out of it than a statement, "Be easy, be easy!? Its five o'clock in the fucking morning, you're just coming in, smelling like more liquor than a little bit. I haven't got a phone call, you ain't return none of my pages, I'm worried sick about you, they outside shooting and you want me to be easy!?"

"Listen, go to sleep I don't even feel like arguing with you right now. Maybe I shoulda just stayed where the fuck I was at!"

At this point I knew Jamel had been drinking, he's like a whole new person once he's got a drink in him.

I stood over him like I was ready to fight, "Nigga you got a lot of fucking nerve! I'm the one who should've stayed where the fuck I was at! I came all the way over here to spend quality time with my man and...," the moment is interrupted by the sound of the ringing phone. Before I could even reach for the phone Jamel jumped up like a bat out of hell, knocking me off balance just so he could answer it.

"Hello," Jamel answered as he made his way to another room at the same time. Just as I was about to follow him he was back inside the bedroom faster than he left. He threw the phone on his bed then started beefing, "Yo, tell that bitch to make sure it's her first and last time calling my house. I don't know why you fuck wit these hoes in the first place. She ain't nothing but a gold digging whore! Tramp bitch…," was the last thing I heard before I picked up the phone, "Hello."

Jackie spoke, "What the fuck is that crab ass nigga saying!?"

I tried to calm Jackie down just as she comforted me only minutes earlier, "Never mind him, he trippin'."

"Well I guess you know his bitch ass is fine now."

"Yeah, thanks Jackie."

"Anyway, I was just calling to let you know he should be there shortly, but I guess I'm too late. My brother said it was Jamel's drunken ass who busted those five shots in the air for each year Sha was locked up. I guess that's what the fuck he calls celebrating. He's a real fucking clown, making shit hot for no reason."

"He is a little tipsy right now."

"Well good luck to you and fuck his ass! I'm taking my ass back to bed now. Get at me before you leave tomorrow."

"I'll do that and thanks for holding me down."

"That ain't about nothing, you know you my bitch all day long."

I smiled before hanging up the phone, "I'll speak to you tomorrow."

By the time I hung up the phone Jamel was in the bathroom taking a shower. Meanwhile, he just left his clothes in the middle of the floor like I was his personal maid. My first thoughts were to just leave them right there but then I decided against it.

Picking up Jamel's clothing I couldn't help but notice the red faded looking stain on the front of his boxers.

Dropping every piece of clothing except for the boxers, I barged into the bathroom as Jamel was just stepping out of the shower. Holding up the boxers I spoke, "What the fuck is red lipstick doing on your boxers!?"

Jamel snatched the boxers from me and threw them on the floor as he ignored me. He calmly placed a towel around his waist as he made his way out of the bathroom and into his bedroom. This only added fuel to the anger I was already feeling. I followed him to the bedroom still demanding an answer to my question.

"So you just gon' fucking ignore me, who the fuck was sucking your dick Jamel, huh!?" Getting angrier by the moment I continued, "I guess this is the reason you couldn't return any of your pages huh, you was too busy with the next bitch!" all the while I'm having a fit Jamel is rested at the head of his bed, wrapped in nothing but a towel, sitting up puffing on a blunt. Still amazed and vexed about how calm he is regarding the whole situation I walk over to slap him. Before my hand could reach his face he grabs my wrist in mid air as he speaks.

"You finished?" Trying to snatch my wrist out of his grip I continue breaking, "No! I'm not finished, you got a lot of fucking nerve, *am I finished*, hell no I ain't finished. I'm up 'til the break of fucking dawn worrying about ya ass, you out with the next bitch getting your dick sucked! You know what though…"

Jamel cut me off, "No! I don't know what!" Yelling in a tone that caught me totally off guard he continued, "You need to calm the fuck down and relax! Before you go jumping to conclusions learn how to ask fucking questions! Always thinking a nigga is up to no good. I made you why the fuck would I play you!?" Tears started rolling down my face as I lay face down across Jamel's bed hurt, upset and confused. Jamel extinguished his blunt in the astray as he walked out of the bedroom.

When Jamel came back he had tissue in his hand which he used to try and wipe my face. Not wanting to be near him I turned my head opposite his direction so I wouldn't have to look at him. This is when Jamel turned me over so I could be face to face with him. He removed his towel from around his waist then laid on top of me wearing nothing but sweat beads from his shower that rested on his pretty, brown, toned body. I didn't wanna look into his eyes that were red and slanted because of the blunt he just smoked. So I tried to look directly at the ceiling. Noticing my attempts to ignore him, Jamel placed my chin in the palm of his hand leaving me no choice but to look at him. Once he was sure he had my full attention he licked his wet juicy lips, planted a kiss on each of my tearing eyes then he spoke.

"Listen to me Mahogany. I'm sorry for yelling at you but you just made ya daddy a little upset that's all. I love you, it's nothing in this world I wouldn't do for you, and you know that baby girl. All I was trying to say is if you wasn't so quick to jump the gun, you woulda seen that the same red stain that is on my boxers is on my shirt too. And no it's not lipstick; it's just a little Sex on the Beach. I ain't seen my nigga Sha in five years and tonight was s'pose to be our night out. I was just tryna have a good time that's all babygirl. Yeah we did some dumb shit that we probably shouldn't have did. We busted shots in the air, poured liquor on each other outside and all that. That's how the Sex on the Beach got on my clothes in the first place. It's all over my shirt, undershirt, boxers, everything mommy. I guess it just soaked through. Take a look at it for yourself its right there," said Jamel as he pointed to his clothes still on the floor. I tried to peek over towards the clothes without letting him know I was peeking, but he caught me and started laughing.

"Look at you," he continued. Then he stood to his feet as he gathered the clothes from off of the ground then placed them on top of me. I saw all the stains he was talking about but I didn't want those clothes on me as I spoke.

"Get these nasty things off of me." Jamel removed the clothes as he grabbed my hand to pull me off of the bed. Standing face to face Jamel wrapped his arms around me and kissed the nape of my neck. A tingle shot through my body immediately. I felt Jamel's dick rise as my pussy began getting wet. Dropping to his knees Jamel held me by my waist as he removed my panties with his teeth. Placing me on his king-sized bed he spread my legs wide open as he began sucking my clit.

We made love until the sun came up. When we finally stopped I cried and cried. I had mixed feelings toward Jamel and it felt so strange. I couldn't help but wonder could the one thing so steady and active in my life go wrong? Was I not living up to my role as the ideal girlfriend, was I not satisfying, not good enough or was I just over-reacting? If I wasn't sure about anything I knew one thing for certain. Time would surely reveal all truths.

Chapter 4

I don't really wanna stay...
I don't really wanna go...

Waking up one o'clock the next afternoon I was shocked to find myself all alone in Jamel's house again. At first I thought he might've went to the bathroom but when I looked on his nightstand the car keys and house keys were gone, I knew he'd left the house. *How the fuck am I s'pose to get out of here* was all I could think about. I picked up the phone to page Jamel but then decided against it. I was not tryna worry myself to death again. Climbing out of bed I found a pair of Jamel's sweatpants to throw on my naked bottom. Heading to the bathroom I brushed my teeth and washed my face.

Looking in the bathroom mirror I knew it was definitely time to call Tammy. Heading back to the bedroom I immediately picked up the phone and dialed Tammy's number, 932-5616. Tammy answered after two rings, "Hello."

"I'm tryna reach the best hairstylist in the world, can you give me her number?" I joked.

Tammy laughed then replied, "I'ma whip ya little ass."

"What did I do now?"

"Don't play with me! Where the hell you been, how dare you leave me all alone to deal with ya pain-in-my-ass-aunt and her fresh ass daughter!?"

"What are they doing coming to your shop? I thought Charlene wanted your sister to do her hair."

"So did I, but evidently she just gets a kick out of being a pain in my ass. They told me you moved upstate, so how is everything up there?"

"What!?"

"You heard me, you thought I wasn't gon' find out huh? What made you act up to the point that they had to ship you away, then ya little ass didn't even say goodbye to anybody. I hope you know I was cursing you out."

I heard Tammy's husband in the background, "Is that Lil' Mama?" "Yeah it's her," Tammy answered.

Then I spoke, "Tammy, I didn't move upstate. I'm still right here. Who told you I..."

Tammy cut me off, "So you mean to tell me you ain't move anywhere?"

I laughed then I heard Uncle Randy still in the background, "Let me speak to her."

Tammy spoke, "Hold up I'ma pass you the phone in a minute. Now back to you little miss, you mean to tell me ya fat ass aunt was lying to me all that time?"

"I guess so, what did she say?"

"What didn't she say, she told me you moved upstate 'cause you was out of control, you was in some type of reform school and you didn't even have a phone. On top of that you wasn't coming to the shop so what was I s'pose to think?"

"I wasn't coming to the shop 'cause Charlene wasn't bringing me. Come on now Tammy, you know how trifling she can be."

"You ain't never lied. I still can't believe she really had me going like that."

"Well believe it."

"When you coming to the shop then?"

"That's why I'm calling now, I want to know when is a good time to come today?"

"Come as soon as you can so you could get in and get out fast."

"Alright then, I'll be there as soon as I can."

"Don't hang up yet, Uncle Randy wants to speak to you."

"Put him on the phone."

Randy picks up the phone, "Lil Mama, what's been going on!?"

"Nothing, I miss y'all so much!"

"We miss you too. What's this I hear about you moving upstate, what's going on?"

I hear Tammy in the background, "Disregard all that shit. Her fat funky aunt was lying, the nerve of her!"

Randy begins to speak, "Word, so they hating on you like that Lil Mama?"

"Yeah, you know the haters always gon' hate."

"Fuck them! Listen I'm giving a bus ride to Great Adventures and I want you there."

"Really, when?"

"It's in two weeks and I don't wanna hear any excuses. You ain't gotta pay nothing, you don't need any spending money just bring you. Anything you need I got you."

"You ain't gotta tell me twice."

"Good. So other than all the hate going on, you alright?"

"I'm good."

"Nobody fucking with you, right?"

Laughing I replied, "Nobody messing with me."

"Alright now, you know I'll kill a nigga for my Lil' Mama."

"I know."

"Alright then, I'ma put my wife back on the phone."

"Speak to you later."

"Be good."

"I will." Tammy picked up the phone and spoke, "So he told you about the bus trip, huh?"

"Yeah, you're going too, right?"

"Of course, but anyway let me get off this phone now, I'll see you when you get to the shop and I'll give you all the details about the trip."

"Alright, see you later."

"See you later."

We hung up the phone. I turned the television to music videos then dialed Jackie's number, she answered, "House of beauty you speaking to a cutie."

"Well I must have the wrong number," I joked.

"Mahogany, don't play with me, you still at Jamel's house?"

"Yeah but I'm about bounce if he ever gets back."

"Well where the hell he went?"

"Who knows, I ain't driving myself crazy tryna figure out though."

"Well have I got some shit to tell you!"

Muting the television I inquired, "What happen?"

Jackie replied, "What didn't!? That nigga Sha came back to my house after I got off the phone with you and it was on!"

"Get the fuck outta here! Where were your brothers?"

Jackie sucked her teeth, "I told you Antoine is too busy chasing after a bitch and Jason is on some other shit right now."

"What about ya damn mother?"

"You know she wasn't here, her and her boyfriend been gone for damn near a week now, but you know she wouldn't have done shit if she was here. Now where was I?"

"You was telling me about Sha!"

"Oh yeah, this nigga came banging on my door five o'clock in the fucking morning like he police!"

"No he didn't."

"Yes he did girl."

"So what happen?"

"This nigga was drunk as a skunk, high as a kite and hard as a rock."

"Yeah-right!"

"I'm so serious, this nigga started sucking on my breast before he was all the way in the door, then he stripped down to his boxer. He started taking off my cute pajama set until I was butt-ass-naked! You won't believe what the nigga did next!"

"What, tell me!?"

"This nigga laid down on my living room carpet, told me to sit on his face!"

"You are lying!"

"Hell no I ain't! Let me finish telling you, after I came all on the niggaz face. I gave him a little head. I swear his dick was just getting bigger and bigger as it was in my mouth. Anyway, after I wet his dick up real nice he told me to get on my knees facing the love seat, so I did what he said. I had my elbows on the love seat, my ass in the air and girl he fucked me just like that until he came! To top it off he ain't even pull out, the nigga came all up in me!"

I couldn't believe my ears, "Y'all ain't use no condom, what if you get pregnant?"

"Girl, a bitch like me ain't even worried about it. I got a doctor named 'Abortion' and a credit card called 'Medicaid' so I'll be aight."

"Uh-uh!"

"Yup girl, so that was my night. I fucked the nigga to sleep."

"Is he still there?"

"Nope, he only stayed for like three hours. His damn pager was going off all night. When he finally saw the number he jumped up and ran outta here like we ain't just had freaky sex one-o-one."

"What he doing with a pager, didn't he just come home?"

"That's the same shit I said, I ain't even know he had a pager until the shit kept beeping in my ear. And I almost felt bad about that hundred dollars I clipped from his pockets while he was sleep. If I would've known he was getting it like that already I would've took a little more. I bet he won't even miss it, he buying pagers and things."

"You stole from him, Jackie?"

"I wouldn't call it stealing; I'm just teaching the nigga how to share."

"What ever happened to giving him a chance to share? I thought you put it on him so bad that he would be ready, willing and able to throw the cash at you, *the bitch who gave him the pussy soon as he came home*, remember?"

"Trust me, I got that nigga whipped."

"Oh really, so you still think you can get his social security number in a week when you already fucked him twice. You ain't even got his pager number yet?"

"Fuck you."

I laughed, "That's just what I thought."

"When you going home?"

"Whenever Jamel gets back."

"Who knows when that'll be?" Jackie sucked her teeth.

"Oops, speak of the devil and he will appear."

"His faggot ass is there now?"

"It's either him or his mother 'cause I just heard somebody open the door with a key."

"You know his drunken ass mother ain't coming home no time soon. That bitch probably swimming in a river of vodka getting her drink on. More than likely it's him. You better find out anyway. Call me back girl."

"I am, let me go see."

"Aight, come check me before you leave."

"I will."

We hung up the phone as I went to see who just walked in the door. Before I could reach the front of the apartment, I was greeted by Jamel on all fours like a dog with a single rose in between his lips. I couldn't help but to smile as I covered my mouth. This is when Jamel took the rose from between his lips and handed it to me. I bent down to give him a kiss as he licked my ear and spoke, "I'm sorry baby."

"Don't worry about it."

"I have to worry about it I let you down, right?"

"We all make mistakes let's leave the past in the past. What happened last night was just a big misunderstanding."

"You know I love you, right?"

"I know baby." I rubbed my stomach, "I need you to take me to Tammy's shop but first we need to stop and get something to eat."

Jamel stood to his feet and grabbed my hand, "Follow me." We entered the Kitchen; on the table sat, Steak, eggs, homefries, pancakes and orange juice. Jamel lead me to the table as he pulled out a chair for me to sit down. I felt like Julia Roberts in the movie Pretty Woman. Jamel spoke, "I didn't know what you wanted so I made a little of everything." After I finished laughing I replied.

"I was born at night but not last night. Which IHOP did you get this food from, because I know you didn't make anything?"

Jamel kissed me on my cheek, "You can't knock a nigga for trying." We both laughed. We ate until our bellies were full then I got dressed and Jamel drove me to Tammy's shop.

It was good seeing Tammy again. We hugged, we laughed and we talked. Before I knew it my hair was done. I was in the passenger seat Jamel's car heading back to Queens. This is when I looked at Jamel with the crooked eye as I spoke, "Where are we going?"

Jamel took his eyes off the road for a split second to look at me, "Where you think we going?"

"I don't know where you think *we're* going but I know I need to go home."

Jamel grabbed my hand, "You ready to leave me already? We ain't even get to spend time with each other."

"That was your choice, remember?"

"So it's like that huh? Fuck me, fuck my feelings and that's that, right?"

"Don't even act like that. You know I have school tomorrow."

"So what that mean?"

"That means I need to go home."

"Why can't you go to school from my house, its closer anyway?"

"I don't have any clothes at your house."

"So you just need me to take you home to get some clothes?" Jamel smiled then rubbed my inner thigh as he bit his bottom lip. I gave in to his persistence, "Fine! Take me home to get some clothes, and then I'll spend the night with you."

"That's my girl."

"I just hope you know my first class starts at seven-fifteen so be prepared to get up."

We pulled up in front of my building. On the scene two female crackheads were arguing, we proceeded pass them and into my building. Once we reached the apartment I was surprised to find no one home. I clicked the light switch on in the dark house. Just to make sure I was alone I yelled, "Shiane, Aunt Charlene?" Jamel was behind me locking the door, "I don't think they're here."

"Thank God!" were the words that came out of my mouth as I proceeded to the bedroom to pack my bag. Jamel was right behind me, "Don't start thanking God yet. It's only one way to really be sure that they're not here."

"Oh really?"

"Yes, really. Watch a pro at work." Jamel placed both of his hands on each side of his mouth then yelled, "Cheese-burger, French-fries, twenty-dollars."

I pushed him; he fell on me and Shiane's bunk-bed

laughing.

"Now we know they're not home for sure," Jamel stated.

I bent down to pick out some shirts from my bottom drawer. This is when Jamel took it upon himself to slap my ass, "Hurry up."

I turned around with a shirt in my hand, "We just got here."

Jamel didn't have to say another word; his eyes said it all. I looked down to see what his eyes were focused on. When I saw his hard dick looking like it was ready to bust out of his sweatpants I knew why he wanted me to hurry up. "Jamel, you're so nasty."

"You know you like it." I grabbed Jamel's dick, his pager started beeping, he looked at the number then grabbed me closer toward him, he hugged me so tight.

"Who was that?" I inquired.

"MD," Jamel replied.

"Who is MD?"

Jamel kissed me then whispered in my ear, "My dick and he wants you to hurry up. I'm going downstairs to wait inside the car, don't keep me waiting long."

"Whatever."

Jamel left the apartment. I continued packing my bag. The more I tried to get my things situated the more frustrated I became. It was clear to me that somebody had been wearing my shit! I searched for a pen and a piece of paper before leaving the apartment, I wrote a note:

Shiane,
Please stop touching my stuff! I know you're wearing my shirts because half of them are stretched out. My

sneakers are too small for you so please stop squeezing your size eight feet inside my six-and-a-half shoes. And, if you're mother is looking for me tell her I'm over Jamel's house. I'll be home soon.

I taped the note to the television and left the apartment. When I arrived downstairs Jamel was sitting in his car waiting for me. I threw my bag in the back seat and hopped in.

"So you rushed out of my house to sit here and do nothing?"

"Why you like starting?"

"I ain't starting."

"Well maybe you should start." Jamel placed my hand on his hard dick.

"Damn, that shit still didn't go down?"

"It's waiting for you to make it go down."

"How am I s'pose to do that right now?"

Jamel pressed a button. The windows on his Lex coupe went up as he pulled out of his parking spot while pulling his dick out of his pants.

"Jamel, how are we s'pose to do anything right now?"

"*We* can't do anything but *you* could."

"You want me to give you head while you're driving?"

Jamel smiled, "Did I tell you you're hair looks nice?"

"You so nasty."

"Can you please make ya daddy happy baby?"

I grabbed the head of Jamel's dick, and then placed the tip of my tongue in his hole. As we cruised our way from Brooklyn to Queens I gave him head without stopping.

When we arrived back in Forty PJ's the nights sky had

just started to fall. The projects looked more crowded than usual. I couldn't help but to think of my mother, I missed her so much. Soon as my feet hit the pavement I heard my name being called.

"Mahogany!"

Fixing the collar on my jacket I turn around to see who's calling me; it's Jackie walking fast toward me. "Jackie, what's up?"

"Girl you missed it all!"

"What happened?"

"Toya just got her ass whipped! That bitch fucked with the wrong person, now she over there crying."

"Toya with the big mouth, get the fuck out of here!?" Jackie grabbed my wrist pulling me toward the crowd, "Come on, she's still over there. I want you to see her face, that bitch is all fucked up!"

Jamel grabbed my other wrist, "You ain't going over there. We ain't got time for that bullshit. You have school tomorrow, remember?"

Jackie became instantly disgusted toward Jamel, "Since when did your name become daddy?"

"Don't you have a dick to suck or something?"

"Been there, done that! You just mad I ain't sucking your dick."

I was shocked and appalled by Jackie's statement as I screamed her name, "Jackie!" I snatched my wrist from both of their grips, "Both of y'all need to cut it out and grow the fuck up!"

"Tell your man's wallet to grow up."

"You slut bitch I could buy and sell you faster than the speed of light."

"You ain't saying nothing but a word Jamel!"

I sucked my teeth and start walking towards Jamel's building, "Y'all both need to chill the fuck out!"

The sound of police sirens causes the crowd Jackie was once pulling me towards to disperse. Jamel follows my lead and walk towards his building. Jackie started walking in the opposite direction.

We arrived in Jamel's apartment. He grabs me by my waist from behind. He puts his arms around me with his chin rested on the side of my neck. Immediately I pull myself away from him, "Get off of me."

Jamel raises his eyebrows, "Oh, it's like that?"

"Yeah, it's like that!"

"You gon' flip on me because of some tramp?"

"Jamel, enough is enough okay! No matter how you may feel about Jackie she is my friend, the sooner you realize that the better off you'll be!"

"Fuck her!"

"What did she ever do to you?" Jamel doesn't say a word. "That's exactly what I thought Jamel. If you love me like you say you do then you'll really understand how upset it makes me when you two argue."

Jamel takes a step back then claps both of hands together, "You know what? From now on I won't say shit to your friend."

"Thank you."

"Just keep her away from me. I shouldn't have to see her every time I wanna see you, you're my girl, she's not."

"Fine, when I'm with her I won't come around you. When I'm with you I won't go around her. So that's the end of that."

"Whatever makes your boat float," Jamel replies.

• • •

As weeks turned into months I continued spending countless days and nights over Jamel's house. His mother was never home. Aunt Charlene didn't care where I was or what I did as long as I wasn't asking her for anything. In some ways I guess you could say me and Jamel had our own apartment, but in other ways you couldn't.

It was a cold winter night in December. I was sitting in Jamel's house all alone again. On this night I was fed up about being constantly left alone while Jamel roamed the streets freely. I didn't even page him anymore because it was pointless. He didn't return my pages, give me a courtesy call to see how I was doing. He didn't even call to let me know he was okay. He used to drive me to school every morning, now I wished for the days I could see him in the morning.

Jamel started making more money in the streets. However, the more money he made the more problems we had. Whenever I entered a room he'd end his phone conversations. Then he would tell me it was nothing personal just business. We made love less and less. I cried more and more. In an effort to hold on to my first true love, I decided it would be better for our relationship if I spent more time at my own house and less time at his. Jamel wasn't thrilled about my decision but I felt it was something that needed to be done. I said hello to Brooklyn and goodbye to Queens.

Chapter 5

Still Hating

I didn't bother asking Jamel to bring me home. Instead, I hopped in a cab. Once I reached my apartment door I realized I left my keys at Jamel's house. In a fit of panic I stomped my foot. I was in no mood to travel all the way back to Queens. I looked at my watch; the time was ten-sixteen at night. I took a deep breath and proceeded to walk towards my apartment. I desperately hoped Shiane or Aunt Charlene was home. I was tired plus I had a mid-term in one of my favorite subjects; English.

As I approached the door I placed my ear against it to see if I heard any signs of someone being home. I heard what sounded like Aunt Charlene on the phone. For some reason a nervous feeling overcame my entire body. I bit my nails as I knocked on the door. From the other side of the door Shiane spoke. "Who is it?"

"It's me," I replied.

"And who the hell is me?" Shiane spat.

"It's Mahogany!"

"Where's ya keys?"

I turned the knob as I spoke in an aggravated tone, "Just open the door."

The door flew open as Shiane stood there with her hand on her hip.

"You got a lot of nerve coming here this time of night demanding shit. Did you forget how to use your key?"

I put my hand in Shiane's face as I brushed passed her. Shaine slammed the door. Aunt Charlene yelled from the kitchen, "Shiane, who's at the damn door?"

Shiane turned the lock on the door and folded her arms as she leaned up against it. With a sarcastic demeanor she yelled, "Its 'Princess Mahogany' mother."

Ignoring Shiane I headed into the kitchen where Aunt Charlene was sitting eating a bowl of spaghetti and talking on the phone.

I cracked a smile, "Hi Aunt Charlene."

"Hold on," Charlene spoke into the phone. Just as I turned to leave Aunt Charlene stopped me, "What brings you here Mahogany?"

"I live here," I replied.

"That's a joke if I ever heard one. Jamel got sick of you, huh?" Charlene laughed.

"I didn't know I needed a reason to come home. And, no, Jamel is not sick of me. I just felt like being here."

"Why did you knock at the door, where's your key?"

"When I got here I realized I left it at Jamel's house."

"Is that right?" Charlene spoke with a mouth full of food.

"Yes, but don't worry I'll pick them up tomorrow."

"Well I guess it's good that you're here after all 'cause I needed someone to wait for housing tomorrow while I go down to my face-to-face hearing."

"Um, I have school tomorrow."

"And?"

"And I have a very important English mid-term that I can't miss."

"That test ain't gon' make or break you. I put a ticket in for housing to come take a look at the socket in my room over a week ago. Of course these motherfuckers wanna come fix it the day I have my face-to-face hearing. I ain't been able to watch television in my bedroom for damn near two weeks. I don't think it'll kill you to miss one day in school. I'm pretty sure you weren't worried about school while you were laying up in Jamel's house."

I frowned, "Excuse me? I went to school everyday. My future is very important to me. If I miss this mid-term then I fail the semester. If I fail the semester then, I won't graduate on time or get accepted to the college of my choice."

Aunt Charlene looked at me as if she was disgusted. She rolled her eyes, sucked her teeth then spoke with the wave of her hand, "You know what? Don't even worry about it. I could always do for motherfuckers but the moment I need a favor it's a whole fucking song and dance."

I had the look of hurt and confusion on my face as Aunt Charlene continued. "I let motherfuckers come and go as they please, rent free at that. Then the moment I need a favor it's...," Aunt Charlene paused then laughed, "You know what Mahogany? Go to school, I'll have Shiane wait for housing. Plus, I hope you know your new bed is the living-room couch. Shiane got too comfortable with the idea of having her own room again. I'm not gonna let you come and go as you please forcing my daughter out of her comfort zone. From now on whenever you do decide to come lay your head here, you'll be laying it right on the living-room couch."

"But Aunt Charlene..." Charlene cut me off, "But my ass! That's how it is and that's how it's gon' continue to be! You're dismissed."

As I exited the kitchen Charlene put the phone back to her ear. Her conversation was loud enough for me to hear as I made my way to the living-room couch.

"Hello, yeah girl...I'm sorry about the long hold. But, I just had to check Mahogany. That little bitch is so ungrateful. And, you know she think she's white, right? Like one fucking day is gonna kill her." Charlene paused as she listened to whom ever she was talking to on the other end of the phone. A few seconds later Charlene was laughing and blabbing again. "Okaaaay, that's what the fuck I'm talking about. People get too caught up in this 'American Dream' bullshit! I deal with the real world, here and now. Did I tell you I finally got my hearing...? Yeah, girl I got a face-to-face tomorrow..." I didn't hear anything else after that. Rather, I wasn't paying attention to anything else after that. I made my way to the living-room couch. Shiane was sitting her fat ass down where I needed to sleep.

"Shiane, could you watch television in your mother's room? I have to go to sleep."

"So go to sleep, I ain't stopping you."

I spoke through gritted teeth, "I have to sleep out here. I cannot fall asleep to the sound of that loud television."

Shiane snacked on her chips as she bobbed her head back and forth, "Well this is the part where my girl getting ready to go to the house and say, 'You told Harpo to beat me?'" Shiane bent over laughing at her own joke. I walked over to the television and pressed the power button. The television went off. Shiane stood to her feet, "What the fuck are you doing!?"

I snatched a pillow and placed it under my arm, "I'm going to sleep, that's what I'm doing!"

"Oh no you not!"

"Just go in your mother's room and finish watching television. You watched this movie a hundred times anyway. "

"Well now it's a-hundred-and-one. Plus the plugs in my mother's room ain't working so I can't watch her damn TV. Therefore, I'll continue watching my movie right here, right now."

"You a bird-brain, you know that? Now, for the last time I need to get some sleep. I have a test in the morning."

"That sounds like a personal problem to me," said Shaine as she walked over to the television and turned it back on.

"You getting ready to have a whole lot of problems if you don't turn that TV off."

Shiane threw the remote control in my direction, it just missed my head as she yelled, "You fucking bitch! You made me miss my part!" shocked and angry I threw the pillow I was holding at her head without missing. Aunt Charlene walked in the living-room just in time to see her daughter being hit upside the head with the pillow I threw.

"Are you out of your fucking mind, Mahogany!?"

"She just tried to hit me with the remote," I cried. Shiane stood behind her mother sticking her tongue out while Charlene carried on.

"I don't give a fuck if she tried to hit you with a brick!

Make that the first and last time you call yourself throwing shit in my house!"

"All I'm tryna do is go to sleep."

Aunt Charlene walked closer toward me as she put her finger in my face, "I don't give a fuck what you tryna do, you'll respect this house! And another thing, the next time you call yourself writing a funky little note talking about, 'stop wearing your shit;' that'll be the day I'll burn all your shit. You're so fucking selfish! It's a damn shame."

Charlene turned around and spoke to Shiane, "And the next time I see somebody whipping your ass and you just standing there like a little punk bitch; I'll fuck you up myself! Both of y'all go to bed before I leave out of here in handcuffs tonight!"

Shiane and Charlene disappeared from the living-room. I turned off the light and said a prayer.

'Dear Lord,

I don't know what I did to Aunt Charlene and Shiane to make them hate me so much but, please make it stop. I love Jamel very much. I just hope he loves me the same way. I know you're probably saying I'm too young to love another human being in the intimate sense of the word but, I feel like me and Mel were meant to be together forever. Plus why would you give me these feelings if I shouldn't feel this way? Is this supposed to be some type of lesson? If it is Lord, I've learned my lesson so please, please make Jamel see I'm the only girl he needs. Please stop him from cheating and staying out so late when I am over there. I also want him to return my pages and answer my phone calls. Lord, I know you can make it work. Mom and dad, I hope I'm making y'all proud. I know it's certain things I shouldn't be doing but I'm only human. Please forgive me for all of my sins. I miss the two of you so much. And of course Lord, I'd like to ace my English mid-term tomorrow so I could move on to bigger and better things, like being the best psychiatrist the world has ever seen! God bless Jamel, Aunt Brenda, Aunt Charmaine, Aunt Charlene even bless Shiane. Last but not least; my crazy friend Jackie needs all the blessings she can get. Amen.'

That was the prayer I said before I went to sleep. It was difficult to get comfortable on the couch. However, I was so tired the minute my head hit the pillow I was already asleep.

When I woke-up the next morning I could barely move my head from the pillow. At first I thought my hair was stuck in between the cracks of the couch. As I tried to separate my hair from the pillow I realized gum was in my hair. I jumped off the couch and raced into the bathroom. Looking in the mirror only confirmed what I was already thinking. I had gum in my hair!

I walked into Shiane's bedroom and woke her up with a big slap across her ugly ass face. Shiane jumped up, "What the fuck are you doing!?" she screamed.

I slapped her again, "What the fuck am I doing…what the fuck am I doing!? Look at my hair!"

"Fuck you and your hair! Bitch you ain't all that," said Shiane as she came charging towards me. I wrestled Shiane to the floor as I stared hitting her like a mad-woman.

"You're gonna learn to respect me even if it's the last thing you do! Do you hear me…do you hear me?" is what I kept saying as I banged her head merciless against the floor. She tried to push me off of her by kicking but she couldn't match my strength. Once I looked down and noticed she'd also used one of my shirts to sleep in I went even more bananas, "And you still wearing my shit!? You just don't learn do you?! It can't even fit you. Look at all ya fat hanging out of my shirt! You nasty!" I slapped her again.

Charlene came running into the room. She grabbed a hand full of my hair and threw me to the cold hard floor.

"Mahogany what the fuck do you think you're doing!? You could have stayed were you were at if you gon' come in my house starting trouble you little bitch!"

Charlene bent down and slapped me across the face. "I'm sick and tired of you thinking you running shit bitch! Shiane, get the fuck up off the floor and come over here so you could whip this bitch ass!"

I placed myself in a fetal position as Charlene continued to hit me while speaking to her daughter at the same time. "Shiane, you better get over here and whip this bitch before I whip your ass! Hurry up, NOW!" Once Aunt Charlene stopped hitting me, Shiane started kicking me.

"Kick the shit out of that little bitch, harder, harder Shiane!" Charlene protested. "You better kick that bitch ass before I start kicking your ass! I'm not playing, she's gonna learn who the fucking boss is around here!"

"Aunt Charlene, it's not my fault, it's not my fault," I cried as I laid on the floor holding my face with tears in my eyes.

"Shut up! I don't wanna hear shit you gotta say!

I continued to cry, "But Shiane put gum in my hair while I was sleeping."

"If you was sleep how you know she did it?"

"It's only the three of us in..." I was cut off by a swift

kick in my mouth. I cried harder.

Still allowing her daughter to kick and punch me as I lay on the floor helpless, Charlene continued to add insult to my injuries.

"The next time I catch you putting your hands on my daughter, I'ma bust ya head wide open until the white meat start to show! If you think I'm playing just try me! Ain't nobody gon' keep feeling sorry for you, ya mother been dead two years now. I think you need to realize that ain't nobody here to spoil and baby ya ass sister girl. I'm telling you right now, all these attitudes you catching and carrying on, better stop today or you gon' see my bad side."

Charlene finally pulled her daughter off of me and the kicks and hits stopped.

"Come on Shiane! Let that little bitch drown in her tears."

Charlene exited the room as Shiane proceeded to follow her. Before the bedroom door closed Shiane turned around to look at me. She stuck her tongue out while raising her middle finger in the air.

Charlene grabbed the door knob, "Cry Mahogany, I don't feel sorry for you! You deserve to cry and while you crying you better clean my fucking house! When me and Shiane get back if this house is not cleaned from top to bottom you gon' have some big problems sister-girl!" the door slammed!

After what seemed like hours of me lying on the floor tasting my own blood, I finally stood to my feet. My head was spinning. I felt like it was the size of a watermelon. My knuckles were bleeding from the many kicks it blocked trying to cover my face. My nightgown was wet from tears and blood. Once I was sure Charlene and Shiane had left the house I went to the bathroom. Looking in the mirror only made me cry harder. My lip was busted, my jaw was swollen and blood was coming from one of my eyes. Plus I still had gummy hair.

I began cutting my hair as it fell like feathers on to the bathroom floor. By the time I was finished cutting my hair it stopped just below my ears.

I picked up the soap dish and threw it hard as I could against the wall. Then I picked up the toothpaste and threw that as well. Before I knew it I was throwing everything I could get my hands on. When there was nothing else to throw I started punching and kicking the wall and door. This is when I discovered a full bottle of prescription pills.

"God, I asked you to make it stop! You didn't make it stop. What happened...what happened!? Huh God!? You said you loved me! You said I was you're child! Why...why...why God!? Please tell me why!?"

I opened the bottle of pills, threw my head back as I allowed as many as possible to fall into my mouth. I turned on the faucet water and drank some of it to help me swallow what I was hoping to be my exit from this cold, cruel world which I couldn't understand.

"Here I come mommy. Here I come daddy. We're all going to be together again. Your Princess is coming mommy. I'm coming home...forever."

I picked up the phone to call Jamel. He didn't answer his phone. I kept calling him but I received no answer. I paged him only to be ignored. The last and final time I paged him I left a voicemail.

"I just want you to know I love you. I always loved

you, remember that. If I never see you again I want you to know you broke my heart. There was nothing in this world I wouldn't do for you. Now, your baby is going bye-bye Mel. Just know that I was true to you. I thought I was gonna be your Kelly Kapouskey to your Zack Morris, your Tapanga to your Corey. You let me down, you let me down big time. You really did. All I ever wanted was your loving Jamel. That's it."

Next I called Jackie to leave her a message. To my surprise Jackie was home. Soon as I heard her voice I spoke, "Jackie, I love you!"

"I love you too bitch!"

"You should be in school right now getting your education. Go to school Jackie."

"School...? Bitch please. School cannot pay my bills but I got a nigga coming at ten who can," Jackie laughed.

"Jackie, I want you to know that no matter what, you are my true, true best friend."

"Mahogany, you starting to sound a little crazy, you alright?"

"Soon I will be, real soon babygirl."

"See now you really starting to scare a bitch!"

"Don't be scared for me. I'm scared for you. You're the one who'll have to deal with this cold, cold world. I'm going to a better place."

"Mahogany! You better tell me what the fuck is going on right now!"

"All I can tell you is that I love you. If you see Jamel, tell him I love him too. Hopefully one day the two of you will get along."

"Is that what this is about? Me and him don't have beef anymore. We decided to keep the peace for you."

"Well, I guess one of my prayers was answered after all. God bless you Jackie."

"I'm coming to your house right now! I know when something is wrong! Is anybody else home?"

"It's no one here but me Jackie and you can't save me. Try to save yourself, save yourself babygirl."

"I'm calling a cab."

"Don't bother. I won't be here to let you in once you arrive." Click. I hung the phone up.

Once I hung up with Jackie I remember shaking, sweating and then passing out.

Chapter 6

Changes...

When I woke up I was in the hospital. Jackie, Jamel, and all three of my aunts were by my side. For a minute I couldn't remember what I was there for; then I saw an I.V. in my arm, I felt a tube up my nose and in my throat. The tube in my throat was hurting me so bad I yanked it out. As soon as I pulled that little stunt a nurse came walking into my room with a white paper cup filled with black, liquid charcoal.

"Well, well, well, look who woke-up, are you ready to drink this charcoal Miss Woods, or are you gonna be difficult again?"

I looked at the nurse like she was crazy as she held that black nasty looking liquid, "I'm supposed to drink that?"

"You are if you don't want that tube back up your nose and throat. Come on don't be difficult, the faster you drink this the faster it'll be over with."

The nurse helped me lean forward as she handed me the cup, "Come on, you're a big girl. I even put some ice in it for you so it could have a little flavor." She slowly shook the cup from side to side. I finally reached for the nasty liquid. I peeked inside the cup then slowly placed it to my lips. With each swallow of the liquid I felt like spitting it back up. Nasty wasn't good enough to describe how truly disgusting the charcoal tasted. When I finally finished drinking it the nurse rubbed my back and gave me a big smile.

"There you go! I knew you could do it. It wasn't that bad after all, was it?"

"It was disgusting!" I replied still trying to get the nasty taste out of my mouth.

The nurse smiled, "Well, I hope you remember just how disgusting that charcoal taste the next time you try to pull an act as foolish as you did."

I put my head down. The nurse continued, "Look at all the people in this room who loves you sweetheart. Just remember no matter who you are, how old you get or how much money you make, you cannot run from your problems. There is nowhere to hide."

I wanted to tell this nurse to go fly a kite, but she seemed so sincere and concerned. I tried to crack a smile.

"I want you to get some rest and feel better. My name is Mrs. Owens and I'll be here until eight o'clock. I'll be coming back and forth to check on you, okay?" I shook my head. Mrs. Owens continued.

"If you need me before I come back just press this button, I'll be right here. I'm gonna leave you alone now so you can spend some time with your visitors."

Nurse Owens left the room. Jamel pulled a chair closer to my bed. His moist lips kissed my cheek.

"How you feeling?" he asked.

I didn't say a word. Jamel grabbed my hand. "You alright, you want something to eat?"

"I need some juice to get this taste out of my mouth."

"You don't want nothing to eat?"

"I'm not hungry." I saw Jackie heading towards the door. I tried to call her.

"Jackie," my voice was more hoarse than I thought it was. I could barely hear myself. Jamel laughed.

"She can't hear you. Jackie!" Jamel got her attention. She closed the door then came back to the bed I was laying in. When she got to my bed Jamel nodded his head toward me.

"Mahogany want you."

Jamel left the room to get my juice. Jackie looked down and smiled.

"About time you got up."

"How long was I sleep?"

Jackie bent closer toward me so she could hear me better. "What did you say?"

I repeated myself. Jackie answered, "You been sleep for what seemed like forever. I just want you to hurry up and get better so I can fuck you up!" I laughed. Jackie continued, "Don't be laughing, you had a bitch scared to death! If you would've died and I met ya ass again in heaven, it woulda been on!"

"Please, you was on your way out the door. You wasn't thinking 'bout me."

"Bitch, I went over there to close the door. These fake ass toy-cops tried to tell me I couldn't come up here 'cause you already had too many visitors. So you know what a bitch like me did?"

"What?" I asked.

"I came up anyway. I stood right by the elevator and when somebody else came down I just took their visitors' pass and acted like I was going to see somebody else."

Inside I was laughing so hard trying to picture the whole scene. Jackie ran her fingers through my hair.

"We definitely gon' need to fix this. Have Jamel put you on a express flight to Tammy's soon as you get out of here!"

"So you weren't playing when you said you and Jamel squashed the beef?"

"I told you I wasn't. Anything for my bitch! You know that. I just know how to deal with him now. Besides, we all growing up and its childish for us to keep this senseless vendetta going."

"You must've just learned that word. I know you couldn't wait to use it. Let me find out you do pay attention in English class whenever you do decide to go."

Jackie stuck up her middle finger. "Oh, Mrs. Gates told me to give you this," said Jackie as she handed me an envelope.

"What's this?"

"It's your English mid-term. I went to school yesterday 'cause my mother and her boyfriend finally came home. You know they had to be getting on my nerves bad for me to go to school instead of chilling in the crib."

"Didn't I just come to the hospital yesterday?"

"Girl you been in this hospital for two days now. I ain't go to school the day you came here. I went to school the day after. Anyway, I went to Mrs. Gates class and she wanted to play twenty-one questions about why I missed the mid-term. A bitch like me ain't even know about the mid-term. Just when I'm 'bout to think up a lie; loud ass Toya come in the classroom talking 'bout, 'I heard Mahogany is in the hospital, what happened?' When Mrs.

Gates heard that she damn near hit the roof. She was like, what happened, what hospital is she in, is she okay? That's when I told her I'm the one who called the ambulance to bring you to the hospital. Then had the fire department break your door down when we couldn't get in. Long-story-short, she let me take a 'make-up' mid-term and she gave me yours to bring to you. She told me not to tell anyone she let you take yours outside of school, but Toya-the-talking-time-bomb was right there so CNN might know by now."

"Didn't somebody whip Toya ass in the projects a few months ago for not minding her business?"

"Uh-hm. Girl, some hoes just never learn," Jackie shook her head.

"Ain't that the truth?" I mumbled.

Jamel walked in with my juice.

"I know you didn't come back with just enough for Mahogany?" Charlene still wanted to 'cause confusion. Jamel looked behind him then straight ahead again, "You talking to me?" he asked.

Charlene replied, "You the only one I see with juice in your hands."

"Yeah, well, Mahogany is the only one I see laying up in a hospital bed. If you want something to drink the store is right downstairs. They also got this thing called a elevator you could get on, press a button and it'll take you the same place the stairs would've took you."

Jackie burst out with laughter. Charmaine cut in, "Jamel show some respect. Charlene is an adult. She's also your girlfriend's aunt."

Jamel laughed, "It's hard to tell that she's any of the things you just mentioned. You gotta show respect to get respect. It's clear to me that she doesn't have respect for Mahogany or herself."

Brenda placed the magazine she was reading down on a chair as she spoke, "It's getting a little hot in here. Let me go down stairs and smoke a cigarette before I have an attack. Mahogany, feel better I'll see you later sweetheart."

Aunt Brenda proceeded to exit the room. Aunt Charmaine yelled to Brenda, "Brenda wait. I'm getting ready to leave too."

"Hurry up," Brenda yelled back.

Charmaine walked closer toward my bed. "I'm leaving now sweetie okay? I just want you to know I love you. I'm also here for you. Your cousins were so worried about you when they found out you were in the hospital, especially Tiffany. You know she wants to be a lawyer, right?" Charmaine looked at the English mid-term Jackie placed on the side of my bed then continued, "If you need help in school she could probably tutor you or something. I couldn't ask for a better child."

"That's nice, but why would I need my younger cousin to tutor me?"

Charmaine laughed, "Don't be silly. You and Tiff are just a few months apart. Plus you know she's the academic scholar between you, her and Shiane. Tiffany spends her Thursdays' and Fridays' tutoring kids who are not as smart as she is anyway. Maybe you'll change your mind and sit in one of her sessions one day, think about it. Your cousin is willing to help you Mahogany." Charmaine kissed my forehead before she left the room. Charlene followed behind. Only myself, Jackie and Jamel were left in the room.

"Ya family is a piece of shit!" Jamel spat.

Jackie sat in a chair shaking her head. Jamel grabbed my chin, "Look at ya face. Jealous bitches! You still the prettiest girl in the world to me." I smiled. Jackie cut in, "Now you can tell us the real story Mahogany. Spill it all 'cause I wanna know how'd ya eye get black, lip get busted and jaw get swollen? I know you ain't do all that shit to yourself. And what made you decide to take all them gaddamn pills? Charlene tried to tell us some bullshit, but I wanna know what really went down!?"

I told Jackie and Jamel the entire story starting from when I got home the night before without having my keys to get in the house. By the time I finished telling the story nurse Owens walked in the room smiling.

"I see you're feeling better Miss Woods."

"As long as you don't give me anymore of that charcoal I'm feeling great." Everyone laughed including the nurse.

"Well, it's all part of the 'pumping' your stomach process. I hope you've learned your lesson."

"Trust me I did."

"That's fantastic, now I'm sorry I have to do this, but visiting hours are over guys. Miss Woods needs her rest."

Jackie gave me big hug, "If any toy-cops come fucking with you, you let me know. I'll be back here soon." I smiled. Then Jamel kissed me, "I'll be back tomorrow. You need me to bring anything?"

"Just bringing yourself is enough."

"I love you," Jamel said.

"I love you too."

"And, I love you all," nurse Owens said as she held the door open for Jackie and Jamel to leave. We all laughed. When Jackie and Jamel were gone nurse Owens walked over to me, handed me some reading material and a puzzle, "The shifts are changing now so I'll be leaving. This stuff I'm giving you should hold you over until tomorrow. You're gonna have a new nurse so be nice," she smiled.

"When do I get to go home?"

"Hopefully soon, we're not going to rush anything. Our priority is to make sure you leave here in tiptop shape. Now, before I leave I'd like to say a prayer for you.

"Dear Heavenly Father,

I come to you as your child, your soldier, your humble servant. I know through you all things are possible. Today I ask for guidance and delivery for not only myself but for Mahogany Woods. Father give her the strength to move on, the wisdom to know better and the light to see through the darkness. May you bless her with enough happiness to make her sweet, but enough trials to make her strong! Father, give her enough sorrow to keep her human, but enough hope to make her happy. Father, help her see that the happiest people don't necessarily have the best of everything; they just make the most of everything that they have. Father, help her see that her future will only be bright if she forgets the past. Father, when she was born everyone around her was smiling while she was crying. Father, help her live her life so at the end she's the one who is smiling and everyone else is crying. Father, help her see that yesterday is gone forever, but tomorrow she can start all over again. Father, I'm asking you to cover her in the blood of Jesus. In Jesus name, Amen!"

"Amen!" I said after I lifted my head up and opened my eyes.

"I want you to know I love you and Jesus loves you

sweetheart. And no matter how hard it seems or no matter how rough it gets you'll always have a friend in Jesus. When you can't even depend on yourself you can depend on Jesus." Nurse Owens hugged me then put her hand in her pocket, "Oh, before I forget sweetheart here's a pen. You can use it for that puzzle book I gave you."

"Thank you." Nurse Owens walked toward the door. Just before she exited she turned around with a big smile on her face, "Your mother was a good woman. I worked with her for eleven years. I see her goodness shining in you, God bless her soul." Mrs. Owens disappeared.

• • •

The next morning Jamel was already in my room before I woke-up. He sat in a chair watching TV. Once he noticed I was awake he walked over to my bed. "What's up pretty?"

I sat up, "What are you doing here so early?"

"I told you I was coming back," said Jamel as he reached for a bag.

"How did the TV come on, did you pay for it?"

"Yeah, I paid for the TV, phone and I bought you some breakfast," Jamel placed the bag in my lap.

"Thank you, but I don't have an appetite, I'm not hungry."

"You don't have to eat the whole thing. Just eat a little bit. Mahogany, you gotta eat something."

"All I wanna do is brush my teeth. I'm not in the mood to eat. I tried to eat yesterday and everything I tried tasted like that damn charcoal," I got out the bed and headed to the bathroom. Jamel reclined his chair back.

"Suit yourself," he yelled as I closed the bathroom

door behind me.

When I finished handling my business in the bathroom I walked back over to my bed. Jamel was handing me a juice, "If you ain't gon' eat breakfast you could at least drink something."

I snatched the juice out of his hands. He sat all the way up, "What's ya problem Mahogany?"

"I should be asking you that."

"What?" he asked confused.

"You heard me."

"Here we go wit ya bullshit. I see you feeling much better today, much better."

"Why it gotta take something like this to bring us closer together Mel?"

"You bugging right now. Word!"

"I'm not bugging. I'm just not gonna sit here and pretend like everything is peaches and cream between me and you."

Jamel laughed, "Chicks kill me. Y'all say y'all want a man who can provide for you financially, sexually and mentally, but the minute that nigga come along y'all wanna bitch and complain. How you expect me to make money if I'm up under you twenty-four-seven or on the damn phone with you every time I'm near a damn phone? Now, if I was a crab-ass nigga sitting up under you all day then that would be a problem too, right? You'll be saying 'why don't you do something?'"

"I ain't asking you to be up under me all day…"

Jamel cut me off, "You might as well. You ain't letting a nigga handle his business. I hate to say it, but sometimes I have to ignore you."

"What!?" I asked heated.

"You heard me right. I have to ignore you sometimes. Let me give you an example. Right now you're in the hospital. Since you been here I been here all day everyday. Now, the only reason I'm able to do that is because I handled my business to the point where I'm not living from day to day anymore! I could stand to stay off the streets for a week or two without worrying about where I'ma get my next dollar from. I'm at a point where I could say I'm well established. And, do you know why? I'll tell you why. 'Cause instead of answering your pages every time you call I was grinding 'cause I knew it would be days like this. That's why!" Jamel sat back in his chair.

I cut the TV off so I could have Jamel's full attention. "Listen, making money and everything is all good but come on now. I'm s'pose to be your fucking girl. When is the last time we went out to a movie or to get something to eat? I remember you used to call me on the phone and tell me you were coming to get me just so we could go to a movie or chill together. Now, I'm lucky if I speak to you once a day. You telling me you don't see anything wrong with this picture?"

"I ain't saying we don't have our share of ups and downs. All I'm saying is stop concentrating on just the negative bullshit if it's nothing we can do about it. Now, I know I can't change our past but I'll see to it that we have a brighter future. You just gotta learn to trust me babygirl. I'm on ya team."

"But how long will it last?"

"Only we have the power to destroy us, right? So I guess we have to wait and see."

My doctor walked into my room.

"Hello, I'm Dr. Rashi, how are we feeling today?" the

doctor asked.

I sat up, "I'm okay. I'll feel even better if you let me go home today."

The doctor laughed, "Not so fast Miss Woods. There are a few questions I need to ask you, okay?"

"Okay."

The doctor looked at Jamel, "Is this gentleman your brother?"

"No," I replied.

"Well I'm going to have to ask him to step out of the room for just a second."

"Why?" I inquired.

"It's for your own privacy Miss Woods."

"Anything you have to say to me could be said in front of Jamel."

"Fine, if that's the way you want it," the doctor closed the door as he looked down at a chart.

"Miss Woods, right now you're seventeen, correct?"

"Yes."

"How's your stomach feeling? Have you been eating, vomiting or feeling any pain in your abdomen area?"

"I haven't been eating because everything I tried to eat tasted like that charcoal to me."

"Yes, yes I understand," said the doctor as he wrote something on the chart. He continued, "That's very normal Miss Woods. Have you been feeling any sharp pains in your stomach?"

"Off and on," I waved my hand.

The doctor wrote something else on his chart before placing it at the foot of my bed as he spoke, "I'm gonna touch your stomach. I want you to tell me where you feel pain if you feel pain at all, okay?"

"Okay," I replied.

The doctor began touching my stomach. Jamel watched as I told the doctor which spots hurt and which spots didn't. The doctor finished then picked up his chart and began writing more stuff. The doctor flipped through a few pages, reading something then looked up, "Is he your boyfriend?" the doctor looked at me referring to Jamel.

"Yes," I replied.

"Well maybe it's good that he's here after all."

Me and Jamel looked at each other. The doctor laughed then spoke to both of us, "Did either one of you know Miss Woods is pregnant?"

My mouth dropped as Jamel stood fully erect on his feet. "What!?" is all I could say. The doctor continued, "From our lab results and judging by your bodies reactions its' safe to say you are pregnant Miss Woods."

I started asking questions non-stop, "How did this happen? How sure are you that I'm pregnant? This has to be a mistake!"

The doctor shook his head as he spoke to me, "I'm afraid this is no mistake," the doctor paused. Then he continued, "I'll give you two some time to be alone."

As he was leaving the room Jamel stopped him.

"How far is she?"

"So far Miss Woods is six weeks pregnant but if you'll excuse me, I'll get the nurse while you two are chatting and she can tell you everything you'll need to know."

The doctor left the room. Jamel walked over to my bed, smiled then hugged me, "I can't believe I'm getting ready to be a father!"

I raised my eyebrows as I spoke to Jamel, "We cannot have this baby!"

Jamel's smile quickly turned into a frown, "Why can't we?"

"We're not ready to."

"Right about now it's really no other option."

"Jamel, you're bugging. I'm having an abortion."

"No you not!"

I looked Jamel in his eyes, "Do you realize what you're asking me to do?"

Jamel looked at me like I was the one with the problem, "Do you realize what you asking me to give you permission to do?"

I shook my head, "If we want a baby later down the line we can always have one. On the other hand my career is not going to wait."

"I got money to take care of all of us."

I shook my head, "Jamel, this is not about the money. We're talking about another human being right now. You're asking me to take on the responsibility of raising a little person who will grow up one day to be a big person. I'm not ready for all the things a baby brings to the table at this point in my life. I have dreams, I have goals and a baby is just not part of the plans. What will happen to me and the baby if something was to have happen to you? You already know my family is a piece of shit, they don't even wanna help me so you know they wouldn't help me and my baby."

"Fuck ya family! We don't need them. Anything you need baby I got you, you hear me? We have to worry about our own family right now."

I begin crying, "Jamel you're missing my point. If I have this baby right now then I'll never be able to become a psychiatrist. What will me and the baby do for income if you were to get locked up, killed, or something else. You're not exactly in a stable or reliable line of work. You have to think about if you went down what would happen to us?"

Jamel wiped my eyes, "Baby, you can still finish high school, go on to college and become the psychiatrist I know you can be. You're gonna have to work a little bit harder but I know you can do it. I got faith in you baby."

"Jamel, I just don't think the timing is right?"

"Ain't no time like the present. Baby, can't you see...this is a blessing?"

The more I tried to convince Jamel having a baby would be a huge mistake right now, the more he tried to convince me that it was just what we needed. We debated over and over about this situation until visiting hours were over. I stayed up most of the night thinking about the news the doctor told us.

• • •

I stayed in the hospital for over a week. Jamel visited me everyday. Jackie visited me every other day. None of my aunts ever came back. When the day finally came for me to get discharged Jamel was in my room bright and early. I was fully dressed and ready to go when the doctor came into my room.

"Miss Woods I'm afraid there has been a mistake."

I frowned, "What kind of mistake?"

"We're not going to be able to release you back to the care of your Aunt Charlene I believe her name is..."

Jamel cut in, "What are you talking about?"

"We've come to a decision that the environment Miss Woods was residing in is not safe enough for her to return to at this time."

"What!?" I asked.

The doctor continued, "Miss Woods, when you were admitted you had a black eye, a busted lip and a swollen jaw. On top of that your Aunt/guardian hasn't come to visit you or called since the first and only time she's been here. We have reason to believe you were being abused."

"Abused!?" I screamed.

"Yes, your aunt should consider herself lucky we're not conducting a further investigation into this matter right now. However, we cannot and will not release you back into her custody unless we can investigate further into this matter. This is the only way we'll release you back to her. Today is the day you're supposed to be discharged and she's not even here to sign you out. That doesn't help you or her much either."

Jamel spoke, "I'm picking her up."

The doctor looked at Jamel, "I'm afraid we cannot release Miss Woods to you either. Since she's still a minor we need a relative twenty-one or older who is going to take full responsibility of caring for her."

"I'm twenty-one," Jamel replied.

"You're not a relative. Miss Woods, since both of your parents are deceased we were hoping maybe one of your other aunts, not Charlene, can come pick you up and sign you out. Otherwise we're going to have to report this to the Bureau of Child Welfare Services."

I started crying. The doctor spoke, "I'm going to give you some time to call some relatives. I'll be back in about one hour."

The doctor left the room. Jamel hugged me tight as he spoke softly in my ear, "Don't worry about it. I ain't letting you go nowhere."

"Why are they doing this to me?"

"Don't worry about it. What's Brenda and Charmaine's numbers'?"

"I don't know. I have to call Charlene to find out," I sobbed.

"Well give her a call."

I walked over to the phone and dialed Charlene's number. Charlene answered the phone, "Hello."

"Aunt Charlene, its Mahogany. I need Aunt Brenda and Aunt Charmaine's number."

"What for, shouldn't you be on your way home? Where's Jamel?"

"Jamel is here but the doctor is not letting me come home to you. The hospital will not release me unless Aunt Brenda or Aunt Charmaine signs me out."

"You little bitch! You tried to get me in trouble after all the shit I did for your ungrateful ass!?"

I moved the phone from my ear, looked at it then spoke, "I didn't say anything about nothing. Look I just wanna get home. Can you please give me the numbers?"

"Well if you can't stay at my house anymore who is your check gonna go to every month?"

"Right now I don't know and I don't care. Can you please just give me the numbers?"

"Well I think you should care because when the ambulance came to get you they broke my damn door down so either you or Jamel paying for that 'cause I lost my face-to-face hearing and I damn sure ain't paying housing, shit I ain't take no pills. On top of that my damn plug socket is still not working so you know I'm pissed. Why didn't Jamel use the key to open the door in the first place?

Didn't you say you left it over his house?"

I frowned, "Aunt Charlene, I really don't know all the details about what went down. Can you just give me the number? And, don't worry about your door. Jamel will take care of it."

"I know one of y'all taking care of it 'cause I damn sure ain't. Now, I'll give you Brenda's number but Charmaine's number I don't know so you'll have to take it from the there."

"You don't know your own sister's number?"

Charlene replied, "You don't know your own aunt's number? And, if you keep getting smart I'm 'bout to forget my other sister's number?" Charlene laughed, "Now, I'm gonna say Brenda's number one time and one time only so I suggest you listen."

Charlene said the number. I wrote it down. Charlene tried to say something else. I cut her off, "Bitch! Thanks for nothing!" I hung up the phone and called Brenda. Aunt Brenda answered the phone singing to the sound of loud music in the background.

"Hello," she screamed over the music.

"Aunt Brenda, its Mahogany. Can you hear me?"

"Hold on child let me turn this music down." Brenda turned the music down then came back to the phone, "What's wrong 'cause I know you ain't calling me for your health?"

"I'm having a little problem being released from the hospital."

"Oh yeah? What kind of problem?"

I explained the situation to Aunt Brenda. I asked her to pick me up then she grew silent for a few seconds. She finally decided to speak.

"Sweetheart you know you can't stay with me because I'm staying with somebody my damn self. What I would suggest you do is go to one of those homes for girls, I hear some of them are really nice and since you're still in the hospital they should have some listings just ask your doctor or nurse."

My mouth dropped wide open as my Aunt Brenda spoke. I couldn't believe what she was asking me to do. When I got over that comment I couldn't hold my feelings in any longer. It was like I was releasing the bitch in me as I spoke.

"You know, it's a shame how sheisty my own family acts towards me. I never did nothing to none of y'all for y'all to treat my like a step-child, my mother was good to all of y'all and y'all know it! If she was here none of this would even go down like this. I know she's turning in her grave right now. Then again maybe she's not 'cause she did tell me how conniving y'all bitches could be. I don't know how y'all sleep at night.

Brenda laughed, "Mahogany, your mother's not here so grow up okay. And, I sleep just fine at night. You on the other hand should be worrying about were you're gonna sleep, because like I said, I live with my man. I met him without having any kids, I moved in with him without having any kids, so I damn sure ain't gon' have no kids around him now. Especially another bitch, I'm the only bitch that's gon' stay up in here. Besides, I ain't got no time to baby-sit a suicidal soon to be grown ass woman. You put yourself in the situation you're in. It's time to be a big girl and get yourself out."

When Brenda spoke I was so hurt I couldn't even cry I just had to laugh as I replied, "Word, I'm happy you feel that way, I'll remember that. But, if you never say another word to me in your life just do me a favor? Can you give me Aunt Charmaine's number please?"

Brenda replied, "Now that I can do, you should've asked for her number in the first place."

Brenda gave me the number and I hung up the phone. As I sat in the chair inside my hospital room I was speechless. Jamel came towards me.

"What happen babygirl, somebody on the way to pick you up?

The tears just started pouring out of my eyes, "No, Charlene is worrying about you paying for her door because the ambulance broke it when they had to come inside to get me. And Brenda is worried about me being around her man."

Jamel grew angry, "What the fuck is up with ya family, they smokin' or some shit!?"

"You're asking the wrong person."

"Well what did Charmaine say?"

I put my head down, "I didn't call Charmaine. I couldn't deal with another rejection, we just gon' have to figure something else out 'cause I ain't staying in this hospital another night!"

"You have to call Charmaine, it ain't shit else we can do. Matter fact gimme the number I'll call myself, it don't hurt to try."

"What if she says no too? I'll really feel like a stepchild."

Jamel grabbed my chin, "Look, stop worrying about if she says no and let's pray that she says yes. You need to get the fuck outta here! And if she do say no then we'll think about what we gon' do then, but right now I'ma just go holla at her and see what happens."

"Fine!"

Jamel called Charmaine. When he hung-up the phone with her he walked over to the chair I was sitting in and gave me a kiss on the cheek before he spoke, "See baby-girl, somebody besides me loves you. Charmaine will be here in about an hour. She said you're more than wel-comed to stay with her."

My face lit up, "My Aunt Charmaine said that?"

"Yes, you're Aunt Charmaine. So sit tight and relax babygirl. Pretty soon you, me and the baby will be outta here."

Chapter 7

Bye Bye Baby...

I moved in with my Aunt Charmaine, her live-in boyfriend; Rome and my three cousins Tyreek, Tiffany and Jessica. We lived in a spacious house in Queens, which made it easier for me to commute back and forth to school everyday.

Upon arriving inside the house I was greeted by my youngest cousin, Jessica. She was five years old – so full of energy.

"Mahogany!" Jessica ran to me as she jumped in my arms.

"Hi Jess," I kissed her on the cheek returning the affection.

"Are you really gonna live with us? My mommy said you are living with us now?"

I laughed as I placed Jessica back on her feet, "Do you want me to live here?"

"Yes!" Jessica's face lit up as she continued, "You can live with us forever and we can play Barbie and dress-up. It's gonna be so much fun!"

"Yes Jessica, Mahogany will be staying with us for awhile," said Aunt Charmaine as she bent down to kiss her youngest daughter. Then she continued, "Has your sister gotten in yet?"

"Mommy, did you forget what today is?"

Aunt Charmaine tapped herself on the head as she threw her keys down. "I forgot today was Thursday."

Charmaine looked at me as she continued speaking, "Tiffany is tutoring the kids I was telling you about. She should be in the house around seven-thirty. I'm gonna show you where you'll be sleeping in the meantime, follow me."

I followed Aunt Charmaine as my eyes wandered around her spacious new home which I was in for the first time.

"This place is nice," I couldn't help but comment.

"Thank you," replied Aunt Charmaine as she opened the door to a bedroom. We entered the room.

"This is where you'll be staying Mahogany." I looked around. Everything seemed pretty decent. There were two beds neatly made-up, a huge window, a walk-in closet and an entertainment system. Charmaine continued, "You and Tiffany will share this room. I know she usually sleeps in the bed closest to the window, so you might wanna get comfortable in the other bed. When Tiff gets home you and her can work everything else out I guess." Charmaine looked down at Jessica, "Is your brother downstairs?"

"Yes, do you want me to go get him mommy?"

"No sweetie, I'll get him myself." Charmaine headed towards the door. "Mahogany, I'm going downstairs to the basement, that's where Tyreek spends most of his day. If you wanna come down to say hi feel free. Or if you get lonely up here he has plenty of video games you can play."

"Thanks, but I think I'm just gonna get in the shower

and get some rest."

"Okay. Come on Jess. Let your cousin get some rest."

"Okay, bye Mahogany," Jessica jumped up to give me a kiss. Jessica and Charmaine made their exit as I prepared to get in the shower.

By the time I was done showering it was a quarter to eight. Tiffany walked in the door. I heard Jessica run to her the same way she ran to me earlier. I hadn't seen Tiffany in such a long time. People often said we looked alike. A few people even mistook us for sisters. We were the same height, same size and same complexion. The only big difference between us was our eye-color. While mines were pretty and green hers were dark-brown.

As Tiffany walked in the room I smiled and she greeted me with a hug.

"What's up Mahogany?" said Tiffany as she threw her book-bag on the floor.

I returned the hug, "Hey girl, look at you!"

Tiffany spun around, "Look at me. I still look good," she laughed.

Tiffany closed the door then hopped on her bed, "I haven't seen you in so long! Tell me how you've been?"

"Besides the obvious I'm doing okay."

"I see you cut your hair but you still looking good."

"That's a whole 'nother story but enough about me, I'm so proud of you! I like how you devote your free time to helping other people with their studies."

Tiffany laughed as she walked over towards the window, "My mother told you about the Thursday and Friday tutoring thing, huh?"

"Yes and I'm so proud of you!"

"I'm so proud of me to," said Tiffany as she reached

inside her pockets to pull out a pack of cigarettes.

My mouth dropped open, "What are you doing with those?"

Tiffany laughed again as she opened the window and put the cigarette to her lips then lit it.

"I'm so proud I'm clever enough to convince my mom that I'm helping tutor a bunch of kids every Thursday and Friday evening. Like I ain't got nothing better to do with my time."

Tiffany puffed on her cigarette as she blew the smoke out of the window. I couldn't believe what she was telling me.

"So you don't tutor a bunch of kids on Thursday and Friday evenings?"

Tiffany sucked her teeth, "Don't get me wrong. I did help the little fucks for a week."

I put a pillow over my face as I did my best to control my laugh. Tiffany continued, "But if you feel like I feel then you got needs and my needs, need to be taken care of!"

I sat listening as Tiffany threw the butt of her cigarette out of the window. She popped a piece of candy in her mouth as she sprayed the room with air freshener. She kicked off her shoes and started unbuttoning her top as she continued, "On Thursdays' I'm with Anthony, Fridays' I'm with Shawn and Los is my fill-in guy whenever one of them can't make it. Today Anthony couldn't make it so needless to say, I was with Los. Now, Los has a little dick but his Puerto Rican ass sure can eat some pussy! That's one tongue I'd kill for. If only his dick was bigger I could see him on the regular." Tiffany shook her head then continued, "Anyway, Los likes to play this game.

Whenever he cum first he has to give me fifty dollars for wasting my time. Whenever I cum first he gets to keep my panties." Tiffany unzipped her skirt as it fell to the floor. She wasn't wearing any underwear. "Today I lost," she said as she laughed and picked up her skirt.

"Tiffany!"

"What? Don't even front like you still a virgin. Ya booty is getting too fat."

I was still in the state of shock, "I didn't say I was a Saint. I'm just surprised to find out that you're not," I replied.

Tiffany shook her head as she put her nightgown on, "Listen, you cannot believe everything you hear, especially from my mother. She loves to make something out of nothing. If you let her tell it, I'm a straight 'A' student who will be a world famous lawyer and I'm still a virgin – negative. In reality I'm an average student who tells her all the stuff she wants to hear to keep her off my back. I don't like to sneak around like I do but she leaves me no choice. She's too nosy and too over-protective. So I do what I gotta do. My mother really needs to get it together. Take this house for example. It's big, it's nice and it's beautiful. You probably said to yourself we are so lucky to live in a place like this. When the real deal is, Rome and my mother had to scrape every red cent together that they could get their hands on just to make the down payment for a house they knew they wouldn't be able to afford. On top of that Rome is never here 'cause he's too busy working just to make sure the bills are paid. They still have trouble paying the bills each month. It's ridiculous! For all the headaches we go through just to keep this house we should have just stayed in the 'hood."

"Things cannot be that bad."

"Trust me, you don't even wanna know. But, tell me about fat ass Shiane. I heard a little about what went down, but I wanna know the real deal. I can't believe you were able to deal with her for that long. I couldn't spend one night with her jealous ass. I can't stand her. Her and Aunt Charlene need some dick in their life."

"They was tryna push up on my baby, Jamel."

A big smile appeared across Tiffany's face, "Jamel? Who's Jamel?"

I started to blush, "He's my Anthony, Shawn and Los all wrapped up in one."

Tiffany clapped her hands together, "This is getting juicy, tell me more, tell me more!"

Me and Tiffany talked for hours. I hadn't been around my cousin in so long that I didn't realize we had so much in common. Tiff was cooler than I could've ever imagined she'd be.

As I was on my way to sleep Tiffany was ending her phone conversation.

"Alright boo. I can't wait to see you. You know I miss that tongue, right?" I heard Tiffany say. She giggled and talked some more, "You know it's on when I see your sexy ass, watch!" That was followed by, "So I'll speak to you later and I'll see you on Saturday," she hung-up the phone. I had to put my two cents in, "So, Los got you open like that, huh?"

Tiff gave me a devilish laugh, "Nope, but Melody do."

I sat all the way up with my mouth wide open, "What!?" I replied.

Tiff brushed it off like it was nothing, "Melody is this twenty-five year old chick I mess with too. I'll tell you all about her in the morning." Tiffany yawned, "Goodnight." Then she turned the lights out. We went to sleep.

The next morning myself, Tiffany and Jessica were up bright and early. Tiffany and Jessica were getting ready for school. I was getting ready for my first appointment with a psychiatrist. Upon discharging me from the hospital one of the doctors orders were for me to visit this psychiatrist, I was on my way to our first visit. Aunt Charmaine entered me and Tiff's room as we were getting dressed.

"Good morning ladies."

"Good morning," we replied in unison.

Holding a coffee mug while leaning on our door Aunt Charmaine spoke, "Mahogany, how are you feeling?"

"I'm okay. Do you know how to get to my psychiatrist's office?"

"It's out here in Queens so it shouldn't be that difficult to find. Tiffany, how was school yesterday?"

Tiffany fastened the last button on her sweater as she replied, "School was fun and exciting. I wish me and Mahogany went to the same school."

Charmaine smiled, "That would be nice. I told her about the kids you tutor on Thursdays' and Friday s'." Aunt Charmaine directed her attention towards me. "It would be nice if you went with her at least once a week Mahogany. I think you could learn a lot from your cousin."

Me and Tiffany giggled as I replied, "I know I can learn a lot from Tiffany Aunt Charmaine. I think she may even be smarter than you give her credit for," I cracked a smile.

Tiffany gave me a look that said "I'ma kill you!" I blew her a kiss then smiled. Aunt Charmaine missed the whole thing. She continued speaking to me.

"I'm glad to hear you feel that way. Would it be safe to assume you're gonna sit in one of her sessions once if not twice a week?"

Tiffany answered the question, "Yes mother! I told Mahogany all about my Thursday and Friday evening tutoring sessions. She was more excited than you could've imagined. She's gonna start going with me on Thursdays' and Fridays' starting next week, right Mahogany?" Tiffany winked at me and smiled. Aunt Charmaine looked at me. I spoke, "Right."

"Well, Good," Aunt Charmaine replied with a smile on her face. Tiffany picked up her book-bag and gave her mother a kiss as she exited the room.

"See you later mom. See you later Mahogany. Oh, before I forget…do you mind if I stay a-half-an-hour to an hour later tonight? I'm tutoring Shawn tonight and he requires extra attention."

"It's Friday I don't see why not," replied Aunt Charmaine. I laughed at how cleverly Tiffany got her way. At the same time I laughed at how gullible Aunt Charmaine was.

"Thanks mom, you're the best," said Tiffany as she gave her mom another kiss. Aunt Charmaine walked out of the room while saying, "Mahogany, we should be leaving in the next twenty minutes."

"Okay," I replied while zipping my pants.

●　●　●

I arrived at my psychiatrist's office on time. I approached the receptionist desk. She greeted me with a smile.

"Hi, may I help you?"

"Yes, my name is Mahogany Woods. I have a ten o'clock appointment with Dr. Klein."

"Okay. You can have a seat, Dr. Klein will be right with you Miss Woods."

"Thank you." I sat down on the comfortable leather couch in the receptionist area. Aunt Charmaine asked the receptionist, "Where is your bathroom?"

The receptionist pointed to a wooden box, "The key is in there. The bathroom is out the door, to your right. You can't miss it. Just keep going straight." Aunt Charmaine grabbed the key and walked out the door.

As I sat waiting for Dr. Klein my eyes wandered all over the nice cool office. "One day I'll have an office just like this with a receptionist just like her," I said in a low tone to myself. "She'll say Dr. Woods will be with you in a second." I smiled at the thought. My dreams were interrupted by Dr. Klein.

"Miss Woods?" said Dr. Klein.

"Yes, I'm Miss Woods," I extended my hand to Dr. Klein's for a handshake.

"Nice to meet you, did you come alone today?" said Dr. Klein. I was surprised the doctor didn't extend her hand as well to shake my hand. I dropped my hand as I answered her question, "No, my aunt is in the bathroom."

"Very well, follow me." The doctor approached her receptionist, "Kathy when her aunt comes back have her wait out here. I can only deal with one of these people at a time, you know how they are."

"No problem doctor," the receptionist replied. I followed the blonde hair, blue eyed Dr. Klein into her office. She looked like she could be in her mid to late forties. Judging from the pictures around her office she was married with two children. Her son played baseball while her daughter danced as a ballerina. Her husband seemed to be into politics. There was a picture of him and her on their wedding day sitting next to a picture of him shaking hands with the governor.

"Have a seat Miss Woods, make yourself comfortable," said the doctor as she took a seat behind her desk. She pulled out a notepad and a pen.

"Okay, Miss Woods, we are going to begin."

I made myself comfortable on the couch as the doctor began asking questions.

"Do you know why you're here today?"

"Yeah, the doctor at the hospital thought it would be best if I saw you. He said you might be able to help me."

"Do you think I can help you?"

"I just think I used poor judgment. I was kind of caught in the moment. I really don't think I need much of your help. But, maybe I can learn other things from you."

The doctor laughed, "I don't think people like you can learn much from people like me although you should. That's a different story all together. Anyway, how did it make you feel staying in the hospital?"

If I didn't know any better I would've thought this doctor was being racist. Giving her the benefit of the doubt I ignored her comment and answered her question, "I hated it. I just wanted to go home."

"Did you like all the attention you received?"

"No. I just wanted to go home."

The doctor wrote something on her notepad then continued, "Why did you take all those pills?"

"I was going through a lot of stuff. You wouldn't understand."

"I do my best to understand people like you and sometimes I just can't, but maybe you can help me understand? Are you going through a lot of stuff now?"

"People like me? Why do you keep saying that? What is that suppose to mean?"

The doctor rolled her eyes in her head, "You wouldn't understand. Anyway, do you feel like the world just doesn't understand you?"

"No."

"Is everyone out to get you?"

I frowned, "No."

"How are you feeling today? Are you stressed out?"

"Are you?"

The doctor looked up from her notepad, "Answer the question please."

"What relevance do these questions have?" The doctor completely ignored me as she continued questioning me and writing, "Fine, then don't answer the question. What does a banana and an orange have in common?"

I sat up, "Are you serious?"

"Please answer the question."

"What do me and you have in common?" I asked.

The doctor dropped her pen on the notepad in frustration, "Look, I'm only trying to help you. But, I cannot help you if you are not willing to be helped!"

"If you're trying to help me then you wouldn't insult my intelligence. What kind of question is 'what does a banana and an orange have in common?' We both know they're fruits."

I was cut off by the doctor, "So you do know what they have in common." She wrote something on her notepad.

"Prior, that means before…so prior to you being admitted to the hospital were you being abused?"

I laughed at how unbelievable and condescending the doctor was being. She continued with her questions, "Are you being abused now?" All the admiration I held for her before we walked into her office went out the window. I headed towards the door.

"Miss Woods, this session is not over. Where are you going?" I ignored her as I kept going. "Miss Woods," the doctor called. I exited and her door slammed!

"Fuck her, I don't need her. I'm a psychiatrist-in-training after all. She can't help me like I can help myself," I said to myself as I walked out of her office. I couldn't believe the nerve of her as I headed home. "I'm gonna show her how you're really suppose to treat a patient, watch!" is what I said to myself as I sat thinking about what a racist bitch she was.

After running a few errands with Aunt Charmaine we finally made it home. I ate something and fell asleep. When eight-thirty came Tiffany ran inside of our bedroom waking me up.

"Mahogany! Get up!" Tiffany shook me.

"I'm up, I'm up," I slowly opened my eyes as they adjusted to the bright light.

"I know you crazy waking me up."

Tiffany was so excited, "Guess what!?"

I sat up as I threw the covers off of me, "This better be good, what?"

"I gave Shawn, head!"

I frowned, "What?"

Tiffany said it again more excited than she was the first time, "I gave Shawn some head!"

I raised my eyebrows, "And?"

"What do you mean, and? That was my first time giving somebody head!"

"Yeah right," I laughed.

Tiffany put her hands in the air, "I swear to God!"

"Girl I been giving Jamel head since the first time we got it on. I love sucking his dick and he loves getting it sucked."

"I think I love sucking dick too." I laughed as Tiffany continued, "I'm serious. Why didn't anybody tell me it was gonna be that much fun!?"

"As much junk as you be popping I would've thought you out of all people woulda rocked a few mics."

"Los and Anthony never put pressure on me to give them head, but Shawn always tried to get me to do it one way or another. I finally got sick of him asking and just said fuck it! I was lying on his chest and he started to push my head towards his dick. Usually I would've picked my head right back up. But, for some reason I just felt like trying it out tonight. It shocked the hell out of both of us!"

I interrupted, "Did you make him cum?"

"Let me finish telling you. So, he's pushing my head down toward his dick. All of a sudden I just grabbed the nigga dick and start jerking it. He started telling me to put it in my mouth. I knew I was getting ready to put it in my mouth, but I didn't want him to know just yet. So, I'm jerking it and jerking it. Then I let the tip of my tongue touch the head. This nigga started going crazy! I gently wrapped my lips around his head as I put the whole dick in my mouth to the point where my lips were touching his balls!"

I cut Tiffany off, "You deep-throated that shit!?"

"Call it what you want. I made it disappear in my mouth and had this nigga screaming like a bitch! It's like the more I saw his toes curl and the more I heard him moan, the wetter my pussy got and the more I spit on his dick. I had his dick so wet that my spit was rolling off his dick, dripping down to his balls. So, I started massaging his balls as I kept sucking his big black dick. Next thing I knew I stopped sucking the whole dick and just concentrated on the head. As I'm sucking the head, I'm jerking his whole dick with my spit all over it. That's when he came! The shit got all over my face and hands. When I finished licking his cum off the head of his dick and my hands the nigga asked me to marry him!" Me and Tiffany burst into laughter.

Tiffany had my full attention, "Why did you wait so long to give him head girl?"

"Don't ask me. But, I'll tell you one thing for sure. He won't have to wait no more?"

"I can't believe how nasty you are."

Tiffany fanned herself as she ran to the window, cracked it open and lit a cigarette. "Neither can Shawn. He don't even believe that was my first time having a dick in my mouth."

"After the way you just described how it went down I wouldn't have believed you either."

Still puffing on her cigarette and fanning herself Tiffany .continued, "I'm still hot just thinking about it! I probably had more orgasms on the way home than I did from sucking and riding the dick put together."

"Well I'm happy one of us is having a good time. I haven't seen Jamel since I left the hospital. Do you think

Aunt Charmaine will let him come over here or do I have to go to his house?"

Tiffany almost choked on the smoke from her cigarette before she threw it out the window, "Are you crazy!? Don't even think about asking my mother anything about you and a guy being together. That's rule number one!"

"Aunt Charmaine be bugging like that?"

Tiff looked at me like I was crazy, "Do you think I do all this sneaking around for my health? If it was that easy for me to go visit a nigga or have a nigga come visit me I'd never leave the house."

"I hope I don't get in trouble 'cause I already gave Jamel the phone number. I didn't know Aunt Charmaine was on it like that."

"Don't worry about that. She don't really care who has the phone number. Her main concern is knowing where we are and who we're with at all times. What we're gonna have to do is get you a fake hobby like I have. We need to make up some event that you have to be at from this time to that time, on this day to that day. These are the days you could chill with Jamel."

"But didn't we already tell your mom I was gon' be with you on Thursday and Friday evenings?"

Tiffany snapped her fingers, "That's right! Thank God you pay attention. Now the only thing we gotta do is figure out what time we'll meet up to come back home together. That'll be a hop, skip and a jump. Then you can come home and tell me stories about how Jamel put that thang on you!" Tiffany did a little dance as I laughed.

I was beginning to feel like we we're long lost sisters. It was something I had to get off my chest. Even though it was bothering me day and night I didn't say a word to anyone about it. In my heart I knew it was time to talk about it. Ignoring my situation wasn't gonna make it disappear. On top of that I knew something had to be done – fast. Since there wasn't any other way to put it I blurted it out, "Tiffany, I'm pregnant!"

Tiffany's mouth fell open, "What!?"

"I'm pregnant and Jamel wants me to keep it."

Tiffany put her hands on her head, "Hell no you not keeping it! You can't keep it! Is that nigga crazy!? This should've been the first thing you told me soon as you saw me!" said Tiffany as she paced back in forth.

I put my finger to my lip, "Shhh! I know I can't keep it but I'm scared. I don't know what to do."

Tiffany lowered her tone but she was still shocked, "I'll tell you what to do. You have to get an abortion immediately. How far are you? When did you find out you were pregnant?"

"When I found out I was six weeks. That was a week ago. I knew right away that I couldn't keep this baby but Jamel is being such an asshole. He won't give me money for the abortion. He doesn't wanna hear my reasons for my decision. The only thing he cares about is me having this baby."

"Fuck him right now! We gotta concentrate on what we're gonna do. The facts of the matter are you're seven weeks pregnant, you need to have an abortion. We need money to do this." Tiff paced back and forth a few more times before snapping her fingers, "I got it," she snapped!

• • •

Me and Tiffany sat in her room as I held the cordless phone in my hand, "Tiff, are you sure this is gonna work?"

"Listen, this may or may not work," Tiffany advised me. Then she continued, "We're gonna try this anyway because when we go to plan 'B' this nigga can't say we didn't try to help him understand."

I bit my lip, "But, I already know Jamel is gonna say no. All he talked about since we found out I was pregnant is the baby this, the baby that. You would think the baby was already born. I should've never opened my big mouth when the doctor asked him to leave the room!"

"It's aight. That nigga gon' pay for this abortion one way or another. He got two choices. Either he gon' give it to us or we gon' take it. Right now the ball is in his court. If he still says no then the ball is in our court. I got game, trust me."

I took a deep breath as I dialed Jamel's number. Lately he's been answering all of my calls. I didn't know if it was because I was pregnant or because he was tryna change. After three rings Jamel answered.

I put on my sweet and sexy voice, "Hi daddy!"

Jamel laughed, "Oh, now you know who ya daddy is, huh?"

"What you doing?"

"I was thinking 'bout you hoping you thinking 'bout me."

"Boy, you need to stop."

"And if I don't?"

"Anyway…"

"Don't anyway me. When I'ma see ya sexy ass?"

"I'm tryna see you real soon," I replied.

"Is that right?"

"Yeah that's right."

Tiffany hit me, "Ask him!" she mumbled.

I covered the phone, "Shhh, I will!"

"What?" said Jamel.

"I wasn't talking to you."

Tiffany stood in front of me with her arms folded waiting for me to ask. I bit my lip as I finally got up the nerve to ask, "Uhm, Jamel...I need you to do me a favor?" I paused.

"What kind of favor?" I could hear the smile in his voice. I knew he thought I was talking about something nasty.

I looked at Tiffany. She was shaking her head, "You could do it girl. The only thing he could do is say yes or no. Remember, you gotta be bold," she whispered.

"Jamel, you know I love you, right?"

"Uh-oh."

Tiffany was still cheering me on in the background. I continued, "Don't say that baby." I covered the phone as I looked at Tiffany, "Do it!" she insisted. I replied, "I'm scared." Tiffany reached for the phone, "Well I'm not," she replied as I kept the phone out of her reach.

"Hello?" Jamel spoke.

"Yeah, I'm here." I took a deep breath as I asked the final question, "Jamel, I really need you to give me the money to have an abortion. We are not ready to be parents. Plus, the longer we wait the more it's gonna cost."

Tiffany moved closer towards me as I put the phone between both of our ears. I sat back and waited for Jamel to flip as I closed my eyes and bit my lip.

"You still talking 'bout that bullshit!?" Jamel paused then continued, "You have a lot of fucking nerve asking me to give you money for some dumb shit like that! I can't believe you, not only do you wanna kill my baby but you want me to pay for it, get the fuck outta here! What's done is done. We ain't changing it now so don't bring that shit up no more, wordamuva! What you should be tryna do is get some fucking prenatal care."

I spoke, "But Jamel…"

Jamel cut me off, "But Jamel nothing! You think you so slick, don't you? Calling me tryna seduce me then ask me to pay for the murder of my child! Ask me again and see what I do? I dare you. Matter-fact I double dare you! Go 'head, ask me?"

I paused then spoke, "I'll speak to you later Jamel."

"Yeah, that's what I thought," said Jamel as he hung-up the phone.

I threw the phone on the bed and looked at Tiffany, "Now what are we s'pose to do!?"

Tiffany shook her head, "Don't worry. We'll just move on to plan 'B'."

"What exactly is your plan 'B'?"

"It's called the-power-of-the-pussy."

"What!?"

"Jamel is ya man, right?"

"Yeah."

"You fucked him before, right?"

I looked at Tiff like she just asked the dumbest question in the world. She responded without me having to say a word.

"Okay. So, if he's ya man and you fucked him. Plus, the dick is good." Tiffany paused, "The dick is good, right?"

I sucked my teeth and hit her, "Get to the point."

"My point is if he's your man then you have access to his stash, right?"

I put my hands up, "Oh, no!"

"Oh yes!" Tiffany stood up then continued, "You better stop being so naïve girl! This is your life we're talking about. You cannot let this nigga dictate your future 'cause you'll be the one stuck in the house wit a crying ass baby. That nigga will be out hitting some new fresh coochie! You might love him and everything and that's cool. Hey, to each is own and all that good shit. But, don't be a fool cousin. I ain't tryna knock you but uhm…think about this? If that nigga left you or got killed tomorrow then where would you and that baby be? Can you handle a responsibility like that on your own? 'Cause if you can't then you'll be doing far worst things than clipping a little cash from your boyfriends stash just for you and your shorty to survive. Is that what you want?"

I didn't say a word but my silence spoke volumes. Tiffany continued, "You better stop being a scared bitch and start being a 'bout ya bidness bitch. Don't think about that nigga being mad at you, he'll get over it. Think about how mad you'll be at yourself if you have this baby and you fuck up your life. Think about that shit. 'Cause once you have a baby ain't no given it back sweetheart. You'll be responsible for that little fuck at least until its eighteen. You might even be responsible for it longer than that. Look at my brother Tyreek lazy ass. He's nineteen, a college drop-out, he don't have a job and he won't even look for one. All he does is play video games all damn day in that basement. You know why? 'Cause he know he has mommy to take care of him, that's why! So if you ain't ready to take care of you and another person on your own then you know what you gotta do. Fuck what Jamel is saying. He ain't gotta open his legs and give birth, you do. Then if he goes to jail you know he gon' expect you to hold down him, you and the damn baby! Oh hell no girl! What you gon' do?"

I laid across the bed staring at the ceiling as I replied, "I'ma do what I gotta do."

"Which is…?"

"I'ma go with your plan 'B'."

Tiffany smiled, "That's what I'm talking about!"

I sat up, "So, Lets hear your plan 'B'."

Tiffany took a seat next to me, "Aight. It's like this, I want you to call Jamel and apologize."

I cut her off, "Apologize for what?"

Tiffany put her hand up as she spoke, "Just listen." She continued, "You have to apologize 'cause you need to get back on his good side. You ain't gon' really mean it 'cause you ain't sorry but what the fuck…? Stroke the nigga ego and tell him you sorry. Niggaz is suckers for love, trust me. Now, you can't call him today 'cause he still a little upset. Give him some time to cool down then you'll call him tomorrow. When you call him you gotta make him feel like he's the man. Let him curse at you if he feels like cursing. He might even wanna yell at you, so what! This is when you put on the sweet-daddy-I'm-ya-bitch voice and tell him you was trippin'. The more you stroke his ego the more he'll forgot about what you said the last time y'all spoke. What you're tryna do is pay him a visit. He's gonna wanna see you 'cause you his 'baby-mother.' Plus niggaz can't say no to some pregnant pussy. He gon' think about how he could cum inside you and all that good shit, whatever. The goal is to get to his house, fuck the nigga to sleep, then clip some money from his stash when he's out cold. In order to do this you're gonna need to spend the night 'cause you don't wanna be limited with time. So that means you'll have to do this next weekend. I don't care if you gotta suck this nigga dick until his nuts is dry! You do what you gotta do! I'll worry about cooking up a lie for us to get out the house that weekend. All I want you to do is concentrate on getting that paper. And we gon' need somebody eighteen or older to go with us to the clinic, but I'll take care of that too. I'm gonna call the clinic and set-up the appointment. After that all we'll need is the money. Don't let me down and most of all don't let yourself down, I got faith in you girl."

"How are you so sure this is gonna work?" I asked.

Tiffany cracked a smile, "Let me explain something to you. You are a female. Females have pussies. Pussy makes the world go 'round. I don't care if you the Prince of Peru or the King of Compton. A nigga is gon' be a nigga and niggaz love some pussy, especially if you know how to work it. If you throw that shit right and wet his dick up real nice then he has no choice but to do as you say. You know why? 'Cause that nigga gon' want some of that pussy again. And don't be fooled into thinking all pussy is the same 'cause it ain't. So, if you got some good shit like I know you do 'cause we fam." Tiff smiled then continued, "Then that nigga will hand you the sun, moon and stars. But it's all a mind game 'cause even though we know we're in control you gotta make that nigga feel like he's the king of the world. Long as you don't forget he's just Jamel from the projects, everything will be all good. Trust me every nigga wants to feel like a king. Why not give 'em what they want if they giving you what you need? You know how that saying goes 'you gotta use what you got to get what you want.' Fair exchange ain't no robbery. Trust me girl, all niggaz fall victim to the power of the pussy at one point or another. How you think baby-mama-drama started? It was 'cause that one nigga met that one chick who he knew wasn't any good for him, but he sampled that stuff and he just couldn't get enough."

Tiffany had me laughing so hard I almost pissed on myself. She had to laugh at herself as she continued, "So, instead of asking what if this doesn't work you should be asking how can this not work?"

"You just got it all figured out girl, huh?"

"Think I don't when I do?" said Tiffany as she walked over to her dresser. She opened a drawer and pulled out a small notebook then tossed it to me.

"What you gimme this for?" I asked looking at the notebook.

"Open it up and turn to the first page. I want you to read it." I did as Tiffany told me to do. When I opened the notebook, page one read,

'I fucked niggaz in places high and low
I fucked them all just to get that doe
They get a whiff of me, now they whipped
I got them doing deep, down, dirty, undercover shit
I make them spell my name and lick my clit
I'm pussy motherfucker
Stop acting like you ain't know I was the shit
I'll make a man forget he has a wife
I'm pussy motherfucker
You need me in ya life
I'm pink and soft
Nigga I'm the boss
You want me in ya life
Then pay the cost
I'll sit on ya face and ride ya dick

When I'm not around
It makes you sick
To all you motherfuckers' who just don't know...
Nigga once I'm in ya life
You can't let me go.'

I closed the notebook and looked up. Tiffany was smiling from ear to ear. She was the proud writer of that poem. She snatched the notebook out of my hand and whispered in my ear, "Pussy rules the world, don't you ever forget that!"

Still in the state of shock I replied, "After a poem like that how could I?"

Tiffany walked back over to her drawer and tossed her notebook inside. She pressed a button on her entertainment system, the soulful voice of Mary J. Blige came banging through the speakers, *'Real love, I'm searching for a real love...someone to set my heart free, real love.'*

Tiffany started dancing in the middle of the floor, "Sing that shit Mary! I'm searching for a real love too. But, I'll settle for a fake love right now long as he got some real money."

I busted out laughing, "Girl do you ever stop?"

Tiffany smiled, "Nope!"

"I didn't think so," I joined her dancing in the middle of the bedroom floor. We danced until we couldn't dance anymore.

• • •

A week flew by so quickly before we knew it and Saturday had arrived. It was time to put Tiffany's plan 'B' into action. Somehow Tiffany convinced her mother to let us spend the night out. Everything was flowing smooth.

Tiffany planned to spend the night with Shawn and I planed on spending the night with Jamel. The next day we would meet up and arrive home together.

Outside the house, one block away a cab sat waiting for us. Once we were seated inside the cab we couldn't help but giggle and smile about how we cleverly set-up our entire operation. Tiffany smiled as she gave me a hug.

"I love you!" she said with so much excitement.

"I love you more!" I replied right back. We told the cab driver where we were going and he pulled off. As me and Tiff sat in the back of the cab we carefully went over the details of our plans again.

"I gave you Shawn's number, right?"

I reached in my pocket and pulled out the number Tiffany gave me earlier, "Yup, I got it."

"Good. Hold on to it and keep it in a safe place."

"Don't worry I will."

"Remember what I said, if you call the first time and we don't answer then we're probably a little busy," Tiffany laughed then continued. "So make sure you keep calling back. Do not leave Jamel's house until you speak to me. I won't leave Shawn's house until I speak to you. I set up the appointment and everything's all good to go. The only thing left is for you to do your part and get this paper. You think you can handle it?"

"I know I can."

Tiffany smiled, "That's what I like to hear."

"Which day is the appointment?"

"I set everything up for Thursday. This way if we need a little more time my moms won't be sweating us 'cause she'll think we're with them damn kids."

"You make sure everything is covered, don't you?"

"I got to," Tiffany replied.

We pulled up in front of Jamel's building. I proceeded to get out of the car. Me and Tiff hugged as she spoke, "Don't forget what I said, work 'em girl, work 'em!"

I laughed, "I won't let you down."

"You better not!"

"I'll see you tomorrow."

The cab pulled off and I walked into Jamel's building. When I reached his apartment he greeted me with a big smile as he spoke.

"Is that Mahogany and Janay?"

Ready to flip, I looked at him real hard as I replied, "What did you just call me?"

Jamel grabbed me by my waist as he gave me a kiss, "Janay, that's gonna be the name of our little girl."

All I could think was "here he go with this bullshit already." I had to remind myself what I was there for as I stayed calm and played it off real smooth.

"How do you know its gon' be a girl?" I forged a smile.

Jamel smiled even harder, "Well if its not then we already know that's gon' be my junior."

I actually started to feel a little bad as I played along, "Jamel Jr. I can't wait."

"Did you tell your aunts yet?"

I hugged Jamel as I leaned my head on his chest, "No, not yet."

Jamel grabbed my shoulders and looked into my eyes as he replied, "What are you waiting for? They're gonna know sooner or later."

I put on my baby voice, "I was waiting for you. I want us to tell them together."

Jamel stroked my hair, "Well, we need to tell them

soon."

"I know," I replied.

Jamel continued, "I like your hair like this. It didn't come out bad as I thought it would. I actually think it's real cute and sexy."

"I tried to do something with it until I go pay Tammy a visit. She's gonna flip when she sees my hair, I already know it."

"Nah, you good mommy, you know who you look like with that style?"

"Who?" I replied.

"That chick from that singing group, 702."

"She wishes!" I shot back.

Both of us laughed. I glanced at my watch. I wasn't ready to put my plan into action just yet. It was still too early.

"Daddy, I'm hungry." As I sat on the bed Jamel caressed my shoulders, "What do you wanna eat?" he replied.

I licked my lips and rubbed my stomach, "I want vanilla ice cream from 'Red Lobster.' I want strawberry cheeses-cake from 'Juniors' and, I want a turkey and cheese sandwich from Blimpie's."

"Gaddamn!" Jamel replied.

I laughed, "Can you please gimme what I want?" I touched Jamel's chest as I kissed him on his cheek and whispered in his ear, "If you give me what I want now, I'll give you what you want later."

A big smile appeared on Jamel's face. To emphasize my point I continued, "And you can cum inside me as much as you want, as many times as you want."

Jamel grabbed his keys and his hat, "Come on," he replied. I followed his lead.

Jamel took me to all the places I wanted to go. He was being such a sweetheart. I was happy I killed two birds with one stone. I got my eat on plus I killed time. By the time we got back to Jamel's place I was ready to put my plan into action.

Fresh out of the shower I was dressed in nothing but black laced underwear. I entered the bedroom. Jamel was lying across the bed wearing nothing but his Hilfiger Boxers. As he watched me strut across the bedroom his dick grew hard. The nipples on my firm round breast grew erect. As I stood up next to the bed, Jamel attempted to grab me but I backed away.

I held one finger up, "Not just yet."

"Why not?" replied Jamel as he licked his lips.

"You gotta show me you want me."

"That's what I'm tryna do," Jamel replied staring at me like he wanted to eat me for dinner.

I put one leg on the bed as I replied, "Try harder!"

Jamel immediately crawled towards me. He moved my panties to the side as he started rubbing my clit. He looked at me like he was my puppy. I rubbed his head like he was my dog. Jamel licked his fingers.

"How does it taste daddy?"

"It taste good, just like that vanilla ice cream you ate a little while ago baby."

As his face was still between my legs I lifted his chin, "Is that right?"

"Uh-hm," Jamel moaned.

"I want you to do something for me, okay?"

"I'll do whatever you want," Jamel replied.

I smiled at his obedience. Then I told him what I wanted him to do, "I want you to sniff it. I don't want you to touch the pussy. I don't want you to eat the pussy. I just want you to keep your face between my legs and sniff it like a good boy. Do you think you can do that?"

Jamel licked his lips as he made the sexiest, nastiest face I've ever seen in my life. I repeated my question, "Can you handle that?"

"I could handle it. You know daddy got you baby!"

"So what you waiting for, start sniffing!"

Jamel sniffed my pussy until I made him stop. It took everything he had to hold himself back from sticking his tongue inside. As I pushed Jamel on the bed I crawled next to him. His dick looked like it was ready to bust out of his boxers. I used my teeth to remove his boxers as he rubbed my chest with his masculine hands. I rubbed his dick all over my face before putting it in my mouth.

Once I was sure I sucked his dick like a nasty slut bitch, I removed my panties. Then I put them over his head as I started riding him like a stallion. He couldn't see what I was doing to him. He could only feel it as I took him to ecstasy in the dark room.

My job was easier than I thought it would be. Jamel was out like a light after the second time I put this thang on him. I quietly got on my knees as I reached under his bed to get the Nike box he used to keep his stash money in. I counted out five-hundred dollars before carefully placing the Nike box back in its place.

I placed the five-hundred dollars in my bag. Then I crawled back in bed with a smile on my face. I eased closer toward Jamel before I fell asleep.

• • •

The next morning I called Shawn's house. Tiffany was

sounding like she had just as much fun as I did. She told me where to meet her then I left. As my cab approached Farmers and one-thirteenth I saw Tiffany standing outside smoking a cigarette. I stepped out of the cab with a smile on my face as Tiffany came running towards me.

"You that bitch!"

I laughed, "I told you," a big smile was plastered across my face as I thought about what I'd accomplished. I took a look around before I asked Tiff, "Why did we meet over here? Where are we going?"

Tiffany took a last pull off of her cigarette before she threw it in the street. She replied, "I'm 'bout to show you, follow me."

I followed her to the side door of a brick house. She knocked on the door.

"Who lives here?" I couldn't help but ask.

"My Boo," she replied.

"I didn't know I was meeting you at Shawn's house."

"This ain't Shawn's house," she shot back.

Suddenly I was confused. The door flew open as a woman with short dreadlocks and a nice figure stood in front of me and Tiffany. The woman wore a tight jean, jumpsuit. At the sight of Tiffany the woman smiled. Tiffany kissed this woman on the mouth as she introduced us.

"Mahogany, this is Melody. Melody, this is Mahogany."

"Nice to meet you Mahogany, come inside." I couldn't believe what I just witnessed. I stepped into the house as Tiffany winked at me then cracked a smile.

"Can I get you something to drink Mahogany? Coke, Sprite, water, Ice-T?"

"Sprite is fine, thank you."

As Melody went into the kitchen I whispered to Tiffany, "Why the hell did you bring me to your girlfriend's house?"

Tiffany laughed, "Relax. Mel is cool people. Since she's the one who will be coming with us to the clinic on Thursday, I thought it might be better if y'all met now."

"What!? Are you crazy!? Why is your girlfriend coming with us to the clinic? Why did you even tell her anything?"

"What you mean, what the hell I tell her anything? Who did you think the person eighteen or older was gon' be that's coming with us? It damn sure wasn't gon' be Jamel! I don't have anyone else in mind, do you?"

"But I don't even know her."

"That's not even important right now. Plus you know me so that's enough. Trust me sweetie, Mel ain't thinking 'bout you. She gotta bigger fish to lick."

I pushed Tiffany, "You so damn nasty!"

"And you so damn scary. You gotta loosen up. Live a little, girl. The world is not gon' wait for you, you better come out that shell you in. I bet you Jamel probably the only nigga you even fucked. How boring is that, the same dick all the time? That gotta be wack."

I put my hand in Tiff's face, "Whatever."

Melody came back with my drink. She also had a bunch of snacks in her hands. She handed me my drink and sat the snacks on the coffee table as she spoke, "I figured I'd bring y'all something to munch on."

Tiffany laughed, "You mean you figured you'd bring preg-o something to snack on. The cat is out the bag now baby, I already told her you know," Tiffany said to Melody.

I hit Tiffany as Melody spoke, "Stop being so mean!"

"I ain't being mean; I'm just kicking the facts."

Tiffany stood up as she stuffed a Doritos chip in her mouth, "We about to leave. I just wanted you and Mahogany to meet."

Melody looked sad, "You're leaving already?"

"Yeah, we got school in the morning," Tiffany replied.

"Am I gonna see you before Thursday?"

Tiffany kissed Melody as she replied, "I'll see what I could do," then she stuffed another Doritos chip in her mouth. She tilted her towards the door then we headed in that direction.

It tickled me how Tiffany really thought she was a pimp. If I didn't see her in action sometimes I don't think I would've believed her. That girl was a trip. We all said our goodbyes then me and Tiff headed home.

• • •

During the next few days all I could think about was my upcoming appointment. Jamel started picking me up from school everyday again. While Tiffany did her weekly routines on Thursday and Friday evenings, mines were spent with Jamel. He looked forward to spending time with me just as much as I enjoyed and looked forwarded to spending time with him. Thursday's and Friday's were the only days I was able to spend with Jamel since I moved in with Aunt Charmaine, we cherished every moment. I didn't have to hunt Jamel down or page him over and over again. Wherever I needed him to be he was there like clockwork. Things were going so smooth. This is why I was so nervous when Thursday finally came.

It was time for me to go to the clinic. I couldn't think of a lie to tell Jamel so I told him nothing at all. I decided it would be best if I told him after everything was over that I had Aunt Charmaine pick me up early from school because I wasn't feeling well. I would later tell him it turned out that I was having a miscarriage. I had all the pieces off the puzzle together but for some reason I still wasn't confident.

As me, Melody and Tiffany walked into the clinic I damn near choked. I thought it didn't get any worse than the group of anti-abortion protesters outside – I was wrong. When I looked around the clinic I never saw so many women in my life. There were chairs everywhere. Women were sitting down and standing up throughout the clinic. A lady wearing a medical uniform held a chart as she randomly called names. A handful of guys were also present but without a doubt, women were definitely the majority up in there.

We walked up to the receptionist desk. Melody did all the talking. The receptionist handed us paperwork as she looked at me and spoke, "You're Mahogany Woods?"

"Yes," I replied.

"Did you eat or drink anything after twelve o'clock midnight?"

"No."

"How do you plan to pay for the termination?"

"Cash," I replied.

"Okay, good. Your total is three-seventy-five. Fill out those papers and bring them back to me when you're done."

I handed her the cash as she gave me a receipt. We all found a spot on the wall as Tiffany rubbed my back.

"Are you nervous?" she asked.

Ignoring her question I asked a question of my own,

"Are all these women here to do the same thing as me?"

Tiffany shook her head, "That's what I'm guessing," she replied.

I put my head down as I spoke, "They could at least give you some type of privacy. Why do they have us all in one big room?"

Melody cut in, "Listen ma, ain't no reason for you to be ashamed about being here. Look to your left and look to your right. All these women are here doing the same thing so ain't no one person above the rest. Just like you here for a reason they're here for a reason too. And, I bet you half of these bitches been in here on more than one occasion. Don't take none of this shit personal you gon' be aight ma. Just like you wanna leave outta here and forget about them, they wanna leave outta here and forget about you. This ain't no meet and greet event. This is a handle ya business and step event. Just thank your lucky stars you ain't gotta get a two day procedure."

I raised my eyebrows, "Two days?"

Melody laughed, "Oh girl you ain't know? This is exactly why I don't fuck with no sorry ass niggaz. I can't deal with all the headaches and heartbreaks they bring to the table. Look at all these women up in here, where they baby daddies at now?"

Tiffany cut Melody off, "Alright already. Nobody wanna hear all that bullshit. The whole world ain't gotta know ya sexual preferences." Tiffany frowned then continued, "For you to be twenty-five you sure need to learn when and where to keep your mouth closed. Sometimes you just talk too damn much!"

Melody rolled her eyes and stuffed her face in a magazine as Tiffany sucked her teeth.

After hours of waiting and speaking with different members of the staff, I was finally called. I was told to go in a room, take off all my clothes and put on a hospital gown. Once I finished I was escorted into a room where the doctor greeted me.

"Hello," said the doctor.

"Hi," I replied.

As I sat on the operating table the doctor gave me medicine that was supposed to put me to sleep as he continued talking, "What kind of music do you like?"

"I like all different types of music."

"Are you into sports?"

"I like…," before I could answer the question the medicine had took its effect. I was out cold.

When I regained consciousness I was in a totally different room lying on a bed, girls were everywhere. It was safe to assume they'd just experienced the same thing I just did since we were all in hospital gowns lying in separate beds throughout various places in the huge room.

When me and Tiffany finally arrived home I was happy the nightmare was over, but sad about the entire situation. Tiffany and Melody were supportive from the beginning to the end. Once we were inside the bedroom Tiffany felt the need to emphasize the doctor's orders to me.

"No sex, no baths, no douches for at least three weeks. We go back for your check-up in two weeks. In the meantime don't forget to take your medicine, otherwise, how you feeling bitch?"

I flopped across the bed, "I don't know what I want more, food or sleep. I know my stomach is killing me though!"

"You lay down. I'll get you something to eat."

"Thank you, Tiff."

When Tiffany came back in the room she had a sandwich for both of us. As she handed me my sandwich she passed me the cordless phone too. I took a bite of the sandwich as Tiffany spoke.

"Don't forget to call Jamel. You know you gotta explain why you weren't there when he went to pick you up from school today?"

"Hopefully he forgot about me today."

Tiffany took a sip of her juice as she replied, "I doubt it."

"You couldn't get me nothing to drink?" I asked.

Tiffany put her glass down, "Damn, I'm only one person with two hands. But, I'ma go get you something to drink this time, only 'cause you know...but next time you're on your own."

"I love you," I said to Tiffany.

"Yeah, yeah, yeah," she replied.

Tiffany left the room as I dialed Jamel's number.

I spoke out loud to myself, "You could do it girl. Handle your business. I was sick, I left school early and I just found out I had a miscarriage. Be strong!"

I took a deep breath as Jamel's phone rung. Jamel answered his phone and I put on my sad voice ready to run my game.

"Hi daddy," I whined. The phone went silent as I spoke again, "Hello?"

Jamel laughed, "Who is this?" he replied.

"What?" I asked shocked that he didn't know who I was. Instantly I caught an attitude, "How many bitches you got calling you daddy?"

"Many as I want, now what the fuck you want?"

I couldn't believe my ears, "Jamel, do you know who you're talking to?"

He laughed again as he replied, "I know exactly who I'm talking to, this Mahogany, right? Or should I call you killer?"

"What?" was all I could say.

Jamel continued, "What's up killer?"

"Excuse me," I frowned. I knew something wasn't right.

"You heard what the fuck I said, I hear you a killer now."

I took a deep breath as I whined harder, "Jamel you wanna explain exactly what you're talking about?"

"Yeah I do, get in a cab and come to my house right now. I just need to feel ya pussy."

"Jamel you know I can't come right now, it's late, I don't feel well and I have to go to school in the morning."

"That's exactly what I thought."

"Jamel what type of games are you playing?"

"Mahogany cut the bullshit aight! Let me just translate 'it's late, I don't feel well and I have to go to school in the morning' to, I'm a lying, conniving, sneaky bitch who took ya money and had a fucking abortion!"

I said nothing on the phone as Jamel continued.

"You might've thought you was playing me but you played ya motherfucking self! I should never have to hear from no dusty ass bitch in these projects that's on my dick, that she saw my girl at the clinic today tryna hide."

I cut him off, "Jamel I can explain."

"Fuck you and your explanation!" Jamel yelled into the phone! Then he continued, "Toya should never have to tell me anything about my bitch that I don't already know. But, that's not even the worst part. You ready for this? What made it so bad was, I barked on the bitch! Now I feel like a real asshole, especially when I went to pick you up from school and ya ass wasn't there."

I began crying, "Jamel I'm sorry!"

"Fuck you!" Jamel yelled! "The bright side to all of this is I'm happy I was sitting up at that school waiting on you 'cause it gave me time to think. I thought about what that bitch Toya said. I thought about you not calling me all day or being present at school and I thought about my money coming up short. Then like pieces of a puzzle it all started to come together.

I cried harder, "Jamel I tried to talk to you but you wouldn't listen. I tried to tell you that I wasn't ready to be a mother, but you weren't tryna hear that. Why couldn't you just take the time to look at the bigger picture? You didn't stop to think about what would've happened to me and the baby, if you went to jail or was found dead in the streets God forbid. I mean damn Jamel why can't you understand that I have dreams to look forward to and goals to reach. Right now just wouldn't be the best time for either of us to have a baby, but maybe one day later in life we will. I promise baby. Please hear me out," I continued to cry.

"I heard everything I needed to hear. Mahogany, fuck you! You just like the rest of these hood rats. I hope you fall in a ditch, bitch!"

Chapter 8

When It All Falls Down...

If April showers brought May flowers then it must've rained a whole lot during the month of April. The flowers bloomed beautifully as the sun shined down illuminating the very presence that spring had arrived.

As the bus I was on rode past my old stomping grounds, Forty Projects, I couldn't help but to think of Jamel. I just couldn't believe how things changed between us. Here it was three weeks since I had my abortion and Jamel still wasn't speaking to me. I called him several times during the first week. However, after being hung-up on, verbally abused and ignored I decided to stop. I accepted the fact that our relationship was over. What I couldn't accept is the reason and the cause of our relationship being over. As I sat on the bus thinking of Jamel my thoughts were interrupted by Tiffany's loud mouth.

"Oh shit! Did you just see what I saw?" she blurted.

As I turned to look at Tiffany I noticed whatever she was looking at outside the window had her full attention. So I directed my attention outside the window as well. I saw about twenty motorbikes heading towards the projects. Tiffany jumped out of her seat and rung the bell for the bus to stop.

"What the hell are you doing? Where are you going?" I replied while jumping up from my seat.

Tiff looked at me like I was the one bugging, "Did you not just see all of those motorbikes? I'm getting off this damn bus. I need me a ride or die nigga!"

The bus came to a stop as Tiffany proceeded to walk down the steps. She pushed the back doors open to exit. I wasn't sure what I should do.

"Are you coming or what?" said Tiff as she looked at me while holding the doors open.

"What about Shawn? Aren't we going to meet up with him and his boys?"

"Bitch! Did you just see what I saw!? Fuck Shawn and his boys I'm tryna get a ride or die nigga! Shawn will be right there whenever I decide to go see him, are you coming or what!?"

"Either you getting off or staying on, but you can't keep holding the doors!" yelled the bus driver.

I exited the bus. A huge smile appeared on Tiffany's face as she proceeded to walk towards the direction the bikers were in.

"Hurry up, I'm tryna get this show on the road!" said Tiffany.

"I can't believe you really got off the bus."

"Well believe it," said Tiffany as she straightens her clothes out. Then she continued, "How do I look?"

"You look fine."

"Well that means I need to look better," Tiffany pulled out her mirror as she applied clear lip gloss to her lips.

"Mahogany, how do I look now?"

"Girl you looking like a million dollars."

Tiffany blew me a kiss, "Now that's what I'm talking 'bout!" We laughed as we made our way toward the projects.

"Tiff, how you know them niggaz stopping there?"

"I'm not a rocket-scientist, but its spring, it's nice and, they are niggaz. They wanna floss and the Projects is right there."

"What if they don't stop? I don't wanna look stupid."

"Didn't you live over here?"

"Yeah, so…"

"So stop acting like you can't pretend we just came through to see one of your homegirls. Doesn't your friend Jackie live over here?"

"Yeah, Jackie is a trip."

"She still got that big butt and curly hair?" Tiffany cracked a smile.

"Yes she does, and she's strictly dickly might I add."

Tiffany laughed, "I don't want her, but we could still pay her a visit anyway," One of the biker's popped-a-wheelie, that got Tiffany's attention.

"Daaaamn don't do it like that boo!" said Tiffany as she walked faster to get next to the action.

"Wait for me," I yelled trying to catch up with Tiffany. When I was next to her I spoke, "How do I look?"

Tiffany looked me up and down. She adjusted my white tennis skirt, fixed the collar on my green and white stripe shirt. Then replied, "I'm loving the ball on the back of your socks, your outfit is definitely gon' make these niggaz sweat and your eyes are making you stand out even more. Plus your hair is growing back. I'll say you almost looking as good as me. You might have to stay away from me 'til I pull the nigga I want," Tiffany joked.

As we walked into the projects all the bikers were right there like Tiffany predicted. Some were riding up and down the strip, while others parked their bikes to watch the show with everyone else. I did my best not to look at anyone but I felt all eyes on me. Just as I turned to say something to Tiffany I saw her leaning on the guy's bike who was popping-a-wheelie just seconds earlier. Tiffany saw me looking. She winked in my direction.

From the corner of my eye I saw a horrible looking guy heading my way. To avoid hurting my eyes and his feelings I headed toward the store. I proceeded to cross the street. Once I reached the middle of the street a chromed-out, midnight blue, Mercedes-Benz rolled up on the side of me. I was stuck like a deer in headlights as the driver rolled down his tinted windows and smiled. His curly hair and Cartier frames made him appear like he was straight off the pages of GQ magazine. He turned down his music and spoke.

"I'm looking for my wife; somebody told me I could find her here. Do you think you could help me? She's young, pretty, sexy and all that!" The driver looked me up and down then licked his lips as he continued, "Today she's wearing a white tennis skirt with some cute k-Swiss to match. Plus her cat-like green eyes would stop any man dead in his tracks. The only thing I can't tell you is her name."

I cracked a smile, "You don't know your wife's name?"

"I will if you tell me. I want you to gimme her phone number while you at it. What good is a name without a number to match? I'ma need to know where I'm sending these flowers I got for her too."

I laughed at his sense of humor, "And if I don't?"

149

"Then I might have to run you over, just so I could come see you in the hospital and bring your flowers there."

He gently stepped on the gas moving his car a little closer to me, "How you wanna do this?"

"Oh, so you really gonna hit me?" I asked.

"I'm spoiled what can I say? I get what I want and what I can't get I take. Now, let me help you understand if you don't already. I want you! What's your name?"

"Well at least let me get to the other side of the street first."

"Nope, I'm holding you hostage until you give me what I want." As we talked in the middle of the street, biker after biker rode by. All of them honked their horn at the guy I was talking to. He greeted them back by slapping his two fists together. All the females stood around watching me like they wished they were in my shoes. Before I had a chance to give this fine motherfucker my number or take his, I heard a familiar voice yell.

"Ayo, get the fuck over here!" when I turned to look in the direction the voice was coming from I saw Jamel. The guy looked at Jamel then looked back to me as he laughed then spoke, "You know him?"

I rolled my eyes, "I wish I didn't."

The guy peeled off a one hundred dollar bill, wrote his number on it then handed it to me, "Call me when you ready to deal with a real nigga. Jamel is a clown!"

"You know him?" I replied shocked! Before my question was answered the guy pulled off and Jamel was so close I could smell his breath. He snatched the hundred dollar bill out of my hand.

"You fucking that nigga now?"

I sucked my teeth, "Jamel, I don't even know him."

"Oh so he just come through giving you money, huh?" Jamel held the money close to my face. Soon as he held the bill up he noticed the writing on it. I tried to snatch the money. Jamel took a step back as he held the bill in the air as he spoke.

"Fuck that nigga and his money," Jamel ripped the money into little pieces then threw it in the air.

"Why the fuck are you worried about me all of a sudden!? You don't want anything to do with me, remember?"

"First of all get the fuck from out the middle of the street!"

"Jamel you wasn't my daddy before and you damn sure ain't my daddy now," I turned to walk away from him. He ran behind me.

"Mahogany, the games are over! You know what's up."

"Ain't nobody playing," I laughed. Then I continued, "Jamel you had your chance to be with me but you chose to let me go. I don't have any hard feelings for you. I hope you respect me enough not to have any hard feelings for me. If you'll excuse me I have to get my cousin and leave."

I headed in the direction where I last saw Tiffany talking to the guy on the bike. When I arrived at my destination I saw Tiffany fastening her helmet to get on the guy's bike. Before I could get closer she hugged the guy tight. He clutched his gears. The bike made a VROOM…VROOM sound. They rode off.

Jamel was still on my trail like white on rice. I tried to walk fast as I could to get away from him. When I couldn't take it anymore I turned around and spoke.

"Jamel, what, what do you want from me!? I'm no longer your girl therefore leave me alone. I'm a killer, a hood rat! You hope I fall in a ditch, remember?"

Jamel grabbed my wrist and pulled me towards him. "I love you," he whispered in my ear.

I tried pushing him away, "You sure have a funny way of showing it."

Jamel wouldn't let me go. Instead he pulled me closer to him as he licked my ear then continued whispering, "Baby, listen, I'm sorry about everything I put you through. I miss you so fucking much! I was hoping you missed me just as much as I missed you. You don't know how bad I wanted you to just pop up at my house. I understand why you did what you did and I'm not mad at you anymore. Can we start over? Can we leave the past in the past? I want you; no I need you in my life! You don't know how bad I been wanting to taste that pussy."

Although I wanted Jamel, I did my best to resist temptation, "You gave up that right, you forgot?"

"Nah, I remember too well. I started this so I'm gon' finish it. I want you back in my life and this time I ain't gon' let you go. Come home to your daddy, baby. I told you I was sorry."

My voice began to crack, "Jamel don't do this to me. Not right here, not right now."

"Why not, you mean to tell me that I can't lick that, I can't smell that, I can't taste that, you don't wanna feel this big dick inside you never ever, ever, ever again?"

To emphasize his point Jamel stuck his hand up my skirt. He whispered, "Come with me in the house."

Like a lost puppy I was so in love all over again. I followed Jamel inside as Tiffany continued to ride up and down the strip on the back of that guy's bike.

• • •

Jamel was still taking care of his business as usual, in between the sheets and financially.

It was the ending of my senior year. I was so excited. Soon I would be off to college. Everything would be all good. Jamel paid for my application fees when I was applying to different colleges. I asked my Aunt Charmaine for the money, but she didn't give it to me so I thought she forgot about it. I'm nobody's beggar so instead of bugging her about the money I told Jamel to pay for it. Once everything was said and done my senior trip had arrived. I wasn't excited because, I wasn't going on the trip. Instead me and Jamel planned a romantic getaway in the Pocono Mountains. Aunt Charmaine thought I would be on my senior trip the entire time.

When we arrived at the resort everything was beautiful! There was a heart shaped bed in our room, a bathtub shaped like a champagne glass with mirrors all over the place. Once I finished looking at our room I ran to Jamel, wrapped my arms around him to give him a huge hug and a kiss, while he still had our bags in his hands.

"Daddy, you really outdid yourself this time! I love you so much!"

Jamel put the bags down then closed the door, "You know I'll do anything for my babygirl." He kissed me softly on the cheek.

"I don't know if three days will be enough time to spend with you. I got some real special surprises in mind for you."

Jamel's eyebrows went up, "Really?"

"Really, I can't remember the last time we spent three

whole nights together! I'm gonna show you just how much I miss you!"

I ran to one of my bags. I pulled out a cassette player and a cassette tape then waved it in front of Jamel's face.

"What you gon' do with that," replied Jamel.

I smiled, "You'll see."

Minutes later I came out of the bathroom wearing red leather shorts, a red halter top and cowboy boots with the matching hat.

"Damn! That shit is looking right on your body, but I want you to take it off right now and ride the shit out of your daddy like you a cowgirl fo'real!"

I smiled as I walked pass Jamel to get to the chair I pulled out for him.

"Sit down," I demanded!

Jamel attempted to sit down, I stood in front of him, "Take all of your clothes off first. The only thing I want you to leave on is your boxers."

Jamel stripped down to his boxers then sat down.

Jamel licked his lips, "Now, why don't you sit on my lap sexy?"

"I'm running this show. You just sit there until I'm finished with you!" a smile appeared on Jamel's face. I went back into my bag. This time I pulled out a scented candle and a pair of plastic handcuffs.

"What you gon' do with that?" Jamel inquired.

"Shut up!" I replied as I cuffed his hands behind the chair. Once I had Jamel in the position I wanted him in I pressed play on the cassette player. 'Justify My Love' by Madonna came banging through the speakers. I started dancing like I was Jamel's personal stripper. For that night I was Jamel's personal stripper.

As he sat in the chair handcuffed his eyes stayed glued to my body as I moved sexy like a snake from side to side. Seeing Jamel's reaction only made me dance even nastier. I watched as his dick grew harder from the pleasure I was letting him see.

I placed one foot in between Jamel's legs, right next to his dick. I stood up in the chair dancing as I threw my pussy in his face! Then I turned around in the chair as I threw my ass in his face. When I was done I hopped off the chair and did a split!

"Sit on my dick right now!" Jamel yelled.

I lit the candle as I looked at him, "I thought I told you to shut up!" I let the candle burn on the dresser then continued dancing. First I removed my halter top as I put my breast in Jamel's face. Then I removed my shorts and my red thong. I threw everything on the bed. Standing butt naked in front of Jamel I stroked his dick as I licked his ear. I kissed him on the cheek then continued dancing. I was wearing nothing but my cowboy boots with the hat to match! Once I saw the candle melting I picked it up. I began pouring hot wax all over my body. Jamel bit his bottom lip as he watched the wax roll smoothly down my body. I picked up the red thongs I threw on the bed then ripped it. I tied it around Jamel's mouth so I couldn't hear him moan as I got on my knees to give him a blow-job.

That was how our first day in the Pocono Mountains was spent! Along with each day we stayed, I had a new surprise ready for Jamel. Each day was better than the day before. Each night was nastier than the night before. On the last night I let Jamel fuck me in my ass! I loved every minute of it after I got over the pain.

• • •

When I finally arrived home Aunt Charmaine called me into her bedroom. She said she needed to speak with me. I just knew I was in trouble. I thought she might've found out I was with Jamel the whole time I was supposed to be on my senior trip, but that wasn't the case at all. Soon as I entered into her room she told me to have a seat as she spoke.

"Did you apply to any colleges because a college called here today looking for you?"

I was so excited I jumped up out of the seat I was sitting in as I asked Aunt Charmaine, "Which college was it, did they say I was accepted, what time did they call?"

Aunt Charmaine laughed at me, "Child please! I didn't ask all that. I just hung up on them and kept doing what I was doing."

I frowned, "You hung up on them? Why did you do that?"

"Why you think? I didn't give you any money for college applications. I didn't even know you applied. How did you pay for the applications anyway?"

I answered the question, "Jamel gave me the money but why do you seem upset about it?"

Aunt Charmaine shook her head as she walked over to close her bedroom door, "I should have known, but I'm not upset I just wished you would've told me what you were doing first. I would've told you not to waste your money."

I sat down feeling dizzy as I replied, "Waste my money, what do you mean by that? Plus I did ask you for the money for the applications, but I thought you forgot to give it to me. I didn't wanna seem like a pest so I just asked Jamel for the money."

"I didn't forget to give you the money. I just didn't give you the money because I don't see the point of you going to a college that I can't pay for anyway."

I could've sworn I was having a nightmare as I replied, "Aunt Charmaine, what do you mean you don't see the point? You know I planned on going to college ever since I was a little girl. Day and night all I talked about was becoming a singer or a psychiatrist. The money shouldn't be an issue because you'll still get my social security check as long as I'm in school. That can help pay for my tuition, plus I'll even get a job and use that money to pay for school as well."

Aunt Charmaine laughed at me again, "Honey that was so cute when you were younger and you wanted to become a psychiatrist or a singer. I admire you for that, I really do. However, that was then and this is now. You're old enough to see that we live in the real world and bills need to get paid."

"But aunt Charmaine..."

"Hold on I'm not finished, you're also old enough to see that nine out of ten people drop out of college or stop going because it's too expensive. Your cousin, my son, Tyreek is the perfect example. I paid for him to attend college, all he did was drop out and waste my money. By now I'm sure you've noticed money doesn't grow on trees around here. So I need every cent that comes my way."

I began crying as Aunt Charmaine continued, "Plus your social security check cannot pay for your college education. You know just as well as I do that check isn't enough to put you through college. Besides, I depend on that check every month so it's already budgeted into my income. If you use it to pay for a college that you're probably going to drop out of anyway it will be an unnecessary waste of money. What I suggest you do is forget about the social security check because they will not keep sending the check if you're not in school. A better solution would be to get a full time job that pays good money. Rome and I cannot pay all the bills around here. We're definitely going to need you to help out with some bills."

My eyes were red and filled with tears, "I really can't believe what you're asking me to do. How could you even fix your lips to ask me to throw my dreams away so I could help you pay your bills? I'm not trying to be disrespectful or anything, but why should I work instead of attending school when your son Tyreek is older than me? All he does is play video games all day. This is not just anything to me, this is my life. This is my future. This is my dream. Aunt Charmaine, please don't look at what Tyreek did as a cause for punishing me. I don't deserve this! Tyreek didn't take college seriously, I do!"

Aunt Charmaine snapped, "First of all let me explain something to you! Nothing in this world is free, nothing! Shit you gotta pay to ride the bus. And, don't worry about why Tyreek is not working right now! Tyreek is a boy so I know how hard it can be for a young brother to find work in this society. You on the other hand are a female. Finding work shouldn't be as hard. Your cousin Tiffany is the only one around here who I can afford to send to college. I've been saving money to send her to school for awhile, so it's not as hard to send her to college as it is to send you. So for the last and final time let me say this; I need you to get a job so you can help Rome and I pay some of these bills! If you plan to live in my house, under my roof then you're going to have to pay bills or start packing."

●　　●　　●

Packing is exactly what I started doing. I wasn't staying with Aunt Charmaine just to help her pay her bills. I figured if I was doing all of that for her then I might as well pay my own bills. I tried to reason with her about different ways I could pay for my education. However, her bottom line was she needed me to help pay some bills.

I hated her because she stole my dreams away. I thought she was different from my other aunts. She really had me convinced that she cared. Time revealed she wasn't any different from the other two. It was all about the money.

I thought about moving in with Jamel then I decided against it. I felt our relationship worked better when we had a chance to miss one another. Moving in together would surely leave no time for us to miss one another. Plus I remember how bad things would get at times when I only spent the night. I knew living together would not work.

I damn sure couldn't afford an apartment of my own, but Jackie insisted I stay with her. Jackie was having problems of her own. One of her brothers was on the run. Her other brother was still sprung over some chick who he moved in with. Plus her mother went back to her old ways of smoking crack. This left Jackie to take care of herself. Me and Jackie became roommates.

Jackie needed me just as much as I needed her. She was basically holding down her apartment all by herself.

She paid all the bills plus had all the say so. She kicked her mother and her mother's boyfriend out. She said she had to much fly shit to live with two crackheads. She couldn't take the risk of coming home one day finding all her shit gone. Her brothers laced that apartment with hi-tech stereo and TV gadgets plus leather furniture. Jackie said that was just the way she planned on keeping it!

Jamel didn't like the fact I was staying with Jackie. However, he did pay my half of the rent. He promised to move me out of that apartment within a few weeks. He felt I should have an apartment of my own.

I wasn't in a rush to leave. I knew Jackie needed my help for the

time being. Plus I wanted to secure a job before I moved even if Jamel did pay all my bills. On top of that I was determined to figure out some way I could pay for school without the help of my family. I had a 'B' average so I was sure financial aid would help.

Chapter 9

You Got Nerve...

It's been two weeks since I moved out of Aunt Charmaine's house. The only person I missed was Tiffany. However, me and Tiff still kept in contact, even though her mom didn't want us to. We spoke over the phone quite often. I didn't get to spend much time with Tiff anymore, but that was cool. I was busy trying to get my life together, while Tiffany was busy spending more and more time with Melody.

I sat in the financial aid office of Borough of Manhattan Community College waiting to be called. I couldn't help but wonder why this was the fourth college I've been to in two weeks, yet none of them granted me financial assistance to attend their school. This wasn't making any sense. I graduated with a high 'B' average with several reference letters from different teachers. My thoughts were interrupted when a beautiful black sister, sporting an Afro called my name. If I didn't know any better I would've thought this woman was Pam Grier herself. The woman smiled as she greeted me.

"Mahogany Woods?" she asked.

I reached for her hand which she had extended as I

spoke, "Yes I'm Mahogany."

The woman popped a peppermint in her mouth as she spoke, "I love your name, follow me."

"Thank you," I replied as I followed her lead. Once I was seated the woman pulled out a folder. She took a deep breath.

"Mahogany I'm afraid I have bad news."

"Don't tell me the financial aid didn't go through."

A sincere concern appeared on the woman's face. She shook her head then spoke, "I'm afraid that's exactly the problem we're having."

I couldn't hold the tears back, "I don't understand! Why is this happening to me? I just want to go to school."

The woman comforted me with a warm motherly hug, "I know sweetheart, I know."

This woman grabbed my shoulders then looked me directly in my eyes. She looked behind her then back at me before she spoke, "I want you to listen to me and listen to me good, do you hear me?"

"Yes," I shook my head up and down.

"What I'm getting ready to tell you could get me fired. So it is imperative that what I tell you doesn't leave this room."

"I understand," I sobbed.

"Not getting accepted into different schools has nothing to do with your academics. The only thing I can tell you is financial aid will not invest in someone's future who they feel can pay for school themselves, have parents who can pay, or someone who has bad referrals."

"But I can't pay, my parents are deceased and all of my referrals are great!"

"I'm not talking about the ones you can see sweetheart. I'm talking about the ones you can't see. Does the name Dr. Klein ring a bell?"

I nearly passed out when she mentioned her name, "That lady is a racist!" I yelled.

"Shhh!" the woman tried to calm me down.

"Dr. Klein is the reason I'm going through all I'm going through!?"

"Sweetheart, first you must calm down before I can go on."

I took a deep breath then closed my mouth. I was still vexed, but I appeared to be calm and subtle on the outside. The lady continued.

"This Dr. Klein seems to really have a personal problem with you. I wouldn't be surprised if she is a racist. All I know is she's connected in some very high places. She has the power to get you banned from many schools with the referral she's written. I cannot tell you what she wrote about you, but trust me; you wouldn't want to know. The only reason I feel the need to share this with you is because I can see the person doesn't match the words written on the paper. Honey, I'm sorry to let you know, but no school I can think of is going to grant you financial aid. Maybe if you pay for a school somewhere out of state you'd have a better chance of being accepted, I'm telling you this because I just don't want you to waste your time applying to school after school knowing what I know. I can look in your eyes and see how bad you want this! I wish there was something more I could do other than just advising you about what's going on. The only thing I can tell you sweetheart is schools do not see you as a person. They judge you on that piece of paper. Then if they do see you, they don't see a beautiful, black, talented, smart child like

I see you. They only see you as a black person. This is America and no matter what they say, no matter what they tell you. The black man or woman can never be equal in this country. To white-America we're still niggaz and slaves. The only difference is instead of keeping us on the cotton field, they try keeping us confined in prisons and projects. Mahogany, you're a beautiful young lady, inside and out, but you cannot let this get you down. You have to stand strong and stand firm. Learn to not let circumstances control your life. Instead you must learn to control circumstances. Right now I'm sure you're thinking theirs no way you can go on, but sweetheart it's always a way, you just have to look a little bit harder."

"Why are you being so nice to me?"

"Because once upon a time I was you!" the way this woman looked me in my eyes, I knew she wasn't talking just to hear herself speak. She was being so sincere.

• • •

The news about me not getting the financial assistance I needed hit home hard. The reason behind it hit home even harder. I was slowly but surely realizing I wouldn't be attending college.

The next day I began my job search. I knew it would be next to impossible for me to find a job where I'd be able to afford to pay for school out of state, plus take care of myself. My new goal became searching for a job just to survive. Jamel was still right by my side if I needed him, but the more he knew I depended on him; the more demanding he would get. He was getting a little out of control all over again.

After one month of searching for a job, I was finally

hired as a customer service representative for an insurance company. The only thing I didn't like was the distance I had to travel in order to get to work.

I worked all the way in Hicksville, Long Island. Thank God Jamel drove me to and from work everyday. If I had to use public transportation to get back and forth to work, I would've been an hour late or an hour early everyday due to the train schedule. That was something I wasn't with. When I explained the situation to Jamel he was more than happy to drive me to and from work everyday. He seemed more excited about me having a job than I was.

As each day passed I'd think about school less and less. Life wasn't fun for me anymore. I was becoming an adult. But, no matter what I could always count on Jackie to make me laugh.

Jackie found herself a job as well. She would come home from work making sure her presence was felt. Jackie would turn the stereo up to its capacity. I'd always have to come turn it down.

"What the hell is wrong with you turning the music up like that!?" I'd shout over the music.

Winding her hips real nasty, Jackie would ignore me then continue dancing. Only when I turned the music off would she speak.

"Bitch, why the fuck are you turning off my music?"

"It's six o'clock in the fucking morning! What do you mean why am I turning the music off?"

"It's only six o'clock? Damn I'm good! That nigga paid me to fuck him and suck him off until seven."

Being a paid hoe became Jackie's new found profession. I shook my head as I looked at Jackie who was still dancing without the music.

"You need to sit down and relax. What are you dancing to, the music is off?"

"I don't need music to fuck and I damn sure don't need music to dance. Dance with me Mahogany!"

Jackie started shaking her ass. She bent over revealing the tattoo on her lower back. The tattoo read in big bold letters 'TEAR IT UP.'

"Jackie, when the hell did you get that tattoo!?"

Jackie laughed, "Don't worry about me boo! Get over here and dance with me!"

I sucked my teeth then shook my head at Jackie, "I'm about to go back sleep. I have to be to work in three hours. It wouldn't hurt you to get in the bed either."

"Please! I just got out of bed if you know what I mean," Jackie laughed. "A bitch is a little tipsy and I'm feeling real nice too. You need to leave that lame ass job of yours alone and come work with me."

"And do what; fuck a whole bunch of niggaz all day? I'll pass."

"I don't fuck niggaz all day so you need to stop!" Jackie shot back.

"Oh, you swing around poles too. I almost forgot about that club, what was I thinking?" I sarcastically replied.

"Now you got it right!"

Jackie was proud of her profession. She laughed like she had the best job in the world. I stepped closer toward her.

"I guess you love your job, huh?"

Jackie looked at me like I was crazy, "I'm supposed to love my job. The times I did go to school my teachers used to say 'get a job you'll enjoy because if you love your job then it's not like you're working at all.' I love fucking,

fucking is my job!"

"You are out of your fucking mind."

"Fucking is a sport. You gotta keep your body tight to be a pro at it. The better you fuck or play, the more paper you get. Then when everybody knows who you are they all want a piece of you. That's just how the games go, fucking is my sport. I'm loving it!"

I turned to walk away. Jackie stopped me, "Don't leave. You gotta start getting ready in a little while anyway. It doesn't make sense for you to go to sleep now."

"If I stay up bullshitting with you, I'll be tired all day at work and you know it."

Jackie threw her hands in the air, "Fuck that job! It's too far, they don't pay you enough. Plus you can't stand your supervisor. Why waste your time? You should work with me and be the hoe I know you can be."

I put my hands on my hips, "Excuse me?"

Jackie rolled her eyes, "I know you ain't tripping 'cause I called you a hoe. I'm only spitting the facts. All girls are hoes so be the best hoe you can be."

"Jackie, fuck you! I'm not a hoe. I've been with one man and one man only!"

Jackie walked in the kitchen to get a glass to pour her Hennessey in. She laughed while pouring her drink, "Mahogany, face the facts; you're a hoe too. The hoe in you just hasn't been released yet. It's gonna come out, watch. Every girl is a hoe, but where I think most people like you get it twisted is thinking every girl is the same type of hoe. There are different types of hoes."

"I can't believe I'm having this conversation with you."

Jackie sipped her Hennessy as she continued, "Believe it, the sooner you realize all girls are hoes; the better off in life you'll be. Matter fact, since you're having a hard time understanding I'll break it down for you."

Jackie sat her glass on the counter. She walked closer to me like she was getting ready to give me the speech of a lifetime.

"In life you have four types of hoes," she said holding up four fingers. "You have the 'money-making-everybody-know-about-her-hoe.' Then you have the 'discreet hoe.' After her you have the 'grimey-set-ya-ass-up in a minute hoe.' Then finally you have the 'dumb hoe' a.k.a the 'broke hoe.' The dumb hoe and the broke hoe is usually the same hoe. The two go together like peanut butter and jelly. Now it's time for the break down on who these hoes fuck with. A grimey hoe will fuck with a stick up nigga. A smart hoe will fuck with a trick they money up nigga. An official hoe will fuck with straight up rich niggaz. The dumb hoes will fuck with a broke nigga just 'cause he got some good dick. So you see; every girl is a hoe. The only thing you have to choose is the type of hoe you want to be!"

Jackie walked away like she just gave me the rules to life. She was proud of her speech.

I burst into laughter at Jackie's 'hoe' speech. I knew that girl was straight up crazy.

"Jackie, I ain't fucking with you. I'm going back to sleep."

"Bye hoe! Sweet dreams." Jackie turned the music back on. I walked in my room. I slammed the door behind me. Jackie continued partying by herself.

• • •

Eight o'clock arrived so quickly. I headed out the door to meet Jamel outside where he waited for me. Jackie was sleeping so hard on the living-room couch. She didn't even hear me exit the apartment.

The humidity outside was enough to fry an egg on the sidewalk. I ran toward Jamel's car. The air conditioning inside his car was just what I needed.

"Hi baby! It's so hot outside," I kissed Jamel on the cheek.

He replied, "They said it's s'pose to be ninety degrees today."

"It feels more like a hundred," I said while fanning myself.

Jamel pulled off as he yawned.

"What's the matter, you didn't get enough sleep?"

Jamel shook his head, "I ain't even go to sleep yet."

"Why not?"

"I was busy," he replied as he turned on the radio.

"Baby, I need you to take me to Tammy's tomorrow after work. I already told her I was coming. She'll be waiting for me."

"I can't take you tomorrow. I got something to do. I'll give you money for a cab though."

"Why can't you take me?"

Jamel glanced in my direction, "Didn't I just say I'll give you money for a cab?"

Jamel's pager beeped. He looked at the number then mumbled to himself, "Damn!"

"What happened?" I inquired.

"Nothing, you got money?"

"Twenty dollars."

Jamel passed me a one hundred dollar bill, "Use that

in case you gotta take a cab home."

"What!? Why can't you come get me?"

A look of disgust appeared on Jamel's face, "Yo, be easy! Didn't I just tell you I ain't get no fucking sleep? I still got some running around to do before I'm able to lay down. By the time you get off I might just be touching the pillow."

I didn't say another word to Jamel. Instead I pulled out a book. I read my book all the way until we pulled up in front of my job.

"Gimme a kiss," Jamel demanded. I pecked him on the cheek. Jamel laughed, "Oh, it's like that?"

"What?"

Jamel laughed a little harder, "You a funny mother-fucker, you know that?"

"Nobody's funnier than you."

"Yeah, aight, I want you to call me at three o'clock."

"For what?" I frowned.

"I'ma let you know if I could pick you up or not."

"How sweet of you," I replied. I cracked a smile then stepped out of his car."

• • •

My day at work turned out to be a nightmare! The customers I dealt with weren't the problem, the people I worked with were. Instead of trying to work together it seemed like everyone tried to bring the next person down. If you were five minutes late coming back from lunch a parade of people would run to tell the supervisor. If you asked for help, they felt you couldn't handle your job. Things were so ridiculous where I worked. I didn't know how I'd be able to deal with it much longer. The best part of my day was speaking to Jamel at three o'clock. He informed me, he'd be able to pick me up after all.

When I arrived home Jackie was sitting in the living-room smoking a blunt. I locked the apartment door then proceeded to walk towards her. Suddenly I heard foot-steps coming from another part of the house. From the sound of the footsteps, the person was coming from the bathroom. Before I had a chance to inquire about who this person was, a familiar voice yelled while jumping in front of me.

"Surprise bitch!" it was Tiffany. She was smiling from ear to ear. We embraced each other.

"What are you doing here!?"

I was so surprised and excited to see Tiffany. We walked toward the couch. Jackie passed Tiffany the blunt. Tiffany inhaled the weed. I sat down next to them.

"I can't come see my cousin?" Tiffany inquired.

"Well it's about damn time! How long have you been here?"

Jackie intervened, "She's been here all of five minutes and already the bitch is tryna get in my pants!"

I laughed. Tiffany took a few more pulls from the blunt before passing it to Jackie then replying, "Bitch, ain't nobody thinking about you!"

"You wasn't saying that shit when you was rolling that blunt. You don't remember putting it under your nose, sniffing it then licking it like it was my pussy?" Jackie laughed. Tiffany cracked a smile. "Yeah I thought so," Jackie added.

"Y'all some nasty bitches!" I shouted.

"Tell that to your cousin. She's the only nasty bitch I see in this house!"

"You know you like it," said Tiffany.

"Whatever," replied Jackie. She stood to her feet while putting her hand in Tiffany's face. Tiffany slapped her on the ass. Jackie's ass jiggled.

"You better keep your hands off of me before I break those shits!"

"Jackie, where you going?" I asked.

"I got a date," she smiled.

"You ain't gotta get dressed. I'm right here," said Tiffany. Jackie snatched the blunt from Tiffany's hands. She inhaled, blew the smoke in Tiffany's face then replied, "See me when you get a whole lot of money and a real big dick, bitch!"

Jackie walked into her room leaving me and Tiffany laughing. She prepared for her date. Me and Tiff continued talking and bugging out. Jackie came out of the room looking like a supermodel! Girlfriend wore four-inch stiletto heals with a backless dress. The dress hugged every curve on her body. Her curly hair hung past her shoulders.

I was the first to comment, "Damn girl! You're trying to make a nigga propose tonight, huh?"

"Fuck marriage, I'm on a paper chase! This nigga got a wife already anyway. He just needs some attention and a quick fuck. I just need some new diamond earrings and a few hundred bucks."

"That's all?" Tiffany inquired. Jackie stuck her middle finger in the air. Tiffany laughed.

"What would you do for the matching bracelet?" asked Tiffany. Jackie ignored her. She looked at Tiffany then spoke to me.

"Mahogany, I hope this carpet licking bitch is gone by

the time I get back."

"You ain't gotta worry about that! We going out tonight too, right Mahogany?"

I sighed, "I wish I could. I gotta get up early for work tomorrow. Even if I didn't have to get up early I still couldn't go."

"Why not?" Tiffany questioned.

I sucked my teeth, "This week is not a pay week."

"What are you a slave? Don't you work five days a week at that insurance company? How much are they paying?"

"Not enough," said Jackie.

"My pay is just fine," I answered.

"It ain't that fine. You just said you were broke," added Tiffany.

"I'm only broke for this week. Matter fact, Jamel did just give me a hundred dollars, but I saw these fly boots I gotta have. I will be picking them up tomorrow before I go to Tammy's shop."

"Then you'll be broke again," added Jackie as she headed towards the door.

"Fuck both of y'all. Y'all bitches acting like y'all rich," I replied.

"I might not be rich, but I ain't broke either," Jackie laughed.

I put my hand on my hip and tilted my head to the side, "So you telling me you never had a broke day, Jackie?"

Jackie looked at me. She took two steps in my direction, placed her hand on her hip, and rolled her eyes as she answered my question, "It's no excuse for broke days when selling pussy pays!" then she walked out the door.

Tiffany couldn't stop laughing.

• • •

Several months passed. I was still working at the insurance company. I also still lived with Jackie. Jackie still worked at the strip club. She also continued fucking guys for cash. Tiffany was in school. She began falling in love with dancing herself. However, Tiffany was a different type of dancer from Jackie.

One Friday afternoon my supervisor asked me to stay at work an extra half-an-hour. Since I was ten minutes late due to the messy roads from all the snow that fell the day before, I agreed to stay. I knew my supervisor didn't like me much. It wasn't hard to tell she was waiting for a reason to give me my walking papers.

When Jamel dropped me at work earlier that day we were arguing. Arguing and having to deal with him disappearing became a regular part of our daily lives. Some days the only time I'd see him is when he brought me to and from work. I was getting sick and tired of our relationship. His games were getting played out. When I called to tell him I was working late, he didn't answer the phone. I left him a message. He never returned my call.

I was happy when I finally finished work. I exited the building. Jamel sat across the street from my job at his usual parking spot. I crossed the street. He started the car. Soon as I entered the vehicle I sensed Jamel had an attitude. I fastened my seatbelt then spoke.

"Hello, I called you earlier."

Jamel didn't bother saying hello. Instead, "Why you ain't tell me you was getting off late?"

"That's what I called you about. You don't check your

messages?"

"Whatever," Jamel mumbled.

"What's wrong with you?" I asked.

"I got shit to do, that's what's wrong. Nobody got time to be sitting up at your job all fucking day!"

I turned to face him, "Look, if you got an attitude then keep that shit to yourself! I ain't do shit for you to be coming at me like you are."

Jamel's phone rung, he ignored it as if it weren't ringing at all.

"Answer your phone," I told him.

"Mind your business please."

"What?"

"You heard what I said. If I ain't worried about my phone ringing then you shouldn't be either."

"You're a fucking punk, you know that?" Jamel said nothing in response. He stepped on the gas harder as he turned the music up.

"I wish this motherfucker had wings! I'm getting you home fast as I could," he mumbled.

"I know you better slow down. You acting like these roads ain't slippery. I'm getting sick of your shit!"

Jamel ignored me all the way home. His phone rung so much, he turned it off. Each time I said something he'd turn his music up to drown me out. We pulled up in front of my building. Both of us were happy we were leaving each other. Before I could close the door Jamel was pulling off. By the time I stepped out of the street onto the sidewalk, Jamel was half way down the block. I proceeded to walk towards my building. Suddenly I was stopped by the sound of a female's voice.

"Excuse me but was that Jamel's car you just got out

of?"

I turned around to see where the voice came from. In front of me stood a slim, brown-skin chick sporting a bad weave. On her lips was the cheap clear lip gloss. I knew it was cheap because her lips were starting to turn white like glue; only the cheap kind turned white. With a little work and some new lip gloss, she could've been cute. I looked her up and down before replying, "What's it to you?"

This female placed her hands inside her pockets. She laughed then replied, "Well I think it's a lot to me since he is my man."

I was shocked by her statement, "Your man, huh?"

"That's what I said. What were you doing in his car?"

I laughed in this girl's face, "Do you mean what was I doing in his car now or for the last three-and-a-half years?"

"Excuse me?" the girl frowned.

"Listen, I'm Jamel's girl so I don't know what type of games you're playing. I appreciate you being a fan of his, but now is not the time," I turned to walk away.

"It sure is hard to tell you're his girl, especially since he left you in the middle of the street the way he did."

I stopped walking and turned around to reply, "What is your name?"

"Ask Jamel, he knows it," she shot back with a smirk on her face.

"Well, I'm not asking him, I'm asking you."

The girl laughed, "You look kind of young. How old are you?"

"I'm old enough to be called legal, but still young enough for you to be insulted since Jamel is your man. Whatever my age, he still can't let this pretty young thing go."

"You're a funny little girl, you know that?"

I laughed, "Are you finished? I have more important things to do?"

"Yeah, and I have Jamel to do. I know he's heading to my house right now."

I laughed, "To your house, huh?"

"That's what I said. He's on his way to visit me just like he does everyday. He's a little late today, but I see why."

She looked me up and down then continued, "I'll straighten him out when I get there. Maybe I'll even punish him. I won't let the nigga eat my pussy tonight. That'll hurt him real bad." The girl laughed, "Yeah, that's what I'll do."

This girl was getting me so heated. I was seconds away from slapping the shit out of her. However, I couldn't let her see I was upset so I played it cool.

"That sure is strange. If Jamel is on his way to visit you, why are you over here?"

"I had to make sure he was alright. I called him a few times, he didn't answer my calls. That's not like Jamel, not like him at all. I thought something might've happened to my daddy. I would be devastated if my child was born without a father," she smiled.

I raised my eyebrows, "What did you just say!?" I could no longer hide it. I was vexed!

She rubbed her stomach, "Jamel didn't tell you...? He's getting ready to be a proud daddy. My Boo is more excited about me having this baby than I am. That nigga checks on my everyday and every night."

"Is that right?" My face began turning red from the

cold weather and heated news. If this girl was speaking the truth, me and Jamel's relationship was over. My bleeding heart could only take so much. This sure did answer a lot of question I had.

Seeing how upset she was getting me, she smiled. Then she continued, "I'm on my third month, don't I look good to be three months pregnant?"

I walked away leaving her to talk to herself. There weren't enough words in the English language to explain how vexed I was. I walked in the apartment. I headed straight to the phone. I called Jamel's phone several times. Not once did Jamel answer his phone.

• • •

The weekend passed, I didn't receive one phone call from Jamel. I knocked on his door, but no one ever answered. I was certain Jamel knew me and his 'baby-mother' met by now. When Monday morning arrived he wasn't waiting outside to drive me to work. It wasn't hard to tell, Jamel was avoiding me.

Taking a cab or the train to and from work became my regular means of transportation. Some days I'd arrive to work an hour early, but I really didn't have a choice anymore. It was either arrive an hour early or an hour late. Carfare was killing my pockets. On top of that, I was paying my own bills. I never realized just how much Jamel was helping me out. I was barely getting enough sleep at night. The time it took me to get home was really taking a toll on my body. My life was become a nightmare!

Close to a month passed before Jamel decided to show his face. I was caught completely off guard by his unexpected appearance.

I stood at the bus stop in below zero weather. I looked at my watch. If the bus was running on schedule it would arrive in the next twenty-five minutes. I thought I'd surely turn into an icicle by that time. Across the street I saw a guy parked in a silver BMW. This guy looked like Jamel, but I knew I was mistaken. Jamel had a Lexus, not a BMW. Plus why would he show up all of a sudden? These are the thoughts that crossed my mind. However, when the guy pulled up in front of the bus stop, I was sure it was Jamel. He sat there smiling like I was supposed to just hop in his car without giving it a second thought. I ignored him as I continued waiting for my bus. Once Jamel realized he was being ignored, he stepped out of his vehicle wearing no coat like a damn fool.

In his hand he held two dozen red roses. He smiled then walked towards me. I turned my back like he wasn't even there.

"Baby look, I'm sorry can I just talk to you?" he pleaded.

"I don't have shit to say to you Jamel. Run home to your babymother."

He tried handing me the roses, "Mahogany let me drive you
home, please. I just wanna talk to you. That's the least you can do, I mean we been through too much shit together to just end our relationship like this. I don't want you to hate me. I just want you to let me learn to love you better."

I laughed, "Is that the best you could come up with Jamel?"

"It's the truth. Can you please get in the car? I just wanna talk to you, please," he begged.

I looked at my watch. It would still be another twenty minutes

before the bus arrived.

"Please," I heard Jamel say again.

I looked at this BMW he pulled up in. It does look pretty warm, is what I was thinking. I looked at him then rolled my eyes. I walked toward the passenger side of the BMW. I saw Jamel smile as he ran back to the driver's side.

I didn't get in Jamel's car because I was falling victim to another one of his lame ass excuses. This was simply a case of me being cold as fuck standing at the bus stop. His heated leather seats seemed to be just what I needed. We drove for about five minutes without either of us saying a word to one another. Jamel placed the roses in my lap. I tossed them in the backseat.

I was getting tired of the silent game, "Well here I am but not for long. Say whatever it is that you have to say?"

Jamel grabbed my hand, "I'm just happy to be wit you right now, I don't even know where to start."

I had enough of his small talk. I replied, "You can start by remembering the condom, you ever heard about one of those? I hear they prevent diseases and pregnancy."

Jamel's smile faded, "You got that one, you right, you right.

Let me tell you this though. I don't love that bitch. You're the only girl who ever had my heart. You will always be the one to have my heart. Mahogany, you are my only wife. No one can ever take that title from you."

I couldn't help but to laugh, "Is this the part where I'm supposed to say thank you then fall in love with you

all over again? If it is, it ain't working Prince charming."
I could sense Jamel was getting upset. He replied, "I'm tryna have a heart to heart conversation with you. Why the fuck you keep getting so smart?"

Jamel was getting me upset. I raised my voice, "The same reason you gotta keep ya dick in anything with two tits and a split!"

"Mahogany, listen. I told you I don't love that bitch! I barked on her for telling you that dumb shit! She was a bird that was on my dick. I fucked her one time when I got drunk. Now the bitch is pregnant. I was gon' tell you. I just wanted to wait until the right time."

"Well, when was the right fucking time, at the baby's college graduation?"

Jamel glanced at me. He held his finger toward my face, "You know we wouldn't even be in this situation if you would've never killed our baby. You was too busy thinking one day you might have a college graduation."

I slapped his hand from my face, "WHAT!?"

"You heard what I said. You had the chance to have my baby, but you killed it, remember? You can't really be upset I'm thinking about my future just like you thought about yours."

"Jamel you know what; fuck you and everything you stand for!"

"Look Mahogany, you taking this small issue and making it into something it's not."

I couldn't believe my ears, "Small? Have you lost your fucking Mind!? This is the biggest issue in this relationship so far. I put up with your late nights out, your sneaky phone conversations with other bitches, your fucked up attitude and anything else you've thrown my way! Now you want me to put up with a baby that's not mine because you don't know how to control your dick!? I have news for you partner, I'm not! I'm drawing the line right here! From this day on I will not put up with anymore of your bullshit! You finally come around after I didn't see or speak to you for damn near a month, now you think I'm supposed to understand? Well think again!"

"Mahogany, all that gangsta shit you popping sounds nice and

everything. It even makes you look a little tougher, but let's cut the bullshit aight. I made a mistake, I'm sorry about it. I'm having a baby, that's just the way it is. It ain't like it's the end of the fucking world! My baby won't interfere with what we have. I'ma still take care of you. You'll still be my number one. We just have to make a little bit of adjustments in our everyday life, that's all."

If I didn't know Jamel was crazy before, I was sure he was now. I replied, "No the fuck you didn't!? I can't believe you even had the audacity to say some shit like that! You must really think you're 'Don-Juan-DeMarco-swear-to-God-don't-get-it-twisted.'"

Jamel laughed, "You a natural born comedian, you know that? All I'm tryna do is save this relationship. You know just like I do; you need me," Jamel patted himself on the chest. Then he continued.

"You can lie to yourself all day long. Tryna convince yourself you don't need me. But, you know what's really up. You know I'm speaking the truth. Who else is gonna take care of you like I take care of you? Nobody! Just be easy! You better thank the Lord above for having a nigga who look out for you like I look out for you! Keep it real wit yourself; you'll be lost without me. Who else is gonna lace you in the flyest shit? Do you know how many girls would love to be in your shoes right now, do you?" Jamel yelled.

We pulled up in front of my building just in time. I replied,

"Well let them walk in them 'cause I ain't fucking wit you!" those were the last words I said before exiting Jamel's car.

I couldn't believe he thought I needed him. I was determined to show him just the opposite. I promised myself I'd make him eat his words. I would show him I could hold my own. I would still be fly. I would have a pocket full of cash. Plus I would get a car to travel to and from work. He would see, with or without him I was a winner! I didn't have the money to get all the things I needed just yet. However, I knew a sure way to get more than enough cash!

Chapter 10

I Gotta Do What I Gotta Do...

"I'm so proud of you!" Jackie screamed excitedly as we sat in the back of a cab heading to New Jersey. She tapped the driver, he turned around.

"Turn the radio up, this is a celebration! My bitch finally saw the light!"

"It's not a big deal, Jackie," I replied while staring out of the window.

Jackie put her hand on my shoulder, "What!? Are you crazy? This is a big fucking deal! Those bitches gon' be mad at you tonight!"

"Are you sure we won't run into any familiar faces?"

"Girl relax, ain't nobody from the hood gon' be up in the spot. These are straight up rich niggaz we entertaining."

"I hope they know I'm there just to strip, not to fuck!"

"It's plenty of hoes fucking and sucking in that club. If one of them niggaz approach you on the fucking tip, all you gotta do is direct them to me. I'll suck a mean dick for five hundred dollars!" Jackie laughed.

"You make that much sucking a dick?" I questioned.

Jackie laughed, "It all depends on whose dick you're

sucking. Not everybody wants to pay like they weigh, but if your 'G' is tight or you're known for making a nigga feel real good – which is my specialty. You could get the sun, moon and stars from that nigga! Most of the men are married, old or both. That makes our job easy. All they're looking for is that attention they're not getting at home. You'd be surprised how many of them just want to talk."

"I don't plan to be there that long anyway. All I need is some doe for this whip, a new wardrobe and enough money to pay these bills."

Jackie applied lipstick to her lips. She pulled out a mini mirror then checked her hair and make-up. When she was done she spoke.

"That's the same shit I said. You couldn't tell me I would be stripping for as long as I have, but that money becomes addictive, you'll see!"

I sucked my teeth, "I have self control. I don't fall victim to circumstances. Soon as I get the paper I need, I'm leaving this shit alone. The first thing I need is a car to get back and forth to work."

"Bitch, I don't know why you just don't quit that job? You don't like nothing about it, it's too far and it's a big fucking headache. This is a better job for you anyway."

"Jackie, this is not a job it's a hustle. Once I get what I need, I'm out!"

"Whatever, hoe." We pulled up in front of the club.

"How much do we owe you?" Jackie asked the cab driver.

The driver smiled, "The usual," he answered.

Jackie handed him a fifty-dollar bill, "When you gon' come watch me work?" she asked him.

The driver started blushing, "Very soon I hope, very soon."

"Don't keep me waiting!" replied Jackie.

We exited the cab. The name of the club was called 'Vinnie's.' In fancy lettering on the outside of the club hung a neon sign that read, 'Vinnie's.'

"Why the fuck you started with that cab driver?" I asked Jackie.

Jackie looked at me, "I ain't start shit. I'm just tryna make that nigga gimme some of that money back I've been giving him all this time! I'm convinced; he's a virgin, gay or just fucking blind! If I wasn't me, do you know how bad I'd be tryna fuck me?"

I laughed at Jackie's vanity, "Girl, you need to stop!"

We walked in the club. The inside of Vinnie's was huge. There were different stages all with gold poles on them. The music was loud and intoxicating. Several ladies walked around the club, none of them wearing a top or a bra – they were topless. On my left a white girl was on one of the stages dancing. She was wearing nothing but platform shoes and a belt. Men threw money at her as she moved like a caterpillar down the pole. Over the music the DJ's voice could be heard.

"She's hot! She's sexy! She's Sunshine! Come on fellas don't miss this opportunity to see the performance of a lifetime. If you haven't seen her up close and personal then you haven't seen anything yet. It's not hard to tell why this blonde beauty is called Sunshine. She can light up any room and brighten any man's day! Don't be afraid to show her some love. Give a lot to get a lot!"

More men rushed the stage as Sunshine performed. I couldn't believe how many people were inside the club. I turned to Jackie.

"Is it always crowded like this?" I asked.

"This ain't shit," Jackie answered. "If you think this is something wait until another hour or two."

"Do you know her?" I pointed to Sunshine.

"Yeah I know her," Jackie answered. Then she continued, "She's trying to pay her way through school. She used to be a rich girl."

I was surprised, "Really? What happened?" I inquired.

"Her family made a few bad investments. They lost most of their money in the stock market. The little bit of money they had left was spent trying to recoup their losses. Needless to say, they lost that money too. Her father took his own life. Her mother is in a mental institution for the rest of her life. That bitch went crazy. She tried to rob a bank. Instead, she ended up killing two people."

"Damn, that's fucked up!" was all I could say.

"That's life," added Jackie.

An older white man with balding salt and pepper hair approached us. "Hello, Rain. I'm glad you're here tonight."

Jackie licked her lips before grabbing this man's dick, "You know I'm here for you baby. I wouldn't be able to live with myself if a passed on giving you some of this fat, black pussy!"

The guy grabbed Jackie's tittie. Jackie moved his hand, "Not so fast big daddy! You're slut has to go get ready for you."

The guy smiled, "That's what I like to hear! Go get ready to be my bad girl. I love you, you slut bitch! Who is your friend? Is she participating tonight?" he said looking at me.

I could tell Jackie didn't know what name to use. "I'm

Ginger," I intervened. Jackie looked at me with the crooked eye. "I won't be participating tonight, but I will be dancing. You don't want to miss that!"

The guy directed his attention away from me. He looked back at Jackie. It was clear that he was ready to get fucked.

"How long will it be?" he asked Jackie. "I've already been here for thirty minutes."

"Not long daddy, not long. Wait right here. You're bitch will be back."

Jackie pulled my arm. We headed towards the dressing rooms.

"What the hell made you come up with the name Ginger?" Jackie asked.

"Have you ever seen that movie *Casino*?" I asked.

"Of course," Jackie replied.

"Well, then you already know Ginger was a fly bitch! That's why I'm Ginger."

"Oh please," Jackie burst into laughter.

"I know you ain't talking, Rain."

"That's right," Jackie replied. "My name has meaning," she added.

"What's the meaning?" I asked.

"When I cum, I get you wet!" Our conversation was interrupted by another female, "Hi Rain," said the exotic looking big breast lady.

"Heaven, what's up?"

"You're up. You know you go on next to dance, right?"

"What!?" Jackie said surprised. She continued, "I can't go on next. I have a date waiting for me!"

"Well you better tell the DJ. He's getting ready to play your song girl."

Jackie looked at me, "Ginger, can you go on next?"

"Me?" I said shocked.

"Yeah, you! Just do this favor for me. I promise I'll make it up to you!"

"I'm so nervous. I thought I wasn't performing until second to last?"

"Nervous?" said the exotic looking female. She continued, "Being nervous isn't going to make you anything but broke. You better have a drink and get on that stage!"

"She's right! Go to the bar, we get free drinks Ginger," said Jackie as she winked at me.

After two drinks I was ready to go on stage. My adrenalin rushed as I peeked through the curtains. I saw a crowd full of men, all waiting to watch me. Jackie ran to give me a peep talk before I burst through the curtains.

"Mahogany I'm proud of you girl! When you get on that stage I want you to own it. I want you to remember you're the star of that motherfucking stage. All them balling ass niggaz is out there to see you! Work your hips and shake your ass like it's never been done before. Get that money, girl!"

We hugged. I heard the DJ introduce me.

"Fellas stand up! You're in for the treat of a lifetime. Coming to the stage for the first time is the green-eye beauty. What you're about to see can turn a gay man straight! She's young! She's beautiful! She's the lovely...Ginger!"

The sound of thunder was heard. I walked on the stage. Janet Jackson's 'Anytime, Any Place' was playing. The entire club was dark except for the stage I danced on. A single light shined down on me. I was wearing a derby hat slightly tilted towards the front with trench coat over a laced teddy. The drink I had before I performed on stage was starting to take its effect. I felt invisible. I threw my trench coat off. All eyes were on me. I wrapped one leg around the pole, money started coming from all directions. The more money I saw being thrown, the more into my performance I got.

When I finished dancing I went back to the dressing room. I counted five hundred and seventy dollars. That was the amount of money I made dancing to just two songs. The night had just begun. Already I was loving the benefits from my new hustle.

The night ended with a performance from Jackie. She embraced the stage like she owned it. Jackie wore a nurse outfit. She also had a stethoscope, four inch white stilettos, white thigh highs and a dildo in her hand.

The music started playing, Jackie walked to the front and center of the stage. She turned her back towards the crowd, bent over just enough to reveal she wasn't wearing panties. The guys went crazy while Jackie kept enticing them. She swung around the pole with one hand, while still holding her dildo in her other hand. Once she finished swing around the pole, she faced the crowd, began undressing then put her back against the pole. Jackie slid all the way down the pole until she was sitting on the floor with her legs wide open. Placing the dildo in her mouth she began sucking it. This drove the crowd wild! However, the highlight of the night was Jackie dancing on stage wearing nothing but a stethoscope around her neck. Then she laid on the floor and arched her back. She looked up in the air as she opened her legs wide. Out of no where an older man ran on stage. He started eating Jackie's pussy!

Two weeks passed, I had all the cash I needed. I was proud of myself for being able to do what I did. I no longer stripped. I continued working at the insurance company instead. However, getting to and from work became a hop, skip and a jump. I used the Honda Accord I purchased as my means of transportation.

Jackie was a little upset with the fact I quit so soon. She had a hard time believing I could leave the life alone just like that. I knew I could do it all along. Stripping wasn't for me. On top of that I had a new Boo. How we hooked up was so sweet.

It was a beautiful Saturday afternoon in the hood. I was headed to the local grocery store. I was dressed in a black and white Versace outfit. My hair was done in spiral curls. The curls bounced with every step I took. I was turning heads, left and right. Me and Jamel's relationship was officially over. We stopped saying hello to one another long ago. However, even he couldn't resist looking at me as I walked passed him.

A group of guys rolling dice occupied the sidewalk in front of the store. As I got closer towards the store all of the guy's attention was diverted from the dice game to me. The guy holding the dice speaks first.

"Hold up, wait a minute, stop the game! We gotta let her sexy ass through. It must be a sin to be as fine as she is."

"Thank you," I smiled.

"Damn ma! Don't hurt nobody!" another guy adds.

"I was waiting for. You broke my heart," says the guy holding the dice.

I turned to look back, "Do I know you?" I ask.

The guy licks his lips then smiles. I proceed to walk inside the store.

Once I entered the store I saw pain-in-my-ass Tazz. Tazz had the biggest crush on me since I could remember. If you looked at Tazz he looked like the average brown-skin guy with braids. The only thing that always made him standout in any crowd was his ability to over accessorize. If Tazz had on a Gucci jacket you better believe he had the matching hat, pants and sneakers. He reminded me of a Jamaican 'rudeboy.'

I hadn't seen Tazz in such a long time. I was starting to forget about him. From his designer clothes and expensive jewelry it was clear to see he was making money. I knew Tazz wasn't getting money in the hood. Only once in the blue moon could Tazz be found in the hood. Nevertheless, I ran into him today. To me Tazz was so annoying. I couldn't stand his over accessorizing and corny pickup lines. I walked in the store, Tazz noticed me. A big smile appeared across his face. I headed to the back of the store to get a soda.

"Girl if I could rearrange the alphabet I would put 'u' and 'I' together," said Tazz.

"Tazz, I'm not in the mood," I shot back.

"You never in the mood. When you gon' stop playing and let me take you out?"

I rolled my eyes then proceeded to walk pass him, "You already know the answer to that. I don't even know why you're still asking."

"Why you gotta be so mean?" said Tazz as he followed

me to the register.

"Why can't you just leave me alone?"

"If I leave you alone then you never gon' go out with me."

"I'm not going out with you now," I sucked my teeth.

"One day you will."

Clearly annoyed I replied, "No I won't, get over it!" I placed my Sprite, Slim Jim and Pringles on the counter.

"Three-dollar-ten cent mommy," said the Spanish man behind the counter. Tazz placed a five dollar bill on the counter. He smiled like he just bought me the world.

"Nobody asked you to pay for my stuff," I told him.

"Nobody stopped me either."

I reached inside my pocket. I pulled out a twenty dollar bill, "You could have your money back."

Tazz threw his hands in the air, "I don't want my money back. I just want you."

I walked out the store. Tazz was right behind me. I turned around.

"Tazz, you cannot have me, not now, not ever!"

Tazz was persistent, "At least let me take you to dinner before I leave."

"I don't eat, sorry."

"Why you acting like that Mahogany?"

It must've been written all over my face that I was annoyed. The guy who stopped the dice game to let me walk through minutes earlier came to my rescue.

"Yo Tazz, what you doing? I hope you not harassing my lady."

Tazz looked at me then looked at the guy. He threw his hands in the air then replied, "Oh word, that's you? My bad. You a lucky man. All men should be as fortunate as you are."

"Ain't that the truth," said the guy. He grabbed my hand then kissed it. Tazz walked away from us. I proceeded to walk away from the dice game. The guy who kissed my handed followed me.

"I hope I didn't mess up your plans with duke," said the guy.

I turned around to see him walking directly behind me, "Are you kidding me? You just saved me. I should be thanking you."

"Good 'cause I was lying anyway," he smiled. For some reason I felt like I knew him.

"Do I know you from somewhere?" I asked.

"Yup. Matter fact, you made me feel so neglected. I think I want a divorce."

"Excuse me?" I frowned.

The guy laughed, "I'm looking for my wife; somebody told me I could find her here. Do you think you could help me? She's young, pretty, sexy and all that!"

I started smiling. I remembered exactly where I knew him from! Once the guy noticed me smiling he started smiling too.

"Why didn't you call me?" he asked.

I couldn't tell him Jamel ripped up the hundred dollar bill he wrote his number on. I thought he was all of that when he pulled up in the midnight-blue Mercedes Benz the first time I met him. Today he was looking even better! His curly hair was freshly shaped up, his caramel complexion glowed. The clothing he was wearing fit him like they were tailor made just for him. He was taller than Jamel. Plus he had a better body. I tried to come up with an excuse for not calling him. However, I came up with none.

So I changed the subject.

"What's your name?"

"They call me Pop."

"Is that right, Pop?"

He laughed, "You a little cutie ma, foreal."

"Thank you," I blushed.

"If I give you my number again are you gonna use it, or will I be wasting my time?"

"I'll call you," I told him. And I was serious about that. This nigga reminded me of a prince, he was just so fine!

He looked at me with the crooked eye, "I ain't falling for that again. Gimme your number too."

I laughed, "Where is the trust?"

"I trust that you gon' gimme your number. I also trust that you gon' gimme a call."

"Do you have a pen?" I asked.

"Yeah, what's your number?"

"Don't you want to know my name first?"

"Mahogany, right?" replied Pop. He smiled as he saw how surprised I was. He continued, "I do my homework," he laughed.

"Well, I see."

Me and Pop exchanged numbers. Before we parted he made me promise to call him the next day. The next day I kept my promise. When I called Pop he was happy to hear from me. I wanted to see him just as much as he wanted to see me. We decided we would hang out together.

I waited for Pop in front of my building. I was outside for less than five minutes before a fire red Porsche pulled up blowing its horn. I ignored the cars cry for attention. I continued looking down the block to see if a midnight-blue Mercedes Benz was within close range. I didn't see Pop's Benz anywhere in sight. I noticed the person inside of the Porsche was still trying to get my attention. I looked at the car. The passenger window rolled down. Pop's smiling face was behind the wheel.

"You waiting for somebody, sexy?"

I smiled then headed towards the car. Once I opened the passenger door I noticed Jamel staring at me from across the street. I smiled even harder.

"I'm sorry I ignored you. I was looking for the other car."

Pop smiled, "Surprise! I never stay in the same thing for too long. I always play it safe."

"That's cool. I'm feeling this color."

"I'm feeling you," said Pop. Both of us smiled as Pop pulled off.

"Where are we heading?" I asked.

"Wherever you wanna go, but first I need to make a few stops. Is that aight with you?"

"Long as it doesn't take all day."

"It'll be real quick. I promise."

The first stop we made was at an abandon looking house. I stayed in the car, Pop got out. He walked towards the house then knocked on the door. I saw a guy peek out of the window. Shortly after, the door to the abandon house flew open. Pop and the guy who opened the door embraced each other with a slap on the hands. Pop entered the house, the door closed.

After five minutes passed Pop made his way back to the car. Before Pop entered the vehicle I heard him yell to the guy standing in the doorway of the abandon house.

"Yo tell that nigga I came through and I'll be back later. Let his little ass know, he better not go anywhere! Tell him he better have all my shit too!"

The next stop we made was at an apartment building. Just like the first stop; I stayed in the car again. Pop headed towards the building's entrance, before he entered the building a kid on a bike rode up to him. The kid pulled a knot of money out of his pocket then handed it to him. I couldn't hear the words being exchanged between Pop and the kid. However, I could tell Pop was yelling at the kid.

When Pop got back in the car he confirmed what I was thinking.

"Some little niggaz are assholes! I think they like to be barked on, foreal. They just do dumb shit!"

I sat in the passenger seat with my legs crossed. I let Pop continue venting before I spoke.

"Don't worry about it, that's life. Hopefully that was our last stop anyway. I wouldn't want anyone else pissing you off. I like it when you're laid back. Plus I'm hungry and I think it's a bit rude how you keep bringing me to wherever it is that you're bringing me, then leaving me in the car while you do whatever it is that you do."

Pop looked at me and rubbed my thigh as he spoke.

"Come on Precious don't act like that. Let me handle my business then we can do whatever you wanna do. I promise. Its gon' be all about you, but I just gotta make one more stop. This time I'll stay in the car, is that fair?"

"One more stop; just one," I replied.

The last and final stop we made was at another building. Pop kept his word, he didn't leave the car. When we pulled up in front of the building some guy ran up to Pop's car. Pop rolled his window down. The guy stuck his head inside the car.

"I'm happy you finally came through. I was just about to page ya ass."

Pop replied, "So that must mean you got all my shit."

"Yeah, I need some more."

"Go call Rah, tell him I said to bring you two."

"That nigga don't be answering his phone!"

"Stop whining nigga, he gon' answer the phone. Matter fact, I'll call the nigga myself, where them other niggaz at?"

The boy pointed, "Oh they in the building, you want me to go get 'em for you?"

"Yeah, tell 'em I said hurry up, my lady is ready to go."

Pop smiled at me. The guy handed him some money.

"Aight, I'ma go get 'em now. Count this, I'll be right back."

Pop counted the money while we waited. Once Pop finished counting, the same guy who just left came right back followed by two other guys. Before Pop rolled his window down he handed me the money the first guy handed him.

"Count that again for me mommy."

I proceeded to count. Pop rolled down the window.

"What's good? How's everything looking out here?" asked Pop.

The boy with the green hoody responded, "It's looking good. I ran through three packs already."

The other guy cut him off, "That's 'cause you a greedy motherfucker, running to sales and shit. Let me get my shit off too!"

"You damn right! Don't get mad at me 'cause ya ass can't make nothing happen," the guy replied.

Pop intervened, "Yo, relax. Y'all niggz play for the same team so don't be fighting and shit! I'm tired of telling y'all this over and over again. Y'all got my shit?"

"I got it right here," said the guy with the green hoody. Pop took the money the guy was handing him.

"What about you?" Pop asked the other guy.

"I'm still not finished."

"What?" Pop asked, clearly annoyed by this guy's answer.

"That nigga keep taking all the sales!"

"Well, you better learn to take some too. I'll be back tonight, make sure you have all my shit!"

Pop pulled off. He didn't bother counting the rest of the money he just received. I tried handing him the money I counted for him.

"How much is it?" he asked.

"It's two thousand three hundred and twenty six dollars."

"Keep it," replied Pop.

I was surprised. I had to make sure I heard him correct, "What did you just say?"

Pop smiled, "I want you to keep it. Get ya self something nice, do you accept my apology?"

"If that's all you got then that's all I'll take," I joked. We both laughed.

"I need to let this nigga piss me off all the time just so he could apologize like this," is what I thought to myself.

We went to a steak house to eat. I ordered the steak and shrimp, Pop ordered ranch chicken and rice. We had a nice conversation over dinner.

"How did you get a name like Pop?" I asked.

"My mother always called me Pop since I was a baby. I guess it just stuck with me."

"Do you have any sisters or brothers?"

"I got two sisters, one is older than me and the other one is a year younger."

"So that's who you live with?"

"Nah, my family still lives in Spanish-Harlem, that's where I'm from. Three years ago I decided it was time for me to make some changes in my life, I moved to Queens."

"So, you're Spanish, huh?"

"I'm Dominican. What are you? You look like you could be mixed with something?"

"I'm one hundred percent black," I said proudly.

"I find that hard to believe. It might be something your mother ain't telling you girl," Pop joked.

"Shut-up!" I replied as I reached across the table to hit Pop's hand.

"Do you have any kids, Pop?"

"Not yet. I love kids though. I want like five of my own one day."

"Five?" I asked. "That's a lot of pushing," I added. Pop laughed. I continued questioning him.

"Are you expecting any kids I should know about?"

"Nah, why you say that?"

"I had a bad experience. It's no big deal; I really don't want to talk about it. Do you have a girl?"

The expression on Pop's face changed, "That's a long story."

I stopped eating, "I have time."

"I really don't feel like getting into all of that."

I was surprised by Pop's answer to my question, "You ain't gotta tell me all the details. I just want to know if you have a girl or not."

Pop said nothing.

"Hello?" I spoke then continued, "Can you answer my question."

Pop sipped on his soda before replying, "Something like that."

"That's all I needed to hear," I replied.

Pop changed the subject, "How would Jamel feel about you being here with me tonight?"

I laughed, "Jamel is not apart of my life anymore. His feelings don't hold any weight concerning me and my life. How do you know Jamel anyway?"

Pop smiled, "Let's just say me and him are not the best of friends."

"So your enemies?"

"I guess you could say that."

Me and Pop continued our conversation as we ate dinner. I wasn't thrilled about the fact that he had a girl. However, I decided I would mess with him anyway. I just knew I couldn't or wouldn't take Pop serious.

For the first two weeks me and Pop was dating we saw each other everyday. I was beginning to wonder when did he have time to spend with his 'something like that' girl.'

By the third week we were dating Pop offered me something that would later change my life forever. He offered me my own independence. How he did this was simple. He moved me out of the projects and into my own duplex in Rosedale. He felt our relationship was growing. He stressed the fact that he couldn't or wouldn't be content with his 'lady' living in the projects.

Pop paid for my duplex to be fully furnished. I did my thing with the design. My walls were peach. The zebra carpet made it stand out even more. Mirrors and plants were everywhere. He paid my rent for three months, plus he still threw money at me left and right. Pop was giving me all this shit without even smelling the pussy yet. The only thing he didn't buy me was a new car. I wondered what would he have done if I put this bomb shit on him? I decided it was time to give Pop a piece of me.

I invited Pop over to dinner. I made shrimp Fettuccini Alfredo with garlic bread. The Moet was chilled, R. Kelly played in the background. I wore a sheer, red night gown that stopped just beneath my butt cheeks. On each side of the night gown there was a split.

When Pop came through the door it was easy to see how surprised he was. He gave me a big hug. We headed to the kitchen.

"Something smells good. What you cooking mommy?"

I kissed Pop on the lips then fed him a shrimp, "It's shrimp Fettuccini Alfredo, do you like it?"

Pop rubbed his stomach, "I love it. How much longer before it's done? I'm ready to eat."

"It's done now. I'll fix our plates."

"Did I tell you, you one sexy motherfucker!"

"You tell me all the time," I winked.

I fixed our plates. We sat across from one another. The candles along with R. Kelly's music playing in the background set the mood just right. Pop couldn't keep his eyes off of me.

"Why don't you come sit on my lap? Let me feed you."

"That's what you want?" I asked Pop.

"That's what I need," he licked his lips.

I walked over to where Pop was sitting, I sat on his lap. He kissed my neck, "You smell so good."

"I taste even better," I whispered in his ear.

Pop begin feeding me. He purposely placed sauce on the side of my mouth, "Oops, I better get that off for you."

I smiled. Pop begin licking the sauce from the side of my mouth. We kissed passionately for minutes. Pop ran his fingers through my hair.

"I wanna know how good you taste," Pop whispered in my ear.

"It's only one way to find out," I shot back.

Pop picked me up. He carried me into my bedroom. As I laid across the bed Pop made sure he kissed every inch of my body. He slowly begins removing my panties. Within minutes, we were both naked, neither one of us keeping our hands off of the other. Pop's tongue felt like a hurricane against my pussy. I laid back as Pop took me to ecstasy.

It turned out, eating pussy was the only thing Pop could do. His sex wasn't the best – it wasn't even close to the best. The sad part about it was I couldn't tell if it was bad because his dick was so small, or if he was just bad without any reason whatsoever. Nevertheless, I continued seeing him. He was still throwing money at me whenever I wanted it, I couldn't be mad at that.

• • •

"Damn girl, I need a Pop in my life!" said Jackie as we walked through Roosevelt Field mall, shopping. Spending money was no longer an issue for me. Pop made sure I wanted for nothing.

I came across a red leather jacket, "Jackie, look at this!" I said while touching the jacket.

Jackie felt the leather Jacket as well, "That shit is bad! Try it on."

I passed my bags to Jackie, "Hold my bags while I try it on."

She held my bags. "How much do they want for that?" she asked.

"Five hundred fifty dollars," I smiled. Without a doubt I knew I was getting the Jacket.

"Does Pop have a brother, uncle, father, cousin or something?" Jackie asked as we walked to the cash register.

I laughed, "Girl, the money is good, but the sex is wack! You should hear me faking it."

"I don't give a fuck," said Jackie. Then she continued, "I could fuck myself or have a nigga on the side to dick me down right, just show me the money!"

I laughed all the way to the register. "Cash or credit, ma'am?" asked the lady behind the register.

"Cash," I replied while placing my hand in my purse.

"Your total is five hundred and ninety eight dollars." I counted six hundred dollars then placed it in the cashier's hand.

Jackie couldn't stop staring at my money, "I see why you got over Jamel so quick, girl," she said with a blank look on her face.

I grabbed my bag with my new leather jacket in it. I threw the receipt and the change inside of the bag as we proceeded to walk out of the store.

"Pop didn't have anything to do with that. Jamel played

his self," I told her.

"Yeah, but I bet Pop's money helped."

"The only thing I can say I miss is Jamel's dick. That nigga was a dog, but when it came time to taking care of business he took care of his! Plus things were different with us. I was Jamel's girl, not his mistress."

Jackie sucked her teeth, "Bitch, you worrying about a fucking title? You better get over it and spend Pop's money."

"Do you think Pop will ever leave his girl?"

"Does it matter?" Jackie asked while looking at me like I was crazy.

"It matters to me. We been fucking with each other for a few months now. At first everything was all good, but now the reality that he has a girl is starting to sink in. Sometimes I don't see or speak to him for two days in a row. On top of that I can't really ask him where he's been, I might not like the answer. Then it seems like this bitch wanna call him every time we're together."

Jackie frowned, "Is that all? If it is then you need to relax. A nigga is gon' be a nigga regardless. If he ain't leave his girl by now then he ain't leaving her. I fuck with niggaz everyday who has a girl, a wife or something, but that don't stop me from getting their money. I wish I did have one nigga I could fuck with and still get all the paper I get. I don't care if the nigga has ten wives. Long as he taking care of me nothing else matters."

A pair of suede boots in the window of a store we we're walking pass caught Jackie's attention.

"Those would be perfect for Atlanta! Come with me inside," Jackie grabbed my wrist. We walked into the store.

"When are you going to Atlanta?" I asked her puzzled.

"I'm going in a few weeks, but I need to get everything out the way right now. You should come with me."

"What are you going to Atlanta for?" I asked.

"Can I help you," a saleswoman interrupted.

"Yes, can you give me these boots in a size seven," replied Jackie.

The saleswoman went to get the boots. Jackie turned back towards me.

"I'm going to the one and only All-Star weekend! It's gon' be nothing but Ballers down there! I told you I was trying to scoop me a Pop. Girl, you thought I was playing?"

I laughed, "I don't think I'm fucking with it, did you ask Tiff if she was going?"

Jackie rolled her eyes, "I'm starting to think your cousin don't even like dick anymore. Every time I see or speak to that hoe, she tryna eat my pussy. If you ain't going with me to Atlanta then I'm going all by my damn self."

The saleswoman returned with Jackie's boots, "Here is a size seven. These boots are two hundred and twenty five dollars."

Jackie looked at me then she looked at the saleswoman, "Did I ask you the price?" she questioned. The saleswoman remained quiet.

Jackie tried on the boots then walked to the mirror. She looked at herself at different angles.

"Do you like these, Mahogany?"

"I love them," I replied.

"Alright, I'm getting them."

We went to pay for the boots. The saleswoman who helped Jackie looked surprised. When Jackie finished paying for the boots she turned to the saleswoman.

"Tell your husband I said hello and thanks!"

The saleswoman's eyes nearly popped out of her head. Jackie laughed as we exited the store.

I tapped Jackie, "You're so mean!"

"Fuck her, I hate bitches like that. She gon' tell me the price of the boots. Did I ask for the price of the boots? I thought her job was to bring me the boots, that's it."

I dropped Jackie off at home then I headed home. I had to make two trips between my car and my house just to get all of my shopping bags upstairs. I detected the smell of liquor – a sure sign that my drunken ass landlord had been around. I never saw that woman sober. Whenever she did come around it only meant one thing, it was time to pay the rent.

I paged Pop soon as I put my bags down. It was time for him to bring me some more money.

I tried on everything I bought at the mall then fixed me something to eat. When I finished eating, I hopped in the shower. The water felt so good against my body. When I finished showering, I laid in the bed completely naked. I fell asleep shortly after.

● ● ●

The next day at work was boring as usual. Pop didn't bother to call me back after I paged him yesterday. This was the part of our relationship I didn't like. Lately he's been getting too comfortable, not returning my calls, popping up whenever he wanted to. I knew he would come around sooner or later. Two days was the longest period we went without speaking to one another. However, it was starting to become a pattern, I didn't like it. This was definitely an issue we had to resolve.

When I got home later that night, Pop finally decided to call. I couldn't wait to give him a piece of my mind.

"Please hold, go ahead," was the sound of an operated voice.

"Hello," Pop spoke immediately after the operated voice.

"What kind of phone are you on?" I asked.

"Mahogany, I'm locked up."

"What!?" I questioned.

"I need you to come see me. I got a visit tomorrow."

"I can't see you tomorrow, I have to work. What are you locked up for?"

"Never mind what I'm here for. I need to see you."

"Well, where are you? When is your next visit?"

"I'm in the Queens House, I don't know how long I'ma be here though. They might be moving me to Riker's soon."

I was silent on the phone.

"Hello?" Pop spoke.

"Yeah, I'm still here," I replied.

"I need you to bring me some shit to."

"How much is your bail?"

"I'm on parole, they ain't tryna let me go."

"So they plan on keeping you for a minute, huh?"

"They talking about some four and-a-half to nine bullshit, but I ain't copping out to shit! We'll talk about everything when I see you. Do you think you could make it tomorrow?"

"Four and-a-half to nine *years*?"

"Yeah, but I ain't tryna hear that. My lawyer is the truth."

I paused, "What happened to your girl?"

"What?" Pop yelled.

"Nothing," I replied. Then continued, "I can't make it tomorrow, but call me to let me know when you have another visit. If they move you to Riker's call so you can give me all the information."

"I'ma call you tomorrow night at nine o'clock."

"Alright."

We hung up the phone. Four and-a-half to nine years was all that kept repeating in my mind. How does a person get themselves into a situation like that? I thought. More importantly, did he expect me to spend those four and-a-half to nine years with him? If I did visit him once would he expect me to visit all the time? What if he went to trial then blew trial and was sentenced to more than four and-a-half to nine years? Didn't he say he wasn't copping out anyway? Plus he's already on parole. He'll definitely lose. These were all the thoughts running through my mind. And I kept thinking about the situation. What did he do anyway? Maybe since I'm not his girl, he didn't feel the need to tell me. It probably has something to do with drugs. Wait a minute, where is his girl? Isn't she the one who is supposed to step up to the plate at times like this? He probably gave her much more than he gave me anyway. On top of that I only have about five hundred dollars left. I spent most of the money he gave me last week when I went to the mall this week. I don't get paid for another two weeks. Plus the rent is due. Who told his ass to get locked up? Not me. Then he wants me to bring him some stuff? Did he ever think about how I would take care of myself? How selfish of him! It was clear what I had to do. I picked up the phone and made a call.

"Hello, this is Cindy. How may I provide you with excellent customer service today?" asked the representative.

"Hi Cindy, I'm calling regarding phone number 718-555-0761."

"Am I speaking with Ms. Woods?"

"Yes you are."

"Great, if you can verify the password on the account I'll be more than happy to assist you."

"Cash is the password."

"Thank you, what could I do for you today Ms. Woods?"

"I'd like to change my phone number."

"May I ask why are you changing your phone number?"

"Does your company wait four and-a-half to nine years before a bill is paid?"

"I'm afraid we do not Ms. Woods."

"Well, that's why I'm changing my number."

"No problem. Give me just a second and I'll have your new number ready for you."

That same night I had a new phone number. I liked Pop, but I had to look out for me first. It was not in my best interest to do a bid with him. I wasn't his damn girl anyway. If he would've came by when he was supposed to I wouldn't be strapped for cash anyway. Now I was left with five hundred dollars. My twelve hundred dollar rent needed to be paid. My car insurance was also due. In two weeks I would get paid. However, my paycheck wouldn't be enough to pay all of my bills even after I put the five hundred dollars towards them.

Moving out of my duplex was not an option. I enjoyed

my independence. On top of that, I couldn't let Jamel think I needed him again. I wouldn't let the world catch me slipping. I made one phone call to solve my problem.

"Hello."

"Mahogany? I just called you, what's the matter with your phone?" asked Jackie.

"I changed the number. Get a pen so I can give you the new number."

"Why you change your number?"

"Pop is locked up, it's a long story."

"What!?"

"I'll tell you all about it on our way to Atlanta, when are we leaving?"

I could hear the smile in Jackie's voice, "Did I just hear my bitch say she's coming with me to Atlanta?"

"Yup, I need to run into one of those Ballers you were talking about."

"That's what I'm talking about! Fuck niggaz, get money! We leaving in three weeks so make sure you get all your shit together."

"Three weeks? I need some money before then!"

Jackie laughed, "Well, you know what you gotta do. Sunshine and Vinnie has been asking about you anyway. It's always money waiting to be made girl."

"Yeah, but this time I don't need a little strip money. I think I might need a little more."

"Well then you know you gotta do a little more. You know how I feel about it. It's no excuse for broke days when selling pussy pays."

Chapter 11

Buck Wild Child...

"I'm glad to have you back, Ginger. I didn't appreciate the way you left before, but I know that's not going to happen again, right?"

I sat in Vinnie's office listening to him pat himself on the back for owning such an upscale strip club. Vinnie was an older Italian man who had a thing for light-skin black girls like myself. Tonight was my first night back at the club. Vinnie felt the need for us to have a meeting in his office which was a hidden back room inside of the club.

"You don't have to worry about that. I didn't understand how serious this business was before, I do now."

"Good, because a lot of girls would love to say they've had the opportunity to work at Vinnie's. However, I'm very careful about who I let work in my place. My reputation is very important, am I making myself clear?"

"Yes, I understand."

"That's excellent. Oh, and one other thing. Rain tells me you have a job elsewhere, is this true?"

"I don't work at any other clubs."

"But, you do have another job?"

"Yeah, I work at an insurance company."

"Do you get paid a lot of money there?"

"Not at all."

"Let me tell you what I'm gonna do for you. I'll give you my all if you promise to give me your all. That means quitting your old job. You probably make in a week there what you could make in one night here anyway, which job is really pimping you, am I wrong?"

"No," I replied.

Vinnie smiled, "I didn't think so. So, you're not afraid to do more than just stripping now, right?"

"That sounds right," I told him.

"Usually when a girl gets a date in the club, she has to give us thirty percent of what she makes. We set the prices for everything. We also collect the money from these guys before we let them go into any room with one of our girls. However, I like you so I'm only gonna take twenty-five percent of what you make, is that fair?"

"Yeah, I think so," I smiled.

"So it's a deal. You're gonna quit that other sorry job, this way you can be devoted to this. Plus I'm gonna give you special treatment. This treatment is for you and only you. I don't want you telling the other girls what I'm doing for you, not even Rain, understand?"

"I understand. Thank you."

"You're welcome. Now, you know I'm only doing this because I like you, right?

"Yes, I know," I replied.

Vinnie smiled, "So, do you like me too?"

"Like you how?" I frowned.

Vinnie laughed, "Come gimme a hug, come mere."

I got up out of the chair I was sitting in. I walked to the

other side of Vinnie's desk to give him a hug. I felt Vinnie's hard dick against my body.

"I promised to give you special treatment now you gotta promise to give me special treatment," Vinnie told me.

"Really?" I said kind of surprised by Vinnie's statement.

"Yeah, really. Can I get a special kiss to?"

I tried kissing Vinnie on his cheek. He purposely turned his head so my lips landed on his lips. Vinnie shoved his tongue down my throat, while at the same time he placed my hand on his erect dick.

"How are you gonna get it down?" he asked.

I tried to break loose from Vinnie's tight grip, "I don't think we should be doing this Vinnie."

"I think you're wrong." He grabbed me tighter.

Vinnie ripped my shirt open. He began sucking my breast. Then he slowly begins to unzip his pants. His pants fell to the floor, his dick stood at attention.

"Look at it," Vinnie demanded. Fearing Vinnie would get even more aggressive than he already was I did as I was told.

Vinnie smiled, "You're not looking at it like I want you to look at it."

"How do you want me to look at it?" I asked.

"You gotta look a little closer, maybe if I sit down that'll help."

Vinnie sat down, "Now you're gonna have to get on your knees to look at it. Once you're on your knees, I want you to look at it very close."

I got on my knees. Vinnie pulled my hair bringing my face closer to his dick. He began rubbing his dick across my lips.

"Are you gonna swallow it for me?" asked Vinnie.

I didn't respond. "I know you're gonna swallow it. Open your mouth."

I opened my mouth. Vinnie forcefully shoved his dick deeper and deeper into my throat until he exploded in my mouth. When Vinnie was done he sucked my breast some more. Within minutes he had another erection. Pushing everything off of his desk, Vinnie instructed me to sit on top of the desk with my legs open. He stood to his feet. His pants were around his ankles. He put his dick in between my legs then began penetrating.

When Vinnie finished having his way with me, I hurried out of his office. Inside the club, the usual activities were taking place. Girls were dancing to the music, guys were throwing money. Everything was happening in slow motion to me. As I headed toward the dressing rooms I noticed all the other rooms were occupied which meant, a lot of fucking and sucking was going on behind those doors.

I did my best to hold back my tears before entering the dressing room. When I opened the door it was like walking into one big party. No one in the room was fully dressed. Most of the girls had a drink in their hand while the others readied themselves for a date or a stage dance. Nothing shocked me more than seeing Jackie along with another girl, both sniffing white powder off of a dollar bill.

Seeing my best friend getting high, plus still trying to act like nothing happened between me and Vinnie was enough to make me breakdown. Before Jackie had a chance to lift her head up, I ran into the bathroom crying.

Shortly after I ran into the bathroom, Sunshine entered. She saw me crying then walked over to me. Without saying a word she began hugging me. I hugged her back.

"Why, Sunshine? Why me?" I cried.

"It's okay, Ginger. I've been there. I know what you're going through." Sunshine held me tight as she rubbed my back.

"No matter what I do, everything always seems to work against me." I cried over Sunshine's shoulder.

"I know, trust me I know. You have to be strong. Whatever it is you're going through it will all be over soon."

"Sometimes it just feels like soon isn't coming fast enough."

Sunshine wiped the tears from my face. She looked into my eyes like she was trying to read my soul.

"Ginger, I want you to listen to me. Since I was ten years old I've lost both of my parents to circumstances. Since then I've been raped, abused and thrown around from one foster home to another. Through it all, I lost my innocence but I maintained my soul. Do you know how I did this? I never let anyone else control my spirits. I didn't lose control, you can't either! Do not let anyone have this much control over you! If you lose control then you lose everything. When I saw what happened after my parents lost control, I made a vow to myself to never let it happen to me. I want you to remember you're here for one reason, to make a better way for yourself. This life isn't going to last forever, but its bringing us a few steps closer to where we want to be."

"Sunshine, I'm so sorry," I said full of sympathy.

"Don't be sorry honey. I'm only speaking the truth. If you really want to make me feel better you can turn that frown upside down." Sunshine placed tissue paper in my hands. I used it to wipe away my tears. I smiled. Sunshine smiled harder. "There you go honey, that's the Ginger I'm use to seeing."

"Sunshine, do you mind if I ask you a personal question?"

Sunshine waved her hand, "Go right ahead honey."

"Is it true you use to be very rich?"

Sunshine smiled, "I'm still rich. My money's gone and so are my parents, but I have a heart full of gold. I'd rather have fifty cent with peace of mind than have fifty million dollars with no peace at all. I have all the finer things in life money could never buy. I have a good friend like you, I attend a great school, and my health is good. Plus I'm alive and breathing. That's what life is all about to me. What's important in life is life. No amount of money is worth me losing my life like my dad, or losing my sanity like my mom. If riches were measured by happiness, I guess I'm the richest person alive. I don't dwell on what could've been... Instead I thank God for what will be... My money can and will be replaced. This is why I'm at this club four nights a week. I'm going to put myself through school, when I graduate I'll open up my own marketing company. Stripping isn't my life; it's just my job for now. I call this my yellow brick road towards a better tomorrow."

"Sunshine, you truly are a ray of light," I told her.

"Hey, just call me a good friend." Sunshine smiled then continued, "I'm not going to sit here and allow you to feel sorry for yourself. Let's get you cleaned up. Have you eaten anything yet?"

"I'm not hungry."

"You have to eat something. Let's go honey."

We exited the bathroom. Sunshine was so sweet. She had a way of making anyone feel good again. I was so thankful I met her.

• • •

The next day I was feeling much better. I put what happened the day before in the back of my mind. However, I couldn't get over seeing Jackie sniffing coke. I would definitely have to have a talk with her about that.

Quitting my job at the insurance company was easy. I simply stopped showing up for work. Quitting that job was something I should've done long ago. I didn't like anything about it. Plus, relaxing in the daytime would give me more strength to be full of energy during my night job. I didn't plan on stripping much longer either. All I needed was enough money to pay my bills and hold me down until I met someone new in Atlanta. Stripping and fucking for cash was definitely the financial outlet I needed.

It was Friday night, the club was jumping. Titties and asses were everywhere. I hadn't been there thirty minutes and already I had three dates lined up for me.

The first guy was a little scary. He was an older, white, fat motherfucker. He looked like a straight up pervert. Once I heard what he wanted me to do to him, I knew he was a pervert.

The entire time I fucked him, he insisted he wore a ski mask while I yelled "stop." He also wanted me to keep sticking my finger in and out of his ass. However, what really confirmed my thoughts about him being a nut was when this motherfucker not only jerked his dick until he came all over me; he also paid four hundred dollars just to piss on me! Thank God Vinnie's had showers. I thought I couldn't run into anyone worse than him – I was wrong.

My next date surprised me for different reasons. The first reason I was surprised by this client is; he didn't look like a nut or a freak. This guy was an attractive black guy with a bald head. He looked about twenty-five years old. On top of that I knew he had to have money because he was in the club, which alone was expensive. I was actually excited and curious to get him behind closed doors. I wanted to know what his problem was.

When we entered into the room this guy wanted nothing but the norm. I was so thankful. The first thing I did was give him a full body massage as per his request. Then I rode him until our time was up and he came.

Once we were done curiosity was killing me so bad, I had to ask him his reason for coming to a place like this. Without hesitation he answered my question.

"I'm in the streets a lot so I really don't have time for a girl, but I do like the things females offer. Plus I could live without the headaches."

"So you like sex with no strings attached?" I asked.

The guy smiled, "Exactly. I'd rather pay for the pussy than deal with the aggravation of explaining my whereabouts to some chick. Plus females get insulted by my honesty."

"Really, why is that?"

The guy laughed, "Whenever I meet a female I like, I'm usually very up front with her. I let her know what I'm into. I tell her about my likes and my dislikes. For some reason they all look at me different, or stop liking me altogether once I tell them I cannot be in a committed relationship with a woman because I enjoy fucking guys just as much as I enjoyed fucking females."

"You're gay!?" I shouted.

This guy was so calm. He replied, "I don't consider myself gay. I'm just a trisexual, I'll try anything sexual."

I didn't care what he said after that. The way I saw it, he was gay! I left the room before he could finish getting dressed.

I finally ended my night with client number three. Client number three was extra surprising for so many reasons. As I was about to enter the room where client number three waited, I saw Jackie exiting another room. When Jackie saw me she became excited.

"Girl, what the fuck did you do or say to get that nigga to leave the bar?"

I looked at Jackie like she was crazy. At the same time I was still upset with her about her coke issue, which we hadn't discussed yet.

"I don't know who or what the fuck you are talking about, I'm just going to my last date. Wait for me before you leave tonight, it's something I'd like to discuss with you."

Completely ignoring the last part of my statement, Jackie replied, "I know you're joking right? You don't know who that nigga is?"

"I haven't even seen him yet. Is he some type of star or something?"

"Bitch, he's that Indian nigga who always sits at the bar. He never got a lap dance or even watched any of us dance up close, but he comes here every night. We used to think he was crazy, but we realized his ass is just cheap. I heard that nigga is paid though."

I suddenly realized who she was talking about. I was nervous and excited at the same time.

"Why do you think he picked me!?" I asked.

"Bitch, that's what the hell I'm asking you!"

"Well, I don't know!"

"I want all the details once you're finished!" Jackie told me.

"Don't forget to wait for me Jackie. I really need to speak with you about some things."

Jackie sucked her teeth, "I already know what you wanna talk to me about, don't even worry about it. I'm grown and I could handle my own habits. I don't need any lectures from you."

She caught me off guard, "You need to worry about it Jackie. I'm not going to stand by and watch you kill yourself."

"I got work to do," said Jackie as she turned then walked away. I entered the room I was heading to.

I was so nervous because I knew I was the only girl he wanted to fuck at this club, I wondered why.

This guy sat on the bed. I began crawling over to him. Since he was my last client, I wanted to fuck him and get it over with so I could leave. Once I was within close range I started unbuttoning his pants. To my surprise, this guy stopped me.

"Please get off of your knees," he told me.

I was confused, "What?"

"I would like you to get off your knees. However, you could go around to the other side of the bed and pick up the two champagne glasses on the floor."

I did just what I was told. I handed him the wine glasses. He poured both of us a glass of Moet. Twenty minutes passed, both of us were still fully dressed.

I took a sip of Moet before speaking, "Do you know you only have twenty five minutes remaining with me?"

The guy smiled then placed his glass down, "I'm aware of the time. If you haven't already realized, my intentions are not to get physical with you. I'd just like to get to know you a little better. What is your name?"

Surprised with his answer I replied, "I'm Ginger."

"Ginger, it's nice to meet you. I can tell you're nervous, you can relax. Companionship is the only thing I seek from you. Sometimes I just need someone to talk to."

"I'm not nervous. This just feel a bit awkward, that's all. What's your name?"

"My name is Mohammad, but you can call me Mo."

"Mo, that's a nice name," I smiled.

"Ginger, you're very pretty. What is a person like you doing in a business like this?"

The question caught me off guard, "What kind of person am I?"

"I can tell you're very smart and caring. This is not the life for you."

"This is just the hand life dealt me. I'm only playing my cards. What brings you to a place like this?" I asked him.

"Like I said, I seek companionship. Sometimes places like this is the only place to find it. However, I don't like being with just anyone, but I feel something special about you."

"Thanks for the compliment," I shot back.

"I'm speaking the truth. You should be at home making some man very happy. You deserve to be someone's wife, someone's queen."

I appreciated what Mo was saying. However, I wasn't in the mood to hear the stuff he was kicking. I already had my conscious beating me down. I didn't need a date at work telling me I should and could live a better life. If his life was all of that then he wouldn't have been here in the first place. I looked at my watch. Thank God our time together was up.

"I'm afraid our time is up, Mo."

He looked at his watch, "I guess you're right. I hope you listened to what I said tonight."

"I did. Thanks for everything."

It turned out Mo wasn't a weirdo after all. I guess Jackie was right; some people just wanted someone they could talk to. However, I was happy to leave him. My night was over, I needed to count my well earned money then relax.

•   •   •

Three weeks later the moment I was waiting for finally arrived! It was time to attend All-Star weekend in Atlanta.

When our plane landed it was clear to me, we weren't the only ones who flew in just for that weekend. There were girls and guys everywhere racing to taxis or other means of transportation. Thank God me and Jackie already made arrangements to reserve a rental car.

Since Jackie couldn't drive, I was our designated driver during our stay in Atlanta.

By the time we arrived at our hotel suites we had so many fliers, we weren't sure which party we would attend. After we turned on the radio and heard a DJ talking about one particular party, where all the major players would be, without a doubt that's the party we knew we would attend.

Our hotel suites were beautiful. Me and Jackie had two separate suites. What I liked the most about them were the connecting doors. It provided the privacy we needed to be alone while still giving us the freedom to choose whether we wanted to be together. While I unpacked my bags, Jackie burst through the connecting doors.

"Damn, you still unpacking?" she asked.

"Why you gotta come over here? You could stay in your room," I pointed then continued, "with all your bullshit."

Jackie took a seat on the bed, "Hoe, please! You know you miss me. What the fuck do you have these for?" asked Jackie. She had a pair of my panties in the air. She twirled them around her finger.

I snatched my panties, "Gimme my shit!"

"You playing yourself if you wearing those."

"Why the fuck are you worried about whether I'm wearing panties or not?"

Jackie sucked her teeth, "Suit yourself then. I know I ain't wearing any panties. I came down here to fuck. My panties would just get in the way. You know I don't let shit come between me and my money."

I ignored Jackie, "What time are we leaving to go to the party?"

"First we go to the game then we go to the party."

"Well, what time are we leaving?"

"Soon as we get dressed, this entire weekend is party time!" Jackie started dancing.

"Why the fuck did I get you started?" I asked.

"You ain't start shit, I been ready for this weekend."

"I'm getting in the shower," I walked into the bathroom.

Jackie yelled, "We ain't bringing any niggaz to our rooms until the last night we down here. If they wanna fuck us, we'll go with them to their rooms. If the nigga ain't got his own room, that nigga probably ain't got his own money either. No money, no pussy! Everything is that simple."

I turned on the shower water.

"Bitch did you just hear me!?" shouted Jackie.

"I heard you!" I shouted over the running water.

"Our last night is reserved for that one balling ass nigga we plan on keeping in our lives."

"Well, our last night needs to hurry the hell up 'cause that sounds like just the type of nigga I need in my life."

• • •

Our first night in Atlanta was the bomb! We partied, fucked then partied some more. Our second night was even better. By the third night of our stay, I already made close to six thousand dollars. I only fucked two niggaz, without a doubt both of them were Ballers! One of them was from Washington D.C. the other one was from Houston. Niggaz from every state was definitely in the house.

However, our third night was our last and final night in Atlanta. This night was important for more reasons than one. This night would be the night I found that one special nigga who would afford me the life of luxury I yearned for so much. Jackie was looking for the nigga who would be her Trump card as well. We hit the club scene.

Arriving at our designated club, people were everywhere. I saw girls sporting the weirdest hairdos. Some females even went far as wearing nothing but a bikini to the club. The guys loved every moment of this cry for their attention. Inside one car I walked past on the crowded street, I seen a girl sucking the skin off of this guys dick. A few feet away from that car sat a gold Mercedes-Benz. One female stood in the center facing the group of guys who were next to the car. Her dress was pulled up, her ass was out. So many hands were grabbing her ass as she posses for the picture leaning on the guys. The freaks were definitely out on this night.

I looked at Jackie then spoke, "Damn girl! I never saw so many niggaz in my life."

"Niggaz?" questioned Jackie. Then she continued, "I never seen so many hoes in my life! Ain't none of them fucking with me though. You remember our goal, right?"

I smiled, "Get that Baller, make him trick, tonight is the night we'll get rich."

Jackie laughed, "That's right!" We gave each other a high five, and then we entered the club.

I was wearing a satin, Chinese mini-dress. I didn't have panties or a bra on under my dress. My hair was full of curls, my body was looking tight. Jackie wandered off to find her Baller, I begin looking for mine.

I wasn't in the club long before a tall, dark and hideous guy with a strong southern accent tried to push up on me.

"You're the sexiest woman I've seen all night," he whispered in my ear. I backed away from him. He was too close for comfort. I looked him up and down. He wasn't wearing a watch, his haircut looked like he did it himself and his shirt looked like it had been put in the washing machine one too many times.

I had to confirm he was broke. I asked him a test question, "How are you trying to talk to me now? Just a few minutes ago you were trying to run me over outside."

He frowned, "Run you over?"

I continued with my fraudulent story, "Weren't you the one driving that white Range Rover? You tried to hit me! Don't try to talk to me now like everything is all good."

The guy laughed then licked his chapped lips, "See, now I know you got me all wrong. I don't even drive a white Range Rover, I wish I did though. I came with my cousin Lil' Rob and 'em. You know who I'm talking about? They right over there," the guy pointed.

Bingo! I got the answer I was looking for. He was a broke ass. I walked away from him. He followed me.

"Hold up a minute sweet peach. I told you I ain't tried to hit you. What's your name?"

"I can't hear you. The music is too loud," I lied.

"I said what your name is?" he repeated himself.

"You're right, I hope it doesn't rain. Bye," I walked away from him again. He stood in one spot with his hands in the air.

"You gon' do me like that? That's cool, that's cool." Defeated, he finally gave up.

I walked over to a different area inside the club. The area was pretty close to the bar. I noticed a group of females, all fighting for the attention of one man. I wasn't sure who this guy was but he damn sure had it going on. His dark skin looked rich and creamy. The waves in his hair only enhanced the beautiful features he already had. When I saw two guys on each side of him who looked like his bodyguards, I knew he had to be an NBA player or something. Since I didn't know any player whose name wasn't Michael Jordan, I had to get some more information about this mysterious guy. I asked a guy standing close by.

"Excuse me, what team does that guy play for?"

The guy laughed, "Team? You think he's a ball player?"

"He's not?" I said surprised.

"He's a player alright. He even got his own team, but he don't play ball sweetheart."

Through the crowd, I caught a glimpse of his iced out watch and what appeared to be a wedding ring. The girls continued throwing themselves on him. He paid attention to none of them.

I knew just what he needed – a real woman like myself. I braced myself as I brushed past all of them. Someone should've taught them how to be smooth like me.

Up close he looked even better. His silk pants fit him perfect. The diamonds in his platinum watch were blue. His skin looked so smooth. Without a doubt, I wanted this nigga to come back to my hotel suite with me. I didn't want our affair to stop there either. I wanted him as my personal cash machine. Goodbye stripping, hello to whomever this guy was! I put my plan into action.

"Let me have Sex on the Beach," I told the bartender seductively and loud enough for that fly ass nigga to hear.

He looked in my direction, I winked. He turned his head back to one of the guys standing next to him. The bartender handed me my drink. I passed her twenty dollars.

"Keep the change," I told her.

"Thank you," she smiled.

In a matter of seconds, I accidentally on purpose spilled my drink all over the top part of my dress. That was all part of my plan. My wet dress revealed I wasn't wearing a bra. This immediately caught the guy's attention. I smiled to myself knowing it would only be a matter of seconds before he would try to push up on me.

I decided to say something to the guy first, "Can I have one of your napkins? I'm all wet," I said in my softest, sexiest tone.

The guy tossed me a napkin without saying a word. Seconds later he was walking away from the bar.

I was shocked and embarrassed! Did I just get dissed? I couldn't believe it! My embarrassment turned into anger. I grabbed a hand full of napkins then turned around to leave. It was just my luck I ran into the last person I wanted to see.

"You thought I wouldn't find you again, huh?" it was the guy from earlier who came to the club with 'Lil' Rob.' I wasn't in the mood to deal with his broke ass again.

"Leave me alone," I let the words roll off of my tongue very slowly. Then I continued, "I do not like you!" I rolled my eyes then left him sitting at the bar like that fly ass nigga left me sitting at the bar. As I walked away I peeped the eraser he had on the back of his earring. That disgusted me even more. I hate a broke ass nigga! Where the fuck was all the Ballers!?

On our flight home, me and Jackie were quiet. We both made money, but neither one of us hooked the Baller of our dreams. At that moment, I knew I would be stripping and fucking niggaz for cash longer than I anticipated. How the fuck did this happen?

Chapter 12

All Things Come To An End...

The night had just begun. Everyone was inside the dressing room getting ready for a date or a stage dance. Jackie was already on stage, dancing.

"Ginger, you sure have come a long way," said Heaven.

"I'm just doing my job," I replied as I continued putting baby oil all over my legs.

Heaven laughed, "I remember when you were 'nervous' to do your job. Do you remember the first night you came to this club? You were so innocent. Now you have regular clients and everything! Even that Indian guy who's never spoken to any of us is your regular client. How did you pull that off?"

"Yeah, how did you pull that off?" another girl inquired.

"Mo just needs a friend," I replied.

"Shit, I'll be his friend. He's a little cute Indian. Plus I'll let him lick all over my big breast," said Heaven. The entire room laughed at that.

"Where's Sunshine? Is she coming to work tonight?" one of the other girls asked. As if on cue, Sunshine entered the dressing room.

"Hey guys," she smiled.

"Here's that cool ass white girl," Heaven joked. Sunshine playfully tapped Heaven. Then she walked over to me. She gave me a kiss on the cheek before speaking.

"Hey honey, you're looking good."

I kissed her back, "Thanks, why are you late?"

Sunshine waved her hand, "It's a long story." Then Sunshine instantly became excited, "Have I got something to tell you!"

My face lit up, "Is it juicy?"

Sunshine shook her head, "Oh yeah, big time!"

"Well let's hear it."

Sunshine started getting ready like the rest of us, "Not now, I have a date waiting out front. Plus I kind of want to tell you in private."

"Okay," I replied.

"Ginger, watch my stuff. I'm going to tell my date I'll be with him shortly. He gets kind of crazy when I'm gone too long."

"You got it! I'll wait right here until you return."

"Thanks honey. This will only take two seconds."

I fastened the last buckle on my platform shoes. Sunshine came racing back into the dressing room. She grabbed me by my wrist.

"Come with me, now!" said Sunshine.

"What's going on?" I asked.

All the other girls watched as me and Sunshine raced out of the dressing room.

"It's your girl," replied Sunshine.

"Who, what are you talking about?" I asked.

"It's Rain. Soon as I went out front to check on my date, she was dancing on stage. The next thing I know, she's falling flat on her face!"

I walked even faster towards the stage. When I got there the bouncers were helping Jackie to her feet. Jackie had a silly smile on her face, her eyes were barely open. Me and Sunshine took over. I was on one side of Jackie, Sunshine was on the other side.

"Jackie!" I slapped her lightly on her face.

"Ginger, is that you?" Jackie asked.

I frowned, "Of course it's me. Are you okay?

"I love you Ginger. Can I have a kiss?" Jackie started blowing kisses in the air.

"What's wrong with you!?"

"She's high out of her mind Ginger!" Sunshine answered.

"We have to get her to a bathroom," I replied. We carried Jackie into the bathroom.

"Ginger, I'm sorry," Jackie said.

"What are you sorry for?" I asked confused.

Jackie started crying, "I don't want you to be mad at me. I know you're mad at me. I'm so, so sorry Ginger."

"Gin, it's the drugs talking," said Sunshine.

"I can't believe she did this to herself," I replied.

"I hate Jason! I hate him so much!" Jackie yelled.

"Who the hell is Jason?" Sunshine inquired.

"Jason is her brother," I told her. "She's losing her fucking mind right now!"

Jackie looked at me, "Are you still my friend? Please tell me you're still my friend Ginger."

"Of course I'm your friend, I love you girl! You have to stop killing yourself like this! Do you hear me!?"

Jackie smiled. "Throw some cold water on her face," said Sunshine.

I began throwing water all over Jackie's face.

"This is just what the fuck I wanted to talk to you about," said Sunshine.

I frowned, "Who Rain? What about her?"

"Not about her. I'm talking about this fucking place!" Sunshine angrily kicked the bathroom door.

"Calm down. Tell me what's wrong."

"I just found out something so sweet. If I share this with you, both of us will never have to do another hard days work in our life!"

"What is it?" I whispered.

"Gin, this is some serious shit I'm talking about. Both of us can walk out of this club without ever looking back. There are some risks involved, but the rewards make it so much worth it!"

"Then tell me what we have to do!"

Suddenly Heaven burst into the bathroom. "What's going on in here? I heard Rain passed out on stage?"

I sucked my teeth, "Nothing is going on! Everything is just fine. Me and Sunshine are taking care of Rain."

Heaven looked at Jackie slouched over the sink, "Everything sure doesn't look fine," she said.

"Heaven, what did Ginger just say? We have everything under control."

Heaven rolled her eyes, "Fine with me! I just hope the two of you remember you're still at work. You ladies still have work to do and he's waiting outside for you, Sunshine." Heaven pointed to Sunshine then exited the bathroom.

"What's her problem?" I asked.

"I don't know, some days she's cool, other days she not. That's the way she's always been. I did forget all about my date though."

"Go ahead. I'll stay here with Rain."

"Are you sure?" Sunshine asked.

"Yeah, don't worry about it."

"You might want to take Rain out of here. I'm pretty sure Heaven told the other girls what's going on by now. I don't want any and everyone to keep seeing her like this."

"You're right. I am gonna move her. Go make that money girl, don't let it make you," that was something Sunshine always said. She smiled before she spoke.

"I'm happy you listen. I'm going to get out of here now. I want you to think about what I said though. Matter fact I want you to fall asleep tonight thinking about it. Once I tell you what's up, there's no turning back. Like I said before, this is some serious shit. Think about what you're getting into long and hard. I'm not coming to work tomorrow. I have some things to take care of. When I return on Friday, you have to let me know if you're in."

"I will," I replied.

Sunshine left the bathroom. Jackie was slowly coming back to reality. I wanted to know exactly what Sunshine was trying to pull me into.

• • •

The next night I stopped in Forty Projects to pick Jackie up for work. We didn't usually ride together because sometimes we'd get to work at different hours, but after what happened to her the night before. I decided to pick her up since she insisted on coming to work.

"You didn't have to pick me up. I'm not a baby you know?" those were the first words out of Jackie's mouth once she entered my car.

"Long as you keep acting like a baby, I'm gonna keep treating you like one." I pulled off.

"Whatever hoe," Jackie stared outside the passenger window.

"Jackie you need to cut your bullshit out, seriously."

"What doesn't kill me can only make me stronger."

I had to take my eyes off the road for a split second to glance at Jackie, "Do you know how stupid you sound?" I asked her.

"If I wanna sound stupid then that's on me. Ain't nobody gotta live my life but me. I don't tell you how to live your life. Please don't tell me how to live mine."

"Those drugs are frying your fucking brain!"

"Long as they ain't frying yours, you don't have to worry."

"Fine, if you wanna kill yourself then go right ahead. Don't say I didn't try to stop you."

"Thank you!" shouted Jackie.

We rode in silence for about ten minutes before Jackie decided to speak.

"I sure can't wait to find out what Sunshine has up her sleeve."

"Excuse me?" I replied.

"Don't act like you don't know what I'm talking about. I heard y'all talking in the bathroom last night."

"I could've sworn you were too high to hear anything after the way you carried on."

Jackie sucked her teeth, "I was high. Not dumb, deaf and blind."

"Whatever," I replied then continued, "If Sunshine wanted you in her business then she would've come to you like she came to me."

"Obviously she did want me in her business. She was talking about it right in front of me. You're acting like she didn't know I was right there."

"I bet you if she knew you could hear and remember everything she was saying, she wouldn't have been speaking about it so freely."

"Well it's too late now. Whatever it is, count me in."

"Count you in nothing! You gotta speak to Sunshine about that."

"Then that's what the fuck I'll do!"

We pulled up to the club. I parked, we exited the car. Soon as I entered the club I was greeted by Mo's smiling face.

"Hello, Ginger. You're just the person I was hoping to see."

"Hey Mo. Gimme a minute and I'll be right with you."

"Take your time beautiful."

Me and Mo had a twisted relationship. He never wanted sex from me – even though he paid for it. Our time together was usually spent talking and drinking. Long as he was spending his money, I didn't care what he wanted to do. The only part I didn't like about our times together was Mo's constant need to remind me why I shouldn't be doing this. I knew what I was doing was wrong, I didn't need him reminding me.

Me and Jackie headed to the dressing room. When we entered, all eyes were on Jackie. Jackie didn't like that at all. She instantly caught an attitude.

"What the fuck is everybody looking at? Do I have diamonds on my face?"

Someone yelled from the back, "Maybe you have a little coke under your nose."

Everyone inside the dressing room started laughing except for me and Jackie.

"Whoever that was can suck my pussy!" Jackie yelled. Then she continued, "As for the rest of y'all bitches. The next time y'all feel the need to look at me. Take a picture, it might last longer."

"Rain, just get ready," I sighed. Jackie felt the need to continue.

"Nah, fuck that! I'm tired of all these jealous bitches in here! Every time I turn around it's always something. I can't help it if I look good plus I got a fat pussy! That's right, my pussy is fat and what!?"

I tried to calm Jackie down. I pulled her to the side, "Do you think all of this is necessary? Ain't nobody in here saying shit to you, so why are you carrying on like this? You flipping on them, you're flipping on me. What's going on girl?"

Jackie didn't answer me. I pulled her closer then whispered, "Jackie, this is me, Mahogany! What the fuck is going on with you girl? Is everything alright, huh? Talk to me!"

Jackie put her head down, "I'm alright."

"Then act like it! You been my bitch for life. I know you ain't gon' let these bitches break you? You better than that! You better than them! I know you already know these things, so why you trippin'?

Jackie lifted her head up, "I'm sorry girl. You right, I am trippin'."

"You ain't gotta apologize to me. Just give your bitch a hug."

A smile appeared on Jackie's face. We hugged.

Soon as I exited the dressing room I ran into Vinnie.
Once I saw him, I tried to head back inside. It was too late,
Vinnie already saw me.

"Ginger! Where have you been? I've been looking all
over for you."

I put my head down, "Hi Vinnie. I've been working.
Matter fact someone is waiting for me right now. I'll see
you later."

I tried to brush pass him. He stopped me before I could
get far.

Vinnie grabbed my hand, "Sweetheart, I'm starting to
feel

neglected. You don't want me to keep feeling this way,
do you?"

"I'm sorry. I have to go," I tried walking away again.
Vinnie held my hand tighter.

"Why don't you come talk to me? Just for a little while.
Come on, it'll be real quick. I promise."

"Vinnie, I really don't want to. Can we do this some
other time?"

"You don't really have a choice. I want a little of you.
I was hoping you wanted a little of me too. So, we can do
this the nice way. Or we can do this my way. How do you
wanna do this?"

I started heading with Vinnie towards his office. He felt
the need to speak to me until we arrived inside his office.

Rubbing me on the back he spoke, "I knew you'd make
the right decision. Ginger, you're a very smart girl. How
do you feel about getting fucked in the ass? Have you
ever tried that before?"

I didn't bother responding. We entered Vinnie's office.
He closed then locked the door behind him as usual.

• • •

By the time I'd got to Mo, he'd already been waiting close to an hour for me. I liked Mo, but I was getting sick of the club, stripping, Vinnie and everything else that came along with the lifestyle. I couldn't wait to see Sunshine the next day. I desperately wanted whatever she had planed to work, not only for her – I wanted it to work for myself as well. I had to get out of this life, fast!

Mo sat at the bar. He saw me heading in his direction. He smiled. I blew him a kiss then sat down next to him.

"Hey Mo. I'm sorry to keep you waiting so long."

"Don't worry about it. I'm happy you're here now."

"Do you wanna go in one of the backrooms now?"

"Sure, I don't see why not. Plus they already took my money so I guess I'm stuck with you." We both laughed.

Upon arriving in one of the backrooms, Mo started his usual line of questioning.

"How was your day today Ginger?"

"My day was good. How was your day?" I replied.

"It could've been better but I can't really complain."

"Sorry to hear that."

"It's okay. It happens. Let me ask you a question."

"Go right ahead."

"I gave you my phone number, why don't you ever use it?"

I took a deep breath, "Mo, I don't mean any harm or disrespect, but I try to keep my personal life away from this club. This isn't exactly Wall Street you know."

"I know, I know. It's just that I worry about you some-times. At least you could call and say you got home safely, that's all."

239

"I guess I can try to do that."

"I'd really appreciate it. Why are you still working here anyway?"

"Mo, don't start this again," I sighed.

"I'm not starting. I just think you deserve better. Wouldn't you agree?"

"I do."

"Okay, then what's the problem? You're young, you're pretty and you're smart. Why must American girls always belittle themselves?"

"Who said I was American?"

"What?" replied Mo.

I laughed, "I'm just kidding. I'm American as they come. Except, I'm not living the American dream, I'm only experiencing the American nightmare."

"Well, then you have to change that."

"I'm aware of that, but sometimes change isn't so easy. Trust me, I've tried."

"Ginger, tell me some more about yourself. I have a few things I'd like to share with you as well."

"Where would you like me to start?" I asked.

"You can start wherever you like. Take your time. I've paid for two forty five minute sessions with you."

I spent an hour and-a-half talking to Mo. Before I knew it, my night was over. I was getting sick and tired of the same routine.

• • •

Nothing could've prepared me for the news I received the next night at work. Before I could reach the dressing room, Jackie ran to me holding the newspaper.

"Look at this shit!" Jackie shoved the paper in my face.

"What happened? What's going on?" I asked.

"Read page four," she replied.

I turned to page four. The first line read, *"Diana Shapiro joins her father Robert Shapiro in rest."*

"Why am I reading this?" I asked.

"You didn't see the picture?" asked Jackie.

"What picture?"

"This picture!" pointed Jackie.

I looked closer. It was a picture of Sunshine! Under her picture it read; *"Twenty-three year old Diana Shapiro found slain on a highway."*

"They're lying! Sunshine is not dead! She's coming to work today so we can talk about leaving this place forever! Why would someone lie like this!?"

Jackie hugged me, "It's not a lie. She's gone baby."

I couldn't stop the tears from pouring down my face. I tried to continue reading the newspaper. The tears were making this a difficult task. The paper went on to talk about Sunshine, her mother and father. Plus the tragic ways all of their lives ended up. They reported there were no motives, witnesses or known reason why Sunshine was found dead on the highway with a bullet in her brain.

I read enough. I didn't want to hear another thing about my friend being murdered. Could it have been over the news she wanted to share with me? Was it a crazy client? I didn't know or understand why someone would want to kill Sunshine. I was hurt and confused.

Jackie caressed my shoulders, "It's gonna be okay, girl."

"Jackie it's not okay! Sunshine is gone, she's never coming back!"

All the other girls took turns reading the paper. I wasn't in any condition to work the rest of the night. I didn't even bother changing. I turned around and headed back home.

• • •

It had been two days since I learned about Sunshine's murder. I hadn't been back to work since I got the news. During that time, I started to re-evaluate my life. Where was I going? What direction was my life heading if I didn't do something to change it, fast? I knew for sure stripping was a dead end. I made plenty of money doing what I did. However, I wasn't happy. I wasn't content. My life was becoming more and more dangerous. I decided it was time to give up that lifestyle.

I counted the money I had saved. The total was a little over nineteen thousand. I knew it wouldn't be enough to last me a lifetime, but it would hold me over until I found something better.

Friday night was the night I decided I'd go clean out my locker. Plus I did want to say bye to some of the girls there. I'd kill two birds with one stone.

Friday came quick. I was at the club cleaning my locker. I said my goodbyes to just about every girl except Jackie. Jackie hadn't arrived at work yet. That was starting to worry me. She didn't even know I was quitting. I wanted to be the one to tell her. When I called her house and no one answered I began worrying even more. Jackie would never be this late to work, especially on a Friday. I decided I was going to check up on her.

When I arrived at Jackie's apartment it wasn't hard to tell she was home. Jackie's music was blasting so loud. Soon as I exited the elevator I heard it. I didn't bother knocking on the door. I knew she wouldn't hear me knocking over the loud music anyway. I used the old key I had to her apartment to let myself in.

Once I was inside, I saw two wine glasses and an empty Hennessy bottle on her coffee table that sat next to a piece of half eaten cake. I started walking towards Jackie's bedroom door, but when I heard loud sex noises I stopped.

Not wanting to disturb Jackie, I headed in my old bedroom. I had to laugh at myself for being so naïve. I should've known Jackie was making some type of money on a Friday night. I was just happy she wasn't passed out somewhere from sniffing that stuff.

I searched for a pen and a piece of paper. I wrote Jackie a note so she'd know I stopped by. When I finished writing the note, I placed it on the bed then I happened to glance outside the window. Noticing Jamel's car made me think about the good times we had together. Then I suddenly remembered it was his birthday. I decided it was time for me to be the bigger person and break the ice between us. Calling to wish him a happy birthday was the perfect opportunity.

I pulled out my cell phone and dialed Jamel's number. I listened to the sound of the rings waiting for him to answer but he didn't. Oddly enough every time Jamel's phone rung, I heard the sound of a ringing phone coming from inside of Jackie's bedroom. I knew that had to be a coincidence, to make sure was just a coincidence. I tiptoed over to Jackie's bedroom door then put my ear close to the door so I could hear things clearly over the music. I dialed Jamel's number one more time. To my surprise I received the same results! At that moment I thought I was having a bad nightmare. Just to be safe, I dialed the number again.

When the third result was identical to my first two results, I kicked Jackie's bedroom door wide open. I found Jackie on her knees with Jamel's dick in her mouth! The two of them looked at me like I was a ghost.

Jackie tried to stand on her feet quick as possible. She grabbed a shirt and tried to cover her naked body. Before either one of them could say a word, I raced out of that apartment before I caught a case! Jackie ran after me.

"Mahogany, come back inside. I wanna talk to you," Jackie shouted down the hall. She was smart enough to keep her distance.

"Fuck you Jackie!"

"This is not even that serious. I promise I can explain."

I flipped, "You can explain what, why Jamel's dick was inside your mouth!?"

"Just come inside Mahogany. We can all talk about this."

"Do I look like I have the word 'asshole' written across my forehead? It ain't shit to talk about! Fuck you! Fuck Jamel!" I pressed the button for the elevator. Jackie kept talking.

"Mahogany you taking this shit the wrong way. Jamel is not even your man anymore. I shouldn't even be explaining shit to you, but I'm tryna be nice."

I screamed, "Jackie! I would suggest you shut the fuck up while I'm still calm!"

"Mahogany, you know what? You're too fucking emotional, that's your problem! If you cared that much about who Jamel was fucking, you wouldn't have left him over some dumb shit. You always think everything is supposed to be a fucking fairy tale. Grow up sweetheart! You're living in the real world, and in the real world people fuck!

My bills need to get paid just like everyone else's so don't knock my hustle."

I laughed then pressed the button for the elevator again, "Jackie, when I slap the shit out of you, please don't ask why. That's my fault though. I trusted a snake and got bit by that bitch!"

Jackie grew angry, "You know what? I'm sick and tired of you Mahogany, foreal! You blowing this shit way out of proportion. You didn't even know what to do with your own man. I was the one who taught you everything you knew. I made you the bitch you are today. I let you stay in my apartment when even your own family turned their backs on you! It was me who saved your ass when you took all those pills, me bitch! Remember that! If it was up to Jamel he would've left your ass in the house that day. All he cared about was me sucking his dick again. I was the one who told him we had to stop fucking and call an ambulance and have it sent to ya house! Then I was the one who dragged him to the hospital after you left all those crazy ass messages on his machine. So the next time you wanna think about something, think about that shit bitch 'cause you owe me your life bitch!"

I heard enough. I started running towards Jackie. Jackie started running towards her apartment. When she reached her apartment, Jamel was coming out. She slid pass him into her house. I heard her bedroom door slam.

"I'm calling the police!" Jackie yelled through her bedroom door.

I slapped Jamel then yelled to Jackie, "Call the fucking police, call them! Tell them you're a cokehead bitch! Tell them your mother's a fucking crackhead and her daughter's a hoe! Tell them about your fucking brother on the run! Tell them that shit bitch!"

Jamel grabbed me by my shoulders. He started shaking me, "Calm the fuck down! Ain't no reason for you to be mad right now. You started this shit, remember?"

"Jamel get your fucking hands off me!" I screamed.

"You knew I loved you, but you just said fuck everything and started disrespecting me. You started fucking with a nigga who you knew was my enemy. When you and Pop had y'all little thing going on, I ain't say shit to you! I wasn't mad at you while you was fucking that nigga – my enemy. So I know you can't be mad at me because I fucked your friend. I don't love her. It was strictly a money-sex thing between me and Jackie."

"Fuck you Jamel! Don't try to blame this shit on me! Jackie already told me everything! I already know you've been fucking her since me and you were together. At least when I fucked Pop me and you were completely finished. You're a fucking dog and I hope you burn in hell! I hate you, bastard!"

I begin crying. The cops arrived, both of them headed in me and Jamel's direction.

"What's going on? We're getting a lot of complaints," said one officer.

"Nothing," Jamel replied. Then he continued, "Me and my lady are just going through some problems."

"I'm not your fucking lady!" I screamed.

Jamel tried to calm me down, "Baby, I'm sorry." He looked at the two officers then continued, "She's just a little upset right now."

"I understand she's upset, but you're gonna have to take this in the house. Do you live here?" the officer asked.

"No," Jamel replied. Then he looked at me, "But we're

leaving right now."

Jamel grabbed my hand, "Come on baby."

I snatched my hand away from his, "I don't need your fucking help." I ran toward the stairs. Jamel followed me. The officers didn't move.

When I got downstairs Jamel was right behind me.

"Mahogany, slow down, come with me inside so I could talk to you."

"That must be you and Jackie's favorite line. Y'all trifling asses deserve each other."

"I love you! Do you hear me? I love YOU Mahogany, not her! We can start over."

Jamel wouldn't give up. He kept following me to my car. When I got sick of being followed I turned around.

"Jamel, eat a dick and die!"

"Why you so fucking disrespectful, huh?"

I laughed, "You're the last person who should be speaking about respect!"

"I love you," Jamel kept saying.

"The only person you love is your damn self!" I shouted. I tried to walk away. Jamel grabbed my shirt. I turned around to slap him, he caught my wrist before I had a chance to hit his face.

"Calm down Mahogany!"

"Fuck you!" I spit in Jamel's face.

Jamel slapped me so hard, my face started to sting. Tears started pouring down my face. Jamel didn't say another word to me. He turned then walked away.

Chapter 13

Happily Ever After...or Not

You don't love me. If you loved me you wouldn't stay out until three and four o'clock in the morning...

So what if that was your cousin. You should've been taking care of home...

What is your thirteen year old daughter doing having sex with thirty year old men...?

I flipped through different channels. All of them seemed to air the same thing; talk show after talk show. I pressed the power button on the remote. The television went off.

I walked into the kitchen, opened the refrigerator. There was nothing I wanted to eat inside of it. I closed the door then opened the freezer. My cookies and cream ice cream was just what I needed. I grabbed a spoon then headed to my bedroom.

I sat on my bed eating the ice cream. I turned the television back on. The same things were playing so I turned it back off. I took a look around my room. Everything was beautiful! I had all the material things a girl could ask for and more. However, the price I had to pay was too high.

It's been two months since I caught Jackie and Jamel in their act. If I wouldn't have seen what they were doing that day, I don't think I would've believed it.

The sudden and tragic death of Sunshine still had me shocked. I couldn't believe her life was over just like that. The more I thought about the recent events that took place in my life. The more I wanted to cry, but I wasn't crying. I was sick of crying. The way I saw it, I was all cried out. My cries started turning into sickening laughs just so I wouldn't have to cry anymore. I didn't have a single friend. My family wasn't shit. I didn't have a man or a job. Life was funny to me. Sometimes I'd sit back wondering could this life I'm living be some kind of cruel joke?

Through it all, at least I knew Tiff was still there if I needed her. Thinking about her made me pickup the phone to call her. After dialing her number twice then hanging up every time I heard Aunt Charmaine's voice, I gave up calling her house for the night. I knew if Tiffany wasn't answering the phone chances were she wasn't there. I decided to call Melody's house thinking she was there. When no one answered Melody's phone, I figured Tiff was spending time with one of her dudes.

I put a spoon full of ice cream in my mouth then turned on the radio. Mary J. Blige was singing what I needed to hear.

"Life can be only what you make it...when you're feeling down, you should never fake it..."

I turned the music up then started singing along. Mary always knew the right words to sing. I zoned out as I continued singing with her. When I finished singing, I laid across my bed staring at the ceiling. I was so lonely.

I jumped up when I heard what sounded like someone knocking at my door. When I got to the door no one
was there. Was I bugging or was or was I just that lonely?
I peeked out the window to make sure no one was parked
in front of my house. I didn't see any unfamiliar parked
cars or people walking away from my steps. It was time for
me to get out the house. I walked in my bedroom then
headed for the closet. I pulled down a shoe box from the
top of my closet. When I opened the shoe box I started
counting the money I had left inside of it. I couldn't believe
I only had six thousand one hundred and seventy three
dollars left. How the hell did I run through thirteen thousand dollars in two months? I answered my own question when I looked around my bedroom. Every top
designer name you could imagine was in my closet. My
bed was wrapped in silk sheets. The new big screen television I bought was bigger than me. It didn't take long
for me to realize I gave up my means of making fast
money. However, I didn't give up my habit of spending
money fast. It was time to make some changes.

As I put my shoe box in the closet. I noticed a piece of
paper with a number on it. When I looked closer, the
name next to the number read Mo. Immediately I started
thinking about how nice he was to me. Then I begin feeling bad for leaving the club without saying goodbye to
him. I decided to pick up the phone and give Mo a call. He
treated me so well, the least I could do was say goodbye.
After three rings Mo answered his phone.

"Hello, can I speak to Mo?"

The phone grew silent. I spoke again, "Hello?"

This time Mo spoke. I heard how surprised he was by
the tone of his voice, "Ginger!?"

I smiled, "Yup, it's me. How'd you know my voice?"

"I know your voice anywhere! I can't believed you called I was worried sick about you, where have you been!?"

"Oh Mo you're so sweet, but it's no need to worry. I'm okay. And you can stop calling me Ginger now. I'm no longer into that lifestyle. Call me by my real name either Princess or Mahogany."

Mo became even more excited, "That's fine with me! I think I like Princess better anyway. I am delighted to see you've finally came to your senses and left that place alone. You deserve to be in far greater places than that."

I took a seat on my bed, "Yeah I finally figured it out. That's what I called to let you know. I also wanted to say goodbye."

"Goodbye? You must mean hello! This is the moment I've been waiting for. Life for you my Princess has just begun. You must let me take you out to celebrate."

I laughed. Mo continued, "Is there something funny about what I just said, why are you laughing at me?"

I laughed again, "Don't mind me I'm just laughing 'cause your accent sounds so cute, and you reminded me of my mom when you called me Princess. She was the only who called me Princess."

Mo replied, "Oh I see. Well I'm happy I can make you laugh and remind you of your mom at the same time. But I'm serious about what I said. I'm really hoping you'll give me the honor of taking you out to celebrate."

"I don't think today would be such a good day."

"I don't see why not. There's no time like the present, beside what are you going to do today, did you find a new job yet?"

"No not yet."

"See? There's really no need for you to sit at home on a beautiful day such as today. Let me take you to a restaurant, or a movie, or any place you'd like to go to. You need to get out and enjoy the fresh air, what have you got to lose?"

I took a deep breath, "Mo, I don't know."

"Come on. What am I gonna do, kill you? I've only seen you everyday for the past few months. I miss your company. Be nice, it's my treat. I'll take you anywhere you want to go. Have you ever been to the moon? We can go if you'd like."

I laughed, "Mo, you are funny."

"I'm even lonelier than I am funny. Princess, let me be your prince tonight. Do I have to keep begging because I will?"

I took another deep breath then paused. Finally I answered, "Fine I'll let you take me out. But make sure you keep our business our business. I don't want any of those people in the club to know what I do on my own private time."

Mo was ecstatic as he spoke, "That's not a problem at all! In fact I'm not even going to step another foot inside of that club. You were my reason for going there, now that my Princess is gone so am I!"

"Mo why are you so sweet to me, what makes me so worthy?"

"Why not? You're beautiful, smart, ambitious, and I can tell you're bound to go places in life. I find those qualities very sexy in a woman. We'll have plenty of time to discuss what I like about you when I pick you up. Give me your address and I'll be there whenever you'd like."

"Six o'clock should be good for me, but there's no need for you to pick me up. I'll meet you in Queens at Uno's restaurant on seventy-first and continental, do you know where that is?"

"Yes I'm familiar with that area. That's an Italian restaurant. Are you sure you want to meet me there? I'd rather pick you up. I'm offering door to door service and it's free, it doesn't get any better than that."

I replied, "I appreciate the gesture but I'd much rather meet you. Let me get off this phone right now so I can get ready for our celebration tonight. I'll give you a call when I'm ready."

I hung up the phone then smiled. I was finally getting out the house. I almost forgot what dating felt like. I ran to my closet searching for something to wear.

• • •

When I arrived at Uno's Mo was already there. He noticed me then slowly began walking in my direction. Mo handed me a single white rose then placed a kiss on my cheek. I smiled as I smelled the rose.

"Thank you Mo. You are so sweet."

Mo smiled, "I try." He extended his hand then continued, "Can I have the privilege of escorting you to our table."

I grabbed Mo's hand, "I don't see why not."

We walked to our table. Mo pulled out my chair. He was the perfect gentlemen all night. The food was great, but our conversation was even better.

Once we were finished eating we spent over an hour outside of the restaurant just talking. I was having such a good time with Mo. He seemed genuinely happy with me.

Both of us opened up to one another more than we usually did at the club. Maybe it was the change of environment. Whatever the case may be, I was having fun! That was something I haven't done in a long time.

Talking to Mo made me feel like I was talking to my best friend. I felt free when I summed up how trifling my family was in as little words as possible. I also shared with him my dreams then explained how they were destroyed. Mo listened to me without interrupting. That meant a lot to me. When I finished talking, Mo started telling me a little more about himself.

I learned Mo suffered as much headache and heartbreak as I did. I also learned he was in the process of opening a shopping mall. Plus he was getting a house built from the ground up. Without a doubt I knew I was speaking to a man who had money. Suddenly I felt more attracted to him. I didn't know if the attraction came from getting to know him better or getting to know he had more money than I thought he did. I didn't bother asking what line of work he was in. It was clear to me whatever his occupation was he was the boss. That was all I needed to know. I decided that this wouldn't be my last time going out with Mo.

When our night was over I headed to my car. Shockingly Mo insisted on dropping me off home even though he knew I drove my own car. I was flattered, but I still turned him down. All Mo kept talking about was my safety. He said he felt obligated to make sure I got home safe. After I assured Mo not to worry then turned him down for the last time, he finally stopped asking. Mo walked to the nearest corner then began flagging a taxi. Shocked and confused I called out to him. He turned around.

"Yes my Princess?"

I frowned, "Where is your car?"

Mo laughed, "I cannot drive very well. Therefore I use taxis as my means of transportation."

Still confused I spoke, "Well, how were you going to drop me home?"

Mo smiled, "The same way I get to and from places. I would've just had the taxi drop you off first. I told you I don't care about the money. It's your safety I worry about."

I couldn't help but smile, "Mo, you are so sweet, I can't say that enough. Instead of asking to drop me home I should be dropping you off." I paused then continued, "Come on, I'm dropping you off."

Mo put his hands up, "No, that won't be necessary. Why don't you go home and get a good night sleep? I'm a strong man. I can take care of myself."

"Mo, don't be ridiculous! Why would you take a taxi and I'm right here? Come on, let's go. I don't mind, really."

Mo shook his head, "But I do mind. The problem is I live very far. I wouldn't take you out of your way like that."

I sucked my teeth, "It can't be that far. How do you know we don't live in the same neighborhood?"

Mo laughed, "I doubt it. I live very, very far."

I put my hand on my hip, "Try me?"

Mo put his head down then looked up, "Okay. You ever heard of the Hamptons?"

"You don't live in the Hamptons!" I shot back.

"I do," Mo replied.

I was shocked! Without a doubt this Indian motherfucker that stood in front of me was one rich bitch. Little did he know; he was stuck with me. I promised myself I wouldn't let this one get away. On the inside I was jumping up and down screaming "JACKPOT!" on the outside I maintained my cool as I continued, "Mo, I had no idea. Why didn't you tell me you lived so far? I would've never asked you to travel all this way, especially since you're not driving."

Mo smiled, "Don't worry about it. I would've traveled to the end of the earth for you. You really don't know how much you're worth to me, do you?"

"Cut it out Mo. I'm just me. Next time we can meet some place like the city. I know it's still out of you're way but at least it's not that much out of your way, plus there's a lot more to do out there. Why do you spend so much time out here anyway?"

"This is where I handle most of my business so I have to spend a lot of time here."

I smiled, "I see. Is that why you're getting a house built out here in Queens? I know you'll spend far less time traveling than you do now."

Mo kissed my forehead, "You're so smart!" he smiled then continued, "When my house is finished being built, I'll spend a lot more time out here in Queens, so you better get use to me," he joked.

"I don't mind at all, but I don't want to hold you up. You have a long ride ahead of you so you better get going." I begin walking away. Mo blew me a kiss, "Please call to let me know you're home safe."

"I sure will," I replied.

I got in my car then headed home. I was pleased with the evening I spent with Mo. As I drove home I thought about how much of a good person he was. I thought about his money even more than I thought about him. I know it was wrong to think that way, but I couldn't help it.

About a block away from my house, I sat at a stop light. In the middle of thinking deep, long and hard while waiting for the light to change, I was rear ended. Shocked from the impact I put my car in park. I grabbed my cell phone then hopped out. My eyes were focused on nothing but the back of my car. I wanted to see exactly how much damage was done. After looking at my car I looked at the car I was hit by. An older lady was stumbling out of the driver's seat saying, "Sorry honey, are you okay?"

Without a doubt, I knew this woman was drunk. Just as I was about to call the police, I realized the lady who hit my car was my landlord. She saw me getting ready to dial the number then yelled.

"Wait! Wait! Don't call the authorities." She walked closer toward me then continued, "Take my phone number and we can settle this our..." she stopped mid sentence realizing exactly who I was. A sudden calmness overcame her as she continued, "Mahogany, sweetheart, thank God it's you!"

I put my hand on my hip then shook my head, "Are you okay Ms. Medina?"

She replied, "I'm okay now. I was ready to have a heart attack thinking you were someone else."

"What happened Ms. Medina, you didn't see my car in front of you?" I asked. Both of us directed our attention to the rear of my car. I spoke first.

"Now look at both of our cars," I pointed then continued, "your head light is out. My tail light is out, and my rear bumper is falling off."

A line of cars behind us started beeping their horns. I

sucked my teeth then put my hands up.

"Go around us. Can't y'all see it's a fucking accident!?"

The cars proceeded to go around us. One guy stuck his head out the window and yelled, "Pull over instead of staying in the middle of the street stopping traffic asshole!" I put my middle finger in the air. He kept going. Ms. Medina looked like she was lost and confused at the same time. Her drunken ass walked over to my car then tried to push my tail light back in place. I stopped her.

"What are you doing?"

Her drunk eyes looked up at me. She shook her head then put her hand over her mouth.

I sighed, "I'ma need to take my car to the shop. It's gon' cost money to get it fixed you know?"

"I know, don't worry about it. Go get an estimate and have it ready for me this week."

"I guess I better hold on to my rent money until we get that estimate, huh?"

Ms. Medina paused. I raised my eyebrow, "Hello?"

"Yeah, hold on to the rent money. Whatever the estimate is we'll just deduct it from that money. Long as we keep the police out of it. I do not need my insurance going up again."

I cracked a smile, "I'm gonna need a paint job too."

I knew she couldn't argue with me. She knew she couldn't either. She replied, "Whatever just give me the estimate. I might as well turn back around now. I was on my way to see you about the rent money, but I guess I can wait."

"I guess you can," I replied. Then I continued, "I'll have the estimate ready by tomorrow."

Ms. Medina stumbled back to her car. "Are you sure

you can drive?" I asked.

She waved her hand, "Don't worry about me. I'll see you tomorrow."

I got in my car then drove off. The minute I arrived inside my house, I kicked of my shoes then headed to the bathroom. I just wanted to take a shower and relax. By the time I cleansed my body then rubbed it down with cocoa butter I was so sleepy. I headed for my bed then fell asleep.

• • •

The next morning I was up bright and early. I wanted to get an estimate for my car as soon as possible. I also wanted to call Mo since I didn't call him when I got in last night. He was pleased to hear from me as usual. Our conversation was going just fine until Mo said something to disturb me. I told him I was taking my car to the shop then he replied.

"Why didn't you call the cops, this way you wouldn't have had to take your car to a shop today?"

Shocked and alarmed I replied, "Excuse me?"

Mo paused. I was silent then Mo continued, "Nothing, I'm sorry about what I said."

Mo's answer didn't sit well with me. I replied, "No let's talk about exactly what you said! How do you know I didn't call the cops last night, how do you even know I was in an accident? All I said was I had to take my car to the shop."

Mo tried to come clean, "Princess I'm sorry I really didn't mean to…" I cut him off.

"Princess my ass! What the fuck are you doing following me!? I try to be nice and give ya sorry ass a chance to take me out and you follow me home! What the fuck is that about!?"

Mo insisted on justifying his actions, "I can explain...remember when..." I cut him off again.

"Explain what!? That you're a fucking stalker!? There is no explaining that shit! Fuck you Mo and stay the fuck away from me!"

I slammed the phone hard as I could in his ear. I crossed my arms as I stared at the phone for about two minutes. I couldn't believe Mo followed me home!

The next two weeks of my life was like a soap opera. I didn't see or speak to Mo. I avoided him altogether. However, one thing I couldn't stop was the roses he sent me everyday.

To be honest, I was really confused about what type of person Mo was. At first I thought he was normal as they come, but following me home was some abnormal shit. Then I said to myself, I must be dealing with some deranged killer or something. Suddenly, common sense kicked in. I knew he wasn't a killer or something like that because if he wanted me dead, he would've killed me already. He knew who I was and he even knew where I lived. Why didn't he do something to me if he wanted to already? The more I questioned myself, the more I wanted answers to my questions.

By the third week Mo realized the roses weren't enough to get my attention. He stopped having them delivered to my house then starting bringing them himself. I continued ignoring him until one day he stood outside in the rain begging for my forgiveness. I decided he had to be dumb, desperate or in-love. I ran downstairs to hear what he had to say. Mo was making a fool of himself yelling how sorry he was at the top of his lungs. I didn't like all the attention he was bringing to me or my place of residence. When Mo saw me standing in my doorway he became silent. I spoke.

"Come in," I waved my hand then continued, "let's hear what the fuck you gotta say, and let me let you know right now this shit better be good!"

Mo entered my apartment dripping wet. His clothes were stuck to his body. The roses he held in his hands were losing petals by the seconds. He looked like a sad lost puppy. I slammed my door then crossed my arms. I looked at Mo then spit, "I'm listening."

Mo looked at me then down towards the floor. He slowly got on his knees as he stood before me and spoke.

"First I would like to say sorry. Words cannot do justice to explain how truly sorry I am, but trust me I'm really, really, really sorry Princess."

I sucked my teeth, "I know that part so let's hear what else ya sorry, sorry, really, really sorry ass has to say."

Mo covered his face with his hands as he stayed on his knees whining, "Princess you're right I deserve that but, let me explain my actions?"

"Like I said, I'm listening," I shot back.

Mo started crying as he spoke, "A long time ago I loved a young lady. I loved her with all my heart. I gave her whatever her heart desired and much, much more. Unfortunately she did the same things to me that you are doing right now..."

I cut Mo off, "The same things I'm doing? I ain't do..."

Mo interrupted me before I could finish my statement, "Princess please don't cut me off, let me finish. Like I was saying, I loved this young lady and I gave her the world. But for some reason she just didn't feel the need to give me her phone number or address, just like you. Suddenly one day she just disappeared. Even today, I still do not know what happened. I don't know if something really terrible has happened to her, or whether she's dead or alive. Maybe she could've just got sick and tired of me, but I will never know." Mo sighed, wiped his eyes then continued, "My point is, I didn't want you to vanish from my life like that young lady did. This is why I followed you home that night. I just wanted to make sure you got home safely. And if there was ever a day you decided you didn't wanna keep in contact with me I would understand one hundred percent and I'll respect your decision, but all I ever want if that day was to ever come, is the peace of mind of knowing you're still alive and okay. I can deal with you leaving me alone, I can't deal with wondering if you're okay like I've dealt with wondering about that other lady's well being over the years. I would've never forgiven myself if I let something bad happen to you, or let you walk out of my life without having some kind of way to get in contact with you. So if you still would like to remain friends the choice is all yours. Just beware that I really care for you and need you more than you know."

I looked at Mo's sorry ass. In my mind I was saying *fuck you*! But in my heart I was saying *we're all humans and we all make mistakes. Give him another chance. Plus he has money, lots of it, remember*? After silently battling my heart and my mind, the winner of the two prevailed. I put my hand on my hip then spoke.

"First of all get up off ya knees!"

Mo looked at me, but he remained on his knees. Then he spoke, "I can't do that, not until I know what choice you're gonna make."

I looked at Mo like he just lost his mind. I shook my head then took a deep breath as I spoke to him, "Look under any other circumstances I would've said fuck you and everything you stand for!"

Mo put his head down looking defeated. I continued, "However, I feel you're being sincere. And I guess you can't be that much of a nut 'cause if you wanted to do something to me, by now you would've already done it. I also feel like our good times together out weighs our bad. With that said, I guess we can be friends. But in the future don't ever let me catch you slipping because if I do then that'll be ya ass and I mean that shit!"

Mo jumped to his feet with a smile on his face. "Princess, thank you! Thank you so much! That was just the answer I was looking for. I know now if I want to make you mine, I have to go about doing things differently. I would like to make sure I never mess up with you again, or let you out of my life, so... marry me!" Mo excited said.

I looked at Mo then laughed, "I know you gotta be joking, right?"

"Princess, this is no joke. I want you to marry me!" Mo got back on his knees. He pulled a red velvet box out of his pocket. Inside the box sat a three karat, princess cut engagement ring. He continued, "Marry me Princess!"

I was in total disbelief. I put one hand over my chest, "What?" was the only word that came out of my mouth.

Mo repeated himself, "Marry me, I wanna make sure we're always together."

I looked at Mo, "But you don't even..."

Mo cut me off, "I know I don't know you as well as I'd like to, but I feel like I know you enough. I also know you're not in love with me, but I believe time will fix that. Once you get to know me better you'll love me unconditionally and it won't be because you're being forced to. Instead, it will be by your own free will. So Princess, I'm ready to be your Prince if you'd just let me, so what do you say?"

I stood there shocked. It was hard to believe what he was asking me to do. I kept looking at the ring, it was beautiful. Then I looked at Mo. I took a deep breath then closed my eyes. I answered his question.

"Yes, I will marry you."

I was shocked by my own answer, so was Mo. His face lit up, "Did you say yes?" he questioned.

"Yes I did Mo, now give me the ring!" a tear fell out of my eye. Mo stood to his feet. He grabbed my left hand then slipped the ring on my finger. We hugged each other.

I looked at Mo then pushed him away from me, "We have to get you out of those wet clothes."

We both laughed. Mo spoke, "We have to celebrate!"

Later that night, me and Mo made love for the first time.

• • •

The next morning I got out of bed early to make me and Mo a nice breakfast. Mo was still sleeping when I started cooking. I knew he couldn't be tired from making love last night because I did most of the work between those sheets. Nevertheless, I was feeling like a brand new woman. I went from being on my last dollar to becoming the wife of a rich man. Suddenly I became excited about marrying Mo. Maybe my excitement was for all the wrong reasons, but so what! I finally got my Trump card after all.

When we finished eating breakfast we showered and

got dressed. Mo said we needed to take a ride, he told me he had a surprise for me. When we got to our destination it was a building in the process of being built. Before Mo got out of the car he looked at me and spoke.

"This is the mall I was telling you about. I wanted you to see it before it was complete. You must not tell anyone this mall belongs to us because people will get jealous and try to milk us for all they can." Rubbing my hand he continued, "So this is our little secret for now."

I sat in the drivers' seat smiling from ear to ear. *Money, money and more money* were the only words running through my mind. Mo kissed my cheek then exited the car. I saw him walk directly over to the only man on the construction site wearing a suit, he was a white guy. They exchanged a few words. I smiled to myself thinking about how life would be from now on.

I sat back in my seat as I started thinking about how deceiving looks could be. Here Mo was, looking like a plain, broke average guy. But in reality he was raking in the doe. I remember being told he had money, but I would've never imagined he had this much. Judging by his appearance, the average person would've never been able to tell he was holding. My thoughts were distracted when Mo came back to the car. It felt like I was wearing a permanent smile. I looked at Mo.

"Is everything okay?" I asked.

"Yeah everything is fine. We have one more stop to make. Would you like me to drive or should I just give you the directions?"

I raised one eyebrow, "I thought you couldn't drive?"

Mo laughed, "I could drive. I just don't have a drivers' license yet."

I frowned, "I could've sworn I heard different," I replied. I waved my hand then continued, "Anyway, where are we going?"

Mo gave me the directions to our destination. Upon arriving there I could've died. The house that was being built was so big and beautiful.

Mo noticed how happy I was. "Do you like it?" he asked.

"Like it?" I replied then continued, "I love it! When will it be finished?"

"It should be finished in a few months. Then it will be all yours to decorate just the way you like it."

I reached over to give Mo a giant hug, "You must've fell from heaven!" I excitedly stated.

"My goal is to make you happy. I'm glad I'm succeeding."

"So am I!" I smiled.

"Mo turned to face me, "Can I be honest with you?" he asked.

"I don't see why not." I answered.

"At first I wasn't gonna show you this until after we were officially married. However, I think you deserve to know now. After all one day it will be all yours."

All I could do was cry. I looked at Mo then spoke, "Mo, thank you so much for everything! I'm sorry about…"

Mo cut me off, "Princess, don't even fix your lips to say that. I understand what you might've thought."

I didn't say another word to Mo. All I did was give him a giant hug.

Mo grabbed my chin then looked me directly in my eyes. I listened as he spoke softly, "Princess, theirs one more thing I want to cover. This is about our marriage. I really don't have much family here, and I remember what you told me about your family. Plus I'm going to be very busy in a few months so I was wondering..."

I cut Mo off, "Yes! Yes Mo, I will marry you as soon as possible!"

Mo smiled, "How did you know what I was getting ready to ask?"

I smiled, "I know everything!" we hugged each other. What I really wanted to say was *I need your money to become my money as soon as possible*. I already had plans about things I'd buy and places I'd go. It was getting ready to be a beautiful day. My plans were figured out.

Two weeks later me and Mo went down to the justice of the peace, where we officially became husband and wife.

• • •

Several months passed and I grew happier with each day. Mo moved into my duplex while we waited for our house to finish being built. Mo became frustrated about how long the house was taking to finish. On top of that, the house in the Hamptons was being renovated. So my place was really the only other option we had for the time being. I didn't mind the delay. I knew in time everything would be all good.

Meanwhile, Mo still checked on the progress of the mall and the house with every passing day. It seemed like the guy who was always at the construction site where the house was being built always had a slight attitude. I didn't hear the words being exchanged between him and Mo. I stayed in the car all the time. And even though that guy always waved to me, it was clear to see he had an attitude judging from his body language.

After awhile I stopped going with Mo to the sites. I was becoming just as frustrated as he was. Another strange thing happened after awhile. I was really starting to love Mo for who he was instead of how much money he had. Mo didn't pressure me for sex, he was very understanding and I felt at peace around him. At this point in our marriage I could really say I was in-love with him, it was a great feeling.

To top things off Mo encouraged me to pursue my dream of becoming a psychiatrist, a dream I let die within me. Without a doubt Mo was paying for my education and I was heading back to school. I was floating on cloud nine. My dream was coming true after all. It just took a little time and patience.

The day finally came when we knew the exact date the mall would be ready and so would the house. We waited two long years before getting this date. I didn't know who was happier; me or Mo. Whatever the case maybe, in three weeks we would be in our new home. The mall would be finished and I would register for school. Before things became overwhelming, Mo surprised me with a vacation to Jamaica so I could relax. I was speechless when he handed me the ticket. I hugged him so tight.

"Baby, when are we leaving!?" I asked.

Mo grabbed my waist, "Sweetheart I'm not going on this trip. This is just so you could relax and release some stress before you come back. We want you to be nice and relaxed when you start school."

"But what about you?" I questioned.

"I'll be alright," Mo replied then continued, "I have a

lot of things to take care of here. Doesn't somebody want to move into their new home soon as they get back from Jamaica?" Mo kissed my cheek and rubbed my shoulders.

"Oh, baby. You're so good to me!" I replied.

"You deserve the best and much more."

"I still want you to come with me."

Mo shook his head, "Next time I will. I promise. Don't you want to come home to a big surprise?"

I made a baby face then wrapped my arms around Mo, "I guess you're right. I want you to be a good boy while I'm gone. Do you think you can do that?"

Mo laughed, "You are something else, you know that?"

I answered Mo with a smile and a kiss. He grabbed the newspaper then headed to the living-room. I was so excited about my vacation to Jamaica I started packing my things. When my flight left next week I wouldn't have to worry about doing anything but heading to the airport. Life was good...

• • •

When I arrived in Jamaica, I couldn't think of a better place for a vacation. Everything was beautiful! I didn't bother wearing anything on my feet as I walked from my room to the crystal, clear, blue water on the island. As my feet touched the sand I felt like I was in heaven. I dropped the beach towel I had wrapped around my waist. My leopard print bikini screamed sexy against my body. The sun shined down on me as I headed to the water. I felt like I was sitting on top of the world.

Later that evening I ate some of the best food I ever tasted. The people in the resort I stayed in were so friendly. Everything was so clean and perfect. I picked up so many souvenirs I had to buy another suitcase. Most of the souvenirs I picked up were for Mo. He deserved every single one plus more. I made a promise to myself that me and Mo would come back to Jamaica, together. I imagined how beautiful that vacation was gonna be.

A week passed, it was time for me to go home. I desperately wanted to stay in Jamaica. However, I knew home was where I needed to be. I had so many things to look forward to. Me and Mo were finally moving into our new home. The mall would be open for shoppers to shop. Plus I was getting ready to start school after not being able to for so long.

My flight landed on time. I was able to get a taxi without putting up a fight. Plus I was heading to my home in Rosedale for the last time. I couldn't wait to see Mo so I could share with him the wonderful vacation I had. Upon arriving at my home, I gave the taxi driver fifty dollars and told him to keep the change.

My car was parked in the driveway. I looked up at my windows. The house looked very dark. Before I walked in the door I knew Mo wasn't home. When I arrived inside the house I dropped my luggage then turned on the lights. To my surprise the entire house was empty. An uneasy feeling overcame me as I tried to recall Mo ever saying we were putting the furniture from my duplex into our new home. I called Mo's name.

"Mo, honey? Are you home?"

Mo didn't answer. The only thing I did hear was my own echo. I took a look around the house. Even the mirrors on the wall were gone. Something just didn't feel right. I headed upstairs to the bedroom. Everything in my entire room was also gone. I headed to my closet. My clothes and shoes were gone. I checked my jewelry box. My jewels were gone. A fit of panic overcame me. I screamed like a madwoman.

"Mo! Where are you!? If this is some type of surprise, I don't like it! If this is some type of joke, it isn't funny! Answer me if you hear me! Mo!"

I ran downstairs screaming Mo's name. Then for I split second I thought I figured it out. We had been robbed! Someone burglarized all of our things, mines and Mo's! I ran in the kitchen to get the phone so I could call the police. Before I had a chance to dial the number, I came across a note tapped to the refrigerator. In Mo's handwriting the note read:

YOU LITTLE SLUT AMERICAN BITCH! HOW COULD YOU POSSIBLY THINK I WAS GONNA SPEND THE REST OF MY LIFE WITH YOU!? YOU ARE PURE TRASH! DID YOU REALLY THINK I COULD LOVE SOMEONE I MET AT A HOE CLUB FOR HOES!? THE ONLY THING I LIKED ABOUT YOU WAS HOW STUPID AND NAÏVE YOU WERE, THAT'S IT! YOU AMERICAN GIRLS WILL DO ANYTHING FOR A DOLLAR BECAUSE YOU ARE THE SCUM OF THE FUCKING EARTH! HOW COULD YOU MARRY A MAN YOU DIDN'T EVEN KNOW? I HAD TO BATHE MYSELF THOUROLY EACH TIME I LAID DOWN WITH YOU! YOU ARE A WHORE AND YOU WILL ALWAYS BE A BLACK, NASTY, AMERICAN WHORE! BY ALL MEANS YOU ARE BENEATH ME! THANKS FOR THE CITIZENSHIP THOUGH. LIKE I SAID THE DAY I ASKED YOU TO MARRY ME; THE LAST GIRL WHO WAS STUPID ENOUGH

TO ALMOST MARRY ME GOT AWAY. I WASN'T GOING TO LET THAT HAPPEN AGAIN! OOPS, DID I LEAVE THAT PART OUT!? HA, HA, HA! OH WELL, YOU WERE STUPID ENOUGH TO BELIEVE ME. THAT'S ON YOU! SO, YEAH, THAT'S THE REAL REASON I FOLLOWED YOU HOME THAT DAY. MY PLAN WORKED LIKE A CHARM. THERE SHOULD BE MORE STUPID GIRLS LIKE YOU TO BE USED! I SEE WHY YOU'RE FAMILY LEFT YOU. YOU ARE NOTHING BUT A SLUT! OH, AND DON'T WORRY ABOUT THE MONEY I'VE SPENT ON YOU. I'VE CREATED A PLAN TO SELL ALL YOUR BELONG-INGS TO MAKE SURE I GET EVERY PENNY BACK, SO THE JOKE'S REALLY ON YOU!

I couldn't believe my fucking eyes! I read the note three more times before I realized I wasn't dreaming! Tears and rage overcame me. I began kicking the walls. Shortly after I cried and kicked the walls I began to curse out loud! Suddenly, a light bulb went off in my head.

Mo thought he was playing me, but he really played his motherfucking self! I would show him in this country called America, the wife gets half of everything he owns – I'd show him the American way alright!

I hopped in my car then begin heading to the place where Mo got the house built. The traffic signs or stop-lights wasn't enough to slow me down. I jetted through all of them!

I was screaming Mo's name before I got to the first step of the house. I saw someone peek out the window, but I wasn't sure who it was. I rang the doorbell nonstop. A red headed white lady opened the door with a smile on her face. The moment she saw how deranged I looked, her smile faded.

"Hi, may I help you?" she asked.

With puffy eyes and a screw face I replied, "You motherfucking right you can! Where's Mo!?"

The lady seemed petrified. She replied, "Who?"

I threw my hands in the air, "Oh, now you don't know!? I'm talking about Mo! As in *Mo-motherfucking-hommad!* Can you understand me now bitch!? Go get Mo! Tell him his wife is outside! I'll be right here waiting! Go get him!" I screamed.

The lady tried to close the door, but I stopped it from closing with my foot.

"Do I look like I'm in the mood to play games with you bitch!? Go get Mo and leave this motherfucking door open!" I demanded.

The red headed woman wasn't able to hide her fear. She replied, "I'm afraid you have the wrong house. If you continue to use such obscene gestures on my property I'm going to have you escorted away from my here in handcuffs."

Before I could respond I heard a man's voice, "Honey is everything alright?" he asked.

"No, everything is not alright. There is some crazy person at the door asking for someone named Mo."

"Bitch, you ain't see crazy!" I screamed. The man rushed to the door. He was drying his wet hair with a towel. Instantly I remembered where I knew him from! He was the same man in the suit Mo stopped and talked to every time I was in the car with him. It was the same guy I saw every time we went by the site when the house was being built. I directed all of my attention to him then screamed!

"He knows me! Now where's Mo?"

Looking confused the man replied, "You're right I do know you, but who is Mo and why are you looking for him at my house?"

I frowned, "Your house!? I think not! You saw me and Mo all the time now you don't know who Mo is?"

The man snapped his fingers then replied, "Oh you must be talking about that guy who stopped by the site so often."

I replied with an even nastier, sarcastic attitude, "Yeah un-huh that guy! Suddenly you know who I'm talking about, right?"

The man laughed, "Of course I know who you're talking about. He came by the site almost everyday asking for a job. He said he admired watching my house getting built. He's such a nice guy is he okay, did something happen to him?"

"What did you just say?" I slowly asked. The man's mouth was moving but I didn't hear the words coming out of his mouth. I was beginning to feel like a real asshole! It didn't take long for me to realize Mo played the shit out of me! His plan was even more elaborate than I gave him credit for. He set me up from day one! I walked away from the house feeling like the lowest of the low. The only thing that kept replaying in my head was Mo's voice saying *you deserve to be somebody's wife, somebody's queen. Why are you working at a place like this?* The entire thing was a set up! Mo was one slick motherfucker! It wasn't hard to tell, if the house wasn't his then the mall wasn't either. I headed back to my empty home.

I laid on the cold floor crying as I begin to put everything together. It all started to make perfect sense. I remembered immigration coming to my house to make sure our marriage was really legit. I remembered Jackie saying he came to the club every night and all he seemed to do was observe different girls. I remembered his cheap clothes and his house in the Hamptons that I never saw because according to him it was getting "renovated." It didn't take long for me to realize he probably didn't have a house in the Hamptons either! He was a bum! That's why he lived with me! I couldn't believe I was so stupid! The more I thought about it, the more sense everything started to make! I remembered it only took two years for an illegal alien to become a citizen in the United States after they were married to an American citizen whether they were divorced or not. The only thing I wondered was how he got all the money to put the entire plan in action!? This motherfucker really had me fooled into thinking he was a rich man! I got fucking played!

I was back at square one. I didn't have money, a job, or a man. School was also out of the picture once again. I didn't have shit! Stripping wasn't even an option. It wasn't the fact that I couldn't go back. I didn't wanna go back. I realized I was better than that. I was worth more than dancing on some stage for money. The bottom line was, I was fucked up and I needed money fast! This time I'd learn to depend on myself. I vowed to never let a nigga have this much control over my life or my money again. This time I would be the boss. I would be the shot caller. I would be in control of my own destiny. This time it was my time to depend on me. I promised to never let anyone take what's mine's from me. It was time for my own independence without having to shake my ass to get it!

Chapter 14

Gotta Get A Hustle...

BANG! BANG! BANG! Was the only sound that could be heard inside of my apartment. I sat on the living-room floor, leaned against the wall trying not to make a sound. Without a doubt, I knew it was my landlord banging on my door like that.

It turned out I owed her more money than I thought I did. All the while I thought Mo was taking care of business by paying the rent. I later learned he stopped paying the rent two months prior to his dramatic departure. I was in deep shit! My landlord began to yell.

"Mahogany! I know you're in there! I see your car parked outside so you may as well stop hiding!" I didn't say a word as my landlord continued, "Okay, you wanna play games, huh? Well, you picked the wrong one to play with. I'm giving you until tomorrow night to have all of my money! If you don't have every single penny, you might as well be on your way 'cause the next time I'm coming to this door it'll be with the po-lice!"

After about two minutes of complete silence, I began making my way up the stairs. Just when I thought the coast was clear, my landlord started banging and yelling all over again.

"Aha! I knew your little ass was in there! Open the fucking door, I hear you moving!" I stopped moving as panic overcame me. My knees started feeling weak. My landlord carried on.

"You think you're slick by putting new locks on the door, but you ain't slick! I'm still gon' get in. Watch! You can't hide forever!" She began twisting the knob. "Open up!" she demanded. I didn't care if she heard my movements or not anymore. I ran up the stairs fast as possible. I walked into my empty bedroom then slammed the door shut! Inside of my bedroom is where I remained hostage in my own home until my landlord finally left. I took a deep breath, looked out the window to make sure the coast was clear. After confirming my landlord was gone, I boated to my car. I knew exactly where I was heading.

• • •

When I pulled up in Forty Projects it looked like a ghost town. The rain was coming down hard, but even that wasn't an excuse for the hood to look as deserted as it did. I hadn't been to my old stomping grounds in quit some time, but everything still looked the same.

I parked my recently uninsured car, *which I shouldn't have been driving.* Too lazy to pop my trunk and get my umbrella, I used my jacket to cover my head. I ran inside the building trying to dodge the rain drops.

Upon entering the building I ran into a few of the local hustlers' I was looking for. They were all posted up inside the building. That explained why the outside looked deserted. Looking past the ones who couldn't do anything for me, my eyes landed on the one who I knew could help me; his name was Jo-Jo. The smell of weed was in the air. I removed my jacket from on top of my head. I smiled and greeted everyone with a head nod and a "what's up?" Jo-Jo was the only one I walked directly up to.

"What's up Jo-Jo?" I smiled.

Jo-Jo licked his lips then grabbed his dick, "What's up pretty? Where you been hiding, wit ya fine ass?"

Laughing, I bit my lip and replied, "You know me, I gotta stay low and try to get that paper."

"Is that right?" Jo-Jo replied. The look on his face spelled, *sucker!* I knew he was open off of me. I laughed to myself thinking about how easy this would be.

I replied, "That's damn right, I'm about my paper from dusk 'til dawn, 'cause if it ain't about making a dollar then it don't make sense."

"I hear that," said one of the other hustlers' while blowing purple haze smoke out of his nostrils.

Trying to capitalize off of the opportunity as it presented itself, I started to put my plan into action, "Jo-Jo can I speak to you alone for a minute?" I asked.

Everyone in the lobby looked surprised, especially Jo-Jo. He pointed to himself, "You wanna speak to me?" he asked like he couldn't believe it.

"Yeah, just for a minute."

Jo-Jo took three rushed puffs of the weed another hustler just passed him. He inhaled the trees' then spoke, "Yeah, we could talk. We could definitely do that." he smiled.

I started walking towards the front door. I wanted to sit in my car and speak to Jo-Jo. He saw me walking then yelled.

"Pretty, where you going? We can talk right in here,

take a ride with me."

Looking back I saw Jo-Jo pressing the elevator button. His head was tilting towards the elevator. I got the picture. I walked over to Jo-Jo, he opened the elevator door. Inside the pissy elevator, Jo-Jo pressed the number seven. He kept looking at me, while licking his lips. The elevator stopped on seven, we exited.

"Where we going?" I asked Jo-Jo.

Jo-Jo headed towards the staircase, "Right here," he pointed. I followed him into the staircase. He took a seat on the steps as he spoke.

"What's up? What you wanna talk about?"

I looked at the bottom of my shoe. I wanted to make sure I didn't step in any piss that was on the elevator floor. I was good. I replied, "You know what I wanna talk about, big business baby!"

Raising his thick, rich eyebrows he replied, "Big business?"

Moving closer I smiled then replied, "That's right, business."

Laughing, he grabbed me by my waist and pulled me closer to him. I was so close that I could smell the weed on his breath, as well as the weed on his clothes. Standing directly in between his legs he asked, "What big *business* do you need to talk about?"

I stepped away from him then started talking, "You know what business I need to talk about! Must I spell it out for you?"

Like a ton of bricks, everything I was talking about hit Jo-Jo at the same time. He shook his head. "Oooooh! I don't think you tryna roll like that!"

"Says who?" I demanded to know.

Jo-Jo's big pretty eyes became bigger. He replied, "Well, listen if you talking 'bout what I think you talking 'bout, maybe you need to slow down and fall back. This drug game ain't for play, play. This is some serious shit. Besides times can't be that hard. You a female so I know a nigga gon' take care of ya fine ass regardless. 'Cause this shit ain't no life for a chick, trust me. Only if you knew how lucky you were you'd look at things different. Everyday in this game niggaz is getting one way tickets to the pen, getting merked out, or just tryna get out. This ain't a walk in the park sweetheart."

I became defensive, "Jo-Jo I ain't no dummy! I know what goes on in the game, my pops was a hustler, remember? I ain't no snitch, I ain't afraid to hold no heat and I ain't a stupid bitch. You talking 'bout the game like it's the worse thing in the world, yet you're still a part of it so it can't be that bad."

Jo-Jo laughed with a deep seriousness in his tone then replied, "Listen sweetheart, this life I live is not by choice. I didn't choose the game, the game chose me! I wouldn't wish this life on anybody. You can't get caught slipping in this game not even for one second, 'cause if you do you lose! You too pretty, you ain't ready for this shit."

"How you know what I'm *not* ready for?" I spit.

Jo-Jo stood to his feet. He replied, "Cause you ain't!" he walked closer to me then continued, "You just a little goldfish ready to jump in a pool full of sharks, they'll eat you alive before you even see them coming! I don't have niggaz out here selling candy, crack, or weed. I fucks wit *that boy*, dope! That pure, white, get-a-nigga-killed-shit! Do you understand what I'm saying? Niggaz will kill you for ya stamp! This shit ain't a game it's foreal! It's more to it than guns and snitches and glitter and gold. You gotta be build for this and know how to stay on ya toes at all times! What you gon' do when ya own man turns state witness on you!? What you gon' do when niggaz is coming for you and ya own team don't tell you 'cause it's ya own team that's coming!? What you gon' do when ya own connect is sticking you up!? What you gon' do when them boys in blue is kicking down ya door at six in the morning, raiding the place!? What you gon' do when you sitting in a cold ass police station with tight ass cuffs on for a crime you know ya man did!? Are you gonna snitch or are you gon' charge it to the game?"

Suddenly Jo-Jo's voice became softer like he was reminiscing. But he continued questioning me, "what you gon' do when even ya lawyer is playing games with you? What you gon' do when you don't know who to trust? Then what you gon' do when the only person you did trust is the person whose been setting you up the whole time? In this game the pressure is always on so what you gon' do? Until you can answer those questions you ain't ready for this! And no disrespect, but instead of looking at the way ya pops lived and using it to wanna get in the game, you should be looking at the way he use to live as every reason to stay out of the game 'cause look at him now. This shit ain't worth dying for you can't take nothing with you to the grave when you go. And if you decide you ever wanna run to the police for help, you could forget about them too 'cause they even more fucked up."

I sucked my teeth, "I hear what you saying Jo-Jo, but we all gotta eat and I'm ready to pledge my undying loyalty to you and ya team."

Jo-Jo shook his head, "I might as well been talking to

the wall. Did you not just hear anything I said? Everybody's loyal in this game until it's inconvenient for them to be loyal. You can't trust anybody, everybody's in it for self nowadays. Ain't no friends in this game only enemies. That's just the basics and you don't even know that, how could you even consider getting in this game? Plus how would Mel feel about that?"

I frowned then looked Jo-Jo up and down, "How would who feel?" I asked.

Jo-Jo cracked a smile, "You know, Jamel, ya man?"

Laughing I replied, "You can't be serious you know me and Jamel's relationship been long gone now. I don't have time for games, but that's another story. Anyway since you can't help me and I can't help you I'll see you later Jo-Jo." I turned to head down the stairs. Jo-Jo grabbed my arm.

"I never said you couldn't help me. I just said the game is no place for you."

I looked at Jo-Jo's hand around my arm. Then I looked at him and replied, "Oh really? How can I help you then?"

"It's a lot of ways you can help me. C'mere Lets talk." He licked his lips. I stood face to face with him.

"Talk about what?" I asked.

"Business," he smiled.

Laughing and shaking my head, I put my hands on my hips. Then I replied, "Business huh? What kind of business?"

Jo-Jo licked his lips then replied, "You know, I heard about you and ya homegirl, Jackie tearing it up in Jersey."

The entire statement caught me off guard. My smile immediately turned into a frown. I didn't think about my stripping days and I didn't need anyone to help me start thinking about them all over again. I took a step back from Jo-Jo then replied, "Excuse me?"

Jo-Jo laughed then smiled, "Don't front like you don't know what I'm talking about. I got ears every where. If you need to eat like you say you need to eat then me and you can go to the 'telly right now and do our thing. And don't worry about time or money 'cause I'm quick and generous. So what's up love?" Jo-Jo licked his lips.

I spit with much attitude, "I don't know where you getting ya information from but um...I don't fuck with Jackie at all! And I ain't no two dollar hoe so thanks but no thanks."

"Baby I know you ain't cheap I'm willing to pay a hundred. So what's up?"

I jetted down the stairs leaving Jo-Jo there speaking to his damn self. I didn't care to hear another word he was saying. I knew exactly what I wanted, and, what I wanted wasn't what he was tryna hear. A long time ago I might've fell for his game, but not now. I didn't feel like being a hustler's girl anymore, *been there done that!* I felt like being the motherfucking hustler! This way no nigga could stop me from getting my paper. I was determined to hustle by any means necessary, my survival depended on it. On top of that, Jo-Jo wasn't even tryna make me his girl. All he wanted to do was use me as a quick fuck. Plus, he wanted to do it all for a hundred dollars. He lucky I didn't smack him with that hundred dollars. *Fuck him!* I said out loud, speaking only to myself. I continued heading down the steps. With each step I took, the angrier I became.

Finally making it down to the lobby, my rage and anger skyrocketed as I saw Jackie. Jackie was waiting for the elevator looking high as a kite. I knew she was high on coke. The sweat beads on her forehead confirmed my thoughts. Plus she kept rubbing her nose and sniffling. Looking at how much weight she lost, I wouldn't have been surprised if she was smoking something else. Jackie looked bad, like a straight up crackhead. Her hair was tangled and her lips were chap. The clothes she had on looked about three sizes too big for her. It didn't take long for Jackie to notice me. She shouted me out like we were the best of friends.

"Hey, Mahogany! How you doing? Long time no see girl!" Jackie's mouth kept twisting like she couldn't control it. I looked her up and down then turned my nose up. I spit at her feet as I kept walking towards the front door. Jackie laughed and looked at my spit like it was a disease. She moved her feet away. Out of nowhere Jackie started dancing and bobbing her head like she heard music. Everybody in the lobby started laughing at her. I had to pause for a minute just so I could make sure my eyes weren't deceiving me. One of the younger hustlers' walked over to her yelling, "Where the fuck did you go last night?"

Jackie put her thumb in her mouth, but she kept talking, "I was waiting for you daddy. I was right upstairs; you know I always take care of you. Can you give me two more? I'll take care of you later, you know I will." Jackie started doing the crack dance. Everybody in the lobby started laughing harder.

"Leave that crackhead bitch alone!" another hustler screamed. Then he continued, "She still owe me forty motherfucking dollars anyway, and, she gon' gimme my money one way or another! Bet that!"

"Chris don't be like that," replied Jackie. My heart was

telling me I needed to save her from herself. Then suddenly I remembered I couldn't save my damn self. I put my head down as I continued to walking towards the front door. Jackie stopped me when she yelled.

"Oh it's like that, Mahogany? You ain't gon' speak? You still mad over some dick that wasn't even yours?" any sympathy I had for her went out the window once she made that comment. I was tempted to slap the shit out of her. But I reminded myself to leave her alone because she was high. I'd rather catch her on a sober day because I wanted her to remember the ass whipping I was saving for her. Still ignoring her I was getting ready to exit the building. But Jackie begged for a beat down when she looked at me for the last time and said, "Oh now you can't hear me, or am I saying your name wrong? Maybe I should just call you Ginger and throw a dollar at you. I bet you'll answer me then!"

That's when I went bananas on the bitch! I charged toward her so hard you would've thought I was charging at a bull. My fist met her face countless times as I kept punching her. Dozens of people crowded around us in the project lobby like it was a championship fight. I banged her head against the ground. We wrestled on the floor. I saw the crowd getting bigger and bigger. The more people that crowded around us, the more closed in I felt. Jackie's frail knee was in my chest. She was so thin that I was able to push her off of me with one swift punch. I stood to my feet. Jackie crawled on the floor like she didn't know what was going on. I kicked her in the stomach, "Get up bitch!" Jackie held on to the wall as she tried to stand on her feet. Once she was standing, I rushed her again. Suddenly I see someone coming in our direction. I couldn't see the face, but I did see a colorful Coogi hat and sweater. Soon as this person opens his mouth, I recognize him as Tazz, the guy with the never-ending crush on me.

"Yo, what the fuck…, why y'all niggaz just letting them fight? Move…move… let me break this shit up. And all y'all nosy ass motherfuckers' should be ashamed of y'all self! Ain't nothing here to see. Take y'all asses in the house. And niggaz wonder why shit is always hot! This is why!"

Tazz pulled me off of Jackie. Jackie's tangled hair was all over the place. Her breathing was deep and hard. She stayed in a corner as Tazz pulled me away. He looked at Jackie and shook his head then he grabbed my arm. Tazz escorted me out of the building with my hair looking wild. My shirt was stretched out of place and my jacket was ripped. The rain came down hard on both of us. Tazz took my car keys from me. He opened my car door, we took a seat inside. I sat in the passenger seat while he sat in the drivers' seat. I didn't know where he was driving when he drove off but I didn't care. I was upset and hungry. I just wanted to get out of the projects.

It was like Tazz was reading my mind. He drove to this food spot on Farmers Boulevard and parked the car. He ordered two trays of chicken fried rice for both of us. When the order was done he came back to the car and sat mine in my lap. I was hungry without a doubt, but the blood in my veins was still boiling from all the tension within me. Tazz was eating his rice as he looked at me and spoke.

"Rocky, what's up? You aight?"

With my seat leaned all the way back and my foot on

the dash board I replied, "I'm good."

With a mouth full of chicken and rice Tazz continued, "This is some good chicken and rice, you might wanna eat yours."

I turned to face Tazz, "Why you stopped me from whipping that bitch ass, Tazz? I would've showed you 'Rocky' foreal!"

"I know you would've champ, but she ain't worth it. Truthfully I was surprised you didn't whip her ass sooner."

"Oh no I tried the minute I found out she was fucking Jamel, but the trifling hoe ran in her house."

"Yeah I heard about that but I was even surprised you was fucking with her then." Tazz paused then continued, "You know because of ya moms and shit..."

"Because of my moms?" I said with a puzzled look on my face, "What about my moms?"

Tazz stopped chewing. He looked at me then continued, "Wait a minute, you telling me you ain't know Jackie's brother had something to do with that foul shit that happened wit ya moms?"

There were cars riding by, rain coming down hard and the radio was on, but everything around me went mute and a chill shot through my body as I focused on the statement I just heard, *Jackie's brother had something to do with my moms death.* Sitting up in my seat and taking my feet off the dash board I looked at Tazz and spoke.

"WHAT!?"

Tazz looked at me like he wanted to cry, but he didn't cry. Instead, he kept talking, "Babygirl, I'm sorry I thought you knew Jason had something to do with that!"

"You thought I knew that Jackie's brother killed my mother? What kind of fool do you think I am? Do you really think I would've fucked with her if I knew her brother was the reason for my mother being murdered all along?"

Adjusting his body towards me he placed his food in between us and continued, "Yo that's fucked up how niggaz is so grimey! I don't even fuck with the hood like that and I knew. I thought you did too that's why every time I used to see you with that broad I ain't understand. And it ain't like you ever gave me the time of day. Every time I tried to get at you you'd just shut a nigga down. But had I'd known you ain't know about that trifling bitch and her family I woulda put you on a long time ago."

"So what really happened that day?"

Tazz put his hand over his mouth then took a deep breath, "Awe man. You sure you wanna hear this?"

I closed my eyes thinking about what Tazz was about to tell me. I felt him touching my hand. I opened my eyes then spoke, "I heard this much you might as well tell me the rest. What's done is done I'm a big girl I can handle it."

Taking a deep breath he began, "I heard the nigga was running from the police and he ran straight to ya crib." Tazz paused then looked at me. Listening attentively with my hand on my chin I said, "Go on." he continued, "then when he got to your door, ya moms didn't open it. He almost got caught."

"How did he know if someone was even in the house?"

"Peep this, you know that fiend that lives on the floor you used to live on?"

I frowned then replied, "Who, Bev?"

Tazz got excited, "Yeah her, well anyway after he was banging on your door and ya moms didn't open it, he was yelling in the hallway saying, *who ever opens their door he got a hundred dollars for them.*"

I interrupted, "So Bev opened her door?"

Tazz continued, "Hell yeah, you know a fiend will open their door for *five* dollars. But check the drama. After he was in Bev's house for a while, everything died down so he was getting ready to leave. Then he saw ya moms taking out her garbage, that's how he knew she was there. Anyway I guess he got mad at the fact she ain't open up the door for him. So he went back inside Bev's house and got a bat. You know the rest..."

Tears came pouring down my face, "Son of a bitch!"

Tazz continued, "I don't know if he meant to kill her or if he just wanted to beat her up, but in the end it didn't matter cause you know..."

I zoned out from that point on. I saw his lips moving but I didn't hear the words that were coming out of his mouth. I thought about the events that happened the day my moms was killed. I thought about me going to the hotel with Jamel, getting my virginity broken. I thought about me calling Jackie on my way back, but no one answered her phone, which was strange. I thought about how some people knew my whereabouts when my moms was killed. I thought about the night in the club when Jackie was so high. Me and Sunshine brought her in the bathroom, she kept saying sorry, she hated her brother and asking me was I still her friend. I didn't know what she was trying to say then, but I knew now. Then I thought about her brother being on the run, it all made perfect sense! The rage I felt inside was like nothing I've ever experienced. I wanted to kill Jackie and her brother!

Tazz broke my chain of thought. He waved his had in

front of my face then spoke, "Yo, either you can tell me where you live and I'll drop you off and call a cab from ya house, or you can drop me off at my crib then drive yourself home. I gotta get ready to make moves. Greensboro is calling me baby!"

I was still hurt, but slowly I began to come back to reality. I spoke. "I'll drop you off. And what you talking 'bout *Greensboro* is calling you?"

Tazz looked at me like I said something wrong, "That's right. That's where I do my thing baby. You know I don't fuck wit New York like that, it's to hot out here. A nigga will never make a dollar, police be out here like roaches.

Ding Ding Ding Ding! It was like an alarm went off in my head. I saw an opportunity to get money with Tazz. I spoke my mind.

"Tazz, what's up? Let me make some money with you?"

Tazz looked at me funny. Then he replied, "Make some money with me?"

"Yeah!" I shot back.

Shaking his head he replied, "Nah, you don't wanna make money with me. I'm a bad boy, I break the law, stay away for weeks at a time and North Carolina is nothing like New York."

"You ain't saying nothing but a word. I could sell weight and break plenty of laws too so what's up?"

Tazz frowned, "Selling weight? Breaking laws? Girl I was talking about running red lights. I don't know what you talking 'bout."

We both had to laugh at that statement. But I wasn't laughing for long because I was dead serious about getting in the drug game. Tazz looked at me still shaking his head.

"Girl you sure are something," he said.

I looked Tazz dead in his eyes, "Nah but on some real shit Tazz, I know you gotta leave something in New York while you're down in Greensboro. I could handle shit for you in New York. You know make sure everything is aight."

Tazz folded his arms and looked at me.

"You dead ass serious huh?"

Waving my hands in the air to emphasize my point, I replied, "I don't play games!"

Tazz closed his eyes while slapping both of his hands together. He replied, "Look this business ain't for you. You're young, pretty and smart why would you wanna put yourself in this mess? You need to let me take care of you because…"

Wasting no time I cut Tazz off, "Here we go again! Why the fuck do niggaz always think a bitch don't know how to hold her own? What is with y'all, do y'all get intimidated by a bitch knowing the game better than some of these lame ass niggaz out here? Is that it? Do y'all think a bitch will put you out of business or take over, I mean what is it? Please tell me!"

Tazz looked at me like he was so shocked. I guessed because I wasn't sugar coating shit. I needed him to know I was dead ass serious about making some money. Taking his hat off and putting it in his lap he began to speak.

"Mahogany, it ain't nothing like that I just want you to know what you're getting yourself into. This is the NBA! The NFL! The real deal! I'm talking about the pros' baby. This is the major leagues! When I does this shit, I does it foreal! Do you understand what I'm saying? Are you ready for that?"

I looked at him with deep seriousness then replied, "I was born ready!"

He looked at me with the crooked eye, "You sure about that?"

"No question!" I answered.

"Aight, I think I got a job for you," he replied.

I tried to play cool but I was excited. I couldn't stop myself from smiling. Tazz continued, "Leaving you in New York is out of the question. You selling weight is out of the question."

I was confused. "Well what do you want me to...?"

Tazz held his hand up, "Let me finish. Like I was saying, I have a job for you that's nice and easy. All you would have to do is hold my bricks when we take trips out of town. Ya pretty little self will be making money and it will be a lot safer than what you're talking about doing, aight?"

I smiled, "Aight." I bit my bottom lip then looked at Tazz. He read my mind.

"Say what you gotta say Mahogany."

"The question is how much money will I be making?" I smiled again.

Tazz laughed, "When I go out of town I take two maybe three bricks. I'll give you sixteen hundred dollars for each brick you hold plus pay all ya expenses while you're down there. Is that cool?"

Tazz pulled out a pen, ripped a piece of paper from the brown paper bag my chicken and rice was in. He started writing his phone number: 917-555-2963.

I flipped my hair over my shoulder and replied, "I'm aight with that. When do we start?"

Passing me his phone number he replied, "Starting

today, I'm driving down but you gon' take the bus. Call Grey Hound and find out the next three departure times of any bus going to Greensboro, North Carolina. Then let me know and I'll give you the money for the ticket plus pass them bricks. I'll meet you down there."

"Tonight? My hair is not even done. Plus I need some clothes and shit to go down there. I'm fucked up. And why can't I ride with you?"

Tazz shook his head, "See what I mean? Look this ain't twenty-one questions, either you wanna do it or you don't. Which one is it?"

"Well if you put it that way I guess I don't have a choice right?"

Tazz smiled, "Welcome to the game baby!"

We arrived at Tazz house within a matter of minutes. Before he exited my vehicle he looked at me while placing his hand on my car latch. He spoke.

"Don't forget to make that call. When you finish, let me know what's what so I can meet you somewhere, and we can take care of everything, aight? Oh, and make sure you get a one way ticket because you can ride back to New York with me."

"Cool."

Just as Tazz got out of my car, he looked at me then spoke again.

"Oh, I forgot to ask you..."

"Ask me what?" I replied.

"Did it hurt?"

Looking at him confused I replied, "Who Jackie? I ain't thinking about that chick."

"Neither am I." Tazz shot back then continued, "I meant did it hurt when you fell from heaven 'cause you truly are an angel."

Smiling and rolling my eyes, I switched from the passenger seat of my car to the driver's seat. As I adjusted the seat and the mirrors I looked at Tazz, took a deep breath then replied, "I'll see you later."

"Don't forget to call me when you get that info."

"I won't."

Tazz walked away. I drove off with a smile on my face. Even the rain stopped and the sun was starting to shine. I took that as a sign from God saying I was doing the right thing. I knew this was the start of something special.

Chapter 15

The Come Up...

In the evening I caught the 7:20 bus to Greensboro, North Carolina. Tazz was meeting me down there. He told me he'd pick me up from the bus station. You couldn't tell me my shit didn't stink! For the first time in a long time I felt like I was in control. I was in control of my destiny, I was regaining my independence. I felt free because I knew this time I was depending on me and I wasn't gon' let myself down.

The trip was a hop, skip and a jump. Tazz met me at the bus station just like he said he would. We drove to what I assumed was his place. I knew my assumption was right when we entered the town house. Besides needing a little dusting, the town house was pretty clean and neat. The central air conditioner that greeted us as we walked in was cool and welcoming. But the over accessorizing of furniture was sickening! The walls were gray with black stripes and so was the sofa. On top of that, parts of the carpet reflected the same pattern as the walls and sofa. From where we stood I was able to see the kitchen, which was also the same pattern as the living-room. I was getting dizzy just standing in the house. I placed the one bag I had on the floor, next to a black table which held a black and gray vase on top of it. I invited myself to a seat on Tazz's couch. Tazz walked over to me. He handed me the remote to his entertainment system, and then he spoke.

"Can I get you some juice, water, sprite or are you straight?"

Yawning I replied, "Well isn't that sweet of you. I'll take some sprite with no ice and a straw if you have any."

Being sarcastic Tazz replied, "Would you like lemons and a little umbrella too?"

I looked at Tazz, "You know what? I guess I better shut up before you change your mind huh? After all you did offer me something to drink and that's shocking enough!"

Heading towards his kitchen, Tazz continued talking, "Shocking? What you think I ain't got manners? Just because I'm from the hood that don't mean I am hood. I wasn't raised by wolves. You are a guest in my home at least until you move in, marry me and have my children."

I sucked my teeth then turned up the volume on the television. Then I replied, "Nigga please!"

Tazz yelled over the television, "Why you gotta be so mean? What you ain't moving in, marrying me and having my children?"

"Bingo!" I yelled. "You must be one of those Rocket Scientist."

Walking towards the ugly striped couch handing me my sprite with a straw, Tazz replied, "Yeah aight smart ass! Get up off the couch let me show you your room."

Putting my hand over my chest I took a sip of my sprite as I replied, "My room? I must be special huh? How many other people have their own room in your house?"

Tazz laughed, "You one dramatic girl you know that? You should really try acting. I'd give you an Oscar!"

Following Tazz to *my* bedroom I replied, "No need for an Oscar. Just give me some clean sheets for the bed 'cause I don't know who you be having up in here. You do stay here alone right?"

"Yeah it's just me."

"Well good because I don't wanna have to be confronted by some deranged chick thinking I want her man. I wouldn't wanna have to beat her ass, you know how I do."

"Yeah Rocky, we wouldn't want that." Tazz laughed.

"Aight I'm just letting you know. Now would you please gimme some clean sheets?"

Pointing to the bed Tazz replied, "It's clean sheets on the bed."

I frowned then looked at the sheets like they had just been dragged through the mud. Then I turned to look at Tazz and replied, "Says who?"

"Says me! I just put those sheets on the bed before I picked you up," Tazz shot back.

I laughed, "Well good because that means you know how to take them off. You could be telling me anything I don't know whose been sleeping and sexing and farting on those sheets. I'd rather have new ones please. Thank you! If you still have a problem getting me some sheets I'll be more than happy to buy my own."

Walking away from me shaking his head he replied, "Girl, you sure are a trip! I don't know what to do with you."

"Whatever." I shouted.

I took a look around the room while Tazz went to get

my sheets. I thought to myself, *if this is the guestroom, I wonder what the master bedroom looked like.* The windows were nice and big. I wondered how many rooms this place had. So I asked, "How many bedrooms are in this house Tazz?"

"What?" Tazz shouted.

"I said..." I thought about repeating myself, but then I said forget it. I yelled back, "Never mind!"

Suddenly Tazz appeared with a brand new set of unopened sheets in his hand as he said, "Three. There are three bedrooms in this house?"

Reaching out for the sheets I replied, "I thought you didn't hear me?"

"I never said I didn't hear you. I just wanted to make sure I heard you correctly."

Both of us began stripping the queen size bed. I continued questioning him, "If you're the only one who lives here, why do you need three bedrooms?"

"I already told you. It's for me, you and our future kids."

"Keep dreaming," I told him.

Tazz laughed then came clean, "Nah, I told you I don't fuck wit New York like that so this is where I stay. I like to be comfortable and have lots of space. Plus sometimes my comrades come over and we get twisted. Then they can't drive home like that so they end up staying in one of my rooms. They damn sure ain't staying in a room with me. And they ain't laying on my couch either! I paid too much money for that couch."

"Fuck that couch!" I shouted.

Jokingly he replied, "I'm 'bout to put you out."

I put on my babyface, "Me? You wouldn't do that to

your future wife, remember? Especially if she still had the three bricks of coke that belongs to you that you didn't get yet."

Rubbing his hands together he replied, "We about to fix that right now! When you finish in here come to the kitchen."

Tazz left the room. I showered and unpacked. The Oil of Olay body-wash felt good against my skin. When I was finished I went into the kitchen to meet Tazz who was sitting at the table eating a bowl of ice cream. A large beige scale sat by his side. It didn't take long for him to notice me. I was wearing a baby tee and short shorts.

"It's nice of you to join me," he said.

I blew him a kiss and replied, "I love you too." I put the coke on the table. A smile appeared across his face. Pleased with myself for getting the job done I took a seat and said real nonchalantly, "Weigh it, it's all there."

Handing me two rubber bands of money he replied, "That's my girl!"

I counted forty eight hundred dollars. I was coming up in the world again. The sound of my growling stomach reminded me that I didn't eat. I put one hand over my stomach and asked, "What do you have to eat?"

Tazz was weighing his product. He answered me, "Crackers, cheeses, butter take ya pick."

I sucked my teeth, "Damn nigga that ain't food! How do you survive up in this piece?"

"You better get with the program. It's a store right up the road that makes some banging ass roast beef sand-wiches," Tazz replied then continued, "I'll take you in a minute."

"Is that all you eat? If I'm staying up in here we gon'

have to do some grocery shopping!"

"*We* could do the shopping as long as *you* doing the cooking."

"You ain't saying nothing but a word," I told him.

Tazz took me up the road to get one of those roast beef sandwiches he told me about. He wasn't lying, the shit was banging! I tore it up. Later on we went grocery shopping.

The next morning I got up and cooked French toast, homefries and beef sausages. When the food was ready I fixed me and Tazz plates. Just as I turned to go get Tazz out of his bedroom, I heard what sounded like someone entering the house. I grabbed the biggest knife I could find like I was ready for war!

"Who is that!?" I yelled. When no one responded I yelled again.

"Who the fuck is in here!?"

Before I could yell another word, I saw a strange man and started screaming! Tazz came running out wearing DKNY boxers with the matching slippers saying, "Yo, what's up?"

"Somebody is in this motherfucker!" I warned him.

The stranger looked at me. I was wearing nothing but shorts and a t-shirt. Then he looked at Tazz and spoke, "Yo Tazz what the fuck is going on?"

Tazz started laughing as he saw me with the knife in my hand. It was easy to figure out, Tazz knew the strange man who stood before me.

"That shit ain't funny!" I said then continued, "Don't ya friends knock before they enter into someone's home?"

The stranger looked at me and said, "I'm sorry Shorty, I ain't mean no harm. That's just how we do 'round here."

I threw the knife on the counter. Looking at Tazz I rolled my eyes before speaking, "The food is ready! I ain't make any extra, I didn't know we were having company."

The stranger kept staring at me in my shorts and t-shirt like he wanted to eat me for breakfast before he said, "That's alright Shorty my name is James Allan and you are...?"

"Call me Mahogany," I replied with an attitude.

"Nice to meet you Mahogany," said James Allan.

I didn't say another word to him. I excused myself and went in the bedroom. Tazz couldn't stop laughing.

After staying with Tazz for a week I got used to the uninvited and unexpected guest. I stopped wearing little t-shirts and shorts around the house. Instead, I wore big t-shirts and sweat pants. For some strange reason I felt comfortable wearing what I wore in front of Tazz like we were brother and sister or something. But, his friends were a different story. I made sure I was covered all the way up when they decided to pop up. After I stopped stripping I became so protective of who I let see my body, don't ask me why. I just did.

I was also learning that Tazz was so cool! I actually felt kind of stupid for dissing him all the time back in our old neighborhood. He still wouldn't give up tryna make me his wife, but even that was funny to me. I liked Tazz not as a boyfriend but as a friend, after all he's the only one who really helped me. I looked at Tazz as a brother. He was mad cool!

• • •

One day I was chillin' on the couch, polishing my toes and watching *All My Children*. My hair was pulled back in a ponytail. I was sporting a t-shirt and sweatpants as usual. By now I was no longer surprised by Tazz friends popping in and out of his house. So when another one of his uninvited, unexpected guest just walked in. I paid them no attention whatsoever. Soon as I heard the door open I knew it had to be one of Tazz friends.

"Excuse me is Tazz around?" I heard a male voice ask. I didn't bother lifting my head to speak to this guy. Instead, I continued polishing my toes, but I did answer his question. "He's out back," I replied.

"Thanks," said the stranger. Then he continued, "Do you mind if I wash my hands real quick?"

I focused my eyes on the show I was watching then replied in *a I don't feel like being bothered tone*, "Don't let me stop you."

He walked to the kitchen sink. I heard the door open again. This time it was Tazz entering. The first thing he said to me was, "Where's Smoke?"

I replied, "Where's who?"

Kicking his sneakers off he replied, "Smoke, my man I just saw him come in here and his car is outside. Where he at?" Just then Smoke came walking out of the kitchen. The two men greeted each other with hand slaps. Tazz came walking over to the couch. He tapped me to get my attention.

"Have you meet Mahogany?" he asked Smoke then continued, "She can be real mean sometimes."

Smoke replied, "Yeah I see, she ain't look at me once."

Tazz begin introducing us, "Smoke this is Mahogany, Mahogany this is Smoke."

I finally looked up. When I saw the man standing before me I couldn't believe my pretty green eyes! I said to myself it couldn't be! It was no way! I must be dreaming or my name is Cinderella! I knocked my bottle of nail polish over then quickly picked it up before any of it was able to fall onto the carpet. I was at a loss for words. I knew exactly who the person was I'd just been introduced to! He was the fine ass, balling ass, chocolate-brown guy who I made a fool of myself in front of at All-Star weekend in Atlanta a few years earlier! I knew it was him. I could never forget his face. He was FINE!! He was standing in front of me wearing a cream, velour Fila sweat suit with the matching classics. To say I was in love with this man would have been an understatement I was like a moth and he was the fire.

I realized I couldn't blow it a second time so I played it cool as I could. At least that's what I tried to do until I realized I was wearing sweat pants, a t-shirt and my hair was in a ponytail. I panicked like crazy, but I did my best to keep it inside. As I stood to my feet to shake Smoke's hand I noticed he was wearing the same ring on his finger he had on at All-Star weekend. However, all of his other jewels were gone. I guessed it was safe to assume he was married. But at that moment, whether or not he was married was the last thing on my mind. Something about him just screamed sexy, masculine, fine! He interrupted my thoughts.

"You are beautiful!" he said almost in a whisper. He extended his hand while looking at me like I was the last female on earth.

I shook his hand then replied, "Thank you."

He looked so defined. I was already open and he didn't even know it. It felt like his eyes were looking into my soul as he said, "Do I know you from somewhere?"

Inside I was screaming, "Hell yeah you know me from somewhere! I'm the girl from the bar at All-Star weekend that spilled her drink on her pretty, satin Chinese dress tryna get your attention, remember?" But I was not about to make a fool of myself again so instead of helping him remember, I just acted like I forgot too. Shaking my head and acting like I was searching my thoughts I replied, "I don't think I've met you before, trust me I wouldn't have forgot."

Tazz interrupted the flow – hating on me!

"Aight Mahogany, finish doing what you was doing. Me and Smoke gotta leave now but *I* will be back. And please don't put my food in the refrigerator like you did last time. It takes away from the flavor so just leave it in the microwave. I'll heat it up when I get back. Thanks a lot sweetheart."

Tazz bent down to kiss me on the cheek then continued, "Oh and if you need me to bring you anything just call. You know I got you," he winked. Minutes later Tazz and Smoke were gone.

Shortly after him and Smoke walked out the door leaving me with only my thoughts, which at the moment were, *Tazz sure does have a lot of nerve trying to make it seem like we were a couple.* I didn't let it bother me though. It didn't look like it bothered Smoke either. That was what really counted. Without a doubt I was feeling Smoke. It wasn't hard to tell he was feeling me too.

The next few days were crazy for me. I went to sleep dreaming about Smoke. I woke up thinking about Smoke. The majority of my days were filled with thoughts about Smoke. If I could've I would've ate, slept and drunk Smoke, I was open! I think I was even beginning to get on

Tazz nerve with my constant questions about Smoke. I had it bad for him! But I didn't neglect my good ol' buddy Tazz. I started helping him out too, not relationship wise. I gave him a little tip about over accessorizing. It started off as an argument, but it ended with much love. I remember it so clear it all started about that damn stripe couch.

Tazz got on my nerves so bad to the point that I told him he always overdo everything. Why did he ask me what does he overdo? I tried to bite my tongue about the situation, but he just kept asking for it so I took one look around his apartment and just let it out.

"What do you overdo? What don't you overdo!? I hate all your over accessorizing, from your matching boxers and slippers to your sweaters and hats, to these fucking stripe walls and matching couches! It ain't hard to tell, shit! Take a look around this bitch!"

Tazz folded his arms into one another then replied, "What's wrong with my couch?"

I looked at him like he had to be kidding, but he wasn't so I continued, "Are you serious? It's a piece of shit! What the fuck ever happened to black? Why must *everything* match!? I mean be foreal!"

"Oh you think you can do a better job?"

I let out a sigh then a laugh as I replied, "I know I can!"

"Alright then miss *know it all* let's go!"

I threw my hands in the air, "Go where?"

"Let's go and you'll see," Tazz demanded.

We left and went to a furniture store. I couldn't believe it, but we were there. I picked out the perfect leather black sectional couch to give his house a much better flava. From that moment on he saw my point of view as far as interior decorating goes. As far as his wardrobe goes...let's just say I was still working on that.

A little over a month passed. Finally, we were on the road heading back to New York. The strange thing is I didn't miss New York. I didn't even miss it for a second. With that being said, I decided Greensboro would be my new home. New York held too many bad memories for me. I didn't bother checking on my apartment or my car. I just abandoned them both. Plus I was pretty sure my landlord wasn't trying to hear anything I had to say. My apartment was still empty from when Mo raided the place. So there was really no need for me to go back there anyway. So I didn't. On top of that, Tazz practically begged me to stay at his place until I found my own place. He claimed it was because he loved my good cooking so much, but I knew it was more to it than just the way I cooked. He was still in love with me. I didn't mind staying with him because after all he was my only link to Smoke. Plus, Tazz was just a cool dude... sometimes.

After Tazz took care of whatever he had to. We were on the road heading back to North Carolina. We rode back together since we weren't transporting any drugs; we still had plenty of coke left in Greensboro. I knew we'd more than likely re-up on our next trip to New York.

As I sat in the passenger seat of Tazz car, one thing I had to give to him was his ability to be persistent. He even tried to do things to let me know he still wanted me. He'd try to be smooth about it to. What he chose to do this time almost made me laugh, cry and slap him all at once. He started playing Puff Daddy and R. Kelly's *Satisfy You*. Then he had the nerve to sing along with them word for word, "*He don't understand you like I do. And he'll never make love to you like I do so give it to me! 'Cause I could show you 'bout a real love and I can promise anything that I do is just to satisfy you..."*

I loved that song, but I was not in the mood to hear it from him. I kindly stopped his tape then popped one of my own in. The sound of my dog came roaring through the car speakers. I started singing along to DMX's *How's It Going Down* and waving my hands up in the air, *"What type of games is being played? How's it going down? It's on 'til it's gone then I gotstah to know now is you wit me or what think I'm tryna get me a nut just 'cause honeys wanna gimme the butt whaaat..."*

Tazz just looked at me and shook his head. I smiled and kept dancing. The only thing Tazz could do was drive. I was in control. I stayed in control of the radio for the duration of our ride. Everything went smooth. When we arrived back in *our* townhouse I was happy for two reasons. The first reason is because I felt at peace in Greensboro. The second was because Smoke stopped by that same night. It just so happened he wanted to take me out. My dreams were coming true. I was large and in charge!

Chapter 16

Beauty Is His Name...

North Carolina was good to me. I started my day bright and early. I treated myself to a day at the spa where I received a full body wax and massage. My eyebrows were freshly arched, and my smooth skin was even smoother than a baby's bottom. Everything had to be just right for my date with Smoke. I received a French manicure for my nails and a French pedicure for my pretty toes. When I left the spa, my next stop was off to the hair salon. After spending three hours there, I found my way to the mall so I could shop! When everything was all said and done, I headed back home.

When I walked in the door I saw nothing but candles lit everywhere. The cherry scent the candles gave off was sweet and intoxicating. On the floor red rose petals laid everywhere. Tazz had really outdone himself this time. While I appreciated Tazz's fight to win my heart, I could not let him stand in the way of my plans. If he thought I'd cancel my plans with Smoke for him, he was sadly mistaken. I briefly admired the scenery around me. Shortly after, I started blowing out candles throughout the house. I didn't want Tazz to even think his plan to ruin my night out was working. I turned on the lights in the house then walked to Tazz bedroom, when I opened the door Tazz was nowhere in sight. Instead, there was a giant teddy bear on his bed. The bear was holding a heart. Inside the heart it read 'Be Mines.' I couldn't stop myself from smiling. I called out to Tazz.

"Tazz, where are you?" Tazz didn't answer. I continued walking around the house, searching for Tazz. When I entered my bedroom another teddy bear holding a 'Be Mines' sign sat in the center of my bed. Different color roses in individual vase were also everywhere inside of my room. It was like I walked into a floral shop. I covered my mouth. Surprise and beauty were the only feelings shooting through my body. I was seconds away from surrendering to Tazz persistence. But, soon as the feeling came, it left.

"Tazz, why are you doing this!?" I yelled then continued, "You already know what I'm gonna tell you. Plus you already know I have a date tonight. You put yourself in these situations then when I don't give in – you make it seem like I'm the bad person." Tazz still didn't answer. I was starting to get frustrated!

"Okay, Tazz, don't answer me! I just hope you understand, I'm going out tonight – and it won't be with you!"

I didn't want to be mean, but I needed to get my point across. I gathered my shopping bags from out of the living-room then placed them in my bedroom. I quickly undressed, wrapped myself in a towel then headed to the bathroom. To my surprise rose petals were all over the bathroom too. Another 'Be Mines' teddy bear sat on the toilet-seat, a bubble bath sat waiting for me, and candles were lit as well. Before I could protest any longer, Smoke appeared in the doorway of the bathroom! Smoke was wearing a three-piece charcoal gray Armani suit. His waves were deep and rich on top of his head. Surprised he was so close to me, I dropped my towel. I stood in front of Smoke completely nude! I tried to cover myself. Smoke smiled, revealing his pretty white teeth. Then spoke.

"You are beautiful!"

I bent down to pick up my towel. Smoke stopped me. He bent down to pick it up himself. Not once did he take his eyes off of me. Smoke wrapped the towel around me then escorted me to the bubble bath.

"Smoke, what are you doing here?"

Smoke removed his suit Jacket, revealing just how good his vest fit. His cufflinks reflected off of the dimly lit bathroom walls. He walked closer to me then spoke, "We have a date, remember?"

"I know, but our date is not for another two hours. I thought you were Tazz and I was about to…" Smoke ssh-hed me by placing one of his long fingers over my lips.

"You don't have to say another word," he told me. Then he continued, "I'm sorry if I'm making you feel uncomfortable, but I want you to know, you should be treated like royalty all day, everyday from the very moment you walk into any door!"

I looked deep into his eyes. He continued speaking, "If you want me to leave, I could do that. But, if you want me to stay, I could do that too." How could I ask him to leave? He caught me completely off guard, and I did feel comfortable in his presence. I removed the towel from around my body then stepped into my bubble bath. The water was warm and welcoming. I grabbed Smoke's hand then looked at him.

"I want you to stay," I said. He smiled as he walked closer to the bathtub.

"I want you to want me to stay," he whispered in my ear. The sound of his voice sent chills down my spine. Smoke sat on the edge of the bathtub. He started sprinkling water all over my back. I was caught up in the moment. His hands were feeling so good against my back.

Minutes later – Smoke carried me out of the bathtub and into my bedroom. Smoke rubbed cocoa butter all over my body. When he reached my feet, he made sure special attention was given to each toe. I laid back while his hands went to work. When Smoke's hands reached my inner thighs, my nipples grew erect while my insides got moist. I looked at Smoke and our eyes locked into one another. Smoke moved my hair off of my neck then kissed me so soft in that spot. When he was done kissing my neck, he kissed my cheeks then whispered in my ear, "You finish getting dress. I'll wait for you out front."

Smoke walked out of the room leaving me naked and horny on my bed. I couldn't believe it!

Before Smoke was able to close my door all the way, I hopped off of my bed. I raced to my shopping bags! I pulled out a pair of new Nola shoes that was a perfect match to the linen Benetton dress I picked up at the mall. I was dressed and ready within minutes. I made sure all of the candles in the house were blown out. Then I meet Smoke in front of the house where he waited for me. The sight of me walking out of the front door brought a smile to his face. I was delighted to see him as well. A black Mercedes Benz stretch limo sat parked behind Smoke. Before I could walk to the limo, the driver was already standing on the side of it, holding the door open for me and Smoke. I got in the limo first. Smoke entered the car shortly after me. The driver closed the door. Me and Smoke smiled at each other. Inside the limo was a fully loaded bar with a television and radio. Smoke pressed a button, the sunroof opened and he moved closer to me. I felt the cool breeze coming through the sunroof as the driver pulled off. I looked at Smoke then spoke.

"Where are we going?"

Smoke smiled, "We're going to a quiet place where the only people present will be the two of us and all of nature."

"I can't wait!" I shot back.

"Neither can I," replied Smoke. Then he continued, "Would you like something to drink?" he asked as he held a glass in his hand.

"Sure, you can pour me something to drink," I answered.

After the long ride, we finally arrived at our destination. We pulled up on a pier next to the water. Smoke escorted me to the yacht that sat in the water waiting for us. As we walked up the ramp I couldn't help but admire how beautiful the stars were spread across the sky. Even the reflection of the moon sat on the water so beautifully! A single table covered by a white cloth sat in the middle of the large, spacious yacht. Two chairs rested on each side of the table. A man wearing a white jacket with a black bowtie placed two glasses and a champagne bottle in the center of the table. Me and Smoke took a seat as more men wearing white jackets with black bowties came to our table. The men carried all types of different food on the dishes they sat at our table. On one dish there was tuna-steak, another dish carried lobster tails. Shrimps of all kind were spread across the table and the men were still bringing dishes. Everything felt like a dream come true. Me and Smoke sat at the table, eating and getting to know each other a little better.

"Smoke this boat is beautiful!" I complimented. My eyes wandered all over the décor of the yacht.

"I'm happy you like it," he replied.

"You really didn't have to go through all of this trouble."

Smoke sipped his champagne then replied, "I believe in working for what I want. To me the trouble was very much worth it, am I wrong?"

I cracked half a smile while placing my hand under my chin, "I don't think somebody right as you could ever be wrong."

"I'm wrong right now. I'm so wrong!"

With an eyebrow raised I replied, "Is that so?"

"Yeah it is so. I wanna express myself to you, can I do that?"

"I don't see why you can't," I replied.

Smoke sliced into the tuna-steak before placing it in his mouth. When he was finished he spoke, "I'm getting ready to be so honest with. I don't want you to take this the wrong way because I'm being so sincere. Please believe everything I'm getting ready to express to you is nothing but the truth."

Smoke had my undivided attention, "I'm listening, go ahead and speak," I told him.

"I don't know how this is gonna make you feel, but I'm married. I've been married for quite some time. I'm not gonna sit here and act like I'm not happy with my wife. In fact I am happy with her, she is the first lady of my life and that's no secret. However, I find myself strangely attracted to you. I don't know how, I don't know why, I just am. And while you may find this hard to believe, I haven't even thought about another woman since I've been married. This isn't by force, it's simply my choice. Not trying to toot my own horn, but I've had plenty of occasions where a female wanted nothing more than a one night stand with me. Those are the females who will lose every time. I can't stand an airhead. A woman with a big booty and a empty brain can't do anything for me..."

I interrupted, "Smoke why...?"

Smoke cut me off before I was able to get a sentence out. He held up his hand then continued, "I'm telling you this because that's just the kind of guy I am. I'm what you would call an extremist. I take things to the extreme because I know that's where it'll end up. That's why you came home to a house full of roses, teddy bears and a warm bubble bath. I believe you deserve the extreme. The same thing applies regarding me being married. I'm telling you this to avoid the headaches later on down the line. I'm giving you the choice to continue seeing me or to leave me alone. I just want to make you aware of my status because it isn't changing. And like I stated, I'm so attracted to you. It's like you have these secret powers over me, I can't really explain it, but I know I want you to be a part of my life. Even if that means we have to be platonic friends, I'm all for it."

I had to take a moment to reflect on everything I was just told. After letting Smoke's words marinate in my mind, I spoke, "Smoke, I'm gonna be real with you. I'm not the one who likes to play number two..."

Smoke cut me off, "That's cool. I guess I gotta respect that."

Before Smoke could proceed, I began speaking again, "You didn't let me finish. Now, like I was saying, I'm not the one who likes to play number two but..." I paused then continued, "I like you." Smoke's eyes lit up, I smiled then continued, "So I guess I would be willing to take a backseat for this ride, but I will not tolerate anything less than your all during the time we spend together."

Smoke reached across the table to grab my hand, "That's just the minimum," he replied. "I plan on making you a very happy lady," he added.

"We'll see," I replied.

The moment was interrupted by the sound of Smoke's ringing phone. Smoke flipped the phone open, "Hello," he spoke. I continued hearing Smoke's end of the conversation. "What you worried about it for...? Didn't I tell you I would take care of that...? Stop acting like a little bitch, you knew what I was doing before I got there... what...? For what...? Yeah aight, hold on!"

Smoke handed me his phone, "It's for you."

I was shocked, "For me? Who is it?" I grabbed the phone before Smoke was able to answer me.

"Hello," I spoke into the phone.

"Thanks for cleaning all these roses up!" said Tazz in a sarcastic and jealous way.

I laughed, "Tazz, I'll take care of that when I get back. I'm sorry. I ain't mean to leave everything the way it is. I blew out all the candles though."

"Aren't you a sweetheart!? When you coming home anyway?"

"I don't know I'm on a date. But when I get there I'll

take care of everything."

Tazz sucked his teeth, "Whatever! What you want me to do with these ugly ass teddy bears 'cause this one sitting in my room definitely gotta get up outta here!"

"You can put them in my room. Is there anything else?" I asked. Tazz hung up in my ear. I laughed then handed Smoke his phone. Smoke wasn't laughing. He didn't find the situation funny at all.

"Let me ask you a question Mahogany?"

"What's up?" I replied.

"What kind of relationship do you and Tazz have?"

"Me and Tazz have a business relationship, other than that, we just cool. I'm his Bonnie, he's my Clyde," I joked.

"Are you sure?"

I looked at Smoke with a crooked eye, "What do you mean by that?"

"Nah, I'm just saying... dude is acting like he has a problem with you being here with me tonight. He bitching and moaning about some damn rose petals like I ain't tell him what I was doing before I got there."

I waved my hand in the air, "Don't worry about Tazz. Sometimes he's just a little crazy, that's all."

"You ever slept with your Clyde?"

I put my drink down then leaned closer towards Smoke, "What part don't you understand about Tazz is my homeboy and I'm his homegirl? That's it! It ain't like we married," I laughed.

Smoke laughed, "Let's make tonight the first and last time we speak about my wife," replied Smoke.

"Fine, let's also make this night the first and last night we speak about me and Tazz's relationship."

In a calm voice Smoke replied, "I don't know if I can

do that."

"Why not?" I asked.

"I know this might sound strange to you, but I don't like to share what's mine. While Tazz may be my dude and I like him, I like you better and I want you all to myself if that's okay with you?"

"It sounds to me like you wanna have your cake and eat it to."

"Ain't nothing wrong with that," Smoke shot back.

I laughed, "You wouldn't see anything wrong with that, but anyway, enough about this. Tell me some things about you, what kind of work do you do?"

Smoke paused before he answered, "I do work, I'm in the uhm... construction business."

I laughed, "You're in the 'uhm construction business' huh? You couldn't think of anything better than that?"

"Foreal, it's my company," Smoke answered.

"What's the name of this construction company?"

"Cracks."

"The name of your construction company is 'Cracks'?"

"Yeah, Cracks construction."

I twisted my face then folded my arms into one another, "You just sat here and confessed the undying love you have for your wife, but you can't even be upfront with me about what type of work you do?"

Smoke sat up, "Listen, the less you know about the business I do, the better off you'll be. Trust me!"

"I'm trying," I confessed. "You wouldn't happen to own a house in the Hamptons or have a mall and a house in the process of being built, would you?" I added.

Smoke looked confused, "No. Where did that come from?"

I laughed, "I'm just thinking about something, that's all."

When the two of us finished eating, we walked around the large yacht. We took a moment to lean over the railing praising the beautiful view of the stars, moon and water. The yacht was moving, but it didn't even feel like it. Smoke grabbed me by my waist then whispered in my ear.

"What is your biggest fear?"

I looked him in his eyes, "I fear losing control. If I lose control, I lose everything. I've been there before, I don't ever wanna go back!" I whispered.

"Well you don't ever have to be scared again. I'm here. I'll protect you, if you let me."

Our eyes meet then our lips touched. We kissed passionately before laying down on top of each other. Smoke lifted my dress and removed my panties. Then he began kissing my thighs. We made love under the stars before falling asleep next to one another.

• • •

I danced around the living-room listening to my walkman as I vacuumed the carpet. I almost had a heart attack when Tazz tapped my shoulder. I turned the loud vacuum cleaner off, pressed the 'stop' button on my walkman then removed my headphones.

"You scared the shit out of me!" I said to Tazz.

"I don't know why. I was calling for the longest, you ain't hear me?"

"How could I hear you, you see what I was doing?"

"Yeah well Smoke wanted you on the phone."

A smile appeared on my face. I walked in the kitchen

to pick up the phone. To my surprise, the phone was on the receiver. I walked back into the living-room. Tazz was sitting on the couch watching television with his feet propped up on his coffee table. I snatched the remote out of Tazz's hand then pressed 'power.'

"I thought Smoke called me?"

Tazz looked at me with no emotion, "Yeah, and?"

I placed my hand on my hip, "And? Don't play with me Tazz! What did you tell Smoke?"

Tazz sucked his teeth, "I told him the truth, you ain't answer me so you wasn't here, right?"

I raised an eyebrow, "Really? You a funny mother-fucker Tazz, you know that? You seen me around this bitch all day, then when Smoke calls I ain't here." I shook my head then added, "You really need to stop trippin'. You knew from the gate this was strictly a business relationship between me and you. So, all this jealous shit you trying to pull is straight wack!"

My cell phone started ringing, "That's probably Smoke now," I said as I ran to my phone.

"Good!" replied Tazz. "I don't know why he ain't call that phone in the first place," he added. I ignored him and answered my phone.

"Hello," I spoke almost out of breath.

"What's up sexy, where you at?" It was Smoke. My big smile got even bigger.

I replied, "I'm in the house. I just had to bark on Tazz. He told me you called after he already hung up on you."

"Tazz is a funny dude. When you gon' move outta there and get a place of your own?"

"Negative. I have to stay here. Me and Tazz have business to take care of."

"You don't have to do nothing but stay sexy, stay mine and die."

I laughed, "Is that right?"

"For sure! I'm coming to get you right now. I got a surprise for you!"

"You're just full of surprises, huh?"

Smoke laughed, "I'll be there in one hour. Wear something sexy for me."

"Of course! I'll see you when you get here baby."

We hung up the phone. Almost as if Tazz was listening to our phone conversation, he walked into my room soon as I hung up.

"Mahogany, let me ask you a question?"

I rolled my eyes, "What you gotta say Tazz?"

"How does it feel to be number two?"

That statement sent the blood in my veins boiling. I looked at Tazz like I wanted to kill him, "Excuse me!?"

Tazz laughed, "Nah, I'm just curious, that's all. I'm curious to know why females will have a nigga right in front of their face who's willing to give them the world if the female would just let them, but they'll rather go with the next nigga who they know could never be one hundred percent theirs. Since you and Smoke been messing around for a few months and you seem happier than I ever saw you before. I'm just wondering if you could help me understand this madness, do chicks like to be treated like shit?"

"Tazz, you know what? I'm not gonna even dignify that question with an answer. Please get out of my room, I have to get dress."

Tazz cracked a smile, "You deserve better than that Mahogany, word. You broke my heart!"

I closed the door behind Tazz as he left my room. I

jumped in the shower, picked out a sexy outfit then waited for Smoke to come.

When Smoke entered the house, I saw Tazz exit the house. Me and Smoke smiled at the sight of each other. Smoke walked over to me then planted a kiss on my lips.

"What's up with Tazz, he aight?" Smoke asked.

I frowned, "I don't have time to baby-sit anybody. I'm here to do a job, that's all. Tazz will be alright."

Smoke hugged me tight, "You so smell good!"

"Thank you," I replied, "I'm wearing Spring Flower's made by Creed," I added.

"That's the perfume I bought you, right?"

"It sure is. Now, where are we going?"

Smoke smiled then grabbed my waist, "First we have to get you ready."

I was confused. I looked at myself then held out my hands and twirled around, "I am ready."

Smoke put one finger against his temple then shook his head, "Nah, I don't think you're ready. It seems like you're missing something."

"What?" I frowned.

Me and Smoke walked into my room. Smoke lead me to the full length mirror. He stood behind me then put his arms around me.

"I don't like those earrings you have on."

I touched my ears, "What's wrong with my earrings?"

Smoke pulled a small box out of his pocket then opened it, "I don't like those earrings because their not these."

My eyes were glued to the earrings inside the box. I was looking at five karat, platinum diamond studs. My face lit up as I about faced and hugged Smoke. He was smiling, "You like 'em?" he asked.

"I love them!" I replied very excited.

"Let me help you put them on." Smoke removed the gold hoops I was wearing. Then he placed the diamond studs in my ear. I stood in front of the mirror smiling. The studs looked beautiful in my ear.

Smoke kissed my cheek, "I still feel like you're missing something."

"What are you up to, Smoke?"

Smoke walked over to my bed where he stretched out, "Maybe I'm bugging. You might not be missing something after all."

When I turned around to walk over to Smoke, he was holding a pair of Chanel sunglasses in his hand.

"Put these on," he said. "You're gonna need them in South Beach, Miami," he added. Before I was able to say another word Smoke showed me two round-trip tickets to Miami. I jumped on the bed then started kissing all over him.

"We're going to South Beach, Miami baby!? When are we leaving!? What am I gonna wear!? Oh my God I have to get my hair done and go shopping!"

I rolled off of Smoke, he sat up. "We don't have time for that baby. We're leaving today. We have to be at the airport in the next four hours."

"Four hours!? Oh my God! My bags are not even packed! How are we gonna make it!? How long are we staying!?"

"We're staying for the weekend, and, you don't need any luggage. Anything you want, you'll get it down there."

I jumped into Smoke's arms, "I love you!"

"I love you back," he stated then kissed my neck.

Me and Smoke walked out the door. I was wearing a one-piece Chanel jumpsuit with my new Chanel sunglasses and diamond studs. Smoke looked sexy in his jeans and t-shirt. We jumped into his 850i BMW then headed to the airport with nothing but our passports in our hands.

• • •

Hopping off of our first class seats on the plane, I thought life couldn't get any better! The Miami heat felt good against my skin. Smoke had a limo waiting for us as soon as our flight landed. We entered the limo then rode to our destination. To my surprise we didn't pull up to a hotel or a resort. Instead, we pulled up to a beautiful brick building which housed nothing but condos. I looked out the window admiring the beautiful building and the clean streets. The door to the limo opened. I looked at Smoke.

"Where are we going? Shouldn't we stop by the hotel first?"

Smoke grabbed my hand, we exited the limo, "This is where we're staying, it's my condo. I haven't spent a single night in it since I purchased it. I was hoping we could spend the night here together. It can be like our home away from home."

I looked toward the pretty, blue sky. I didn't see tall buildings like I was use to in New York, or half dead trees like I've seen in North Carolina. All I saw was beautiful palm trees and birds soaring in the air. The scenery reminded me of something off of a postcard. I wrapped my arms around Smoke's neck, "This is beautiful! I could stay here forever! It can be our home away from home!"

Smoke lead me towards his condo. Once we were inside it was breathtaking!

Inside Smoke's condo there were two levels. The spiral stairs leading from one floor of the condo to the other looked like they'd never been stepped on. The kitchen was big and fancy. It looked like it was straight off the pages of a magazine. What I loved the most was the beautiful view of the beach. Through the clear glass patio doors, I was able to see the sand and crystal-blue water. People on the beach looked like they were having the time of their lives. I opened the glass doors then walked onto the patio. Inhaling the fresh air, I turned around to find Smoke making his way to be with me.

"Do you like the view baby?" he asked.

"I love it!" I replied. "I have to get a bikini for the beach! I can't wait to feel the water against my body."

"We can go handle that right now. I know the perfect spot," Smoke replied.

"Then let's go!" I shot back.

Me and Smoke ended up going to *South Beach Couture*. It was a shopping area with designer labels. I was in awe of most of the things we came across. There was so much to choose from I wanted almost everything. Dragging Smoke into so many different stores, he found it cute at first, but later he became tired of me running him raggedy. I wasn't denied anything. I had clothing, shoes, beachwear and accessories. I even picked up sexy sleepwear so I could wear it for Smoke. Smoke was spending money like it grew on trees. Each time he pulled out one of those fat knots, it made him look even sexier. I laughed out loud thinking about something he told me on our first date. "I own Cracks Construction Company." Yeah right? I thought to myself. I knew he was lying then, I still knew he was lying now. I knew his type.

When we arrived back at the condo, Smoke only had two shopping bags for himself. The rest of the bags belonged to me. I had so many bags it looked like I was staying for two weeks instead of one weekend. Smoke undressed and headed for the shower while I tried on my new things. When Smoke finished using the shower, I jumped in. Before I was all the way out of the shower, Smoke was standing in the bathroom waiting for me to get out. He was wearing a wife beater and boxers. His hard dick peeked through his boxers. Smoke grabbed my naked body then gently placed kisses all over me, from my head to my toes. I returned the affection. Smoke slowly came out of his boxers as I removed his shirt. His large hands picked me up by my waist. He sat me on top of the sink as he buried his face in between my legs. I moaned uncontrollably from the pleasure Smoke bestowed upon me. I grabbed the back of his head causing his face to become buried deeper and deeper into my pussy. When Smoke was done pleasing me with his fat, wet tongue, he lifted his head slowly. When our eyes meet, he stuck his tongue down my throat. Our tongue's wrestled leaving both of us wanting each other bad!

I slid off of the sink. Smoke ran his fingers through my hair. I slowly backed away from him.

"Where are you going?" Smoke asked.

I grabbed his wrist, "Follow me," I whispered.

We went into the master bedroom. I laid Smoke on the waterbed. Then I placed a honey-lemon halls cough drops in my mouth. I used my tongue to play around with the halls. Once I felt the tingling sensation in my mouth that the halls gave off, I proceeded to give Smoke head. And just as I predicted, Smoke was feeling the same sensation on his dick that I felt in my mouth. His moans were loud and clear! His eyes couldn't stop rolling in the back of his head, and his toes were curled so tight they were starting to look like a fist! His dick was sticky and wet from the halls mixed with my spit. It wasn't long before I started riding him backwards.

The next morning we were up bright and early. I was wearing my new all black Dolce & Gabbana bikini with the Chanel shades Smoke surprised me with. The bikini looked like it was made just for me. And the shades were a perfect fit for my face. Smoke surprised me when he informed me we'd be jet-skiing! I was excited and nervous at the same time!

When we finally got to the beach, only us and a handful of other early-birds were out. Smoke didn't waste any time hopping on his jet-ski. I didn't waste any time hopping on the back.

"You ever been jet-skiing before?" asked Smoke.

"Uh-uh," I replied.

Smoke cracked a smile, "Well hold on tight, I don't wanna lose you, understand?"

I didn't reply. I simply held Smoke tighter and leaned my head against his back. Before I could blink, we were in the water, jet-skiing! We rocked from side to side as the water splashed us every step of the way. I fell off of the jet-ski a few times, but Smoke was right there laughing and helping me up every time. The experience was so fun I didn't ever want it to end!

Later that evening we found ourselves at *Osteria del Teatro* a casually elegant restaurant. The atmosphere was cool and calm. Countless Italian eateries surrounded the place, but none of them was a match to the delicious, fresh seafood we ate at *Osteria del Teatro*. Our waiters were friendly and welcoming. Even the music playing in the background was nice. It wasn't too hard or too soft. It was a balance, just the way I like it.

On our final night in South Beach we decided to go clubbing. We walked into a place beautiful enough to stimulate anyone's mind. The illuminated glass-enclosed water walls which lead to the grand lobby were breathtaking! The dancers and savvy crowd added an exotic flair to the scenery. Tables were lined along the balconies. High-tech lighting and futuristic raised platforms were present throughout the club. Me and Smoke danced the night away as couples around us did the same.

When we finally exited the club the sun was setting. I didn't realize we spent so much time in there. I accredited that to having such a good time. Before we were able to get in our car, a guy ran up to us asking if we'd like to take a picture. Smoke thought about what the guy said for maybe two seconds. Then he threw his hands in the air and replied, "What the fuck, why not!?" I smiled and so did the picture guy. Me and Smoke moved closer to each other then posed for the picture. I was standing in front. Smoke was standing in back of me with his hands wrapped around me and his chin resting on my shoulder. The camera guy kneeled on one knee then positioned the camera on me and Smoke. "Say cheese!" We smiled and the camera guy snapped the picture. The flash nearly blinded us. When the Polaroid was dry, the camera guy handed it to us. "That will be ten dollars," he said. Smoke peeled off a twenty and told the guy to keep the change. The picture came out beautiful. That was our last night in South Beach, Miami.

Chapter 17

Slow Down...

Arriving back in North Carolina was bitter-sweet. I was happy to be home, but I was sad me and Smoke were parting. I always dreaded leaving him. But at the same time I knew I couldn't get upset, he was a married man and I was nothing more than his mistress with benefits. I was beginning to miss Miami already and we weren't even back home for two hours yet. I stared out the window not saying a word as Smoke drove towards my house. So many thoughts were running through my mind, most of them about Smoke. I was happy for the time we spent together, but bitter for the time we spent apart. I couldn't imagine Smoke touching or kissing someone the way he touched and kissed me, but if I told myself he didn't do those things to his wife I would've been in denial. I ain't gonna even front. At first I thought I'd have a chance to convince Smoke that I was the only woman he'd need. I really thought one day I could possibly be his wife. I was slowly learning I was waiting for a day that would never come. I knew what he told me in the beginning about not leaving his wife, but I still thought I could change that. After coming to the reality that Smoke wasn't leaving his wife, I tried to convince myself that I was cool with just having him in my life, but I wasn't. I wanted a real relationship that had room for growth. Smoke interrupted my thoughts with a pat on my thigh.

"You're so quiet over there, you aight?" he asked.

I forged a smile, "I'm alright. I just wish we could've stayed longer, that's all."

Smoke continued rubbing my thigh, "We'll go back. I promise. I wouldn't have mind staying longer myself. I could use a long vacation."

"So why didn't we stay Smoke?"

Smoke took his eyes off the road for a split second then looked at me, "C'mon Mahogany. We both know the answer to that."

"Mmm hmm. We sure do," I replied.

"What's that s'pose to mean?" he asked.

"Nothing, it is what it is. That's all."

We pulled up in front of my house. I looked at Smoke then put up the peace sign.

"Call me when you get a chance," I told him. Then I exited the car. Smoke came running around to the passenger side.

"Mahogany, what's wrong with you?"

"Nothing, what's wrong with you?"

"I'm fine, but I don't know what's your problem!? Since when do I get the peace sign? No hug, no kiss, no nothing, it's like that?"

I sighed, "Smoke what you want me to do?"

Smoke nodded his head, "Yeah, you got a attitude. You just straight flipped somewhere between the airport and on our way here. It's all good though. Let me help you in the house with your bags."

I grabbed a few bags, Smoke grabbed the rest. We entered the house. Tazz seemed more upset than I was.

"Oh, so you remember where you live? I thought you and Smoke took Totoe and moved to the wonderful Land of Oz!"

I sucked my teeth and kept walking towards my bedroom, "Not now Tazz!"

Smoke was so upset he dropped the bags right where he stood then turned to face Tazz, "Yo, what's up Tazz? You aight man 'cause every time I come here you acting like you got a problem with me seeing Mahogany, what's up with that?"

"I ain't got no problem. You and Mahogany could do whatever the hell y'all want!"

"You sure about that?" asked Smoke.

Tazz laughed, "I'm sure about that. If Mahogany wanna play second to your wife, I ain't tryna stop her any longer. She a grown ass woman, and you and her can do whatever the hell y'all want, word!"

Smoke frowned, "What was the first part of that statement?"

Tazz replied, "I said if Mahogany wants to play second to your wife, Melissa, remember her?" Tazz asked sarcastically then continued, "Then that's her business. I'm not tryna stand in the way of this thing y'all got going on any longer. Straight like that!"

Smoke gritted his teeth as he moved closer to Tazz, "Listen duke. You my man and I'm tryna keep it that way, but you better check the way you coming at me! All this extra shit you call yourself doing ever since I hooked up with Mahogany is unnecessary! Quit while you ahead. You don't wanna keep pushing my buttons, I'm telling you."

Tazz looked at Smoke then nodded his head. Without saying another word Tazz walked away from Smoke. Smoke picked up the bags he placed on the floor then proceeded towards my bedroom. I didn't want him to know I was ease dropping on their conversation, so I picked up a magazine, ran to my bed then laid across like I had been reading the magazine the entire time. Smoke entered the room then closed the door.

"You gotta get the fuck up outta here!" he told me.

I closed the magazine then sat up, "Why, what are you talking about?" I asked.

"I'm talking about this nigga Tazz. I can't continue seeing you like this! I don't wanna be uncomfortable every time I wanna see you. This dude is really like obsessed with you! We need to get you outta here soon!"

I grabbed Smoke's shirt, "Don't worry about Tazz. He just be bugging sometimes."

Smoke pushed my hand away, "Nah, fuck that! I am worried about Tazz. You can't continue seeing me while you living up in here, it just ain't gon' work!"

I raised an eyebrow, "Excuse me? Was that an ultimatum?"

"It is what it is!" Smoke shot back.

"You got a lot of fucking nerve, you know that?"

Smoke pointed to himself like he was confused about who I was speaking to, "I got a lot of nerve?" he asked.

"Yes you!" I replied.

Smoke frowned, "It's funny that you say that 'cause I'm starting to think the same thing about you. You tell me you love me, I know Tazz get on your nerves about our relationship just as much as he gets on mines, but you don't wanna leave his house. That sounds like two people who are fucking to me!"

I hopped off my bed outraged by Smoke's Statements. I got up in his face real close then said what I had to say. "You want it raw Smoke, then I'ma give it to you raw! My mother was kilt the day after my fifteenth birthday! Since then I was living with different members of my family, if that's what you wanna call them! My dream of becoming a psychiatrist that could've been a reality, you might as well say died with my mother! I was with one guy who I loved deeply for a long time! I left him when he basically told me I had to play his way or not at all! To survive I stripped and fucked niggaz for cash! The girl who I thought was my best friend turned out to be a lying, conniving, sneaky bitch whose brother had a lot to do with the death of my moms, not to mention I caught her with my one true love's dick in her mouth! When I got sick and tired of stripping I left it alone then married a guy who I thought cared for me plus had lots of cash! I later learned this guy just married me to become a citizen! One day I came home to nothing! All of my shit was gone, he took it, he robbed me! With no one to turn to and my back against the wall, Tazz saved me! He gave me what no one else would – a chance! So don't expect me to turn my back on him and just leave. And like I told you a million times before; me and Tazz's relationship don't have shit to do with fucking, it's strictly business!"

Smoke didn't say a word. He kissed me on my cheek then left my bedroom and left the house. A week went by and I still didn't hear from Smoke.

• • •

I sat on my bed looking at the picture me and Smoke took in Miami. We looked so happy, so complete. Where did it all go wrong? I thought to myself. A tear fell from my eye then I heard a knock on my bedroom door. I quickly wiped the tear, hid the picture under my pillow then answered the knock.

"Come in."

Tazz stuck his head in my room then finally he walked in. Holding a comb in his hand he looked at me, "Can you braid my hair?" he asked.

"Yeah, just gimme a minute," I told him.

"Aight, cool! You alright? You look like something is bothering you," asked Tazz.

"Who me?" I pointed. "I'm good. My allergies are just bothering me, that's all." I lied. "Thanks for asking though."

"I'll be in the living-room," Tazz stated.

"Alright, I'll be out there in a minute."

Tazz walked out of my bedroom closing the door behind him. I picked up the picture I hid under the pillow. I reminisced about me and Smoke's time in Miami then I kissed the picture. What happened to us? I asked.

A few minutes later I was in the living-room braiding Tazz's hair.

"How do you want it?" I asked Tazz.

"However you wanna give it to me," he replied.

I tapped him with the comb, "Boy! You better cut it out! I'ma just do zigzags parts straight back, is that cool?"

"Do you," Tazz replied.

I took a look at the couch we were sitting on, "Ain't you happy you got rid of the old ass, ugly ass, stripe couch you had!?"

"You gon' stop talking about my shit! I liked the couch!"

"Whatever," I replied.

There was a brief moment of silence between us. Then I spoke.

"Tazz, let me ask you a question?"

"What's up?" Tazz replied.

"Why you always trippin' whenever Smoke comes through? You're the one who introduced us."

Tazz sighed, "You still think I'm trippin' over that dude? I ain't thinking shit about him. It's you who I'm concerned for, I know he can't love you like you deserve to be loved. You're compromising yourself when you shouldn't have to. It's no secret that he has a wife, and harsh as it may sound, if you're messing around with a married man then you're nothing more than his slut. No matter how much money he spends on you, or how many trips he takes you on, at the end of the day he's still a married man who has a wife waiting for him to come home at night."

"Tazz, I hear what you're saying, but I don't think you hear where I'm coming from. If I choose to be with someone, whether you like that person for me or not, no one has to deal with the consequences of my actions but me! It's not up to you to pick and choose the guys I date. I'm not a child and I shouldn't be treated like one. So if you feel like you don't like a person for me, that's okay. I'm not saying you have to. It's okay to disagree. All I'm asking is that you give me the same respect you would want me to give you."

Tazz replied, "But don't you think you deserve better?"

"Yes I do, but let me handle my own issues my way. You cannot play daddy and hold my hand for the rest of my life. Let me be my own woman."

Tazz sighed again, "Listen Mahogany. All I'm saying is you know how I feel about you, you've known how I felt about you for years. I use to dream of the day we'd be together living happily ever after, the white house, the picket fence, the dog and two kids, the whole nine! But you never had time to even look my way. I was always getting brushed off, shot down or looked over. So when the opportunity finally came to have you become a part of my life, there was no way I was letting you get away. I thought by you being around me you'd see just how much I could love you, but I was wrong. Then slowly I was learning to deal with that and accept the fact that we could just be cool, but then you let Smoke knock down that door I've been tryna get in for years knowing he has a wife. My mind kept telling me to leave it alone and let y'all be, but my heart was saying something else. My heart wouldn't allow me to sit back and watch you settle for less when I know you deserve the best! I wouldn't mind losing you to a man who knows your worth and he's willing to take care of you like you should be taken care of. But to lose you to someone who only sees you as second best…that's something I cannot live with. That's like me watching you get up every morning driving a broken down Prelude, all the while knowing I got the Bentley waiting right here for you. You asking me to sit here and watch you settle when I know I got the key to take you on that ride you deserve! All I want is what's best for you, you feel me?"

I paused in the middle of braiding Tazz hair, "You

know what Tazz? I've been doing a lot of thinking and I think it might be time for me to get a crib of my own."

Tazz turned around, "Oh, it's like that? Now you wanna move out over this nigga? Where you gon' go?"

I sucked my teeth, "It's not even like that! Maybe I'll stay down here, maybe I'll go back to New York. I just don't think us living together is gonna work out. I truly believe the feelings you have for me are too strong for you to ever accept the fact of me being with someone else. And since I like you as a friend and a brother, I think I should probably leave before things turn ugly. What's gonna happen the next time someone you don't approve of wants to take me out? Are you gonna shake everybody down?" I laughed then continued, "I just think our friendship will last longer if we didn't live together, that's all."

"What you gon' do if you go back to New York?"

I replied, "I don't know. Maybe I'll go to school and get my cosmetology license to do hair. Or I could open up a small business or something. Maybe I could even try to get a record deal. I always had a passion for singing and songwriting, and I did take a few lessons when I was younger. Who knows... maybe the demo I'll make can fall in the hands of the right person. I guess there's a lot I can do in New York."

"And what you gon' do if you stay here?"

"Maybe I'll get a real job or I could keep working for you."

Tazz interrupted, "You tryna say my job ain't real?"

I laughed, "Tazz you know what I mean. We all gotta get it together sooner or later."

I finished the last braid in Tazz hair. He stood to his feet and so did I. We hugged each other, then Tazz looked me in my eyes, "I hope you know what you doing baby-girl."

I nodded my head, "I hope so to."

The next morning Tazz helped me pack my bags. I hadn't decided where I was going just yet, but I knew I needed something to call my own. I packed my bags early to give me more incentive to find an apartment. I didn't need anything big and fancy, I just needed something I could call mine. Me and Tazz sat on the floor reminiscing about the good ol' days.

"Remember your parties?" Tazz asked, "Those joints use to be off the hook! I don't know what ya moms use to put in that chicken, but that shit was good like a moth-erfucker!"

"That chicken was the bomb right?" I laughed then continued, "But yo, you 'member Dey-Dey? His ass use to tear that chicken and them Cheese Doodles up! And his ass couldn't dance for shit, but my moms always made sure he won the contest."

"Hell yeah!" Tazz replied, "I use to be tighter than a motherfucker every time he won! I was tryna get a little change back then myself, but that nigga kept winning every year!"

I laughed so hard I was holding my stomach, "Those were the good ol' days! I wonder what happened to Dey-Dey?"

"Dey-Dey is good," Tazz replied then continued, "He got a football scholarship and that nigga got a baby."

"Word?" I replied surprised. "I guess Dey-Dey came a long way from being the fat boy at all my parties with the tight ass superman shirts, huh?"

"Yeah, he did. I'm hoping he gets drafted. He's s'pose

to be real good so most likely he'll make it to the pros'."

I paused for a second then looked at Tazz. Holding up one hand I spoke, "Hold up! How the hell you live way out here, but you always know what's going on in New York?"

Tazz smiled, "C'mon baby, you know me! I am the streets! My eyes and ears are on everything!"

Suddenly my bedroom door was pushed open. Smoke stood in the doorway with a smirk on his face.

"Am I interrupting something?" he asked. I looked at Smoke. Tazz looked at me. I didn't say a word. Tazz rose up off the floor. He walked over to Smoke and replied, "Nah, you ain't interrupting nothing." They sized each other up then Tazz left the room. Smoke pushed my door closed then took a seat on my bed.

"You going somewhere?" he asked looking at my suitcases.

I rose to me feet, "As a matter of fact I am," I replied.

"Smoke licked his lips, "So you was just gon' leave without saying bye to me, huh?"

I rolled my eyes, "You gotta be around for me to say goodbye to you. It was obvious to me that you had better things to do than to come check me."

"So where you going?" Smoke asked.

"I don't know yet, but I'm outta here!"

"I'm supposed to believe that?" Smoke laughed.

"You could believe whatever you want, but I'm telling you, I'm out!"

"I want you to take a ride with me Mahogany."

"Ride with you where?" I asked.

"You'll see. It'll be worth your wild, trust me."

I shook my head, "I'm not getting on no planes with you. I don't have time to be stuck on a yacht, and I'm not tryna spend much time with you. As long as we have an understanding, we could take that ride." I folded my arms, one into the other, "Now where we going?" I asked.

"You ain't gotta worry about none of that." Smoke assured me. Then he continued, "The place we're going to is only about a half-an-hour ride from here. I'll be outside waiting in the car." Smoke left the room.

Minutes later I was sitting in the passenger seat of Smoke's ride. We drove for about thirty minutes like he said. Then we arrived inside of a gated community in Cramer Mountain, North Carolina. I was looking at the prettiest mini mansion I'd ever seen. I turned sideways to look at Smoke, "Why are we here?" I asked.

"I got some things I wanna show you," Smoke replied in a calm voice.

Both of us hopped out of the car. We walked up the brick path, which lead us to the huge wooden doors of the house. Smoke turned the gold handle on the door. The door flew open, we entered the house. I was like a kid at an amusement park, my eyes wandered all over the place. Fine Italian leather furniture was present throughout the house. The ceiling was so high. I wondered how anyone was able to get the beautiful chandeliers up there. Royal-red wall-to-wall carpet covered the floor and the stairs. Pictures of Malcolm X, Dr. King, Assata Shakur and other strong black leaders covered the walls. Smoke grabbed my hand. He led me towards the curved stairs which were long and wide. Before I put one foot on the steps I pulled Smoke back.

"Who lives here?" I asked.

Smoke smiled then kissed my cheek, "You do!" he replied.

"Smoke, stop playing," I warned him.

Smoke sat on the steps then pulled me closer towards him, "I'm not playing! This is all yours. When I gave you that ultimatum I realized I did it out of anger. I didn't give you much of a choice or a solution. I basically told you it was my way or no way. Now I'm giving you a choice and a solution. The solution is this house is yours. The choice to move in is completely up to you." Smoke stood to his feet, "So what do you wanna do Mahogany?"

I took another good look at the gorgeous mansion, looked at Smoke, then jumped on him like a big kid! My legs were wrapped around his waist. "Let's go get my stuff!" I told him.

• • •

Picking up my things were easy. I explained to Tazz where I would be staying. To my surprise, Tazz didn't get upset at all. In fact, he was happy I was staying in North Carolina instead of moving back to New York. We said our goodbyes and promised to keep in touch. Then I was off to my new home in Cramer Mountain.

I was so excited about my new home! It took a little while to let the reality sink in that this was my mansion, mine, mine, mine! Smoke took me on a tour through the house. He was just full of surprises! I became even more excited when he escorted me to an indoor garage where a purple Range Rover with lavender seats and purple piping sat. He made it very clear to me that the Range Rover was mines as well! I was beginning to love it more and more. My heart raced as I came in contact with a giant fish tank once we made our way back into the mansion! The tank was so tropical and beautiful!

"What kind of fish are those?" I pointed while asking Smoke.

He hugged me tight, "Those are called red belly piranha fish. Do you like them?"

"I like the different colors they're changing!" I replied, "Oh, look at that one! And that one! That one too!" I pointed. I was enjoying watching the fish. As we made our way through various parts of the house, I oohed and ahhed at nearly everything we came in contact with. Inside of my walk-in closet was a big safe! I knew there had to be plenty of money in there for me. I couldn't wait to open it and view its contents. I ran towards the safe.

"Baby, open it up!" I shouted while rubbing it down as if it was my own body. Immediately Smoke came towards me and the safe. He grabbed my arm and pulled me away from the safe.

"That safe is not yours, it's mine! I don't wanna see you near it, understand?"

I snatched my arm away, "Alright then! Why do you have it in my closet if it's yours?"

"How many times do I have to tell you my business is my business?"

"I'm sorry," I replied.

Smoke walked out of my closet, I followed him. When I was close enough to touch him, I wrapped my arms around his waist.

"Baby, I'm sorry. I'm just so excited, that's all. Why don't you let me make it up to you?" I put my hands under his shirt then continued, "I'll run you a nice bubble bath. I'll feed you strawberries and whip cream with a little Mahogany on top. Then in the morning, I'll make steak, cheese-eggs and grits! C'mon daddy, let me take care of you," I persisted.

Smoke removed my hands from underneath his shirt. He kissed and licked each individual finger of mine before he spoke.

"Baby, I can't stay tonight. I wish I could though."

Smoke might as well have stabbed me in the heart with that statement. This was the part of our relationship I hated. Just when everything felt so right, he did something to remind me of how our relationship was so wrong! I loved the beautiful house he put me in, but was I supposed to stay here alone every night while he went home to his wife? I was ready to flip right there! However, I didn't say anything. I simply laid on my huge bed and curled up in a fetal position. Smoke took a seat next to me. He ran his fingers through my hair. I stopped him then spoke in a soft voice, "Please leave, Smoke."

Smoke must've thought he heard me wrong, "What did you just say?" he asked as if he was confused.

"I said please leave. If you're leaving I'd rather see you leave now. It's no need for you to stay here and patronize me any longer. Whenever you get a weekend pass gimme a call, otherwise I'd like you to leave right now."

Smoke stood to his feet. He took a set of keys from out of his pockets then placed them on the nightstand. Without saying another word to me Smoke left the house. Tears came rolling down my face.

What was supposed to have been the best time in my life was turning into a nightmare! Yeah, I had all this money, a nice big house with a fancy car, clothes and jewelry most girls only dream of having. But I still wasn't happy. The man who was supposed to be mines wasn't mines at all. While I was dedicated to him – he was dedicated to someone else. Sure Smoke bought me nice things, gave me plenty of cash and rubbed me the right way whenever he had time to come around. But I still felt like a void wasn't being filled in my life. It was for this reason I decided it was time to move on with my life.

I was only in my new home for about two weeks before I decided to leave. While I liked the life of luxury Smoke was providing me with, I didn't like the games being played with my heart.

I came up with an elaborate scheme to get away from it all. I made up a story I knew Smoke would go for. I told him I was going to New York to handle some personal business that required my immediate attention. When I finished handling the business I'd be back in North Carolina.

The truth of the matter was I purchased a one way ticket to New York with no intentions on coming back. I had to lie to Smoke, I knew if I told him my true feelings he wouldn't do anything other than try to stop me from leaving. I realized no matter how much expensive things he got for me, he was never leaving his wife to be with me. That was enough motivation for me to move on with my life.

Between the money I made working with Tazz and the cash Smoke threw my way, I had close to one hundred thousand dollars. That was more then enough cash for me to carry out my plans. Soon as I got back to the big city I would find an apartment I could call my own. Then I'd start school where I'd obtain my cosmetology license. After the license was obtained, I'd open up my own shop. I purchased and read every book I could find about starting a small business. I had my plans down packed. Smoke would never hear from me or see me again. But the thing I was most excited about doing was visiting my mother's grave. I missed her and yearned for her so much that I just had to pay her a visit, speak to her, and let her know what was going on in my life. For me that moment couldn't come soon enough.

I turned out my bedroom light and went to sleep with a smile on my face. I knew the very next day my life would never be the same again. Smoke was picking me up to drive me to the airport at six o'clock in the morning. Little did he know – that would be his last time seeing me.

• • •

The next morning I was awoken to the sound of foot-steps racing up my stairs. I turned on my light then looked at the time. It was only eight minutes after four a.m. Smoke was very early. He and his wife must be going through some problems is what I assumed, after all, he was the only other person with a key besides me. I climbed out of bed and slipped on my slippers. Just as I reached to open my bedroom door, about twenty men with nine mil-limeters and shotguns were standing on the other side. All the guns were pointed directly at me.

"FREEZE FBI!" one of the men shouted. "Put your hands up! Put them up in the air where I can see them, NOW!" another man shouted. I complied with their every command.

"What the fuck is going on!?" I managed to ask. Before anyone could answer me I was thrown facedown to the ground. I heard more footsteps racing up my stairs. FBI agents with big guns and ugly looking dogs were tearing up my house, searching for something! I heard the sound of helicopters, it sound like the helicopters were on top of my roof. The light from the helicopter shining through to the inside of my window was blinding and bright. All I could do was cry as I laid on the floor handcuffed. I was clueless about what was taking place!

Chapter 18

... And It All Ends

All my life I was known as Mahogany Princess Woods.
Today I'm known as 63930-054 – inmate Woods. The
night the Feds raided my house, I thought I was having a
bad nightmare. It turned out, I wasn't lucky enough to
be dreaming. The Feds really were raiding my home and
I really was laying facedown on the ground with my hands
cuffed behind my back.

I already served two years of my sentence, but I still
have five more to go. According to the Feds, I was lucky
to get such a 'light' sentence. My co-defendants, Robert
Miller and Melissa Miller weren't so lucky. Robert Miller
was Smoke's real name. Melissa Miller was his wife. It
turned out another set of FBI agents were raiding their
mansion around the same time mines was being raided.

The entire time I was dealing with Smoke, I thought he
was hiding the fact he was involved with drugs, and that's
how he made his money. I knew his story about owning
'Cracks Construction Company' was a lie soon as the
words left his mouth. Although he couldn't fool me about
owning a construction company, he still managed to fool
me about what he really did. Smoke's real profession was

robbing banks.

Not even in a million years would I have thought Smoke was a bank robber! The authorities estimated Smoke robbed between fourteen to twenty banks in a five year period. They said his M.O was get in and get out. He never left with less than half a million dollars. His wife never helped him with the robberies, but she was aware of what he was doing. In the eyes of the law, she was just as guilty as him. They slapped her with a fifteen year sentence. Smoke was sentenced to life.

As for myself, my crime was 'money laundering' and 'obstruction of justice.' According to the authorities, I was aware of what was going on just as much as his wife was. I tried to tell them they were sadly mistaken. And in my heart, I still believe they knew I wasn't involved in Smoke's activities. But one thing I quickly learned about the Feds is; they hate to be wrong and they hate to be outsmarted. Needless to say, they took the handful of 'evidence' they had placing me involved with the crime, and built a case against me with it. Although the house I was living in was in Smoke's name, just like the other houses he had throughout the states of Miami, Washington, Philly, Atlanta, Virginia and North Carolina. The pigs still managed to turn me into just another statistic so some dumb fuck could get another star on his badge, or stripe on his sleeve.

The strongest part of the entire case built against me was the steel, black safe they found inside of my walk-in closet. The safe contained floor layouts of numerous banks, guns and one-point-two-million dollars in cash that could be traced back to different banks. Another thing which helped the Feds build a case against me was the things I had packed in my suitcase. I had books about starting my own business, the plane ticket to New York and ninety-six-thousand-dollars in cash which I couldn't explain where it came from. That's how the 'money laundering' charge came about.

Nowadays I reside at a medium security level woman's federal prison in Greenville, Illinois. I always wonder how things could've been if I would've went to New York the day before, continued staying with Tazz or snitched like the Feds tried to pressure me into. And although I think long and hard about what would've happened if I moved to New York or stayed with Tazz. Snitching was never an option for me! First of all I didn't know much about Smoke's business to snitch. Even if I did I would've never compromised my integrity and the bond we shared. But somehow the Feds had been convinced I knew more than I lead them to believe. They found it hard to believe Smoke robbed all of those banks alone. They wanted to know where the rest of the money was and who his accomplices were, and they were convinced I could help locate them. Never that! I wouldn't tell them pigs shit stink! But they were persistent. One of the agents played the bad cop while the other one played the good cop who was tryna save me *if only I would cooperate.* They promised me everything but the sun, moon and stars. In the end, they saw their promises fell on deaf ears. I took my seven years like a trooper! Everything in all of Smoke's houses including the houses themselves were seized and auctioned off.

As far as friends and family goes, I keep in contact with Tazz and my cousin Tiffany. Tiff writes often, she always keeps me informed about what's going on. I received a letter from her just the other day informing me about what's going on in her life.

Dear My Bitch!

What's going on with you? Holding it down, I hope! You know I'm maintaining as usual. I miss you so much girl! Melody has been asking about you. You know I don't fuck with her anymore, but we still cool. That bitch was too emotional for me, word! Anyway, I have a new boo, her name is Korine, she a little cutie, you should see her. I stopped fucking with niggaz altogether, I guess I just got bored with them. I finally got up the balls to tell my moms the real deal about my preference. She was more embarrassed than she was concerned, but I don't give a fuck, I'm happy! What my mother should be embarrassed about is Rome leaving her plus losing that damn house her and Rome tried so desperately to keep. They kept missing payments and the bank repoed that shit! Jessica is staying with me now. But my moms and her shadow, Tyreek is staying in the projects with Aunt Charlene and Shiane's trifling asses. Speaking of those two...they ain't nothing but hoodrats who gon' be in the hood forever. Tell me why they was fucking the same eighteen year old boy!? Nasty ain't even the word girl! Circle, circle, dot, dot, now I got my coudie shot! (smile). Aunt Brenda is still the same, all she's concerned about is her and her broke ass man. It's a shame.

In other news those dance lessons I used to take finally paid off. Next week I'll finally choreograph my first music video! Could you believe it? Me a choreographer!? I still

*find it hard to believe myself. Well, that's it for now girl.
Call and holla at me sometimes. Anything you need, you
know I got you! I love you! You know you my Bitch for
life! Hold ya head and write back soon!*
Ya Bitch Tiff!

I was glad to be getting the support I needed. Even
Tazz came to check me occasionally. On our visits we
mostly reminisced about ol' times. The last time I saw
Tazz he surprised me a lot.

The moment I spotted Tazz he was wearing brown
Gucci loafers. I don't know why I looked at his feet first.
I guess it was just a habit I had. Before I could look at
the rest of his outfit I burst into laughter. I knew he would
have on the entire Gucci ensemble. But to my surprised
Tazz toned down his wardrobe a lot! The only thing he
wore similar to his loafers was the brown Gucci belt holding up his brown pants. Through his brown sweater it
looked like Tazz had been working out. His braids were
cut off, now I was the one sporting cornbraids. Me and
Tazz hugged.

"You still looking good," he whispered in my ear as
he kissed my cheek.

"You look like a piece off shit," I joked.

We both laughed then took a seat. "How was your ride
here?"

"It was a piece of cake. I'm use to it now, what's up
with you, you maintaining?" Tazz asked.

"I'm good, just taking it one day at a time now. What's
going on in North Carolina?"

"Actually I'm staying in New York for a minute," Tazz
said to my surprise.

I shook my head, "That's cool, you in the hood?" I asked.

"I go through the hood every now and again, but that's not where I'm staying. Shit is hectic over there. You should see ya girl Jackie! That bitch look like she from another planet!"

I shook my head, "She looks that bad, huh?"

"Hell yeah!" Tazz shouted. Then he continued, "They saying she on that crack bad! She sold all that fly shit she use to have in her crib, her spot is a straight crack spot now. And if you ask me, I don't believe it's just the crack making her look the way she do. I know a few niggaz who dun ran up in that, now them niggaz is dying or dead."

"Word? So you think Jackie got the monster?"

Tazz shook his head, "That's what it look like. She got one foot in the grave and the other foot out. It's sad man. She don't even have all that pretty long hair she use to have."

"How's Jamel looking?" I asked.

Tazz sighed, "It need to be an APB out on that nigga. Supposedly he went out of town three months ago. Nobody seen or heard from him since... Niggaz don't even know if he dead or alive."

"That's fucked up!" I replied.

"You know Jackie brother got kilt right?"

I raised an eyebrow, "Nah, which one?"

"The one who had something to do wit ya moms death." Tazz leaned forward then whispered, "I heard he crossed the wrong nigga. Some dude named Randy from Harlem put that in?"

"Randy?" I asked surprised. "Do you know if he has a wife named Tammy?" I whispered.

Tazz put his finger to his temple as if he was in deep thought. He looked toward the ceiling then replied, "Yeah, he do got a wife named Tammy, you know them?"

I smiled before answering Tazz. I shook my head then replied, "Nah, I don't know them." I winked at Tazz, he winked back. We both laughed.

"So what's going on in your life Tazz? Who you staying with in New York?"

Tazz put his head down like a little kid. Then he looked up and spoke, "I got this special lady in my life. I'm staying with her right now. We thinking 'bout moving out to Chicago."

I couldn't believe my ears. I blushed and frowned, "Does your 'special lady' know you're here visiting me?"

"Of course, me and you is peoples. I ain't got nothing to hide."

"You know Tazz, I'm sitting here thinking about my life and I'm saying this shit could be a book!"

"Then maybe you should write one," Tazz replied.

I shook my head, "Yeah, I could do that, but who would we get to publish it?"

Tazz frowned and sucked his teeth, "We don't need nobody to publish it. We could do the shit ourselves. I'm sick of the game anyway. Nowadays they got a million police and a million snitches. It only takes one of each to get a hundred years. I ain't tryna go out like that. I'm ready to walk the straight and narrow. So yeah, you write the book, I'll find out how to go about starting a publishing company. This way we'll have power and control. We need to have both because one means nothing without the other. This way at least you'll come home to something solid. I think I already got a name for the company.

The only thing we need now is a title for the book." "What about calling it *The Game Chose Me*?" I asked. Tazz repeated the name to himself, "The Game Chose Me...I like it!"

THE END.

ALSO AVAILABLE BY EBANDTE INC. PUBLISHING:

THE HOOD

A STORY BY DANTE "TE-SHOOTA" CLARKE

WRITTEN BY EBONY STROMAN

THANKS FOR YOUR SUPPORT!

SNEAK PREVIEW OF

CRITICAL CONDITION

A NOVEL BY

EBONY STROMAN

COMING SOON!!!

CRITICAL

CONDITION

INTRODUCTION

"Sadé!"

"Sadé!"

"Sadé!"

"Over here! Look over here!"

"Can you tell us why you did it!?"

"Do you have any regrets?"

"Are you going to enter a plea of insanity!?"

"Sadé!"

Sadé could still hear the reporters' voices loud and clear. It seemed like everything happened just yesterday, but that clearly wasn't the case, time could affirm that.

Placing her hands on the rusting metal sink Sadé looked up at the thin dull metal on the concrete wall in front of her. This was supposed to be a mirror, but it was more like looking into a piece of aluminum foil, she could hardly see a thing. However, she did manage to notice the gray hairs that had snuck up on the widow's peak of her head. She turned to her left then to her right.

Yeah. She was getting old. Time had preserved her girlish figure and radiant skin, but nothing could prevent the crows' feet that rested on the corners of her eyes.

Today was June 23rd and Sadé would do what she did every June 23rd for the past 25 years. She about faced and took the three maybe four steps necessary to reach her bed. Lifting the thin mattress off of the cold hard steel Sadé grabbed the news article she'd clipped from the newspaper years ago.

Sadé Campbell is what the article read: ***Resurrected! Captured! Convicted!***

Sadé sat down on her bed and she felt the metal as it seeped through the thin mattress causing a pain in her ass. She moved over a bit but it was no use, it still felt as if she were sitting directly on the metal, the mattress might as well have not even been there, it didn't serve its purpose at all. She shook her head as her gray eyes looked over the article she held in her hand.

"Campbell! Mail!" a correctional officer yelled through her cell.

Sadé placed the article back in its place as she stood to her feet waiting for her mail. She knew if she only had one piece of mail there wasn't a doubt in her mind that it would be from Becky Gallagher. Even though Sadé hadn't replied to Becky's mail, not even once in the 25 years she's written to her, she knew Becky would still write. She was persistent; you had to give her that. Although Becky's letters had slowed up within the last few years she never managed to miss the anniversary that Sadé's life was changed forever.

Upon receiving her mail Sadé had to laugh. Becky Gallagher didn't write every month like she used to, but once a year she managed to follow up with Sadé. Sadé on the other hand couldn't understand how or why a person she'd never met constantly thought of her, wrote her letters and asked her questions she knew or at least Sadé hoped she knew she'd never get the answers to. This was beyond crazy to Sadé. Nevertheless, she bypassed Tiana and Rick's mail to see what Becky had to say this time.

Dear Sadé:

So, here it is 25 years to the day and I have yet to hear from you. My only hopes were to assist you and your situation. So far I know you've denied my visits a total of 16 times, you've lost 2 appeals, transferred to 4 facilities during the duration of your time, managed to get your Masters degree in criminal justice and pass the BAR exam on your first try. So why is it that you constantly ignore me? Am I some kind of monster, did I do or write something to upset you? If so please, let me know! What have I ever done so wrong that I am not even worthy of a reply? To be honest I don't even know if you read my mail at all. As a matter of fact I won't even waste anymore time with the small talk because who's to say if you will ever even get this. So let's get to the point, right? Right! I will start off by asking what I've been asking since I've started my study on women prisoners in New York over 25 years ago. For one reason or another that behooves me your case in particular has captured my attention from the very beginning. Your story, rather the bits and pieces that I know about your story has kept me intrigued and inquisitive. Please don't think of me as just another reporter trying to get your story, instead think of me as someone who's here to help. With that I'll ask the three questions that puzzles me almost daily. Why did you do it? How did you do it? And, why after 25 years of major publishers offering you million dollar deals, film executives offering bigger million dollar deals for the rights to your story, several different versions of unauthorized books on your crime and conviction being printed, why after all of this, why now did you decide to go with a fairly new, relatively small publisher such as Ebandte Inc. Publishing for a rather small $10,000 advance compared to what you were being offered from the majors?

Desperately seeking answers,

Becky Gallagher

Sadé placed the letter back in its envelope then she did something she'd never done before. For the first time ever, Sadé was going to reply to Becky. Grabbing a yellow note pad and a black ink pen Sadé began writing.

iv

Dear BG:

I know my reply may come as a pleasant surprise to you but I'm gonna keep it short and sweet. If you want my story; read my book, it's due to release nationwide within the next two weeks. All the questions you may have and even ones that you may not have are answered in that book. And you'll also see why I waited 25 years to release my official story; everything I do is for a reason. As far as signing with a smaller publisher such as Ebandte Inc. Publishing goes... it's like this, they feel me and I feel them. For me it was never about the money. All that cheddar that those majors were throwing my way was nothing but cheese to me, and if you've been checking up on me like you say you have then you would know it was never about the money, I got my own money and plenty of it... check my records. What was and still is important to me is establishing a relationship and an understanding with my publisher so that my story is not only told but told right. I feel with Ebandte Inc. Publishing being a smaller publisher who works closely with their authors I can accomplish that. I am confident that they can give me the time and dedication that me and my project deserves, with the majors I know I wouldn't have got that. Plus I can't write for shit! And being a fan of Ebony and Danté's work way before I joined their roster made me feel even more comfortable in my ability to tell Ebony the story knowing that she would translate it on paper just right, no embellished, remixed or chopped up shit! I knew she'd write it just like I told it. So if you want the truth about Sadé, the no holds barred truth, then pick up my book, I already told you when it's due to release.

Becky couldn't believe what she was reading! Was it true? Did this really happen? After all these years in the dark had Sadé Campbell replied to one of her letters to finally shed some light?! For a split second she thought she was dreaming, but no, it couldn't be! She clearly remembered checking her mail and finding Sadé's letter.

"She wrote back!" Becky shouted out loud to herself. "Finally, she wrote back!"

The next two weeks would be the longest two weeks of her life! She would finally know all the facts to Sadé Campbell's story!

Two weeks later nothing or no one could stop Becky from reaching the bookstore before the doors were officially open. When the doors finally did open she raced inside the store in search of the book she'd waited 25 years for. Once the book was in her hand she felt a chill shoot through her body. Becky practically threw the money at the cashier before racing out of the store.

Becky thought about taking the subway but then quickly decided against it. No! This was urgent! She needed to get home to her Manhattan loft as soon as possible. She didn't want to be disturbed while reading this book nor did she want to stop once she started it. Becky hopped in a yellow cab and within ten minutes she reached her loft in the SoHo section of Manhattan.

Once inside, Becky raced to the phone. She placed a call to her news station informing them that she'd be out for the next three days. She grabbed her cell phone out of her purse then turned it off; it would stay that way for the next three days. The ringer on her house phone would also remain off.

Turning on her shower, Becky dropped her clothes on the bathroom floor. After fifteen minutes of cleansing her body and washing her hair she exited the shower with her head wrapped in a towel. She grabbed a short white baby-T and a pair of hot pink terrycloth shorts. Her red polished toes sunk into the fluffy brown carpet as she made her way to the couch. She retrieved her book and a warm cup of apple juice. Sipping her juice and making herself comfortable Becky opened the book to page one.

This book is dedicated to Rick, Tiana and all my people in the struggle! I'm with ya'll, I love ya'll, I thank ya'll! Here is my story.

-Sadé

CRITICAL

CONDITION

COMING SOON!!!

ALSO COMING SOON FROM Ebandte Inc. PUBLISHING IN 2009:

CAN' T KNOCK THE HUSTLE
BY KAMAL BRADDOX & EBONY STROMAN

CREATION OF A GANGSTER
BY DANTÉ "TE-SHOOTA" CLARKE

PULLING ME BACK
BY G. STARR

Somebody in his click wanted him found! The Mob wanted him dead! Police wanted him questioned. But Chilli didn't give a damn; he had a tank full of gas, a car full of cash and a low spot in New Jersey where he thought he was safe from it all.

But, when Tammy; a low-down-dirty-tramp mixes business with pleasure, cops with criminals and the Grimes brothers with The Mob, the end result can only mean one thing; complete chaos! The Grimes brothers' has a long history and a team just as sick and vicious as The Mob's.

When Deadeye gets caught up in the mix and labeled a snitch he only wants what he thinks is rightfully his; his money from the bank robbery, his name cleared and Chilli's life!

Brace yourself for the bloodiest saga of semi-automatic madness ever to spill its guts on paper, at the orders of an infamous Mob family and the ruthless and well respected Grimes brothers.

In a game where friendship means nothing, and strangers mean everything, who will you trust?

"I 'on't know what you think you doing with this wanna be tough guy shit 'cause you ain't scaring me! So if you ain't here to talk about my lawyer or me going to Central Bookings to see the judge; you could suck my dick because I don't know shit and I ain't saying shit!"

-Peter Grimes Stop Snitching!!!

CAN'T KNOCK
THE HUSTLE

The year was 1988. It was a heat blazing summer in New York City. At 1pm the day was busy like any other day in the Williamsburg section of Brooklyn, traffic was backed up, horns were honking and people were everywhere.

From the outside looking in – everything seemed to be normal, but at Chase Manhattan bank that clearly wasn't the case!

"It's hotter than a muthafucka in here," Tammy spat while fanning herself. "When are they going to fix the air conditioner?" she turned and asked her co-worker who was also a bank teller in the Chase branch they worked.

"Girl! You better watch yo mouth befo' Mr. Thomas hears you and you lose yo job for cussin' like that."

Tammy waved her hand at Tracy's country ass like she didn't give a damn. Tracy shook her head then continued in her notorious country accent. "Fool with these people if you want, but you better remember you black – not white girl! You know they fire us fo' anything then won't even think twice about it."

Tammy rolled her eyes then looked at Tracy. "I just know it's too hot to be working in here like this! They gotta do something about this heat!" Tammy stated wiping her brow.

"I hear you," Tracy assured, "but getting fired ain't gon' help the situation none."

"You're right. Let me go make this money, I know my break is over by now."

"I'll be over there in a little bit," Tracy looked at her watch, "I still got about five minutes left on my break."

Tammy simply nodded her head and kept on walking. Once she arrived at her booth, she set up then opened her bank draw to count the money.

No sooner than Tammy counted the last bill she had in her hand she looked up and noticed four black males with afros and sunglasses enter the bank! If she didn't know any better judging by their appearance alone she would've sworn these brothers were a part of the notorious Black Panthers Party. Then there was the reaction of everyone else inside the bank. The look on everyone's face seemed as if time had stopped! The four males' presence was felt without a doubt. All eyes seemed to be focused in their direction. The air inside the bank suddenly felt tensed! Before anyone could utter a word, one male, referred to in the 'hood as Deadeye, a big black grizzly looking muthafucka with gorilla arms pulled out his pistol and grabbed the unsuspecting security guard all in one motion!

A young lady who'd just been talking with the guard tried to run towards the exit once she figured out what was going on. But she was stopped short when another male, the short, dark and stocky one out of the bunch, better known as Kev, pulled out his Colt 45 then smacked her in the face with it. The impact of the gun was enough to make the young lady fall to the ground screaming and holding her face.

Screams of terror and women crying could be heard throughout the bank.

Another one of the bank robbers pulled out his .38 revolver, let off two shots then ran to the middle of the crowded bank waving his gun.

"Don't nobody fucking move! Everybody shut the fuck up and stay down or you gon' get laid down in this bitch! If I hear a pin drop I'ma turn this bitch into the Fourth of July up in this muthafucka! Don't nobody try and be a hero, ya dig? Just do what the fuck I tell you and you'll walk out of this bitch alive!"

The two shots the robber let off in the air assured the people inside the bank that they were there for business and they weren't playing any games – not Atari, not Nintendo, nothing!

Silence filled the air as everyone froze in fear. You could still see the mist of gun powder in the air. Two out of the four men proceeded towards the bank tellers with their guns out and fierce looks on their faces.

"Open the gate bitch!" one of the robbers demanded while pointing his gun at Tammy. Tammy wasn't anybody's fool; she did just as she was told. Once inside the gated area the robbers demanded to know who the manager was. Everyone inside the teller area pointed to the man crouched underneath a large oak desk. It was clear to everyone that Mr. Thomas was shaking and scared.

Mr. Thomas was grabbed by one of the men who then put the nozzle of the gun to his temple and demanded the keys to the safe!

Scared and stuttering, Mr. Thomas tried his best, "I...I..I don't have any keys."

BOOM! The robber smacked him with the butt of the gun causing his head to spill blood everywhere.

Tammy screamed out, "Mr. Thomas! For God sake give them the keys off your keychain, please! Or they're going to kill us all!"

With his hands shaking Mr. Thomas nervously handed over the keys to the safe room.

Unaware and uninformed that anyone would be inside of the safe room. It almost appeared as if the security guard fell out of the clear blue sky with his gun blazing!

BLOCKA! BLOCKA! BLOCKA! Two shots hit one of the robbers in the chest before the security guard's gun jammed. The second robber, who everyone called Chilli, turned around then opened fire on the security guard hitting him in his neck, chest and head. His dead body fell like a feather hitting the ground. The once shinny marbled floor was now covered with blood.

Screams and cries for help rang throughout the bank. The dark, short and stocky male quickly calmed the crowed down with life threaten words.

The robber who lay bleeding on the floor was badly wounded and it wasn't hard to tell that he didn't stand a chance. Chilli reached for his wounded comrade but Kev stopped him, yelling across the bank, "He's gone man! He ain't gon' make it, leave him alone!"

The wounded robber heard what Kev said then pressed on his elbows trying to pull himself up, but to no avail. Gasping for air he turned towards Tammy.

"Ta... Ta... Tam... Tammy," he stuttered. "Please don't let Kev leave me."

Tammy was crying hysterically looking at the young male. Meanwhile, Mr. Thomas was looking at Tammy suspiciously and wondering how the wounded robber knew her name.

Two out of the three remaining robbers cleaned out the safe then made their way to the exit with their guns still in plain sight. The third robber followed the other two out while walking backward and still holding everyone at gunpoint.

Once outside the trio bumped into two uniformed officers who were talking, shooting the breeze. Immediately one of the officers noticed the three men with their guns out! Without any hesitation he took cover, drew his gun then yelled out "GUN!" The other officer who he'd been talking to turned around, but it was too late. The gunmen lit him up like a firecracker! The pig was dead before he hit the floor.

The other officer retaliated with gunfire hitting one of the robbers five times. Then he called for back-up.

By the time the back-up arrived it was too late. The other two robbers had gotten away with over $151,000! Now the police set up the crime scene. Blocks surrounding the bank were cut off in each direction as the investigation began. Detective Napola was one of the first responding officers on the scene. He was also the lead detective covering the case, at least for now.

Napola did a thorough inspection of the crime scene, checking the dead bodies before they were shipped off to the morgue, interviewing employees and customers alike. Then he ran into Mr. Thomas.

"Hey, Mr. Thomas," Napola extended his hand. "My name is detective Napola and I'm in charge of this investigation. Are you alright Mr. Thomas, do you think you can tell me what you saw?"

Still a little shaken from the day's events, Mr. Thomas replied, "Yes I can officer."

Napola pulled out his pen and pad as Mr. Thomas rattled off the day's events. He explained everything to a T. But, just when he thought he was finished he snapped his fingers and remembered the most important thing of all.

"And, oh, how could I forget the thing that puzzled me the most?!" Mr. Thomas pulled Napola a little closer to him then spoke in a whisper. "One of my employee's; Tammy Clark, when the robber was shot and dying he said her name like he knew her. He also said another name, but I'm not sure what that was, but I know he said Tammy's name and that struck me as odd."

"Me to, me to," Napola replied shaking his head. "Where is Tammy Clark right now?"

Mr. Thomas pointed, "Right over there! She's the one wearing the red shirt."

Napola then called one of the uniformed officers and asked him to take Miss Clark down to the precinct so he could interview her in the interrogation room.

Napola held up his index finger and pointed in the uniformed officer's face, "Now, listen rookie!" The young cop wasn't a rookie but Napola's been on the force so long that he'd made it a habit to call all young cops rookies', to him everyone who came on the force after him was a rookie. He continued, "I want you to bring her down to the station and keep her in that interrogation room until I get there! Got it?" Napola raised his brow.

"Yeah, yeah. I got it," the young cop replied.

"Good! Don't fuck this up." Napola turned and walked away.

"**Y**o, you think Kev is dead to?" Chilli asked. Chilli's real name was Gary Carter, but since he was so grimey and always had some evil shit on his mind people got cold feelings whenever he was around. This is why everyone called him Chilli.

With a deep scary voice the other robber replied, "He was hit pretty bad. I don't think he could've made it out of that, ya dig?" This robber was known as Deadeye. He never told anyone his real name because he didn't like it. He was the only black kid with a Jewish name and that never made any sense to him. He never knew his father but he hated his mother for giving him the name she did. Do you know how many fights he got into growing up because all the kids made jokes about his name? All the jokes he'd heard about himself made him stop laughing and he became very cold-hearted. He wore his pain and his anger in his eyes; therefore he was hailed as Deadeye.

Deadeye was much smarter and crazier then Chilli. Yet, he let Chilli think he was in charge.

Chilli sighed, "Well, we got to find out what happened! I can't just sit up in here not knowing. If Kev still alive he could be sending the pigs to our spot right now, but if he dead then we probably good. But one thing is for damn sure, I gots to know something!"

Deadeye shook his head, "Nah, even if Kev is alive I don't think he would send the pigs at us. I mean come on, this Kev we talking 'bout!"

"Yeah, that shit sound real good 'til the pigs is kicking down the door, running up in our spot. All I'm saying is if Kev is dead we don't know if he died right away. Who knows what could've been said before that man closed his eyes? And, if he still alive then there's still a chance that he might give us up, ya dig?"

"You right," Deadeye agreed. "What time is it right now?"

Chilli looked at his watch, "Its 5:00."

"Aight sun, this what I'ma do. You wait here and I'ma go to the coffee shop on the corner and get some cigarettes and watch the news. Now if they say Kev is alive we gots to leave right away. But, if he died at the scene, befo' the pigs got there then we good. We won't have to go anywhere 'cause dead men don't talk."

Chilli sighed while shaking his head, "Yeah, okay. But I'm telling you I don't trust this shit! I think we should bounce anyway."

Deadeye held up one hand, "Listen, I'ma go watch the news then when I get back we gon' take it from there."

"Aight," Chilli replied still sounding a little unsure.

"I've been here for four hours! Can somebody please tell me what I'm doing here?" Tammy snapped with much attitude.

The officer responded annoyed by Tammy's questions, "You'll know when Detective Napola comes back. He didn't say why and he didn't say for how long, he just told me to hold you and that's what I'm doing."

Almost as if on cue, Napola walked into the precinct studying a stack of papers he had in his hand. Just then the officer who Tammy had been annoying noticed Napola and raced over to him quickly.

"Hey, boss! What are we doing with this Ms. Clark? She's getting on my fucking nerves!"

Napola diverted his eyes from the papers in his hands to the officer that stood before him. "Is she in the interrogation room?"

"No," the officer shook his head. "She's right over there," he pointed towards a desk.

"But, didn't I tell you to put her in the interrogation room? If she was in there she wouldn't be getting on your fucking nerves, now would she?"

"No, no. I guess not," the officer replied dryly.

"Okay, then put her in that room. Tell her I'll be in in a few."

The officer walked off into Tammy's direction. Twenty minutes later Napola walked into the room where Tammy was being held.

"Hello Ms. Clark. My name is detective Napola. Do you know why I'm interviewing you here instead of in the bank?"

"No. Why?" Tammy asked with much attitude.

"Because we have information that lead us to believe you knew one of the assailants."

"What! What! What?" Tammy asked shocked! "What makes you say that?"

"The information we have makes me believe that."

"Well, what's the information?"

Napola laughed then interlocked his fingers as he sat up in his chair, "Listen here Tammy--"

Tammy cut him off, "I prefer Ms. Clark."

"I prefer if you stop bullshitting with me and tell me the truth. We know you knew them and we want the names of the two who got away. Don't give me any bullshit because I have no time for the stupid games you're playing!

"Excuse me?!" Tammy exclaimed looking and sounding mad as hell! "Who do you think you're talking to?" Tammy demanded to know.

KNOCK! KNOCK! KNOCK! came the annoying sound of someone interrupting Tammy and Napola's battle.

"What is it?" Napola asked clearly annoyed.

A young officer pushed the door open then entered without being invited in. "Ah, sorry Napola but I have some news you might want to hear."

"Sure. Gimmie one minute," Napola replied. The officer shook his head then exited the room as fast as he entered.

"Listen, Ms. Clark! You better have your shit together by the time I come back or I promise to make your life a living hell!"

"Yeah, whatever!" Tammy waved her hand as if she wasn't worried. Napola exited the room.

"Yeah, what's up?" Napola asked the officer standing outside of the room.

"I just got word from the hospital that the other suspect died."

"Shit! When did he die?" Napola asked looking worried.

"About twenty minutes ago."

"Shit!" Napola exclaimed. "Shit! Shit! Shit! This ain't good! This ain't good at all!"

"But, we did manage to get identification of the perp," the officer added.

"Well what is it?" Napola asked. "Who is he? What's his name? Who are his friends?"

"I can find out more information later but for now I know his name is Kevin Reynolds. He lives over on 321 Blake Avenue in East New York, Brooklyn."

"Good, good!" Napola patted the young officer on his back. "Now I need you to come back in this room with me and just follow my lead. Take your cuffs out," Napola ordered.

They both walked into the room where Tammy was seated.

Tammy kicked her feet out from under the desk as she pushed the chair outward and stood to her feet. "Can I go now?! You can't hold me here like this!"

"Shut up bitch! We can do whatever we want to do, we're the police!" Napola put one foot on a chair and leaned forward in Tammy's direction. "I got some good news. Good news for me, but bad news for you. Your friend said hi."

"What friend?" Tammy asked looking puzzled.

"Kevin, Kevin Reynolds," Napola replied with a smile on his face.

Tammy's face dropped! It looked as if she had seen a ghost. Napola caught on immediately.

"I thought that might ring a bell," he sang out.

Napola could feel it! He knew he had her in his grasp! Her facial expression told it all.

As Deadeye entered the coffee shop he noticed the news was just starting. So before he bought his cigarettes, he sat at the table and watched the news.

"In breaking news I'm here on the scene where a bank robbery gone badly has left 3 dead and 1 in critical condition at Woodhull Hospital. Police say four men entered the bank armed and dangerous and somehow got into a shootout with security guard Danny White, who fatally wounded one of the gunmen but in turn he was gunned down by another of the robbers. Shortly after the remaining three gunmen exited the bank they exchanged gunfire with two on duty police officers. One of the officers was pronounced dead on arrival and one robber was wounded badly and taking to Woodhull Hospital where he still lies in critical condition as we speak. Police do not know the whereabouts of the two gunmen who got away or the names of any suspects. If you have any tips, please contact the police,

thank you. I'm Vanessa Hasslehoth reporting for channel 11 news."

Deadeye didn't know what to think at this point. They had Kev, he was still alive but they didn't know him or Chilli's names or where they were staying. But, *could they be bluffing?* Deadeye wondered. But bluffing or no bluffing they had Kev and that put them in harms way. Deadeye mumbled something he learned long ago. *"Three men can keep a secret as long as two of them are dead."*

Deadeye eased from the table then walked swiftly toward the exit without thinking about purchasing his cigarettes. Once outside he blended in well with people commuting to or from work, school or just the local grocery store. His stroll back to the hideaway was just as smooth as when he left.

As Deadeye approached the door to the safe-house he noticed it was cracked. He then drew his gun and lightly pushed the door open and quietly stepped in. He moved through the house like a ninja.

Searching.

Peaking.

Watching.

After a thorough inspection of the house, it was safe to say Chilli and the money was gone!

Here Deadeye was; possibly facing the rest of his life in jail and now he had nothing to show for it. He couldn't believe this! Deadeye could feel his whole world fall from under him. He was furious! But on the flip side of things, Chilli was chillin' with a tank full of gas, a car full of cash and a destination that no one knew about accept for him and the people who were already there.

"Hey, baby!" His grandmother greeted him with open arms, happy to see her favorite grandson. "What are you doing here?"

"I came to see the best grandmother in the world," Chilli hugged his granny tight.

No matter what, Chilli knew he could always count on his granny. He was her favorite and that was made very clear. He spent as much time at her house in Newark, New Jersey as he spent at his home in Brooklyn. He had a set of keys to come and go as he pleased and his own room that his granny made sure was always sparklin' clean just for him.

Granny kissed Chilli on the cheek. "You're just in time. I finished cooking exactly six minutes ago!" she announced, excited by her grandson's surprise visit. "Now, go wash-up for supper and tell your grandfather that the food is ready. Maybe you can get him up and off of his ass from in front of that TV watching those damn sports all day." She winked at her grandson then proceeded to set up for dinner as Chilli headed upstairs to stash his bag for the time being and get his grandfather. Chilli's grandfather loved him just as much as his grandmother did.

By the time Chilli finished stashing his bag, both his grandmother and grandfather were seated at the table waiting on him. When Chilli finally took a seat at the table his grandfather smiled hard exposing his gold capped tooth on the left side of his mouth as he asked, "What you doing out here Gary?"

Chilli raised the palms of his hands skyward, "You act like I need a reason, but if you want to know it's because I miss y'all."

"Ain't he the sweetest thing ever?" his grandmother said looking at her husband.

"Boy, you know that girl Kelly has been bugging me about you." His grandfather informed him.

"That girl is nice. Why don't you call her?" Granny asked. "You're getting old and you need to find a wife and she's a good one. She cooks, cleans and she even has a job."

"You're right granny," Chilli replied while dipping one of his granny's famous biscuits into the heavy brown gravy sauce. "I probably give her a call or stop by her house tomorrow." He bit into the gravy soaked bread. Granny smiled, "See, Arthur. He gets his brains from my side of the family."

CAN'T KNOCK THE HUSTLE

BY KAMAL BRADDOX & EBONY STROMAN

COMING SOON TO A CITY NEAR YOU!!!

ABOUT THE AUTHOR
Ebony Stroman-Clarke

Ebony is a gifted and creative young writer. She brings not only a new way of story-telling to this game; this twenty-three year old Queen brings so much more. She brings her courage, wisdom and the strength to move on, under any circumstances. She's currently raising her two younger sisters due to the death of their mom in 2002. She's married to whom she refers to as "The Best Man in the World." (Dante Clarke) who she says "inspired" her along with her sisters to start her own Publishing company; EBANDTE INC. PUBLISHING. Ebony is a Queens, New York native who has plans to change the world! To learn more about Ebony, her company and her titles, visit her website: www.ebandte.com

EBANDTE INC. PUBLISHING
P.O. BOX 341147
JAMAICA, NY 11434
ORDER FORM

ALL TITLES ARE $14.00 EACH. PLEASE ADD $4.05
FOR SHIPPING & HANDLING

AVAILABLE NOW!!!

QUANITY

THE HOOD -by Ebony Stroman & Dante "Te-Shoota" Clarke

THE GAME CHOSE ME-by Ebony Stroman

UNFALLEN ROSES: PETALS & THORNS-by Anthony Walker

BOOK TITLE: $14.00 + $4.05 S&H TOTAL = $18.05

*PLEASE NOTE: Ebandte Inc. Publishing deducts 25% off of the sale price for orders being shipped directly to **colleges** and **correctional facilities.**

Cost are as follows:
BOOK TITLE: $10.50 + $4.05 S&H TOTAL = $14.55
MAKE ALL PAYMENTS TO EBANDTE INC. FORMS OF ACCEPTED PAYMENTS ARE MONEY ORDERS & INSTITUTIONAL CHECKS. WRITE THE ADDRESS YOU'D LIKE YOUR ITEM(S) SHIPPED TO ON THE BACK OF THIS FORM

"A BOOK BY EBANDTE GOTTA BE GOOD!"